Hiatus

SAM POLAKOFF

HIATUS

Published by Komodo Dragon, LLC

Forest Hill, Maryland

Book design by GKS Creative
Cover image used under license from kwest/Shutterstock

Author photo courtesy of Ed Polakoff
www.photosbyed.net

ISBN (print): 978-0-692-96229-9
ISBN (EBook): 978-0-692-96230-5

Library of Congress: 2017918182

First edition

Printed in the United States of America

www.sampolakoff.com

This book is dedicated to my grandfather, Abraham Allan Polakoff.
After his death in 1967, I experienced a recurring dream for many years
that became the inspiration for this story.

PART I

CHAPTER 1

Courage, strength, patience, wisdom.

"Those four words will get you through any situation," advised his grandfather long, long ago.

"Bringing people back from the dead has always been impossible for a reason," his mentor, Albert Harmon, had cautioned.

The voices cascaded upon him in a torrent, flooding his brain as he stood on the precipice of a miracle.

A miracle? Yes, to some. To others, it was playing with fire. Albert had warned of unintended consequences but Ben Abraham was strong in his resolve to move forward. Others used fear to create reasons for staying in a comfort zone. But no scientific breakthrough ever occurred in a comfort zone.

He tried to collect himself. His stomach contained a swirling cauldron of acidic witch's brew; at least that's how it felt. Being nervous was okay, he told himself. After all the years of research, experimentation, trial and error, arguments and debates among his team about next steps, and a string of interwoven successes, he had finally arrived at the crescendo. This day represented a vicissitude of human existence. Sylvia Bresling had been dead for a year. If things went well, she would become a household name for being the first human to resume life after lying in a chemically preserved state of death.

The daughter and son-in-law of Sylvia Bresling were waiting, eagerly positioned in an observation mezzanine high above the floor where he, Rachel, and Tomi, members of his scientific team, were preparing the body. The required year of hibernation had passed quickly.

Ben looked up at the mezzanine. Bresling's daughter, Molly Kendrick, seated beside her husband, Jeff, had a death grip on the rail before her. She was clearly a wreck, a woman of weak constitution, someone who would likely fall apart at the hint of the smallest complication. He hoped she could keep it together. As a precaution, he stationed two members of his team, Bock and Weiskopf, in the observation deck with her.

Before him lay the body on a metal table lined with a thin mattress and pillow. Sylvia Bresling wore nothing but a hospital gown and was hooked up to the standard array of life-monitoring equipment. Above her, on an oscillating platform welded to the ceiling, was the Liferay. The newest iteration was barrel shaped, with a variety of rotational capsules, each roughly half the length of the main unit. He gave the order and Rachel Larkin slowly activated the device. The quiet mechanism efficiently and effectively began its work and one by one the capsules on the side of the machine rotated in proper sequence until Sylvia Bresling's body had been enveloped exactly twelve times for the prescribed time limit. The group in the observation deck all sat forward, anxiously waiting, watching for any sign of life. All of the monitors were silent, offering little hope.

The Liferay completed its sequence. Nothing.

Seven precious minutes passed. Still nothing. All of the research had led Ben to believe the awakening process would begin immediately. The despair in the room caused the oxygen to vanish. His colleagues looked as dejected as he felt. With his head hung low, embracing the realization that there was nothing else to do, Ben began to ready himself for the difficult conversation with Molly and Jeff Kendrick.

Courage, strength, patience, wisdom.

Then a single, solitary blip from the heart monitor. And then another, and another. Sonofabitch, they had actually done it! Any shade of doubt had been eviscerated by the audible beep of the machine registering cardiac activity. From the remaining medical apparatus, he could see that Sylvia Bresling's lungs were taking in air. She was breathing on her own. All indicators were progressing toward normal ranges, including her heart rate and blood pressure. He kept a watchful eye for reflexes and muscle tone as well as any pupillary activity.

Molly screamed in joy while the others tried to calm her. Ben had worried all along that Molly's emotional euphoria might disrupt her mother's awakening. No one could be sure what the mother's mental state might be.

After making sure her vitals were stable, Bock and Weiskopf escorted Molly and Jeff to the floor. Molly and her mother were about to be reunited. Ben watched as they came through the double doors and walked toward the table where the body of Sylvia Bresling lay. She was breathing, her heart was pumping, but she was not yet conscious. They stood around her for a few minutes discussing all of the "what if" questions for which no one had definitive answers when suddenly Sylvia's left eyelid began to twitch, and then her right did the same. Her face tightened briefly as if she were about to sneeze and just as quickly, it subsided.

Sylvia's eyes opened. She seemed alert.

Ben flashed his trademark smile, the one that told the world how confident he was. "Hello, Sylvia, welcome back. I am Dr. Abraham. Do you remember me?" But Sylvia did not reply. "We are going to get you up slowly, Sylvia. Your daughter and son-in-law are here and anxious to spend the day with you."

Sylvia sat up slowly. Tomi was behind her, supporting her upper torso in case she collapsed. Rachel was ready with a sip of water from a long, flexible straw. Sylvia refused the water, cleared her throat, and looked around.

"Mom!" Molly cried. "Mom, oh my God, my heart won't stop fluttering. I can't believe this is really happening."

Jeff stood by her side and smiled. Sylvia stared blankly at her daughter. Her face contorted grotesquely and she snapped, "Who are you people and why am I in the hospital?"

At that instant, Ben Abraham knew he had reached an impasse. Years of research and experimentation, endless scientific permutations, algorithms, chalk talks, and debate, and no one had considered the possibility of an awakened patient being devoid of memory.

CHAPTER 2

Three years earlier

Silent, Ben Abraham sat alone at the mortuary, elbows on his knees and his head drifting listlessly near his lap. Why had he arrived so early? Given his discomfort with funerals, and this one in particular, he should have waited for the other members of his team to arrive. Their colleague was dead. A medallion hung metaphorically from his neck, his enemy. Despite his extraordinary intellect and record of scientific accomplishment, he knew little of this foe. For thirty years, since the death of his grandfather, it weighed on his spirit. On days like these, it choked him without warning. The ability to swallow was neutered in the face of reflux, rising through his body like an atomic fireball. He began to sweat. His skin felt prickly, even clammy to the touch. He wondered if he was getting sick, but deep down, he knew better. It was the same old feeling. The temporary, unwinnable fight with an enemy he barely understood.

Death.

He wondered how such a place helped the grieving family and friends in a time of sorrow. The viewing room was depressing. The forty-year-old wallpaper, the gray carpet, faded from too many years of heavyhearted footsteps and falling tears. His own experience with funerals was sparse. Upon consideration of this point, he was equal parts grateful and bitter.

When death had occurred around him, it always seemed that somehow, it was his fault. Today was no different.

The guilt over Gramps' death enveloped him to this day. Try as he might, he couldn't shed the feeling. The stigma was moss grown over an ancient cobblestone wall, causing him to carry the neverending burden and its unyielding torture. Like the forecast of an approaching storm, his parents explained the cancer and its ravaging effects. It seemed ominous. Fear caused him to withdraw. His schoolwork suffered. Precious weeks, days, and seconds had withered away like the man he once thought of as his best friend. Why did he forfeit those moments? He could have told Gramps how much he loved him. He could have helped take care of him when he became ill. He could have fought his parents, rebelling against the loving attempt to shelter him from the harshness of the cancer and its ultimate fate. He blamed himself—not for Gramps' cancer, but for the way he withdrew.

He knew Gramps saw something in him he did not see in himself. Gramps had trusted only him with his secret. A secret Ben had no idea how to handle. It's what kept him up at night. Not knowing why, not knowing how.

A light touch settled upon him. "You look like you went away for a minute there," said Rachel Larkin.

"Yeah, sorry. Deep in thought." Rachel was outfitted in a simple black dress. He wasn't used to seeing her in anything other than slacks and a white lab coat. The other members of his team would be filing in shortly. They would all pay their respects. Ben would try but he knew it wouldn't be easy. He was the reason Andrew Kauffman was dead.

Guilty of driving his team beyond the point of exhaustion, Ben was willing to push himself beyond what a reasonable person could do. So should every member of the team. His work ethic proved both a blessing and a curse.

Andrew had been his lead biologist. A foremost leader in his field. Ben recruited Andrew from a research laboratory at nearby Johns Hopkins in Baltimore. He was needed at what Ben called the Lab, his privately held research center in the backwoods of Maplebrook, a sleepy hamlet in farm and forest laden Harford County, Maryland. Ben could be persuasive. "We," he had told Andrew, "are on the cusp of something truly magnanimous."

It didn't take much convincing. The opportunity to provide the biological know-how as part of a team attempting to preserve and activate deceased cells from once-living organisms was too tempting. After making that first visit to the Lab and meeting Rachel and Ari, the physicists, and Harrison, the chemist, Andrew had readily agreed. The other biologist on the team, Tomi, had intoxicated Andrew with her work to date. He was all in. Ben viewed Andrew as the missing piece. Now he was gone. Ben wished he had handled things differently. Why couldn't he contain that demon pushing him beyond the limits? Yes, he thought, a blessing and a curse.

Ari Weiskopf approached, extended his hand, and then drew in the much taller Ben Abraham for an awkward bro hug. Ari looked drawn. *I don't know why they stay*, Ben thought. *I'm not sure I want to work with me some days.*

A woman he didn't know approached him. He attracted attention from strangers, mostly unwanted.

"How did you know Andrew?" she asked.

"Colleague," was all he said, somewhat mundanely. Without asking, the woman launched into a monologue about how she and Andrew had been neighbors when he first came to Baltimore from New York. Ben feigned interest but admitted to himself, he couldn't care less.

Mostly he just wanted to get the hell out of the funeral home. Another hour, maybe.

Suffocation. Darkness. A recipe for his anxiety. Those prickly burrs rising under his skin. It was all beginning. Was there no escape?

Courage, strength, patience, wisdom. His grandfather had taught him the axiom as a recipe to get through any difficulty.

Ben spied Harrison Bock. As tall as Ben but 150 pounds heavier, Harrison's ascension upon the dour crowd could not be ignored. Ben felt the anxiety begin to abate. Friends since college, Harrison had a way of making him laugh. His zany personality and their shared fondness for causing trouble made them instantaneous friends. Ben thought about how his work and life had forced him to grow up and get serious, yet Harrison still maintained his boyish charm and a mischievous streak.

Needing to temporarily get his mind off the events at hand, he recalled Harrison had been on a first date the prior evening. While strangers tended to annoy him. Harrison was part of the inner circle, the group to which he maintained fierce loyalty.

"How'd it go with the blonde from Federal Hill?"

"She wanted to go to dinner and then see the symphony at The Meyerhoff. Not my thing but she was hot, so I was like, what the fuck?"

"Did you wind up liking it?"

"The music was cool but I don't get the whole conductor thing. The musicians are focused on their instruments, making some good sounds, and this guy is standing up there waving his arms and the little stick. I'm like, dude, no one is paying any attention to you. You don't add any value to the performance."

Ben laughed. Harrison had a way of trivializing everything. He wished he could be more like that, not taking it all so seriously. He frequently had to remind himself to lighten up. It was tough getting back to those days when they were young and carefree. Harrison, he had it all figured out.

"Are you gonna see her again?"

"I don't know. I'm thinking she'll be fun to hang with for a while. You know, until the sex gets stale."

"Man, you really are *that* shallow," Ben remarked.

Rachel and Ari came toward them; Tomi was close behind. There they were, his scientific team, all together. Would they blame him for Andrew's death? His throat began to close. *Oh fuck!* He tried to take a deep breath but couldn't seem to inhale. Back to that place.

The room began to spin. Sweat formed on his brow. A shooting pain seared down the back of his neck. His vision blurred. His legs felt weak. Dizziness overcame him. Momentary blackness . . . enshrouded by that feeling. He was alone in the empty room, pitch black, gripped with fear. Suddenly, his eyes sprang open, face awash with perspiration. The beefy arm of Harrison Bock was around him, helping him, guiding him.

"C'mon, let's get you outside for a little air."

"Sorry, I think I just zoned out. I saw Andrew's parents and sister and it kind of just set me off."

"Dude, it's not your fault. His family doesn't blame you. No one blames you. Stop beating yourself up."

Easing himself onto a cement bench with wooden slats, he looked up. His friends' concern was evident. Rachel offered a bottle of Dasani, Ari a handkerchief. Across the parking lot, the aging figure of his mentor, Albert Harmon, was moving through the sea of cars. As Albert approached, Ben looked into the concerned faces of his team.

"Forgetting the auto accident that killed Andrew, don't you see the ironic twist of fate here?" Ben asked desperately.

The words hung in the dry, still air as Albert broached the three metal steps under the burgundy canopy bearing the name of the Wesley Funeral Home.

"Judging from the parking lot, there's quite a crowd here. How's everyone holding up?" inquired Albert.

"Okay," replied Ben. "We just stepped out for some air. C'mon. Heading back in now."

Ben's resolve to pay his last respects outweighed the desire to run. He'd stick close to his team, view the body one last time, and then retreat.

The dismal parlor holding the body of Andrew Kauffman was now overflowing. A beloved figure unexpectedly taken much too soon.

Andrew, its Ben. Yeah, I know what time it is. No, it can't wait till morning.

Ben recalled his own words with clarity. It was 1:30 a.m. Andrew had left the Lab only two hours earlier, following an eighteen-hour day. He said he was exhausted. Ben's life was his work. Going home was not his priority. He would just as soon take a power nap in the meeting area he called the Dugout. And even then, with reluctance. He thought he had a breakthrough. Waiting until tomorrow wasn't an option. They were trying to infuse life into once-living cells. Andrew needed to come back to work. Where was his sense of urgency? Why couldn't everyone share Ben's level of commitment to the science? When Andrew wasn't back to the Lab within the hour, Ben left urgent messages on Andrew's cell phone imploring him to hurry back to the Lab.

In his haste, Andrew forgot to fasten his seatbelt, then had fallen asleep at the wheel. The car veered off the road, culminating in a high-speed crash against a medical building's cinder block wall. Police surmised that Andrew died on impact.

The line of mourners crept slowly toward the coffin. Andrew's family was receiving people at the head of the casket. Dreading the encounter, Ben worried, was Harrison right? Would the Kauffmans hold him blameless?

Ben could see from the advancing line that Andrew's parents were handling things pretty well. Just a few more in front of him. He stood behind Rachel, Ari, Tomi, Harrison, and Albert. He wanted to hang back. Delaying the encounter was the only option to running as fast as he could from the funeral home. Just a few more minutes and it would all be over.

Now, at the foot of the casket, he looked forward and saw Rachel hugging Andrew's mother. Albert and Harrison were shaking hands with the father. Tomi and Ari, in full embrace with the sister. From his position, Ben was able to look down into the casket. His last look at the calm face of Andrew Kauffman. The irony, he thought again. If their work together had been further along, this scene might have been avoided. Ben's emotions and experience over the past hour had been part tornado and part wildfire. As he stared down into the still face of the man he called friend and colleague, the one with whom he had worked so closely to bring the world a gift, his mind became awash with the formation of an idea. He imagined a faint white light beginning to shine down on Andrew's cosmetic laden features. With each passing second, the light, shaped in a hollow cone, became gradually more brilliant in its intensity. An apparition? The illumination deposited a smile on Andrew's lifeless expression. In his grief, a state of high-stakes anxiety, the key to Ben's quest appeared in the narrow ray of imagined bright light. In spite of his foe, clear as day in his mind's eye, he now held the answer to a previously unsolvable puzzle. Death, he thought, could soon be on the run.

CHAPTER 3

The jet black Rolls-Royce Phantom, polished to perfection, pulled into the cobblestone driveway deep in the heart of Alsace. The house was nestled within the vast farmlands, which were common to the area but not unreasonably far from the highway, offering both access and privacy. Anstrov Rinaldi had been ready for ten minutes. Inherently irascible, he kept peeking out the window. Finally, he saw the driver, uniformed with white gloves, step out of the sleek, burnished Rolls, open the rear door, and patiently wait for him to emerge from the residence.

When the high wooden door with the moon-shaped crown finally opened, Rinaldi, with a brown hardwood cane, negotiated his way toward the sedan. The chauffeur, an experienced valet who had good history with him, knew better than to offer assistance. Rinaldi, who was proud or stubborn, take your pick, walked slowly but with decided determination down the companion cobblestone walkway. His left leg shouldered the burden.

Once seated comfortably in the back of the Phantom, the chauffeur closed the door and prepared to drive south to Basel. Through the adjacent village town, the car passed by the multi-colored shops that, once upon a time, defined the vocation of the building's inhabitants. Although they were in France, the architecture of the village was most definitely of German influence. Rinaldi was well versed in the Alsace culture, architecture, and language, which was a German derivative known as Alsatian. A similar dialect of German was spoken in Basel. Not to worry, he was fluent in German, English, his native Italian, and Russian.

Anstrov Rinaldi was the Chief of Scientific Research for Swiss Pharma Ingenuity, the world's fourth largest pharmaceutical company. Despite being only in his early forties, he had held this position for many years and reported directly to the CEO. His employer, SPI, maintained its worldwide headquarters in Basel, a sixty-minute drive with no traffic. Rinaldi oversaw the company's most prestigious research and development facility located in Colmar, France, the seat of the area known as the Upper Rhine—or to some, Haut Rhin.

Today, Rinaldi had been summoned to Basel for the type of event he absolutely loathed, a senior management meeting. He prided himself on his ability to "play along" with the corporate types but he held them all in low regard. He believed that the SPI leaders were imbeciles, did not appreciate real science, and quite frankly, weren't very good businessmen. SPI made piles of money on the back of his innovation, not because of their business acumen. In Rinaldi's view, SPI succeeded in spite of the leadership.

Greedy bastards, he thought. The only reason he could truly tolerate them was because he needed the world-class facilities they had in Colmar. He gave them some simple pharmaceutical products, they made billions, and he got to concentrate on what he considered real science . . . the science that drove and sustained life itself. All the Executive Directorate was concerned about was the almighty euro and their precious pills, liquids, and ointments.

Because he had never operated a motor vehicle, one of the perks Rinaldi negotiated when he came onboard was a hired limousine service whenever he had to travel within the region. Having made the ninety-eight-kilometer ride countless times, Rinaldi knew he had time to work or ponder. The chauffeur, Clifford, offered a bottle of Evian but Rinaldi politely refused. He pulled out a tablet to scan the morning headlines but quickly became bored. He was preoccupied with whatever drivel he would have to address at yet another senseless, waste-of-time meeting in Basel.

The Phantom made its way to the A35 motorway and began the southbound trek. Rinaldi looked out the passenger side window and took in a distant view of the Vosges mountain range. The range, although not nearly as pronounced, made Rinaldi think of his beloved Italian Alps. As a young boy, he had been quite athletic and favored both skiing and horseback riding. The passing scene carried him back to that day where, as a boy, he had been made the fool, humiliated and hurt both physically and mentally.

In the distance, he recalled hearing the discharge of a hunter's rifle. The sound was stark. The frightened horse reared up, tossing him from the mount. Only twelve years old, he was thrown ten feet in the air, landing hard in the dirt-based ring. Another blast from the nearby woods and the spooked horse of seventeen hands was fully upright. "Ni . . . co," mother shrieked. His parents hustled down a steep, grassy hill toward the faded, split rail fence that guarded the ring. Before they could get there, the horse thundered down hard, fifteen hundred pounds slamming full force into his right knee. Another shot was heard. The horse careened away, its hooves throwing loose dirt and gravel at his face as he lay there writhing in pain.

A horn blared on the highway, jarring his psyche back into the moment. For now, he thought, the idiots at SPI will get what they want. He would play his part. Not forever . . . but for now.

The sedan entered the city limits and rolled past Rathaus, Basel's Town Hall, and through the old European streets until coming to rest in front of the world headquarters of Swiss Pharma Ingenuity.

The office tower was a dark building, flying fifty stories and brightly adorned with mirrored glass and horizontal steel crossbeams lining each level. The building screamed unabashed wealth and was almost unseemly in a city married to tradition and influence from bygone generations.

"Shall I wait for you, sir?" asked Clifford.

"No, Clifford, thank you. Unfortunately, I expect I will be here all day. I'll call you when I am ready to head north."

With that, Rinaldi made his way into the building, displayed his ID, and proceeded to the bank of elevators for the ascent to the executive conference room on the fiftieth floor. In the lift, a young secretary whom Rinaldi had never seen before appeared startled by his appearance. Rinaldi understood. A lifetime of ridicule had followed him. His outward front wore shame like a badge of honor. Blind in his right eye, he did not wear a patch. Rather, a glass eye stared straight ahead, never in harmony with the movement of its partner. Rinaldi's eyes were far enough apart from one another as to appear unusual at first glance. His face was pockmarked and red. His right knee, long ago crushed by the spooked horse, barely had any useful remaining function. Standing only one hundred and seventy centimeters (five feet, six inches), Rinaldi's stout frame contributed to the aura he presented. Knowing how he appeared to people, his first instinct was to attempt a smile and some friendly banter but because he spoke with a low, scratchy voice, an attempt at a kind gesture dribbled out of his mouth like unwanted saliva. The young woman appeared even more frightened as Rinaldi laughed for no reason at all, and she bolted out of the lift at the first opportunity.

At the building's summit, Rinaldi hobbled down the long corridor to a set of glass doors. He shook his head at the lavish paintings and sculptures commissioned by supposedly gifted artists. He appreciated art he deemed relevant but saw these items as nothing more than a complete waste of money, funds which could easily be diverted to the company's real purpose—or at least, *his* real purpose. He passed through the frosted glass entry and was greeted by a familiar face.

"Good morning, Dr. Rinaldi. Fresh coffee and tea are in the executive conference room. You are the first to arrive."

"Thank you, Frieda." Rinaldi liked Frieda. She had been the executive receptionist for thirty years and treated everyone with respect, regardless of what they looked like. His Executive Directorate peers were not held in such high esteem. Rinaldi cynically thought how odd it was that he was the first to arrive. These guys had to get their morning rubdowns, workouts, or whatever. Work wasn't their priority. The blasted meeting started in fifteen minutes. Rinaldi was coming from nearly one hundred kilometers away and these arrogant, do nothing suits couldn't get here before him? Rinaldi took several deep breaths to regain his composure. It was show time.

"Maverick, you are looking spry on this fine morning," remarked Gerhard Lanzinger, SPI's CEO.

Rinaldi bristled at the use of the distasteful nickname given him by an obnoxious uncle on his mother's side. Rinaldi's mother was a banker from Moscow; his father, a highly paid consultant to the Italian Minister of Economy and Finance. They had met and fallen in love at an economic conference in Milan. Rinaldi was raised in his father's hometown of Florence. His boorish uncle proffered the unwelcome nickname many years ago to commemorate what he saw as the young boy's "spirit to be different." After his terrible childhood accident, Rinaldi felt the nickname to be most insensitive. He had regrettably mentioned the nickname during his interview with Lanzinger to set himself apart from other candidates. Rinaldi's real name was Niccolo Abandonato. While in high school, his father had been arrested in a national embezzlement scandal. Embarrassed, he legally changed his name, assumed a new identity, and never returned home.

He forced a smile and replied, "It is good to be with you again, Gerhard. These gatherings are always most productive." The lying came easy.

The ornate room filled with members of the prestigious Executive Directorate. Rinaldi, dressed simply in a black sport coat and charcoal button down shirt open at the neck, scoffed to himself as the stuffy group of prima donnas filed in. The colors and patterns varied but in each one, Rinaldi saw only the finely tailored suit, starched shirt, silk necktie, and shoes refined to a gloss, enabling one to see his own reflection. This "old boys" group comprising the management team of one of the world's pharmaceutical behemoths was all male. Each one, starting at the top with Lanzinger, fancied himself a quintessential businessman capable of running any company with precision. Lanzinger, the arrogant son of a bitch, was the biggest clown of all, at least in Rinaldi's eyes.

The twelve men took their assigned seats around a rectangular conference room table made of the world's purest glass, nearly five centimeters (two inches) thick, with polished edges rounded at the corners. The high-backed chairs were a fine, soft black Italian leather contoured perfectly to complement the stress of sitting for long periods of time. The chairs were the only thing about this room Rinaldi admired. The comfort of the chairs helped keep his sanity in check as these meetings pushed well past their natural saturation point. Everyone settled in and Lanzinger got down to business.

"Our primary purpose for today's meeting will be a thorough review of products in market and products currently under development. The morning will be dedicated to sales, marketing, and product enhancement possibilities for existing lines, the afternoon to future product possibilities. Lanzinger turned the floor over to a series of quacks who, one by one, spoke in front of PowerPoint shows designed to dazzle. After thirty minutes, Rinaldi had mentally checked out. *They actually think they are accomplishing something,* he remarked to himself.

By 11:30, Lanzinger was already focused on what would be served for lunch. The head chef from SPI's executive dining room and his staff were setting up the extravagant meal to be served in the adjacent dining room. Appetizers, including caviar, were to be followed by the fresh catch of the day washed down with the finest in French wines, hailing from a vineyard in Alsace, near Rinaldi's home. Desperately needing a break from this madness, Rinaldi excused himself, pulled out his cell phone, and summoned Clifford. Two-hour lunches were not uncommon for an SPI Executive Directorate meeting. He would take the time to recharge for the afternoon session.

Rinaldi hobbled out the main lobby and found a waiting Clifford standing by the shiny Rolls, which had just been unnecessarily washed and waxed. It was a crisp, cool day in Basel. He climbed in the backseat, cracked the window, and told Clifford to drive along The Rhine to Basler Münster, the old, red sandstone church that had been standing for hundreds of years. While not a religious man, Rinaldi found solace in architecture. Basler Münster would prove a peaceful departure for his weary mind.

A block from the exalted church that resembled a castle, the Rolls came to a halt at a red light. Rinaldi watched as the notable green tram passed by. While stopped, Rinaldi spotted a takeout café offering a quick lunch. The rich foods being consumed in SPI's executive conference room would have upset his digestive system for a week. His tastes in cuisine were simple. Rinaldi made his way to the café window and proceeded to order flammekeuche, something akin to pizza without the tomatoes. He liked his with mild cheeses and fresh ham. To wash it down, he purchased a bottle of his favorite beer, Kronenbourg. The hustle and bustle of Basel seemed to relax him. Seated on a stone curb in the shadows of Basler Münster, his mind wandered back to the horrific childhood day that now fueled his every move.

A doctor from the Maryland hospital came in to discuss the diagnosis. He heard the doctor express relief that his parents were highly educated and spoke perfect English. He listened intently as the doctor explained.

"I am sorry to tell you that the boy's right knee has been damaged beyond repair. Surgery will help with pain management but the boy will likely walk with a bad limp for the remainder of his life."

Mother began to sob. Father's emotions were evident through his tired eyes. His shoulders slumped forward and his face turned haggard as the doctor continued.

"I am afraid that's not all. Your son will be permanently blind in his right eye. He has a cracked rib, multiple contusions, and a few minor lacerations. We'd like him to remain here in the pediatric ward for a few days for observation before making the journey back to Italy."

Upon hearing the news, he remembered becoming distraught. His usually stoic demeanor evaporated and he had openly wept. His parents tried to calm him but his uncharacteristic furor left them not knowing what to do. Fully enraged, he swept his arm across the surface of the wheeled serving tray poised above his hospital bed. A water jug flew the expanse of the small room, landing violently against the glass window and cracking the pane. The tray, cup, and bedpan clanked to the floor and came to rest in a puddle amid the dated linoleum.

In his fit of anger, the youngster cursed loudly, through his tears, slipping unconsciously between Italian, his mother's native Russian tongue, and English.

"Perché io? YA ne mogu prodolzhat. Why me? I cannot go on!" he recalled crying aloud.

In the ensuing years, he visited with numerous counselors and therapists but the rage he felt remained long after his stay in the rural Maryland hospital.

The horseback riding session had been a way for him to feel better about being rejected in what he felt was a very subjective process. The school simply did not comprehend the brilliant mind of young Niccolo, the prodigy. A day that had started badly finished as a complete and total tragedy.

He had scored a perfect 100 on his written examinations. It had to be the interview! In preparing for the interview with the school's headmaster, he had taken counsel from his assigned student ambassador; a boy roughly his own age who was asked to show him the ropes and be his guide for the day. As he replayed the prep session in his mind, he clearly remembered being told that the headmaster looked for risk takers. *Anyone can deliver the expected answer. You need to set yourself apart by showing you are different from every other applicant.* He recalled the words with clarity. He heeded the advice. The headmaster had not responded in the expected manner. In fact, he had been admonished and told that he needed more discipline if he wished to be successful in the competitive world of scientific research and development. He was shocked at the verbal tongue-lashing. The headmaster dismissed his candidacy on the spot.

For the previous five years, young Niccolo and his parents had planned his admission to the highly regarded American school. In one fell swoop, a man's words and a horse's fear had shattered his dreams and his body. As he moved through a range of powerful emotions, he had come to the realization that the student ambassador had been toying with him. Someone he presumed he could trust, a peer assigned for his benefit, played a joke and brought his entire world down upon him. Feeling betrayed, he vowed never to forget.

A marching band played nearby. The beat of the drum caused him to take note of the time. The temporary reprieve with real food, good drink, and fresh air under the shadow of Basler Münster had come to an end. He instructed Clifford to take him back downtown for an afternoon of misery.

Lanzinger reconvened the gathering as Rinaldi entered the room. The glazed-over faces around the table appeared to be in a state of food coma, or maybe it was the wine. Nevertheless, Rinaldi just wanted to get it over with. Tomorrow he would be back at the Colmar facility, pursuing the advancement of his life's work, the reversal of the human aging process.

Unfortunately, Rinaldi found that the endeavor had to take a back seat to creating the more mundane discoveries that created profits for Lanzinger's effusive lifestyle.

"Maverick, could you please update the team on the products slated for release in the next eighteen months?" asked Lanzinger.

"Certainly, Gerhard. Nothing would give me greater pleasure."

For the next hour, with the most basic of visual aids, Rinaldi astonished the team with an assessment of three new pharmaceutical products. One was a rescue aerosol inhalant for asthma patients. The idea, he explained, was to expand bronchial tissue, easing breathing difficulties in half the time of existing bronchodilators. A second product was an eye drop for glaucoma that would last one week, as opposed to the daily application currently on the market, and third was a pill to halt hot flashes in menopausal women. Rinaldi walked the team through each product, its efficacy, its cost to manufacture, suggested dosing, and potential side effects. The men around the table showered him with questions on each product, most of which he found amusing based on their simplicity.

When the questions came to an end, Rinaldi meandered back to his seat at the table and began to sit down when Lanzinger said, "As always, Maverick, a fine job. Your research in Colmar has kept us on track for projected earnings for the next two years. I am very proud of your contributions. However, I wish to share with the team that there has recently been talk of a hostile takeover of SPI. Our board is obviously opposed to such an action. They have asked me to double down on our research, to stretch the limits of our imagination, and to open a line of pharmaceuticals with the potential to define a new market. The board feels that such a development would make us less desirable as a target because of the added risk. It will also help to elevate us above the competition."

Rinaldi grimaced to himself. The request reinforced his belief that Lanzinger was an idiot. *What CEO of a billion-dollar multinational firm would take on expensive and unnecessary uncertainty to stave off a hostile takeover?*

"Gerhard, are you sure this is a wise course for our company? The additional risk could place SPI in a position of jeopardy if such undetermined product exploration failed to yield results."

"I understand but I assured the board that you, Maverick, are the one person who can pull a rabbit out of the hat. Any thought on how to proceed?"

Rinaldi paused, took a deep breath without making it obvious, and replied, "Yes, Gerhard, I think you should revisit your conversation with the board. Try to talk some sense into them. Foolish exploration for the reasons stated would not please our shareholders."

When Lanzinger proved too stubborn, Rinaldi knew he had to come up with something to appease the egotistical CEO. With forethought, he dangled out, "What if I told you I think I can reverse the aging process?"

"What are you saying? You mean like a Fountain of Youth?" asked the stunned leader.

"Something like that. In my free time, I have been toying with research giving me hope that through a process called programmable cell death, I can theoretically control cell division in quantity and quality, a process that naturally changes as people age."

"That's fascinating!" replied Lanzinger. The rest of the team followed Lanzinger's lead. If the leader appeared interested, they were as well. None of them dared to say a word, knowing full well that upstaging the self-absorbed CEO was a bad career move.

Lanzinger commissioned a full report assessing the viability and timing of the antiaging product. Rinaldi wasn't sure he should have revealed his secret research to the Executive Directorate but as he had thought it through, he concluded that he could manage expectations in exchange for greater resource allocation. His penchant for strategic thinking turned this into a banner day.

Unexpectedly, his pet project jumped to the top of the corporate priority list. This meant more money at his disposal for staff, equipment, and research. Rinaldi reveled in the unexpected development. He enjoyed the adulation heaped upon him by Lanzinger and the Executive Directorate. While he didn't respect this group, he longed for affirmation of his skills. Never again would he be told he wasn't good enough. Never again would he be rejected by people with inferior intellect. He would succeed at all costs. Nothing and no one would get in his way. When the dust settled, those who had disrespected him would understand, completely understand, that they had committed a grievous error.

CHAPTER 4

Ben drove his beat-up Blue Pearl Honda down the meandering road. His private research facility resided atop a long and winding maple tree-lined road barely constituting a known county thoroughfare. That's just what he wanted . . . tranquility and seclusion. He was anxious to get back to work. Years of effort were finally beginning to culminate in what could prove to be the most fascinating scientific breakthrough of the twenty-first century. Scientific discovery aside, the work represented a small degree of sanctuary from the prior day's funeral.

Ben brought the Honda to a stop at a wrought iron gate controlled by a remote transmitter emitting an untraceable frequency. The gate was too high to traverse and its connecting fence surrounding the property was treated with a special resin to make climbing impossible. He thought electric fences for security might prove barbaric. With the push of a button, the heavy gates came to life and slowly welcomed the old Honda and its owner.

The Lab resided on a substantial tract of fifty acres deep in the woods of suburban Maryland. He chose to build the research center near The Harmon School for Gifted Scientific Youth to avail himself of young, innovative talent and be close to his mentor, the school's founder and long tenured provost, Dr. Albert Harmon. Many years ago, Ben labored at The Harmon School under the watchful eye of Dr. Harmon. The proximity to DC and New York was also helpful, as he made many trips to Capitol Hill and Manhattan in the never-ending quest for additional funding.

"I swear to God, the answer just came to me at the funeral home," Ben declared in an animated fashion as he shrugged with outstretched arms. "Staring down into the casket, I realized why our experiments keep bombing."

Rachel and Tomi were running most of the fruitless trials but it was Ari who was the first to protest.

"What? You are saying that staring at a dead guy in a casket gave you the answer we've been seeking for nearly two years? If only I knew it would be so easy, I'd have been hanging out in the local mortuaries."

Ben noted the sarcasm and flipped Ari the bird.

"At the funeral yesterday, I had an epiphany. It occurred to me that years of failure in animal trials were the result of a certain rare protein that exists in most animal cells but not human cells. If we eliminate the protein from our work, the results will materialize."

Tomi offered, "And that means taking the animal cells out of play." With the death of Andrew Kauffman, Tomi was now the team's biology lead.

"That's right."

Rachel shifted nervously in the old brown side chair Ben nicknamed "the catcher's mitt." He had an affinity for baseball.

"Do you have any idea what the Liferay will do to human cells?" Rachel was Ben's right-hand person. In addition to being an accomplished physicist from Southern California, she was the person on the team with the strongest sense of organization. He valued her nurturing capabilities and inclination to always stress the positive. She was the glue that made the team successful.

"Based on computer modeling Andrew and I were working on, it should work," added Tomi, a noted biologist who was a third-generation

Japanese-American hailing from San Francisco. Her prior work in cell restoration theory had earned her a coveted award from The World Biology Institute. Tomi still held the record as the youngest recipient in history.

Ari winced and tore the wire rim glasses from his rotund face. "This is total bullshit. I think we're still a long way from human cell trials. What's the rush? You're not bringing Andrew back—or any other dead person, for that matter." Ari was a physicist from Philadelphia and a graduate of The Harmon School. He was the eldest member of the team at the ripe old age of forty-five, just five years older than Ben. It was Ari on whom Ben relied the most to drive his concepts toward reality. When Ben was out of town, Ari assumed the team lead.

Still replete with guilt over Andrew's accident, Ben wanted to flip off Ari again. He settled for throwing him a hairy eyeball denoting his extreme displeasure. Ari caught the drift.

"Sorry, I was out of line."

"Forget it," Ben replied somewhat insincerely. That familiar pain ran down the back of his neck. Like a vise, it gripped the muscles in his upper back and squeezed.

Ben was determined. He always was, no matter what the task at hand. The new summit was to successfully infuse life into human cells more than eight hours after death. Anxiety morphed into adrenaline. He had that twinkle in his eye. He flashed it when he was feeling confident in his ability to solve the most complex equations. No stranger to scientific success, at a young age he had built an international reputation by developing technology for inexpensive, renewable energy, greatly reducing America's dependence on foreign oil. The fortune he made from that technology fueled the construction of the Lab and his current quest to restore life to the recently deceased. Inspired by a recurring dream and motivated by the secret Gramps bestowed only upon him, Ben forced himself to continue failing forward. Physical limitations were signs of weakness. Despite his self-awarded culpability in Andrew's death, he understood that his overarching goal pushed him to be relentless.

Before he could conclude the meeting, Ari's inhibitions had to be dealt with. Ben would appeal to his sense of adventure. He knew Ari would bite on the opportunity to experiment without restriction. Scientists were naturally regimented people. Once in a while, when circumstances warranted, one had to step out of bounds. It was that string he needed to pull. Everyone else was getting onboard with the plan. Except . . . *where in hell was Harrison?*

At that moment, the burly and immense Harrison Bock busted through the doors of the meeting space they referred to as the Dugout. "Sorry I'm late. Did I miss anything other than the normal early morning coffee talk?"

"You might say that, Harrison," quipped Ben.

○ ○ ○ ○ ○

After several weeks consumed with data validation, brainstorm meetings, and in-depth research, Ben and his team finally gathered in the main scientific theater, the largest in the facility and the one reserved specifically for use by his team. Retina scans were required to enter the main lab. The cell samples had been extracted from patients at nearby Upper Chesapeake Medical Center. This was done with cooperation from the hospital and the patients. Consent forms were executed stating that, in the event of death, tissue samples could be biopsied in small quantities and used for cell restoration trials. Similar to the transport of an organ awaiting transplant, the samples were placed in a temperature-controlled cooler and driven fifteen minutes by a special medical vehicle from Bel Air to Maplebrook. The samples Ben had before him were from a patient that died at 9:21 that morning. Ben's research indicated that human cells remain active, on average, for about eight hours after death. It was now 5:30 p.m.

Upon arrival, the cells were immediately treated with a chemical formulation developed by Harrison. Its intended purpose was to "preserve" the cells from further degradation until the Liferay could restore them to their former state. The Liferay was the name Ben gave to his crowning achievement, a femtosecond laser designed to restore preserved human cells by emitting a series of ultra-short pulses in varying colors to address different cell types. While Ben had conceived the Liferay, it was Ari who built the first prototype.

With his team gathered around, donning protective eyewear, Ben took the Liferay and gradually pulled back on a small, metallic lever, which began the process. The Liferay's rotation hit the samples, causing the cells to glow inside the Petri dishes. The whole process lasted mere seconds.

Monitors displaying the energy of the cells were set high above the surface on which they worked. When the monitors registered the building energy of the treated cells, Ben threw a celebratory hug in Ari's direction. Rachel, Tomi, and Harrison were high-fiving and then hugs all around. The scientific team of Ben Abraham had just gone beyond what anyone in its field had ever dreamed of accomplishing. The implications of success were immense, to say the least. A commercial Liferay device in hospitals and ambulances around the world could routinely save lives.

○ ○ ○ ○ ○

Four hours later, his body was rebelling. His head was splitting and his eyes were burning. A new pain emerged in the bone behind his left ear. Probably just exhaustion, he reasoned. Minutes after he had closed his eyes on an old couch in the Dugout, Rachel burst in the room.

"Ben, Ben . . . wake up!"

His head in a fog, he rubbed his tired eyes and replied, "What's the problem?"

"The cells—they've mutated."

○ ○ ○ ○ ○

Thirty minutes later, the entire team was back in the Dugout to review the latest debacle.

"Any idea what went wrong?" Ben queried in his weary and frustrated state.

Ari ran his fingers through his thinning hair in an anxious manner and removed his wire-rimmed glasses with his left hand. "Hell, I don't know. My best guess would center on the Liferay. Something to do with the duration of the laser application, maybe. It could be off by a femtosecond. I mean, it could be anything."

He was troubled by Ari's assessment. A femtosecond was *a quadrillionth, or one millionth of a billionth of one second.* Being off by a single femtosecond left a margin of error wide enough to baffle the world's most powerful supercomputers. He knew the problem would not be solved on this night.

Dejected and not wanting to quit, he reluctantly said, "We're all beyond tired. Everyone knock off for the night and let's pour through the data tomorrow. There has to be a clue in the data."

With that, Rachel and Tomi headed out with Harrison and Ari. Ben lingered. Let the others go home. He was likely to work all night. With black coffee in hand, he retreated to his office to start unearthing clues to the damaging mutations.

Ben sat down behind his desk, moved aside stacks of paper and books, and set his coffee down. Empty coffee cups were overflowing in his small metal waste can. He believed in the science. His team had been at it for two years. They were so close. In fact, the day's short-lived success was enough to bring most scientists a lifetime of satisfaction. Would Andrew know what to do from here? Tomi was more than capable of taking over the biology aspects of their work. Ari didn't have the answers. He would have Rachel work with him to validate the femtosecond laser calculation. That was due diligence. Harrison? For some reason, the laser and the preservation chemical were not playing well together. Instinct told him the answer they sought was rooted in the preservative. He had the utmost faith in Harrison. He had the ability to see difficult equations through a prism different from anyone else he had ever worked with. This time, however, Ben wasn't sure. This equation was like no other. Harrison seemed to be stuck. Given the unprecedented nature of what they were attempting, Ben began to worry. What if the equation were simply unsolvable?

CHAPTER 5

In search of her soul, Dr. Rachel Larkin looked deep within and tried to process the void. Religion was never a big part of her formative years. She understood their work would naturally raise moral issues. Focus on the prize, she reminded herself. *Saving lives, helping people—that's what you signed up for.*

She pulled a long lock of light brown hair away from her swollen and bloodshot green eyes. She had no personal life to speak of. Like the other members of the team, her work was her life. Rachel was tired. Her face showed it and her body screamed it. She quickly dismissed those physiological reminders. She and the senior scientific team had just completed an experiment, a promising building block that could change the world. Reveling in the day's monumental accomplishment, she concluded that no time was available for nursing tired bodies and worn out souls.

She and Tomi went to the Lab's main theater to check on their work. The monitors set up to gauge the energy of the neoteric cells infused by the Liferay had once again gone dark. A yellow, rectangular error message greeted them. Rachel knew instantly that their latest efforts to build upon the recent purported breakthrough had culminated in yet another failure. Not that the monitors would lie but visual confirmation of the cell samples told the full story. To Rachel, it was as if a beautiful bouquet of lilies, her favorite flower, had wilted before its time.

The team remained in search of the missing key. Ben's epiphany about removing animal proteins showed real promise. Something was still amiss. As instructed, she had validated the Liferay settings. She and Ari were confident that they were accurate to the femtosecond. Although they were attempting to solve an impossible equation, the formula seemed somewhat straightforward. The essential elements remained the Liferay, the preservative, and time, but in what quantities? That was the question. As she wrestled with the morning pangs of morality, she knew they were so close, yet still so far away.

She was on her way to the main scientific theater. Ben's office was outside the entrance. Before getting down to work for the day, she wanted to bounce some thoughts around with him. As she neared his doorway, from behind, she heard his suave voice reverberate through the corridor.

"He's not in there."

She turned to greet him. Ben had an armful of folders and donned his usual attire. Jeans, an unbuttoned plaid sport shirt, and a T-shirt underneath bearing the logo of his favorite baseball team, the Dodgers. His shirt sleeves were rolled up a third of the way. How many of those T-shirts does he own, she wondered?

"Got a few minutes? she asked. I want to run some ideas by you before we get going today."

"Yep, just need to drop these files off in my office."

She followed him into his office and watched from behind as he encountered an unusual site. Harrison sat back in the faded and torn faux leather chair with his size-thirteen dogs plopped squarely in the middle of the desk, atop mounds of haphazardly arranged paper. The chair squeaked under his girth as he shifted and waited. Rachel noticed his impatience dressed in the form of a shit-eating grin.

"Harrison, mind telling me what the hell you are doing behind my desk?" asked a troubled Ben Abraham.

"Oh, is this your office, Dr. Abraham? I must have gotten lost in my euphoric state of delirium."

Rachel, at Ben's side, chimed in. "I know that look, Harrison. Out with it."

"All I can tell you guys is that the breakfast cereal people are gonna be really jealous. I just nailed the preservative to end all preservatives."

Understanding the magnitude of Harrison's revelation, she watched as Ben's angular face cracked a smile that truly went from ear to ear.

"Are you saying what I think you are saying?" Ben asked.

"Does a bear shit in the woods?"

"How long?"

"Best guess, eighteen months at most."

Ben looked right at her. Their eyes locked and their restrained sense of professionalism gave way to unrestrained joy. Instinctively, Ben threw his long arms around her neck and proffered a celebratory embrace. Surprised, she felt her body move close to his, absorbing the warmth of the unforeseen occurrence.

Harrison, still sitting behind Ben's desk with his feet perched up top, said, "Easy there, Stretch. No love for the big guy? She didn't invent the new preservative."

Rachel blushed. She chuckled like a schoolgirl when Ben looked over to Harrison and in a most collegial fashion replied, "If you get your feet off my desk, you can have a hug, too."

Harrison smirked. Ben suggested they assemble the team and share the breakthrough.

In the Dugout, the team listened as Harrison took them through his process. It took an hour to get through the scientific machinations, particularly with Harrison's inclination for theatre. Rachel half listened to Harrison's tale. Her mind was spinning. The discovery was of paramount importance. With an advanced chemical preservative to properly seal the cells for a later awakening, she knew they had taken a major step toward commercializing the ability to reunite people with their deceased loved ones. The Liferay, the preservative, and time. The first two elements appeared in order. Harrison was now able to estimate the time a cell could survive in a preserved state. Eighteen months, he guessed. Their goal was twelve. Now knowing that they could keep preserved cells viable for a year or more, the last barrier to knock down was understanding how to keep damaging mutation from occurring for at least twenty-four hours after awakening with the Liferay. It was her job to figure out how to get there. At that moment, she really had no idea.

ooooo

That was a year and a half ago. God, how many times had they failed since then? As a scientist, she knew all about failure. Dr. Oswald "Oz" Moore, one of her former professors, once told her, "For every success, expect one thousand failed attempts." She recalled thinking at the time that the guy was off his rocker. Now she knew the truth. There was no teacher like real life experience and Rachel and the team had logged no fewer than twelve hundred futile attempts at successfully awakening preserved human cells.

One night, long after most everyone had departed, she and Tomi began reviewing the experimentation of their oldest samples. They had been at it since 8:00 am. Old Dr. Oz used to say, "When all else fails, try what others deem impossible, if not improbable." Rachel had begun to feel a sense of fatigue with the situation but she found her resolve. Displaying the grit and bulldogged determination with which she ultimately attacked everything, she said, "Tomi, I ran the latest Liferay trial on human cell samples that are six months old. I was able to stave off mutation for twelve hours."

Rachel experienced that old, familiar rush of adrenaline. Despite the near physical exhaustion, all of her senses came alive. The energy was liberating.

"That's encouraging," Tomi replied as she retied the bright red band around her short, black frizz ponytail. "Did you try the nine-month-old samples?"

"As a matter of fact, I did."

"And?"

"That got me to eighteen hours."

"So, that begs the obvious question."

"Right. What's the oldest sample we have?"

"We started collection and storage just after the first cell mutation eighteen months ago."

"Great. Get me a set of twelve and eighteen month samples. It's time to see if we can make old Dr. Oz proud."

"Too late," she laughed. "We've already blown his thousand to one success ratio."

Whenever Rachel Larkin was on the verge of a great discovery, bile rose from her gut and a metallic taste enveloped her mouth. It was her sixth sense that she was onto something really good. Rachel, a star physics student at The University of California, had been experiencing this dynamic dating back to her high school days in the sleepy hamlet of Lobo, halfway between San Diego and Los Angeles, due east from San Clemente.

They loaded the aged cell samples into a small rectangular chamber and activated an electronic vacuum, causing the cells to be hermetically sealed within the small space. Rachel watched as Tomi guided the Liferay's titanium exterior through a lens at the chamber's topside. Rachel activated the Liferay by slowly depressing a trigger on the device's underbelly. The two scientists observed through separate eye-protective magnifying scopes as a thin beam of alternating, varicolored light streamed into the outer edge of the year-old cells.

Rachel remarked, "It never ceases to amaze me that the concentration of Liferay into the perimeter of a cell offers a completely different result than streaming into the center."

"I remember those early trials. The cells just got obliterated when we hit them in the middle."

"I know, right? Maybe it's the little girl in me but I love watching the outer edge of those cells light up and then begin glowing from the outer edge inward."

"Don't tell Ben. He'll tell you to grow up."

"Yeah, I need to loosen him up. He's all work and no play."

The cells seemed to come alive all at once. Attached to the chamber was a monitor indicating live, normal cell activity, a most positive sign.

"Tomi, let's fire up those eighteen-month-old samples while we're at it. Then we can take a break. The monitors will text us if any of the samples go into a state of distress."

"A break" for Rachel meant another infusion of caffeine and then a few more hours of work. She didn't mind the long hours. That journey into an uncertain future had always been part of who she was. Yet somehow, she knew, she would always find her way through. Her sense of organization and determination enabled her to plow through obstacles like a bushman with a machete in the midst of a dense jungle. Rachel fed off the discovery and craved whatever came next.

○ ○ ○ ○ ○

Two days later, Rachel gathered the team to present the results in the Dugout. Ben was already stretched out in the catcher's mitt while Ari fell into the folds of the beat-up sofa. Tomi leaned against the mural in such a way that she appeared to be up against the metal railing above the painted cement steps. To no one's surprise, Harrison arrived late, unshaven, curly blond locks uncombed, wrinkled shirt untucked, and with the latest astonishing excuse for his tardiness.

"Guys, you won't believe this but my cat gave birth this morning.

Heck, I didn't even know it was a 'she.' I've been calling her Herman," laughed Harrison.

Ari fought back the tears from his amusement and said, "Bock, your whole life is nothing but a hot mess."

"That's funny, Ari. You're a riot. Hey, anybody want a kitten?"

Rachel waited for the lighthearted fun to subside and then got the meeting in gear.

"Well, Tomi and I have good news and news that's not so great."

Rachel showed the team the data from the experiments with six- and nine-month-old cell samples. She proceeded to elaborate on the next set of trials with twelve- and eighteen-month-old cells.

"We had our first major success with the twelve-month sample. The awakened cells remained viable for nearly twenty-four hours."

Ben replied, "Terrific news. What do you attribute the success to? It doesn't seem to make sense that the Liferay won't work on cells younger than a year."

"As near as we can figure, it seems that the cells need to 'cure' after being treated with Bock's preservative."

"Do we get extended viability when we use the eighteen-month old samples?" asked Ari, pushing his round wire frame glasses back up the bridge of his nose.

"No," replied Rachel. "That's the not so good news. Research is clearly indicating that cells much younger or older than one year mutate badly. After eighteen months and more than one thousand experiments, we haven't been able to crack the twenty-four-hour threshold."

Knowing Ben was not one to give up, Rachel guided the conversation to the next phase.

"Ben, I am recommending a short series to validate the data on the twelve-month-old samples. If all goes as expected, I think it's time to enlist some candidates for human trials."

Ben looked at her quizzically. Rachel would not be deterred. Her rich, emerald green eyes and the arched right eyebrow maneuvered into position as if to say, "You know I'm right."

Inwardly, she laughed at his reaction every time she threw him "the look." She knew he got the message. Whereas both she and Ben were driven to succeed, Rachel knew Ben could stay too long in the blue sky of endless improvement opportunities. She understood he was trying desperately to overcome an innate sense of occasional recklessness. As a result, he could sometimes be too careful, too deliberate. She, on the other hand, settled on a course she knew would work and put the wheels in motion. Perfection was a goal to which they both aspired. The difference between her and Ben was that he needed to get there all at once. She was content to get there by building one small victory on top of the other. It was Rachel who had to give Ben the push to get him moving down the road to success.

"Before I agree," said Ben, "tell me we're not moving too fast for our own good."

CHAPTER 6

Eighteen months later

Coping with her mother's death had been the most difficult period of her life. The ensuing year had passed agonizingly slowly. Each day felt like torture, every moment a limitless void in a deep, dark abyss. Molly Kendrick knew she was weak, both in physical stature and constitution. Her mother had been her best friend, her rock. As an only child growing up in a rural Maryland town, it was her mother who had proved to be friend, mentor, and armchair psychologist every time she fell apart, which was often.

Sylvia Bresling was, by all accounts, a saint. She was described as selfless, congenial, giving, and generous. She was the first to volunteer for church committees, nurse a sick friend, or rescue a stray animal. She was the light in Molly's life and the lives of so many others. Today, Molly had prepared for her miracle. She imagined the reality of the impossible. She would be reunited with her mother, not through death but through life. Her impossible dream had been almost close enough to touch.

At her lowest moment, Molly never fathomed the heartache she now felt. It was inconceivable that her mother would have memory loss. These jokers had reams of legal documents for her to sign but no one had warned of this possibility. As she stood by the metal table where her mother lay, her leg muscles began to acquiesce to the overpowering strain. Almost by instinct, she clutched her husband's arm and squeezed, partly for emotional support, partly to keep herself steady. Her stomach gurgled. Nausea stripped the façade of any bravery she sought to display. With tears rolling down her cheeks, Molly glanced around, wondering what might happen next.

On one side of the table were Drs. Abraham and Larkin and on the other, Drs. Oka and Weiskopf. The big man, Harrison, who had helped escort her to the floor, was stationed alone at the far end. As Molly stood there softly crying, she watched in horror as her mother became agitated and irrational. Sylvia stood on wobbly legs, her gown askew, and lurched past Weiskopf and Oka. Before they could catch her, she fainted and slammed into a control panel. Her left shoulder depressed a button activating the Liferay device. Without guidance, the device spun out of control and began emitting its rotational bursts one hundred and eighty degrees from its normal destination, directly into the forehead of Harrison Bock.

The laser pounded into Harrison's head. Still on his feet, he was paralyzed where he stood. His mouth locked in an open position and his eyes went wide. Molly was horrified. Although her mother was on the floor and in distress, she could not look away. When the Liferay finished its programmed cycle of rotational bursts, it let Harrison go.

Harrison fell backward, cracking his head on the cold, tiled floor. To Molly, the terrifying scene played out in slow motion for what seemed like forever. In reality, only thirty seconds had passed.

She rushed to her mother's side. Jeff went with her. They could detect a faint pulse. All of the other lab people rushed to the far end of the table where the immense body of Harrison Bock had fallen.

"My mother needs help, now!" demanded Molly.

She felt badly for their friend, a victim of the unfortunate incident caused by her mother, but her mother was not going to be ignored. After all, she was the focus of the day. Molly felt trapped in the most chaotic occurrence of her life. As she waited, she heard Rachel Larkin scream, to no one in particular.

"He's not breathing!"

After she had seen three paramedics struggle to lift the huge man off the floor and onto a gurney, Molly and her husband were shown into a private office. On the door, a small sign indicated that it belonged to Dr. Benjamin Abraham. Although Molly was a neat freak, in her frazzled state, she barely noticed the disheveled nature of her immediate surroundings. She sat and waited, the familiar package of travel-sized Kleenex firmly in her grasp.

Molly had seen her mother come back for a brief period. But it wasn't her mother at all. It was her mother's body but in no other manner was that crazed woman her beloved mother. Molly knew her mother as the world's most gentle soul, a selfless sort who volunteered at soup kitchens and gave generously to charities. The person she saw today was someone else entirely. Jeff rifled through her purse, looking for the Xanax. She took double the prescribed dose. She calmed, but just a bit.

Fifteen minutes later, a haggard Ben Abraham walked through the door, greeted them warmly, and sat down behind the messy desk.

"How are you doing, Molly?" he inquired.

"I am a wreck, in case you couldn't tell."

"I understand. Today was not at all what any of us had hoped for. We think that your mother was affected by a neurodegenerative disease, sort of like Alzheimer's, that caused her not to recognize you. None of this showed up on her prescreening forms or tests. Did she ever display any signs of memory loss in the years before she died?"

"No, none at all. In fact, her mind was as sharp as a tack. She had amazing recall," she replied. A growing resentment was building in her tone.

"It is possible that the hibernation process might have caused proteins in her cells to act unnaturally, creating the condition upon awakening."

"Are you suggesting that your process caused this condition to occur?" asked Jeff.

"Yes, that is possible," replied Ben.

"So, what's the next step? How do you cure her?" asked Molly, as she fought through the tears.

"Unfortunately, there is no cure. Medical science cannot cure such diseases in the living. We have no other choice but to place your mother back into a state of permanent sleep and turn the remains over to you for a funeral."

Molly lost it. Her sadness had shifted to full-fledged rage.

"You mean to tell me that you plan to euthanize my mother? Like an old dog? Are you out of your mind?"

"I understand you are upset. Without a way to reverse the neurodegenerative condition, we cannot place your mother back into an effective hibernation and reawakening in accordance with the original plan."

"So, you want me to have a funeral for my mother? She died a year ago. We skipped a funeral because you were going to bring her back, and keep bringing her back, year after year, for a day at a time. That was the deal, right? We expect you to make it right. Do whatever you need to do to bring her back the way she was," she demanded.

"Molly, I feel your pain. There is nothing I would like to do more than that. It just isn't possible."

Molly reverted from anger to despair. She sobbed uncontrollably. She felt Jeff gently take her hand, indicating it was time to leave. Molly Kendrick left the Lab defeated, her spirits crushed. The trial was over and so was the chance that she would ever have another conversation with her mother. She had been robbed of the treasured opportunity.

CHAPTER 7

The long, flat head of the Komodo dragon shimmied. His muscular tail might have been called magnificent. In fact, it was. In the wild, the lengthy accoutrement served these beasts well. His beady eyes looked around, always curious, as the rounded snout ascended into the air. The bowed legs puttered slowly across the countertop in Rinaldi's Colmar office. Nearly three meters long and weighing seventy kilos, accompanied by scaly skin and shark-like teeth, he proved frightening to many. Not so for Anstrov Rinaldi. In an odd way, Rinaldi felt a kinship with his unusual companion.

It was time to make sure the subordinates understood his expectations. In Rinaldi's mind, the expectations had always been crystal clear. Those he placed faith in frequently let him down. Rinaldi, however, struggled with delegation.

The door to Rinaldi's office withstood a gentle knock.

"Come in," he barked through the closed door to Moretti and Ivanov, his top two people in Colmar. Dr. Vanessa Moretti was the chief scientific assistant and Dr. Maxim Ivanov, the chemist. Moretti entered first. Rinaldi noticed with irritation that Ivanov had stopped to chat up a colleague.

"Ugh! Shouldn't that thing be in a cage?" asked Moretti.

"My dear Vanessa, Drago is highly trained. If you are nice to him, he will gladly reciprocate. On the other hand, Komodo dragons have been known to eat almost anything. In fact, Drago can consume up to 80 percent of his body weight in a single meal. Given that he weighs a little more than you, I'd say that places you in line as a candidate for the main course on his luncheon menu." Rinaldi was enamored with his own attempt at humor. He was amused when Vanessa looked over at Drago and watched the elongated, yellow, forked tongue slither out of his mouth, as if aimed at her. "Thanks for the information. If it's all the same to you, Doctor, I think I'll keep my distance."

Rinaldi had the largest office in the Colmar facility. Vanessa would have no problem avoiding close contact with Drago. Ivanov meandered into the office. Rinaldi smiled to himself at the fear engendered in the timid soul that was Maxim Ivanov.

"Oh, it's loose. Dr. Rinaldi, I have previously requested that your giant lizard be in his cage when we meet. He makes me nervous."

Dr. Maxim Ivanov, Rinaldi's talent overseeing the development of the anti-aging drug, was a slight man, balding and very much a timid soul. Rinaldi sensed that it took all of the courage he had to merely suggest that Drago be in a cage.

"Not to worry, Maxim. Vanessa has already expressed her concern and offered to serve as lunch." Neither Vanessa nor Maxim laughed at Rinaldi's awkward banter.

Despite the setback in the schedule for the yet-to-be named antiaging drug, Rinaldi was in a reasonable mood. It had been eighteen months since the bittersweet victory in Basel. In exchange for an outlandish promise and enduring a day of abject boredom, he had received hundreds of millions in additional funding. Only eighteen months in and that lout, Lanzinger, was already on his case about results. Rinaldi had explained to his boss on numerous occasions that something this magnanimous takes years to develop. Since Lanzinger had an absence of backbone, he refused to be forthright with the board. *Idiot!*

Rinaldi hated the thought of having to depend on Moretti and Ivanov for results this important. He silently hoped he would not have to take over the project himself.

Ivanov began, "Based on the timetable you had given us at the commencement of the project, which we all felt was terribly aggressive, I have had teams literally working around the clock, seven days a week."

"And?" replied Rinaldi.

"And what, Doctor?" came Ivanov's sheepish reply.

In a millisecond, Rinaldi's mood deteriorated. His response to the weak-minded Ivanov thundered down on the little man like death by a thousand cuts. *"And . . . when in hell will I have a working formula?"*

Ivanov cowered in fear. In an attempt to rescue her colleague, Vanessa chimed in. "Dr. Rinaldi, as you know, it's not possible to deliver the results you require in such a short time period. Even with the resources you provide, it simply cannot be done."

This only served to send Rinaldi into full-scale rage. He felt his good eye bulge as if it were about to pop, his normal red complexion bordering on purple. He stood up and walked toward them with his polished, dark wood cane.

"Don't ever tell me something is impossible! Your excuses are tiresome. Tell me what is possible."

Ivanov was so frightened, Rinaldi was sure he was going to shit himself. Vanessa was better able to take these frequent outbursts in stride.

"Dr. Rinaldi, I believe we can have a working formula within six months and enter animal trials within a year. From there, timetables will be established by the degree of success at each trial phase. If animal trials go well, then we proceed to stage-one human trials."

"Do not patronize me, Dr. Moretti. You are here earning what you earn because you purport to be the best in the world. I gave you the formulaic concept. You simply have to shepherd it into production status. Any team of fools can surely do that. You two get out of my office. Come back by week's end with real results. If you fail, I will make sure your reputations precede you."

Moretti and Ivanov left as quickly as their legs would carry them. The door closed behind them. Rinaldi looked at Drago and chuckled, "I really need to get better help."

Drago seemed to smile as he looked at his benefactor and extended the forked tongue. Rinaldi made a mental note to call Lanzinger and buy time with stories of amazing progress. *That simpleton will believe any line of crap that serves his purpose.*

○ ○ ○ ○ ○

"*Guten morgan*, Gerhard. How are things in Basel?"

"Maverick, I am catching a ton of heat from the board on this antiaging drug. I need to deliver some good news."

Every fiber of Rinaldi's being stiffened as he heard the unwelcome use of the loathsome nickname. He shifted uncomfortably in his black, leather chair and tried to keep his expression even for the Skype transmission.

"I understand, Gerhard. You may explain to the board what they already know. In endeavors such as these, patience is the appropriate route. It takes years and billions to bring a new drug to market. For something as revolutionary as what we are discussing, even more time."

"I sense the board may be running low on patience. Even though we were able to fight off the takeover attempt, earnings for the past two quarters have been flat and the antiaging drug is the most promising thing we have in our pipeline."

"Tell them we have names that will win the hearts and minds of our target market. For the ladies, our product could be called Belissimo and for the gentlemen, Vigoré."

"Are you suggesting separate formulations by gender?"

"No, that will not be necessary. However, this will not prohibit us from giving the customer the idea that each gender requires its own formulation."

"Brilliant," exclaimed Lanzinger. "And the names you suggest—forgive me but I am rusty on my Italian."

"Belissimo, for the ladies, means 'beautiful' and 'vigoré' for the men implies strength and spirit of the young."

"You never cease to amaze me, Maverick. I will get marketing on this immediately. A press release would be prudent to boost confidence in our stock. Don't you think?"

"You are brilliant as well, Gerhard. Of course a press release would be in order. Please let me know if I can assist in any way. As you know, you have my complete loyalty and full cooperation."

"Thanks. We will need to feed the media some modicum of an idea regarding when these 'products' will hit the market."

Rinaldi considered his next words with extreme deliberation. "Tell them we anticipate market launch in eighteen months."

Lanzinger looked astonished. He loosened his necktie, and asked, "Are you sure? That seems aggressive, given that we have yet to get to a phase-one human trial."

"I understand Gerhard, but you must pave your way as a CEO who accomplishes what others cannot. This sets your company apart and distinguishes you as its leader."

Rinaldi knew he could prey on Lanzinger's ego. Lanzinger appeared to relax just a bit and reluctantly said, "I trust you, Maverick. If you can pull it off, I will put it out there. I can tell you though, if we fail, the board will have my ass on a platter."

"We will not fail, Gerhard. Do not worry."

They clicked off and Rinaldi sat back in his sizable leather chair. Letting Lanzinger get axed wouldn't be the worst thing in the world. Rinaldi could always tell the next CEO that no respectable scientist would have promised the timelines Lanzinger put in the press release. Who are they going to believe? Rinaldi was perfectly fine with Lanzinger taking the fall for introducing two formulations when only one is required. *Regulators will not care for this tactic*, he thought.

Rinaldi called Moretti and Ivanov back into his office. "I am sorry for earlier," he said. "I have been thinking about our conversation. You are right. We must be professional and cautious with how we proceed. Draw up a project plan enabling a potential market launch in three years."

CHAPTER 8

Ben had driven ninety miles per hour all the way to the ER. He had been scared in his life but he had never witnessed anything quite like the scene in which his best friend took a prolonged laser to the head. How Harrison was still alive was beyond comprehension. Ben just shook his head at the thought of it all. Just an hour earlier, the failed awakening of Sylvia Bresling had been the catalyst in a day's events gone awry.

In the hospital, doctors examining Harrison had no logical reason why he survived the accidental assault. Ben marveled at the fact that Harrison's hard head finally did him some good.

Since Ben was the closest thing to next of kin at the scene, he was allowed in the examining room. He paced back and forth in the small room, continuously bumping into the thin, blue curtain separating Harrison's unit from the adjacent one.

Courage, strength, patience, wisdom.

He forced himself to sit while he waited on the ER doctor to return.

Groggy and in a slow draw, Harrison came to, looked up at Ben and asked, "What in hell happened?"

Ben relayed the horror of the ill-fated awakening of Sylvia Bresling, how she tumbled into the control panel and accidentally activated the Liferay and its directional settings.

"Man, I have one lollapalooza of a headache."

"You are lucky to be alive. In fact, you are lucky you don't have brain damage."

"Are they sure I don't?"

"Preliminarily, yes. Still a few more hurdles to clear. The doc overseeing your case told me your thick skull saved your fat ass."

"Really? He actually said that?"

"Not in so many words, but yeah."

Ben knew that Harrison would be anxious to get back to work. Although he desperately needed Harrison's knowledge to unlock the mystery that was the failed awakening process of Sylvia Bresling, his primary concern was for the health of his friend. He still felt pangs of guilt over the death of Andrew Kauffman. While he gave Harrison the assurances he knew he would need to stay calm, the truth was the doctors *were* worried about permanent brain damage. Ben did not have the courage to tell his friend and chief chemist that he might never return to work.

○ ○ ○ ○ ○

Ben's brain was used to functioning like a powerful Intel chip. He could handle seemingly endless numbers of concurrent processes. The process got messed up only when one of two variables was introduced; exhaustion or emotion. On this day, he was feeling both. His brain was in overload, in need of a serious reboot.

Ben was overjoyed to see Harrison back at work in only one short week. He was mollified when doctors had cleared Harrison of any neurological issues. Ben was still concerned. Harrison needed to take some time off but he could not convince him to do so.

Completely lost in the fog of preoccupation, he was rattled back to reality by the persistence in Ari's voice. Today was the team's first opportunity to download on the Bresling case.

"Amnesia?" asked Ari.

"No," said Ben. "Amnesia is more likely the result of a head injury, a severe illness, or a seizure. Even certain types of drugs could cause it. Sylvia Bresling had none of these indicators."

It was Tomi who spoke next. "Bock's preservative is designed to keep proteins in the cells folded during death so that during awakening, they can resume normal function. If, for some reason, the proteins didn't fold properly, the patient could exhibit signs of an advanced neurodegenerative disease."

Harrison asked, "You mean like Alzheimer's?"

"Yes, or even Parkinson's or Huntington's," replied Tomi.

Ben simultaneously rubbed one hand across each of his tired eyes and somberly stated, "While I feel terrible for Bresling's family, the larger problem now becomes evident. If our process is flawed relative to protein folding and cell preservation, then every other patient we currently have in trial will awaken to a neurodegenerative disease."

"Oh Lord," exclaimed Ari. "That's eleven other people in trial that we are talking about."

"Do we terminate their trials?" asked Harrison.

"That would be inhumane," snapped Rachel.

The level head of Ben Abraham took over. "No, I think the wisest course is to inform the families of the remaining eleven patients that their loved ones will potentially wake with a condition rendering their memory dysfunctional. Each family will need to make a decision as to whether they wish to remain in the trial."

Ben continued, "The conundrum we currently face is the one-year curing period for the preservative process. Every time an awakening results in failure, the corrections we make will each take a year to prove out. That means we could be years and years from taking commercial applications."

With that proclamation, the mood turned bleak. Ben watched Tomi as she nervously flicked her ponytail, which he knew was her way of slipping into deep thought. Then, with the notion fully formed, Tomi ventured, "You know, if we switched from a human trial to one using a member of the simian family, we may be able to reduce the one year waiting period for the curative process. Simian DNA is close to human and the smaller body mass should require less time. It would be harder, though, to understand the before and after relative to personality."

Harrison smirked. "Tomi, the curative process of one year has nothing to do with body mass. A cell in a monkey won't take significantly less time to cure. It will be roughly the same. Besides, we don't want to reintroduce animal proteins."

Just then, with the team at the brink of breakdown, Rachel had an idea.

"Protein folding is normally viewed using NMR spectroscopy. If we added new holographic technology, I think we can simulate a proper sequence validated by computer modeling. This would enable us to prove a change in weeks or months instead of years."

Ben liked the idea. NMR spectroscopy, or an imaging process called "nuclear magnetic resonance" was sort of like an MRI for a cell. Adding holography and a supercomputer might just be the ticket. The team bounced the idea around and found it promising. The spirited conversation gave Harrison the impetus to consider adding a "chaperone" to his preservative. A chaperone involved a chemical process to induce proper and elongated protein folding within a cell. If this could be achieved, Rachel's holograph model might be even more effective. After discussing the ideas, Ben authorized the new avenues of study. In his own mind, however, he knew he could not take this service to market without successful human trials. Despite the positive pathways embarked upon during the Dugout session, Ben knew he was facing a long delay in bringing his dream to life. With his head ringing, his body aching, and his eyes stinging, he began to seriously question his sanity. Had he committed his own life and millions of dollars to a dream he could never actually realize?

CHAPTER 9

Absent direction, feeling like a rudderless ship, Ben returned to a place of seminal restitution. The Harmon School and its founder were the genesis of his formative years, a place where he never failed to find guidance.

"Ben . . . an unexpected pleasure. You know how to brighten an old man's day!"

Albert greeted him with heartfelt warmth and surprise. Ben knew he was the closest thing Albert ever had to a son.

Ben studied Albert, who was now seventy-two years old. He had a lot of energy but had aged demonstrably. He founded his school thirty-five years ago. Originally located in Washington, DC, Albert ultimately opted for the tranquility of Maryland's countryside. He figured that beyond the preferred setting that Maryland offered, his young charges would get in far less trouble being forty minutes north of Baltimore in the quiet, backwoods town of Maplebrook.

After a warm embrace, Albert motioned for Ben to sit down. The old man took off his always-present baby blue lab coat, which bore the embroidered, handwritten surname of his own mentor, Dr. Emmerling, and sat down behind his desk. There was something so consistently familiar about Albert. Under the lab coat, Albert wore his standard, button-down white dress shirt and the same old black slacks with a pair of well-worn, heavily scuffed black loafers.

Ben laid out the details on the disastrous awakening of Sylvia Bresling.

"Ben, why are you driving yourself so hard? Have you considered that bringing people back from the dead has always been impossible for a good reason?"

Nervous energy consumed Ben. He rose and plucked a memento from Albert's bookshelf commemorating his invention of a device advancing the time-tested slide rule. Ben recalled the story Albert had told a thousand times. Albert's device had won the top prize at the Kansas State Fair. Albert's work served as the precursor to the handheld electronic calculator. Although he was in his seventies, Ben viewed his mentor as the ultimate prodigy. Albert had created his calculation machine at nine years of age.

For a moment, Ben said nothing as he paused to gather his thoughts. As he sat silently, he took note of the old black and white photo on the wall. It was of Albert as a boy being given the award at the Kansas State Fair. The man standing by his side was the renowned Donald Emmerling, the noted science professor from The University of Kansas. The image of Emmerling reminded Ben of his beloved Gramps.

"It's my grandfather, Albert. He's my driving force. After he died, I've had this recurring dream where he comes back to life and spends a day with me and . . ."

"And what?"

"There's more . . . it's just that I've never . . ."

"Never what? C'mon Ben. Spill the beans. You know you can tell me anything."

"Gramps died with a secret, a big one. I'm apparently the only person he told. I have always believed the secret manifests itself in my subconscious and comes out in the form of the recurring dream."

"I'm no psychiatrist but it might help if you just tell me about the dream."

He hesitated and slowly offered, "Are you sure? It might sound kind of hokey."

"If it's important to you, it won't sound hokey to me."

"Okay. When the dream begins, I travel alone to a building that looks like any other you might see in passing and choose to ignore. It could have been anywhere. When I arrive, I am shown into a small, sterile room. The walls are white, as are the floors and the ceiling. A chair and a shiny metal table are placed along the far wall. A vault-like door with a black handle stares me down. I sit in the chair and begin a most anxious period of waiting. So many years after his death, I am being given the unimaginable gift of spending the day with my grandfather, a central part of my boyhood years and someone for whom my love and admiration knew no bounds. Yes, through the miraculous advances of science, I am to be granted a single day with my grandfather. He would be alive and healthy!

"My foot begins tapping nervously on the floor, all on its own, up and down, up and down. The waiting is maddening. I wait and wait and wait some more. I hear his voice in my head reminding me: *Courage, strength, patience, wisdom. Those four words will get you through any situation.*

"A man in white pants, shirt, and shoes enters the room. From the vault door, he activates a hydraulic lift, lowering the casket gently onto the shiny metal table. The casket opens without human intervention, as if it were magic. I stand there, astonished, and I watch him awaken.

"He is as I remembered him. He sits upright in healthy splendor, his gray hair combed straight back with just a smidge of gel to keep things in place. He wears the familiar vertical-striped, black and white, short-sleeve button down shirt reminiscent of so many family photos. His warm smile places me at ease. I approach him cautiously, wanting a hug, but not truly believing what is before my very eyes. His big, outstretched arms are inviting, as are his clear blue eyes, and so we embrace. Love and warmth are what I feel nestled in the comforting hold of my grandfather.

"In an outpouring of emotion and adrenaline, I tell him about our family, my studies, and, of course, our favorite baseball team. Gramps is keenly alert and listens intently, wanting to just watch me and soak in every precious moment.

"We stroll the grounds. The beautiful red bricks cut a path through a cherry tree orchard, fully in bloom and able to provide a modicum of shade on this warm spring day. I am preparing to tell my grandfather—who in life was my best friend, someone I could tell anything to—my biggest secret.

"As I am trying to find the words, Gramps' face turns gray. His eyes roll upward and he collapses in a patch of grass on a small hill. The attendant in the white outfit was immediately by his side. I was told he would be alive for a full day. I watch in horror as my grandfather lay dead on the grassy hill . . . and then I wake up."

"That's powerful," remarked Albert.

"I don't know how to explain it. My love for my grandfather was fierce. You know, I love my parents more than anything but my bond with Gramps . . . that was something special. I can feel his presence, Albert. It's like he is always with me. Even to this day—and in a way, he is."

Ben sipped from a timeworn white ceramic mug bearing The University of Kansas moniker and gave his mentor another glimpse into his past.

"If it weren't for Gramps, I might never have explored my scientific calling. He bought me my first chemistry set. If you ask my mother, she'd tell you he nearly blew up his own house trying to help me figure out how to use it. Gramps didn't know anything about chemistry but I loved and respected his playful sense of curiosity."

He saw Albert smile. His eyes began to grow slightly moist.

The secret. The knowledge haunted him. Share with Albert? Or continue to bury it?

"Ben, let's go back over where the team has been. There must be a stone we have not yet turned over. Tell me again how this awakening of cells is supposed to occur."

"Well, it might seem complicated but it's not, which, in a way, adds to the conundrum. We know that a cell has proteins on its outer membrane and that these proteins interact with other substances in a "lock and key" fashion during the cell's lifecycle, which signals the cell to perform its normal functions. During hibernation, a chemical preservative Harrison developed blocks the normal interactions. This causes a slowing down or suspension of normal processes without damage to the cell or its function. To awaken the cells, we bring in the Liferay, a multicolored, femtosecond pulse-emitting laser device that reverses the cell preservation process. In essence, the Liferay removes the preservative, allowing the protein to interact with its environment. The cell is now allowed to be energized and thus becomes functional for a defined period."

They poured over data, questioned each other until their brains ached, and developed a new regimen of tests that infused different degrees of artificial mitochondria, a cell's energy source, in an attempt to keep the regenerated cells from failing.

Ben knew the probability of success with the new "recipe" was miniscule. His resolve to prevail overshadowed his sense of logic.

"When I was in grad school at MIT, I remember messing around with color lasers that were needed to penetrate different types of cells. Even then, I knew I would use those experiments to create the Liferay. I had the idea for a sequenced, multicolored laser blast. After so many trials, I wonder if I'm even doing the right thing anymore. I guess what I am asking, Albert, is, do you think I'm screwing with the natural order of things?"

"You've asked me if you are on the proper path, doing the right thing, and I say using science to make the world a better place is always the correct choice."

"Geez, I would have bet anything you were about to give me the old cheesy line of how 'Science is a gift to mankind. We are but vessels that will propel the world to new heights.'" Ben mused.

"Nah. I save that bit for the youngsters." Albert smiled his paternal smile and continued. "We've been through this already. The concept of the Liferay device has enormous implications for the betterment of mankind. All scientists on the verge of discovery have doubts about their work. My only caution is to beware of The Law of Unintended Consequences."

Ben slumped in his chair. He had that tired feeling again. Maybe he just needed a pep talk.

"What's an unintended consequence look like to you, Albert?"

"This science can work well in a tightly controlled environment. Go outside those lines and anything can happen."

Ben paused to contemplate the suggestion.

"No disrespect intended but I haven't been able to get the science to work well in a tightly controlled environment. Until then, I can't worry too much about unintended consequences."

"Suit yourself. I think you need to just brainstorm with your team and just keep working at it. As long as you don't have investors or any other stakeholders looking over your shoulder, what's the hurry?"

"No one is looking over my shoulder, it's true. I understand that we will fail and in failing, we learn how to move forward. But you know how I am."

"Yes, I do. With brilliance comes impatience," Albert remarked with his trademark, know-it-all smirk.

Ben always felt better speaking with Albert. Albert challenged him in a way no one else could or would. It had been that way since his boyhood studies at The Harmon School. Albert asked the tough questions and made him reexamine everything he was planning to do. Yet Albert was right—brilliance does breed impatience, at least it did with him. Ben knew he would relentlessly pursue his quest with reckless abandon. He would have to rely upon Albert's counsel to keep him grounded. He grabbed his jacket off the coat tree in the corner of Albert's office.

"Before you go, would it help ease your mind to tell me your grandfather's secret?"

Ben froze. Inwardly, he wanted desperately to confide in someone. It couldn't be his parents. As close as he was to them, Gramps' instructions forbade it. Harrison? Rachel? No, they would ridicule him. Unburdening himself would be a godsend. Albert was the only one he could trust with this one.

The White Owl cigar box.

The lingering smell of tobacco permeated the cracked, yellowed pages of a handwritten brown leather diary encumbered by a wide, dry-rotted rubber band. A lawyer in New Jersey had been holding his grandfather's most private thoughts and last wishes. He remembered opening the parcel delivery while at MIT, shortly after his twenty-first birthday. The diary contained information so private, his grandfather withheld it from everyone, including his own son. Only he, the grandson, would eventually be told. His mouth went dry and his throat felt like sandpaper. Gramps saw something in him, even as a boy. Their bond was unbreakable.

Ben cleared his throat and finally managed to stammer out, "Gramps had himself cryogenically frozen."

CHAPTER 10

Ben understood the implications of the message. In astoundingly rich, beautiful color, the holographic, 3-D image of the world "floated" and danced gleefully with a secret to reveal. In large, bold text, the words, "SEQUENCE COMPLETED" rotated around the globe in capital letters. The team had been at it for months, always nonstop, always working to the point of exhaustion. He knew no other way and by extension, neither did his team. The day had started like any other but for the pouring rain that pounded the streets of Maplebrook with abandon. With absolutely no scientific basis for their objective, Ben's team had once again resorted to "logical tinkering," a phrase Ari had coined to achieve further progress when no one knew for certain what to do next. The phrase made Ben smile, probably because it was so nonsensical.

With the sequence now complete, the team was able to view detailed 3-D imagery of properly folded proteins, enabling patients to awaken normally, as themselves, after a year of death. More important, the algorithm they had been running had produced the exact formula needed in all aspects of their application. The upshot was off the charts. Ben now held the exact formulation for Bock's preservative and the Liferay. In fact, the model even gave them a precise curing time for the preservative: 359 days, 37 minutes, and 14.75 seconds. Their prior assessments settling on a year for the curing process had been damn near perfect. Ben understood that the phrase "imperfect science" had no role to play at the Lab.

"I could have trained that puppy a thousand different ways and not come up with that exact formulation," laughed Harrison.

"The same goes for the Liferay settings," exclaimed Ari.

"Ben, how did scientists accomplish anything without the benefit of computer modeling and holography?" asked Rachel rhetorically. "Hell, even reaching back five or ten years, no scientific team on the planet could have done what we have, let alone scientists from prior centuries."

"Albert always taught me to respect scientific discoveries that helped mankind to progress. Every breakthrough, in its own era, was outstanding in its own right for its contribution to the world," responded Ben.

"So Ben, what comes next?" inquired Tomi.

"What comes next is seeing the inside of my eyelids for seven or eight hours, a hot shower, a cheese omelet and plenty of black coffee . . . in that order," laughed Ben.

Tired eyes and sleep deprivation were not a good mix for dark, winding country roads on a night beset by torrential downpour. The way the strong wind drove rain toward the old blue Honda, Ben thought it might actually penetrate his windshield. As he navigated the rainy abyss in the backwoods of Maplebrook, Ben thought of his grandfather. The tenseness in his muscles subsided when he imagined his grandfather's voice saying, in his most Jewish, grandfatherly way, "You know, if you were that good of a scientist, you could invent a car to repel the rain and dry the road so you could drive home safely." Ben laughed out loud and said, "Sure, Gramps, that'll be my next project." The rest of the drive melted away as Ben pulled into the parking lot of his apartment.

The apartment was large by any standard but decorated in simple tastes. His mother urged him to hire a cleaning service but Ben thought this unimportant. His apartment resembled his office at the Lab. Ben liked to call it early American clutter. His mother, Marcy, called it a sty. Tired as he was, he grabbed a bottle of water and stood by the long, picture window in the middle of his far living room wall. He leaned against the wall and watched the rain. He heard a cracking sound, which he failed to identify, and his head whipped around the room. Suddenly feeling melancholy, his attention shifted to the painting above the flat screen by famed sports artist Stephen Holland. It was one of the few things Ben actually spent money on and he did so to pay homage to his grandfather's most revered sports hero, Sandy Koufax. While long before Ben's time, Gramps impressed upon him that Koufax was the best left-handed pitcher in the history of the game. The Holland piece had been purchased at an estate auction in New York, not far from the borough of Brooklyn, where Koufax and Gramps both got their start. Gramps reminded him that Koufax, early in his career, had the talent but not the achievement. Like many famed inventors, Koufax achieved remarkable success after numerous failures. Koufax was the bond between his Gramps and his own burning desire to achieve greater success as a scientist. Ben hoped that, somehow, Gramps was able to see that Holland painting in his living room. He took comfort in the thought as he chugged the last of the water.

As he brushed his teeth in preparation for much-needed sleep, Ben took stock of the image in the mirror. *Christ, I look like the Wolfman*, he thought. His normal few days' of beard growth were clearly out of control. His thick, brown hair was almost long enough for a ponytail, but not quite. Again, his mother came to mind. She definitely would not approve. Ben's eyes were bloodshot and the underlying bags, along with the beard with its hint of gray, made him look ten years older than he was. Tonight, sleep; tomorrow, a rendezvous with a razor and a trip to the barber. Five minutes later, he was out like a light, sleeping deeply to the rhythm of the pouring rain.

○ ○ ○ ○ ○

Morning came all too quickly. In the Lab, Rachel was leading the customary review in the Dugout. Since its inception, the team always met immediately after a major failure or achievement. The primary objective of these sessions was to determine what came next. On this day, it was the Lab's founder who was late. Ben arrived nearly thirty minutes after the scheduled meeting time to find the team in the thick of it.

"You know, Ben, it really is disrespectful to the rest of us when you can't get here on time," chided Harrison.

"Harrison, you are, as always, the man. I stand here humbly apologetic without so much as a bullshit excuse about my cat giving birth," replied Ben.

"Touché, Dr. Abraham, touché," said Harrison.

"Dr. Abraham clearly has a good excuse for being late today," said Rachel. "He shaved and got a serious haircut. You clean up nicely, Benjamin."

"Is that sexual tension I detect?" said Harrison, never one to resist the temptation to tease his friends.

"Harrison, you are an ass," remarked Tomi. "Can't someone give a compliment without it turning into a sex reference? For the record, Ben, I think you look great—speaking strictly as a friend, of course."

"I wish I knew years ago that a haircut and shave could generate this much energy amongst the team. It might have inspired me to indulge more often," said Ben. "So, what brilliance can you grace me with this morning, esteemed colleagues?"

Rachel chimed in. "Look, Ben, we know how you feel about shortcuts and we feel the same but with the computer modeling and holography, we have the golden ticket. Our success is guaranteed."

"We all agree, Ben," offered Ari. "None of us would ever take a shortcut but with the benefit of the sophisticated computer modeling we have, the results are irrefutable."

With his affirmation, Ari grinned. Ben had great respect for Ari, the eldest of the group and by far the most conservative in approach. If Ari was recommending they skip another human trial with the recalibrated Liferay and preservative, that was really something.

Ben felt duty bound to offer some measure of resistance, although his willpower was wilting slightly under the pressure from his collegial team. "What would oversight agencies say about skipping another round of human trials?"

Harrison retorted, "Who are we worried about? Which agency exactly, US or otherwise, oversees the restoration of dead people for a day?"

"He's right, Ben," offered Rachel. "We've been down that road. There really is no oversight. If we are successful, there most certainly will be one day but for now, we get to call the shots."

"I can't argue with anything you guys are saying. In my heart, the right thing is to go one more round with human trials and make 100 percent sure the algorithm is correct. We've come so far. This conversation has been years in the making. What's another 359 days, 37 minutes and 14.75 seconds?" replied Ben.

In the end, Ben did not waiver. To validate the algorithm with data from human trials was hitting the mother lode. Ben needed to feel comfortable that long-term success in the marketplace was achievable. He was sensitive to the emotional needs of the families who would become his company's clients. The distress of Sylvia Bresling's daughter was still very fresh in his mind. No, on this point, Ben Abraham redoubled his resolve to go down the correct scientific path and do what he felt was right. Time was not the determining factor. The strength of what he had to offer the world, a chance to procure continuity of sorts for people and their loved ones, was the overriding factor. While the process could never bring back his Gramps, he thought lovingly about his parents. If they were to agree to submit to the process, he would be able share them indefinitely with his own future children, extending their special relationship with their grandparents beyond death.

Ben Abraham knew he was playing a zero sum game with both the living and the dead. Sylvia Bresling's daughter had had one shot of bringing her mom back for a day each year and now it was gone forever. Ben felt that pain. He now had a new weight upon his shoulders. Within days of notification following the Bresling debacle, all eleven families had given their consent to terminate the trial. None of them wanted to take the chance of having their loved one come back with a neurodegenerative disorder. Now, with the exact formula for preservation and hibernation in the palm of his hand, he knew he could have saved them all.

CHAPTER 11

One year later

Rachel Larkin was nervous. She sometimes felt like they were playing God. Although she had no religious upbringing, she felt a spiritual connection with a higher being and hoped her work would be viewed in a positive light. The rest of the team, like Rachel, believed deeply in the algorithm and its precise calculations. However, when one was playing with life and death, all bets were off.

Rachel coordinated the orderlies who had already brought the preserved body of David Allen to the Awakening Suite. David Allen, dead just under a year, had been a successful businessman in Dallas. In life, he stood a shade under six feet, was of medium build, and had a reputation as being tough but fair. His cause of death had been an undetected pulmonary embolism. Doctors had told his widow that despite being in reasonably good shape for a man his age, these things sometimes come out of nowhere. The family had been devastated.

David's business had involved selling insurance within the medical community. Because he was highly specialized in designing insurance policies for unique medical endeavors, his agency had been referred to Dr. Ben Abraham for liability insurance covering the activities of Hiatus Centers, LLC. In speaking with Ben, David had become intrigued and asked, on the slim chance that he passed and was eligible, that he be considered for human trials. Papers were drawn up and upon his sudden death, the body was properly treated with Bock's preservative and then airlifted from Dallas to Baltimore in one of Hiatus Centers' specialty temperature-controlled caskets. The body of David Allen was now fifty-seven years old.

Rachel and the other four members of the scientific team were on the floor. Ben, working alongside her and Ari, administered the Liferay with its recalibrated settings. David Allen's body received the rotational bursts in precise sequence. After the twelfth pass, the wait was on. Rachel felt relief when the heart monitor registered its first beat. She studied David Allen's face and upper torso, hoping to see his chest rise with the intake of breath. And there it was! David Allen was showing signs of life faster than any prior awakening. Now, she prayed, please let him be lucid. Allen's face began to twitch slowly and his eyes opened. His big, brown eyes were alert but at ease. His body temperature had risen to 96°F. Everything was proceeding as planned. Rachel noted the pleased look on Ben's face.

"David, it's Ben Abraham. Do you know where you are?"

David Allen, still flat on his back, looked over in Ben's direction and said with a scratchy voice, "I . . . I can't see. Everything is a blur."

Rachel's heart sank. Everything had gone so well. What would cause David Allen to wake up blind? Negative thoughts flooded her mind. *Maybe his retinae deteriorated. Maybe the portion of the brain controlling sight was damaged. Maybe the optic nerve . . .*

Tomi knew exactly what the problem was. "Mr. Allen, I have your glasses. Let me help you put them on."

Rachel felt foolish. She knew David Allen had been extremely nearsighted. This had been one of a thousand details they had covered in the Dugout before the awakening. She had simply forgotten. At least Tomi had it together. David consumed a small paper cup of water and began to sit up.

"Ah, much better. It's good to see you again, Ben. You are a gift from God," said David.

Rachel beamed with pride for the entire team as she watched Ben in action.

"So, you know who you are, you know who I am, and you know where you are and why," said Ben. "We're off to a good start. Your wife, Liza, and your son, Trey, and daughter, Ava, are waiting to see you. You will have approximately twenty-four hours to spend with them. You will not be permitted to leave the grounds of the Lab. A Hiatus Centers' staffer will be with you and your family the entire time. In accordance with the agreement you signed when you entered this trial, we will be filming the entire twenty-four-hour period of your awakening. At around the twenty-third hour, our staffer will summon me, Rachel, Ari, Tomi, and Harrison and we will help you and your family prepare for the "hibernation" of the next year. Do you have any questions?"

"Ben, I understand. I'm scared. My family, will they still love me? Will I be viewed as something other than human? Will they be afraid to touch me? What if they ask me about heaven?"

Ever the scientist, Ben looked lost. Rachel knew these types of questions could not be addressed with math or science. She felt for Ben, who did not know how to answer such inquiries. In truth, none of them did but Rachel knew she had to come to his aid.

"Mr. Allen, you are as human as the day you died. Your family is here because they love you very much. As for touching you, I would be honored if I could be your first hug."

David smiled. When the embrace ended, Tomi looked at him and said, "Mr. Allen, you said you won't know what to say if your family asks you about heaven, maybe you could try telling us what that answer might be . . . that is, if you are comfortable doing so."

Tomi smiled at David. Her smile could melt away anyone's inhibition. David looked at Tomi quizzically and said, "Truthfully, I know I experienced something beautiful, something unlike this world. There are simply no words with which to accurately describe it to you. I can say that it brought me an inner peace I never knew in life. Yes, a magnificent sense of peace."

Rachel touched him affectionately on the shoulder and said, "Mr. Allen, I think you are ready to see your family."

CHAPTER 12

After David Allen's successful awakening and hibernation, Ben's team achieved similar results with the remaining patients in the second round of trials. He was ready to open the first commercial center. After months of research and a modicum of debate, the lawyers agreed that no governmental approval process existed for their service. The lawyers merely insisted that, for now, Hiatus Centers acquire a mortuary license. The Baltimore city government gladly issued the license. Ben shunned publicity and preferred to get the business up and running before shouting his value proposition from the rooftops. Because of this position, Hiatus Centers planned a quiet opening with little fanfare. He knew it was bound to get far more complicated as time went forward but for now, he sought to operate from behind the curtain. So far as anyone in the public domain knew, a new funeral home was coming to the neighborhood. *Who could have a problem with that?* he reasoned.

Through a mutual acquaintance, Ben had met Ruben Bannister, a city councilman who was hailed as a visionary. He recalled his first encounter with Bannister, a seasoned politician at the age of seventy and an ardent supporter of anything that would generate good paying jobs in the economically depressed community.

"We could support a mortuary license," Bannister had offered, "even though we know what your true purpose is. Hell, I'd go so far as to say that the City would be amenable to tax credits for every job you create. If you locate your headquarters here, as well, I'll see that we double the tax incentive. I have a lot of pull on the city council. Mayor Goldstein and I are old buds. We go way back."

He silently laughed at the manner in which Bannister stretched his pronunciation of the word, "*waaaay.*"

Ben was surprised at how easy it was to get something done when the politicians saw a benefit that didn't historically grace Baltimore with the frequency with which they desired. Bannister had been true to his word. Ben would be true to his. He committed both the Hiatus Centers headquarters and the first commercial location to the city's beautiful Inner Harbor.

Ben had found and purchased waterfront property in Canton that gave them close proximity to the airport, universities, and major hospitals. The location left them a tidy forty minutes from the Lab and the up and coming talent in The Harmon School. Ben had begun the construction process two years earlier by tearing down buildings that once housed a family owned retail furniture store and its warehouse. His goal was to have the construction done in time to coincide with the conclusion of human trials.

The first Hiatus Centers' location would occupy a full city block with a building that, once fully operational, would be able to house up to fifteen hundred clients. The building sat on a tract of land with high, soundproof, city-approved, decorative walls on the street side. The street side walls were made of red brick, stood twelve feet high, and held treelined walkways with antique lamps reminiscent of Baltimore in the early twentieth century. These touches offered security and privacy so that the harbor side view could be entrusted to what Ben would call "the virtual experience."

The city was elated by having Hiatus Centers open its flagship location in Canton. Beyond job creation, it emboldened Baltimore's growing, desired reputation as an innovation hub. By virtue of the service it provided, Hiatus Centers would eventually gain world acclaim and Baltimore would share in the rewards. Mayor Goldstein was extremely happy that Hiatus Centers planned a national expansion with headquarters to be located downtown. It was a boon to the local economy. Ben shared with city officials the design of the eight-foot, forest green awning that would bear the simple moniker of the white letters H and C, in overlapping fashion. So far as anyone knew, the reserved structure and its surroundings screamed "mortuary."

CHAPTER 13

They were down to the final days. On Monday, Hiatus Centers' first location would officially open its doors. Rachel was conducting the final walkthrough. By and large, it had been a massive undertaking. Given the enormity of the job, the pressure had weighed heavily on her mind. Forgetting a single detail could be the difference between life and death.

Rachel walked to the basement facility to check on Harrison and Tomi, who were tasked with overseeing the finishing touches on the casket containment area. With all going well in the basement, she proceeded to visit Ari as he worked on the Awakening Suite. Finally, she wandered to the back of the sprawling facility where Ben focused on the design of his crowning jewel, the Virtual Experience Theater. It was here where, using a combination of multimedia and virtual reality, awakened clients would be able, if they chose, to relive a favorite moment of their life, along with their family, without leaving the grounds. No awakened person would ever leave the grounds so Ben wanted to provide the best technology available to recreate special moments. Rachel stood in awe as Ben explained how it all would work.

Rachel was satisfied. They were ready. She smiled as made her way back through their flagship location. One of the first things she had volunteered for was overseeing the interior design. Having seen Ben's office and apartment, she knew this project required a female touch. If

Ben had his way, the building would be done in early American baseball or what she called "that crap." Rachel had nothing against America's pastime; in fact, being a Southern California girl, she shared a love of the Dodgers with him. She just didn't believe the sport should serve as a decorating theme, particularly given the sensitive nature of the services they offered.

Ben gave her free reign and was comforted by the fact she hired the top interior design firm in the city. At the end of a very long process, he had stood with her in the lobby to admire her handiwork. The lobby and consultation rooms were filled with soft pastels and artwork that she hoped said "life." Her goal was to avoid the funeral home feel. The extensive, three-level serenity fountain, with its colored lighting and abundance of live plants, reminded her of the rainforest in the nearby National Aquarium. Rachel was pleased. Things in this place were living and growing. The décor spoke in welcoming tones. Ben told her how proud he was of her. She had achieved her goal. Yes, they were ready. She was sure of it.

Tonight, Saturday, Ben had promised the team a celebratory dinner to commemorate years of hard work and remarkable achievement. The five scientists met in Little Italy, Baltimore's hidden alcove of Italian restaurants, most family owned, which had served generations of Baltimoreans the best Italian food one could find this side of Rome. There was no shortage of great restaurants from which to choose. Rachel reveled in Ben's choice of venue, Speranza's, a place he deemed his lifelong restaurant of choice to honor special occasions. She had always heard great things about Speranza's but had never been.

The restaurant was in a very old building that essentially had no lobby. Rachel thought the entrance said "New York" more than Charm City. One walked through a glass door and was greeted by the smallest of foyers and a stairwell rising three levels. A valet parked cars out front while the hostess greeted patrons with an oversized reservation book atop a wooden lectern at the foot of the stairwell. They climbed the stairs to the third level and were given a table by a window overlooking Albemarle Street in the heart of Little Italy. Rachel looked longingly at the horse-drawn carriage meandering down the street with a happy couple nestled comfortably against one another. For a moment, she fantasized that it was she and Ben.

"Rachel . . . Rachel . . . the waitress wants to know if you would like something to drink," said Tomi.

"Huh, oh yeah, sure," she said, coming back to reality. "A glass of Chardonnay, please."

Three courses later, the scientific team of Doctor Benjamin Abraham was quite full. While they tried to resist, the homemade cannoli and cheesecake were to die for. Rachel had the strawberry cheesecake. After too much wine, she no longer had any regard for how many calories she was ingesting. They were all feeling no pain. By 9:30, Ari, the old man of the group, bailed, mumbling something about it being past his bedtime. Harrison was next and he was Tomi's ride, so they left together. Seemingly all of the sudden, it was just Ben and she, pondering one more glass of wine. Pondering didn't take long; nor did consumption.

"Wanna go for a walk in the city? Maybe catch a horse-drawn carriage ride somewhere?" asked Rachel.

"I'm up for walking."

They strolled a bit. Rachel had guided them to Fells Point and its array of unique drinking establishments. She wasn't ready for the evening to end. After frequenting three such taverns, they were both inebriated beyond immediate repair. They stumbled out of the third bar and Rachel lost her balance; Ben instinctively reached out to help. She felt his arm move around her waist and he pulled her slowly up to his large frame. They found themselves in an untimely but accidental embrace. They both burst out in laughter. Ben let her go and they began to walk toward the Inner Harbor. The horse-drawn carriage slowly drove by and its operator asked if they wanted a lift. Before Ben could reply, Rachel accepted.

"Would you just take us around the harbor for a little while?" she asked.

Ben was too drunk to offer resistance. Rachel knew that for him, fun had been a long time coming. He helped her into the plush, upholstered carriage and guided his tall, lanky frame in next to her. Rachel cuddled as close to Ben as she could and laid her head on his chest. He looked down at her, she back at him. Their eyes locked and slowly, under the bright light of a full moon, they kissed. The cool evening air balanced the warmth of their exchange. It seemed to last forever.

"We've circled the harbor three times now. Not sure you've enjoyed any of it," said the driver.

"Oh, trust me," said Rachel. "We've enjoyed every last second."

"Where can I drop you folks?"

Without consulting Ben, she said, "The Pier V Hotel, please." They disembarked. Ben shoveled some money at the driver and they stood outside the hotel. They kissed again and Rachel said, "Ben, neither one of us is driving anywhere tonight. It's too far to take a cab back home and I am not letting you out of my sight."

Ben smiled and they walked into the lobby and requested a room. Once inside, Rachel asked Ben to get some ice from down the hallway. She noticed that he managed to get a sense of his legs and how they should work to accomplish the task at hand. When he came back with the ice, he was without his key. She heard him knock but chose not to answer. She listened and heard him jiggle the handle, indicating the door was unlocked. She waited and listened from her vantage point. She knew he was now in the room, wondering where she was. Slowly, she emerged from the bathroom. She was wearing nothing but a scientific lab coat she had wadded up inside her purse. He looked at her in a way he never had before. Rachel opened the lab coat and let it drop all around her.

"Ready for some experimenting, Doctor?"

Rachel saw Ben approach and her brave façade began to fade. He wrapped his arms around her and gently kissed her on the mouth. She felt herself becoming putty in his hands and decided to just let things go where they may. When their lips separated, he whisked her from her feet, as if it were magic, and carried her across the threshold to the double bed on the other side of the room. She was lowered gently onto the bed and watched through dreamy eyes as he removed his clothes. Rachel was in complete submission.

She moaned quietly as Ben explored her body, gently and unselfishly. She held tightly to his long, athletic shoulders. Their interaction with one another was both curious and caring. She had dreamed of this moment and savored the time. They made love till they no longer could.

Rachel woke six hours later to find Ben still asleep. He was stirring. She ran her fingers through his thick mane and smiled. Her soft brown hair was tousled.

"Good morning Benjamin. Did we sleep well?"

Ben stretched, his eyes were glassy. His stream of consciousness was beginning to return. Somewhat tentatively, he replied, "God, you are beautiful." She warmed as their eyes locked. Then, just as quickly, worry took over.

"Ben, tell me we didn't make a huge mistake."

Rachel saw that Ben wasn't sure how to reply. She wasn't sure how to proceed. They had been friends and colleagues for so many years. Would one night of drunken sex ruin it all? She sat up in bed and wondered whether she would need to find another job. Worry was beginning to consume her. She mustered the courage to step outside her comfort zone.

"You do know that I've always sort of had a thing for you, right?"

Rachel waited patiently for a response but got only a nod in the affirmative. She thought her declaration came off lame but didn't say anything more. In a rush, Ben got up to say a quick prayer to the porcelain god.

She lay there and thought about the things that attracted her to Ben. He was good-looking for sure, but she'd always been drawn to his intellectual curiosity. To Rachel, it was like a contagion. She couldn't get enough. His enthusiasm for discovery energized her like nothing else did. Maybe it was because she found success in smaller units. Her need to complete sequential tasks complimented Ben's ability to soar in the wild blue yonder.

When he came back to bed, he apologized and waded into a conversation she knew he found extremely uncomfortable.

"Rachel, I've always sort of had a thing for you, too. Our friendship means everything to me. I think, though, for the time being, it's best if we both just focus on work. One day down the road, when the time is right, I'll be there for you."

Dejected, Rachel knew that he was right. *Damn! He can even boil love down to logic. And the irony is he doesn't even know he's doing it.* She kissed him on the forehead, put on the wrinkled lab coat, and headed off to the shower, all the time wondering why he couldn't give himself to her the way he did with his work.

CHAPTER 14

Anstrov Rinaldi did not receive many guests in Colmar. Today would be one of those days. Rinaldi did not know Johann Bagstrom, the SPI chairman, but had done his research and through a recent business exposé learned quite a bit about his makeup and accomplishments. Bagstrom had made a career of corporate turnarounds, mostly in the pharmaceutical sector. He held CEO positions across the globe and was highly regarded for his accomplishments. Now, at the age of seventy-four, he served as chairman of the board for Swiss Pharma Ingenuity, one of the largest pharmaceutical companies in the world. Bagstrom had been chairman for three years. In the article, Bagstrom boasted of his ability to find untapped talent within an organization, change the culture, and get things moving quickly in the right direction. Rinaldi couldn't be sure but he suspected this was the reason for Bagstrom's unorthodox visit to the company's main R&D facility in Colmar. Rinaldi, like always, decided to lie low to see how the conversation unfolded.

The Colmar facility was a single-level white sandstone building that, if viewed from overhead, would resemble the letter "U." Architects had chosen the white sandstone for its artistic qualities. Sandstone, being a "softer" rock, made it easier to create unique features. A prior CEO had commissioned the architect to use raised images of famous inventors on the front walls surrounding the main entrance. The facility's founder wanted the building to inspire innovation. Since Colmar experienced little precipitation, the use of white sandstone was a perfect choice.

Bagstrom entered the office and sat opposite Rinaldi, away from the desk in a sitting area surrounding a round wooden conference table. Rinaldi studied Bagstrom carefully. He had a gift enabling his good eye to bore into a subject, taking in every nuance without the other person being aware he was doing so. Every detail he could glean would be used to his advantage. An administrative assistant brought in tea service for two. Drago looked on from a large cage on the other side of the room. After pleasantries were exchanged and some small talk about Rinaldi's unusual "office mate," Rinaldi shifted into gear, as usual, with focus and determination.

"Herr Bagstrom, I was most surprised to receive your call. You are here in Colmar for a facility tour?"

"Not exactly, Dr. Rinaldi. I come with news from Basel. Yesterday, the board terminated the services of Herr Lanzinger. I have assumed the task of finding the next CEO of Swiss Pharma Ingenuity. I am known for pursuing unconventional pathways, for thinking differently. That is why I am here, Dr. Rinaldi."

Rinaldi smiled to himself. He played the "innocent" role well but every word, every action, was carefully measured toward his desired outcome.

"I am sorry to hear that. Lanzinger was a good man. I do not understand, however, how I might be expected to assist you in this endeavor."

Bagstrom was a man who did not mince words. "Lanzinger was a buffoon. I'm not sure how he got the job in the first place. The company needs new, fresh, and different leadership. It needs someone who understands the market and is dedicated to innovation. I would like to consider you for the CEO position, Doctor."

Rinaldi had been planning for this day. For Bagstrom's benefit, he arched his eyebrows in a feigned state of shock, doing his best to appear humble and honored.

"I am flattered to be considered for such an important role. May I inquire as to the exact reasons for Herr Lanzinger's downfall? If I were fortunate enough to earn this position, I would not wish to repeat the mistakes of my predecessor."

"It's quite simple, Doctor. In a large, publicly traded multinational corporation, one must meet earnings projections. Those projections must be based on honest assessments of new products and when they will be ready for market. Lanzinger had deliberately provided the board with false information regarding the antiaging drug. Our understanding is that the drug's state of readiness is still far in the future. Lanzinger led the board to believe it would be ready in eighteen months. This 'miss' has upset the board and our shareholders. The displeasure is reflected in our stock price."

Like a trial lawyer, Rinaldi never asked a question for which he did not already know the answer. He was in complete control of the conversation.

"But Herr Bagstrom, surely you see that I am the one in charge of the antiaging drug. If its failure to hit the market sooner versus later is a cause for Herr Lanzinger's demise, then why would I be considered to take his place?"

Bagstrom grinned. He crossed his right leg over his left, took a sip of tea from the Royal Copenhagen cup, and said, "Doctor Rinaldi, I understand the nature of your question but rest assured that before I would spend the time to travel to Colmar and conduct this conversation, I have undertaken a thorough investigation of the antiaging drug development process. In interviews with key personnel at this facility, we learned that your leadership had scripted a much different course, a more reasonable three-year development plan that, while longer, remains honest and practical and would resonate with shareholders. Every internal email and document we reviewed told the same story; Lanzinger lied to the board and manipulated the truth about the antiaging drug while you, Dr. Rinaldi, were willing to take longer to do it properly.

That is why I am here. Leadership like yours might have saved SPI a ton of international embarrassment. Lanzinger was issuing press releases to perpetuate his story."

Bagstrom paused, took a sip of tea, and continued, "The board has already discussed this in great detail and your candidacy is highly regarded."

Rinaldi relaxed for just a moment. He found orchestration of his plans to be like child's play.

"It is an honor to be considered. For a man dedicated to science, it seems that the business end of what I do has always been better left to others. But I must say, this conversation has piqued my interest. I have often wondered how a company like ours might benefit with a scientist leading the way."

The meeting was more a conversation than an interview. Bagstrom and Rinaldi spoke for four hours. During the course of the morning, Bagstrom explained that two other candidates were being considered, both from outside the organization, neither of whom was a scientist. The board hoped to make a decision in the next few weeks. Bagstrom would act as interim CEO during the interview process. Yes, there would be at least one more interview session to go through, most likely in Basel with members of the board's search committee. If he were to receive the job, he would not have to worry about compensation. He would make more money than he had ever seen in a given year. The package included a substantial base salary and bonus program dependent upon hitting specific financial metrics. A job offer would also come with an employment contract offering risk mitigation for both sides. If the board terminated the contract for anything other than negligence, Rinaldi would be paid in full for the balance of the contract. The payout would be equivalent to his historical average total compensation for time on the job.

Rinaldi inquired about his current arrangement with a private car and driving service. Bagstrom was one step ahead. Having done his homework, he knew about Rinaldi's disabilities and that he did not drive. He readily agreed that if a job offer were to be forthcoming, he could add the driver to the payroll and lease the vehicle of his choice.

After Bagstrom departed, Rinaldi sat back in his leather chair and smiled. Everything was going according to plan. He now had the names of the other two CEO candidates and was already plotting on how to anonymously discredit these individuals. He believed in leaving nothing to chance.

CHAPTER 15

One month later, the SPI board hired Anstrov Rinaldi as the new CEO. Rinaldi was pleased with everything except the pain of commuting from Alsace. He had added Clifford to the payroll and leased the latest Phantom. The luxury sedan was well equipped to make the daily trek as productive as possible. For this reason, he considered the expense a reasonable one. Rinaldi contemplated leasing an apartment in Basel on the company dime but he did not for two reasons: one, he did not want to spend the money on something he deemed wasteful; and two, his home in Alsace was his sanctuary. He knew he would not be there forever. He chose to enjoy it to the maximum extent possible, while he could.

On the morning of his first full day as CEO, he sat back in the Phantom and pondered the days and weeks ahead.

His first order of business would be to meet with that wretched Executive Directorate. They would learn that the days of being fat, dumb, and happy were over. Most of them would be replaced. He required competence and absolute loyalty. The company needed leaders who were serious about science and less so about massages, caviar, and other such frivolous nonsense. With Vanessa Moretti now in charge of Colmar, Rinaldi knew he could concentrate on ridding the company of waste. The antiaging drug would be recast as one formulation for both men and women. He would push the name BV3000. His logic was that for the ladies, they would still feel "belissimo," hence the "B" and the men would still feel "vigoré," hence the "V." The number 3000 had absolutely no meaning other than to sound futuristic.

Because he would eventually need to hit the road and visit SPI's major customers and facilities around the world, he would look to hire a Chief Operating Officer to mind the corporate noise while he got the enterprise moving in the right direction. He had already reached out to his first choice for COO, Henri Marceau. Marceau was the former CEO at a small French generic pharmaceutical manufacturer where Rinaldi had worked earlier in his career. They had kept in touch. Henri had recently accepted a golden parachute, a forced buyout that was difficult to refuse. At the age of sixty-two, he looked and felt younger and was not done working quite yet. The opportunity to be COO at the much larger SPI would be most welcome. Rinaldi had Marceau's employment offer at the top of his to-do list.

○ ○ ○ ○ ○

It had taken three weeks to schedule his first Executive Directorate meeting as CEO. His first few weeks on the job had involved an inordinate amount of time with Human Resources to accommodate for the numerous terminations of incompetent Executive Directorate members.

The look and feel of the room had transformed from one of ceremony to a place where people rolled up their sleeves and got work done. Gone were objects of opulence. Rinaldi had ordered all symbols of riches removed. Save for the conference table and the chairs he enjoyed, everything else was gone, including the executive chef and his staff. The members who survived the change in leadership were those who were relatively new to the company and had not yet been polluted by Lanzinger's lavish regime.

Rinaldi entered the room, said good morning to his newly assembled team, and took his seat at the head of the glass table. He brought his dark, lacquered walnut cane to rest along the table's edge. Eleven faces stared back in a state of anxiety. All they knew of the leadership style of their new boss was that he had essentially come in and cleaned house in his first few weeks on the job. They were starting off scared and that's exactly what Rinaldi wanted.

To Rinaldi's left sat Dr. Vanessa Moretti, to his right, his new COO, Henri Marceau. Rinaldi would rely on these two to get things moving fast. Each knew of his temper but understood how to withstand the "storms" and emerge relatively unscathed.

Rinaldi cleared his throat and, in a voice that never seemed strong enough to match his stature, began to welcome his team in the egotistical manner he owned.

"If you are seated around this table, it is because you have been chosen to do so—chosen by me. The reason you have been chosen is that I presume you are serious about science and the business of making and selling world-class pharmaceuticals. You are here because you believe in our ability to lead the world in this regard. You, of course, recognize that any pharmaceutical company of SPI's size can pump out great products to rack up revenue and profit and yes, we will continue to do this. However, SPI will also assume the mantle of industry leader by creating products for which demand is currently unknown."

Rinaldi glanced around the room and paused before delivering his next remarks. *Half of these dimwits seem bored or maybe they are just too stupid to follow what is common sense. We shall see,* he thought.

"Now, that statement may seem foolish to you. Why would we spend years and billions to develop products for which there is no known demand? Simply stated, people don't know what they want until we show them what is possible. Our antiaging drug is a prime example. None of our competitors are pursuing such a project. People are naturally vain and do not wish to suffer the ill effects of growing older. This is a product that will change the world. And that, my friends, is why we are here, in this room, around this table, on this team: to change the world."

Rinaldi completed his opening monologue and smiled his crooked smile. He was pleased with his remarks and their delivery. He sat back in his formfitting leather chair and waited to drink in the adulation that never came. Undismayed, he elected to press forward.

○ ○ ○ ○ ○

The black Phantom arrived in a park in the outskirts of Zurich. It was near midnight. The place was deserted. The long sedan came to a stop. The passenger door opened slowly. The lacquered walnut cane appeared first and was used as a prop to gain footing as Rinaldi made his way out of the car. He shuffled along the path toward a playground and waited, alone, on a wooden park bench. After a few minutes, a man appeared from the nearby woods. He walked toward Rinaldi, greeted him warmly, and took a seat on the bench.

Rinaldi looked at the man and said, "You have done what I asked?"

The man replied, "Ja, Herr Doktor, I have made the required change in a completely undetectable manner. No one will ever know the rods are imperceptibly bent."

"I am pleased," replied Rinaldi. "You have done well."

With that, Rinaldi handed the man a thick envelope overflowing with cash and hobbled back toward the Phantom. Adrenaline expended, he allowed himself to succumb to the rich leather of the Phantom. His head melded with the plush headrest. All in all, Rinaldi thought, it had been a good day's work.

CHAPTER 16

Rachel found herself with butterflies fluttering freely in her stomach. The chairman of the board was coming for his initial look at their first commercial location. To Rachel, Albert's blessing would be a critical validation of all they had worked so hard for.

She was pacing about in the lobby until she spotted him walking under the long green awning out front. To Rachel, Albert was part teddy bear, part favorite uncle, and part wise sage. She greeted him with a hug befitting a cherished elder colleague.

Although Albert was not a businessman, he was able to assemble an impressive array of scientific business people to form the inaugural group of directors. In Rachel's mind, Ben would never have asked anyone else to serve in the role as board chair. She knew Ben needed someone he could trust implicitly.

"I think you may have missed your calling," he said. "It seems you have a flair for interior decorating. What does Ben think?"

She reveled in his positive reaction to the tranquil setting she had created for Hiatus Centers' first location. The pressure she had placed on herself to impress Albert began to fade. Rachel hoped Albert did not notice her body language at the mention of Ben's name. She felt the muscles in her neck and shoulders tighten. Since their tryst at The Pier V Hotel, things had not been the same.

"I haven't heard any complaints," she replied.

"So, we are taking a tour this morning?"

"Yes, but first we have a new client here for intake. I want you to observe and listen to the process."

They moved to a room adjacent to the intake office and stood behind the two-way glass. The lighting in the intake office was ten times brighter, enabling those on the other side of the specialty mirror to observe the application process of a new client without being seen or heard.

"My priest says I should be at peace with the path I choose," exclaimed Jocelyn Murphy, a widow whose husband had left her very comfortable. She was one of the first people requesting an appointment during their inaugural month of service. Murphy was fifty-nine years old, thin as a rail, and had graying hair worn shoulder length and parted to one side. She had never worked a day in her life. Since her husband had passed ten years earlier, she relocated her elderly mother from Jackson, Mississippi, to her home in Severna Park, a stone's throw from Annapolis. On this early winter morning, she sat in the beautiful new Hiatus Centers office in Baltimore, wearing a simple teal blouse and black pantsuit, to discuss the possibility of her mother entering the program upon death. Rachel wondered about Jocelyn Murphy's mother. *Why wasn't she here with her daughter?*

Rachel noticed that, much to the chagrin of the intake clerk, Shelley McAllister, Murphy prattled on. McAllister appeared ill prepared for this conversation. "If your priest told you to be at peace with the path you choose, then that is what you should try to do."

"Father Thomas told me that. He also said the church wouldn't approve. They don't approve? Can you imagine? I mean, jeepers, I don't know how to handle it. I want to bring Mom back more than anything but if I defy the church's teachings, am I defying God?"

"What else did Father Thomas say?" inquired McAllister.

"When a person dies, the spirit or soul separates from the body and lives on. When you stand before God, you must be worthy to do so.

Everyone goes through purgatory. You have to be very holy to skip it. Everyone goes through a state of purification. He told me that a person in a chemically preserved state is not viewed to still be that person. He made me feel like I won't be worthy to stand before God when I die because I placed my mother into a chemically preserved state. Do you agree with that?"

Upon hearing Murphy's question, Rachel looked at Albert in amazement. *Holy shit,* she thought. I wouldn't want to be McAllister tackling that one. Albert looked back at her to acknowledge the incredulity of the inquiry.

"Mrs. Murphy, I am not a religious person. I think that your priest is a wise man and if he told you to be at peace with your decision, I think that is what you should focus on."

"Do you think that when Mom comes back the first time, she will be able to tell us about purgatory or whether she stood before God?"

"There's simply no way of knowing, Mrs. Murphy."

McAllister paused for a moment and took Jocelyn Murphy's hand in her own in a moment of empathy for the conflict she was feeling. Jocelyn smiled through thin lips and the anxiety dissipated.

"I want to see Mom once a year," she said with resolve. "That's the most important thing to me."

McAllister smiled again before delving back into the details of the intake process.

"And how old is your mother?" asked Shelley McAllister.

"She turns seventy-eight on Saturday."

"How nice! Wish her Happy Birthday for me. Now, we need to get a thorough medical intake form completed for pre-qualification. Once your mother clears this step, we will need her to come to Baltimore for a comprehensive physical," explained McAllister.

"Mom had a physical recently. Does that count?"

"I'm afraid not, Mrs. Murphy. The Hiatus Centers' physical is a full body scan that will instantly tell us if your mother will be a successful candidate for this program. There is also a comprehensive blood screen."

"Why wouldn't she be accepted?" asked Murphy.

"A successful candidate cannot have any medical condition which might cause internal or external degradation."

"What happens if the candidate passes the physical and develops a degenerative condition at a later point?" Albert asked Rachel.

"Unfortunately, they forfeit their spot."

"Degradation? I'm sorry, I don't understand. I thought you just, you know, wake her up once a year for the day."

"Well, Mrs. Murphy, we do. We just need to make sure that—for the process to work properly, your mom can't have any sort of illness that will radically change the way she looks or destroy internal organs required for a successful awakening."

"Oh, I see," Murphy replied.

"Ben has a great team of lawyers," remarked Rachel to Albert. "They literally have thought of everything, which is really impressive in view of the fact that there is absolutely no legal precedent for what we do."

"What about her mother's will?" inquired Albert. "Does that interfere with Hiatus Centers' contracts?"

"Part of what you will see if you watch the entire intake process is that each incoming client must alter their will to provide the authority to enter the program upon death. The family members must also sign declarations, waivers, and disclaimers," she replied.

"How would a lawyer preparing a will even know what to write? This has never been done before," queried Albert.

"Like I said, Albert, Ben has a great team of lawyers. They came up with the language to be inserted into the will. Shelley McAllister, our intake specialist, will give that language to Jocelyn Murphy today and her mother will have her will altered. We require a copy of the revised will before we administer services."

Rachel propped her glasses atop her head to hold back her mind-of-their-own bangs. She smiled warmly at the board chair and said, "Albert, if you listen to the rest of the intake procedure, Shelley McAllister will cover all the bases on process and liability."

They looked on and listened as McAllister continued.

"Mrs. Murphy, if your mother is deemed a viable candidate, she will wear a monitor for the remainder of her days. This can be a wristlet or a necklace, her choice. The device is waterproof. Once she passes, the device will notify you, if you are the designated party, and the Hiatus Centers' computer. If she is still living in Severna Park when she dies, we will bring her here immediately, no matter the time of day, and treat her body with a special preservative. If she is out of town when death occurs, the preservative will need to be applied at the place of death and the body placed in a temperature controlled unit and brought to Baltimore. In the event this occurs, a Hiatus Centers' staff member will be dispatched to oversee this process on an emergency basis. There will be significant additional charges if this were to occur. Once the preservation process is complete, your mother's body will be stored in our containment area."

Rachel and Albert listened carefully. McAllister had a real knack for this job, thought Rachel. She relayed all of the pertinent information, seemed empathetic, and didn't dwell too long on tangential subject matter. Rachel looked over at Albert, who was studying every detail. Knowing him as she did, Rachel understood his desire to learn everything he could. After all, he always preached that information is power. She stretched for a moment, extending her arms skyward and turned her neck from side to side. Rachel felt the earlier tension melt away. She knew that before too much time had passed, she would need to have another conversation with Ben. Since that night, sleep had been hard to come by. Her head screamed the logic of the situation but her heart yearned for both the work and love relationship. Albert suddenly sneezed, causing her to refocus on the intake process.

"Each year, approximately thirty days prior to the anniversary of your mother's death, you will get an email requesting that you contact us to make plans for the awakening. You will be able to spend the day with your mother on the grounds of the Hiatus Centers in either a solarium, the outdoor gardens, or in our Virtual Experience Theater. Awakening will last up to twenty-four hours, but visitations are limited to eighteen hours. At the end of eighteen hours, we will begin preparation for the twelve-month hibernation."

Rachel was distracted again. Damn if Albert wasn't wearing the same cologne that Ben wears, or something similar. *Crap*, she thought. *Here I go again.*

McAllister continued.

"Hiatus Centers has the right to terminate an awakening session at any time if things go awry or to terminate hibernation, all at our sole discretion. For instance, if neurodegenerative disease sets in, patients may become irritable, angry, or even violent."

Despite her best efforts, Rachel's thoughts continued to drift. Watching the intake was for Albert's benefit. She was already well versed in the details. She wondered why men could not approach love and work in the same way as women. If men could think like women, she reasoned, the whole world might be better off. Her glasses slipped down; she readjusted them and once more redirected her attention back to the interview.

"You should realize that you will have aged and changed but your mother will not. This will become more profound with each year's awakening. We will prepare your mother for this each time she is awakened but you must be prepared, as well. During awakening, no more than two people will be allowed in the room for the first six hours and no more than four at a time thereafter. You agree that your entire session will be recorded and/or monitored by Hiatus Centers' staff . . . for scientific knowledge and your safety."

"Where did you find this intake employee?" Albert asked.

"We ran an ad on Monster. She had prior experience as a triage nurse at Upper Chesapeake Medical Center so she was familiar with the combination of legal and medical paperwork."

"Why did she leave Upper Chesapeake?"

"She left years ago to start a family and was looking to get back into the workplace. I think she's fantastic!"

"I concur," replied Albert.

They watched Jocelyn Murphy, who was totally absorbed in McAllister's every word.

"We realize that this is challenging for the surviving family members who will be visiting but we encourage you to treat your mother with the same affection as if she had never died. Spend some time considering how you would like to allocate your awakening time. We will send you periodic communication with suggestions and ideas. Our Virtual Experience Theater can recreate almost any life event that your mother may have enjoyed. To accomplish this, we will need a good deal of information from you to get the details and create an accurate, lifelike experience."

As the intake continued, Rachel noticed Albert taking copious notes. She admired people with photographic memories but she also knew that most of the human population suffered from a malady she jokingly referred to as CRS: *Can't remember shit.*

Rachel knew McAllister was coming down the home stretch.

"Some things she will not be permitted to do during awakening include strenuous movement of any kind. This includes sexual activity, running, jumping, lifting, or exertion. Muscles, bones, and organs simply cannot withstand the strain after lying dormant for so long. We encourage you to limit conversation to avoid any unpleasant topics. We do not wish to upset your mother during awakening."

Rachel and Albert continued their observation. There were a seemingly endless number of forms to complete, waivers to execute and disclaimers to acknowledge, all of which were reviewed and agreed to on a touch screen resting on McAllister's desk, angled toward Jocelyn Murphy.

"Come on Albert; let's head over to the Containment Area. I want you to see the finished product."

They proceeded toward the elevator and pressed the button for the lower level. When they finished viewing the Containment Area and the Awakening Suite, Rachel and Albert returned to the main level, toward the back of the building. They were headed to the Virtual Experience Theater.

When they arrived at Ben's pride and joy, Rachel took Albert's hand.

"Now, Albert, we have a little surprise for you. This part of the tour was customized for you."

They walked into an expansive round room. Rachel sensed that Albert had not grasped the unique aspects of what he was about to see. He moved slowly in the room, looking at everything but appearing to be less than enthusiastic. This was the part of the tour that, for Rachel, held the most promise in the quest to impress the board chair. Of this, she was confident.

Movie screens surrounded them from floor to ceiling. Rachel had him take a seat in one of two chairs docked in the center of the space. She handed him a virtual reality headset and he slipped it on over his thinning gray hair. He brought the unit to rest on his head and his eyes were covered by the latest, most advanced 3-D technology with internet access. Once he was comfortable, Rachel pushed a button and told him to relax.

She watched as Albert sat back and began to experience the walls illuminate in preparation for some sort of video presentation. His headset came to life at the same time. Instantly, she observed, he was transfixed. As if he were actually there, he saw a young boy at the Kansas State Fair, long, long ago. The nine-year-old was dressed in a tweed suit and black bowtie, befitting a bygone era, and was accepting an award from a panel of judges seated on a wooden bench behind a table adorned with red, white, and blue bunting. The middle judge was Dr. Donald Emmerling from The University of Kansas Science Department. The boy spoke.

"Thank you all. This is a tremendous honor."

"Oh my God, Rachel, that's me. This is unbelievable!"

Albert watched in amazement and felt a breeze created within the theater, coinciding with his 3-D view of a brown dust cloud around the old Kansas tents.

"Rachel, I am without words. You, Ben, and the team have outdone yourselves," exclaimed Albert.

"Albert, I couldn't wait to show off the Virtual Experience Theater. We've been working on this for quite a while."

"But how? Where did you get the source material?" he asked.

"Don't call the cops on us but Ben snuck into your office at the school and found some old 8mm tape of your science award. He wanted to be here to see your reaction but he had to go to DC for the day."

"I'll give him a call this evening. As your board chair, I can only tell you that I am most impressed and I know the clients will be, also."

"Thanks, Albert."

They walked along from the Virtual Experience Theater outside to the gardens overlooking the water. Rachel took on a troubled look.

"Rachel, you seem down all of the sudden. Is something wrong?" asked Albert.

"Albert, you've known Ben since he was a boy. You are like a second father to him. Do you think he will ever make room in his life for something other than work?" she asked.

Albert seemed to immediately grasp the magnitude of the situation. He looked at her in a patriarchal manner, put his arm around her shoulder, and replied, "Yes, I do think he will. One day, he will make the time. Some men, my dear, are in love with their work. Eventually, they all learn that they really love something, or someone, else. When it hits him and he looks into your beautiful green eyes, he'll kick himself for not noticing sooner."

A tear dropped from her eye. She reached to wipe it away with her hand but Albert was quick to offer a fresh handkerchief.

"Does he know how you feel?"

"Yes . . . yes, he does. But he told me he would be there for me, one day, when the time is right."

"And do you believe him?"

"Uh huh," she said through soft, almost undiscernible tears. "I just don't know how long I am prepared to wait."

After seeing Albert on his way, Rachel returned to her office at the nearby corporate headquarters building on E. Pratt Street, closed the door, threw her white lab coat over the back of a guest chair, and kicked off her heels. She grabbed a scratch pad, plopped on a beige, upholstered sofa parked against the windowless wall, and began to contemplate the words that would help take her back to a happy place, a destination with no cares, one enabling her to energetically emerge with the focus she would need to be productive.

Growing up in a small California town as an only child, Rachel Larkin had plenty of time on her hands. A nerd, late to blossom, she had always found solace in words. When she was down, her parents were often occupied with work or chores, friends were few and far between, so she threw herself into her studies. When that became tiresome, she turned to poetry. Rachel enjoyed reading and writing poetry. Unlike many young girls of her day who kept a diary, Rachel would express her emotions through verse, a line here, a line there, until eventually, a finished product would emerge. She once took two years to write a complete poem. Another time, her despair caused her to knock one out in fifteen minutes. Words had always been her outlet. Even when she couldn't find the words to say, they came easily when constructing a poem. When she was seventeen, she often thought she could make a career out of writing poetry, perhaps even as a songwriter. While her sense of pragmatism won out, along with her love of physics, she never abandoned her secret hobby.

She stared blankly at the lined pad but the words would not come. The urge to cry began to overwhelm her but she fought back. She gathered her emotions, returning to a favorite poem from her teenage years. She had written it on Valentine's Day when she was sixteen. A boy for whom she had feelings didn't seem to know she was alive. All these years later, the twisted knot in her stomach, the headache from crying, and then the desire to punch something all came rushing back. Her mother had tried to comfort her but to no avail. That evening, her mother brought her a gift; a pink ceramic mug with a large, red hand-drawn heart outlined in subtle rings of pink, red, and lavender. Hundreds of cups of tea and cocoa later, that old pink mug still went with her everywhere she went. She spotted it on her desk and smiled, wishing Mom was here to fill it with love. The anxious moments began to tone down. The energy, as always, transformed her from emotional wreck to wordsmith. The familiar lines from her youth flooded the forefront of her mind and returned her to a state of inner peace. She scribbled the title "Unbreakable" diagonally across the upper right hand corner of the pad and the words began to flow.

Dry
Dusty
Dirt
It all surrounds my skin
A thick, green sheath
Covered in thorns
A tough disguise
But soft in the middle
In this parched place

I stand alone.
Burnt out
Bushed
Beat up
I'm tired of being deserted.
Arms outstretched,
Aiming for the sky
My sharp spine is chilling.
Decades go by
I sprout taller
And I stand alone.
Distinct
Diverse
Different
More peculiar than the rest
On a sunny day
Others shy away
That's when I turn out my best
In a climate where most don't survive
I yearn to thrive
And in that I stand alone.

Budding
Blossoming
Blooming
I have endured the front line
One day my flower will bloom
And bright it will shine
In the darkest sandy dune
At the top I will stand,
And I will stand alone.

Rachel loved her old cactus-themed poem. It never failed to bring her back from the brink of emotional disaster. Today was different. She only got part of the way there. While the poem was comforting, it couldn't erase the innate conflict searing into her brain. Her period was three days late.

CHAPTER 17

The air in the building was heavy and stale. No circulation after 11:00 p.m. *You think I'd be used to this by now, after all the years of late-night sessions in the Lab,* thought Rachel. Her eyes were weary from reviewing endless reports relating to the performance of their first commercial center in Baltimore. The Lab was close to home. Many days, she reasoned, her old digs in the research facility were perfect for what she had to do. Plus, it saved the forty-minute commute to Baltimore. Given the hour, she was hopeful that Ben might also be working late and they could have a few minutes, or maybe more, alone.

Rachel plodded slowly down the corridor toward the main research area where Ben was most likely to be working. She was exhausted. Maybe it was the anxiety of being late or maybe this is what pregnant women felt after a long day. Rachel didn't really know. She still hadn't worked up the nerve to take a pregnancy test and pondered whether to even bring this up to Ben. After all, Rachel wasn't apt to let emotions stir the tide and leave a disastrous trail of debris. She elected to wait a few days more before deciding what to do. It was still possible that she was simply late. *If that turns out to be the case, I never have to broach a pregnancy with Ben,* she contemplated. *That would be a relief!*

Admittedly, Rachel felt despondent when she heard two voices coming from inside the main lab. Both Ben and Ari were working late. After submitting to the retina scan in the outer vestibule, she pushed through the double doors and witnessed a menagerie of scribbled notes and formulas on the whiteboard that stretched ten feet against the long wall. She quickly tried to discern the meaning but even with her advanced knowledge of physics, it made absolutely no sense.

"You boys need a life."

"Thanks for the heads up," replied Ari, with his trademark lopsided smile.

"What are you guys working on?"

"Well, Ben said Einstein got the theory of relativity all wrong and I say he nailed it. So we decided to beat it up from the beginning," said Ari. Rachel had always admired his dry sense of humor. It was characteristic of a real intellectual, she thought.

"So, what's really going on?"

"Actually, Ben and I have been having these occasional late nighters to see if we can't create some sort of instantaneous awakening."

"You mean, without a preservative and one-year curing process?"

"Yeah, something like that. You just zap the deceased and they come right back."

"Shouldn't this be a team project?" she asked, somewhat taken aback at the profound nature of the project.

"Probably," conceded Ari. "You've been consumed with the commercial center in Baltimore and Harrison and Tomi would be pissed off if they knew we were working on a process that eliminated the major aspects of the chemical and biological implications."

Rachel felt her anger diffuse. "Okay, points well taken. How far along are you?"

"Does that mess on the board look like anything meaningful?"

"Not even a little bit."

"Well, there you have it."

"You are quiet this evening, Dr. Abraham." She enjoyed the playful banter associated with tagging him by his degreed status.

Rachel looked on at Ben, who didn't reply. To her, he looked pale. She noticed that he was rubbing his neck, trying to work out a kink. His left hand moved to one eye and then the other, rubbing meticulously. Before she could ask him if he was okay, he doubled over the white Formica countertop and puked up everything he had eaten that day. A few seconds later, another round poured out like a faucet all over the floor.

"Ben, whoa, the smell! You okay, buddy?" asked Ari.

Rachel rushed to his side. The odor of the vomit was overpowering. She tried to lend a hand as he slowly straightened up. As Ben looked down at her from his tall, lean frame, Rachel noted that he looked gaunt, thinner than normal. *Ben didn't respond to Ari's question,* Rachel thought. It was as if he never even heard him speak. The look in Ben's eyes spelled confusion. Clearly, he had some sort of bug and was a little disoriented from the sudden heaving. Rachel and Ari helped him to one of the high-back stools and waited for him to regain his senses.

"I've got the worst headache ever," he finally managed to say.

Rachel saw his right eyelid start to droop and then he fell off the stool, out cold and flat on the floor. Ari knelt by one side, she on the other. Rachel searched in vain for a pulse, holding Ben's wrist. Her fear started to build as the color evaded Ben's face. Ari measured for a sign of life on Ben's neck. Nothing.

Rachel began to well up but summoned the inner strength that somehow served her well in emergencies. Long ago, she discovered she possessed an ability to focus in the face of calamity. Quick thinking overpowered fear and emotion as the man she loved lay on the floor, unconscious. A moment earlier, all had seemed lost. But now she knew she could save Ben! She began administering CPR. As she alternated between compressions and exhaling into Ben's mouth, she felt Ari reach down to her shoulder.

"It's no use, Rachel. Ben is dead."

CHAPTER 18

Anstrov Rinaldi had little tolerance for meetings. He regarded himself as a man of action. Only so much talk was needed. He saw most people as being intellectually inferior, which only fueled his impatience. BV3000 was selling briskly in every major market across the world, except the biggest of them all. The excuses from his Executive Directorate were lame. Why they couldn't find a way to get past the bureaucracy of the FDA was beyond comprehension. After all, there were ways of dealing with such matters. That is, of course, if one knew what to do.

Rinaldi shook his head at Drago, who hovered on a long, flat shelf domiciled behind his desk.

"Time to meet with the best of the worst," he said aloud to the Komodo dragon.

Drago responded by fully extending his forked tongue. For effect, he curled the tip inward and then rotated it clockwise, like a twisted rubber band.

"No one likes a showoff, Drago."

Rinaldi looked toward the door and watched curiously as his chief operating officer, Henri Marceau, walked timidly through the doorway. On his heels were the vice president of sales, Stefan Lowenstein, and the CFO, Bjorn Stenson. True to form, Rinaldi began with an attempt at humor to quell the natural anxiety he seemed to invoke in those he encountered.

"Good morning, gentlemen. I called this meeting to discuss the sales progress of our antiaging drug. I fear I will myself become old and decrepit before we reach the pinnacle of success."

The three men in his company stared back blankly, ignoring his pursuit of a laugh. Rinaldi outwardly displayed a big ego. Inwardly, he knew he was insecure and fragile. His sense of humor landed on others more as sarcasm and condescension. This only fed Rinaldi's lack of self-worth. This was a known flaw he shared with no one, not even Drago, his only living confidante.

Lowenstein, ever the salesman, decided to lead off with what everyone in the room already knew.

"Dr. Rinaldi, sales of BV3000 are strong throughout Europe, Asia, South America, and Australia. We can't make the product fast enough to satisfy demand."

"Sales in most of the world are admirable but do not flatter yourself. This product is so good, it practically sells itself."

Lowenstein sat back, looking deflated. His body language strongly suggested that he would be passing the baton to Marceau or Stenson. Neither mustered the courage to speak. Disgusted, Rinaldi got up from his desk and walked over to a large world map on the far wall. With his cane, he tapped on North America.

"Here," he tapped on Canada, "and here," he tapped on Mexico, "sales are good, but here," he pounded angrily with the cane on the United States, "our sales are zero."

He glared down at them with his good eye and let the comment sink in. Then, like lava rising up through an active volcano, the rage appeared.

"ZERO," he screamed. "Our sales in the largest market in the world are nothing, nada, zip," he continued. "And why, you might ask? Because our team of pharmaceutical experts can't seem to appease the fucking FDA, that's why!"

At that moment, Rinaldi's presence, although small in physical stature, loomed large.

"Now, I want you to explain what you are planning to do about it."

The three men sat frozen and just stared at Rinaldi. With every moment of silence, he felt his disdain for these men increase. He almost wished he could pull the revolver from his desk drawer and just blow them away. A deep breath and common sense prevailed.

"Henri, what is the latest with the FDA?"

Rinaldi waited for a response. He thought Marceau would be so great when he hired him but he was really no better than the other jokers on the Executive Directorate. In fact, Rinaldi thought this meeting alone had aged the old man another ten years. He appeared meek and frightened.

"There is some silver lining in the FDA cloud," he began slowly. "We have passed Phase 3 trials, the FDA has approved our application, our manufacturing facilities, product labeling, and even our NDA."

Rinaldi knew the Americans called the New Drug Application an NDA. Their fancy acronym described a lengthy submission detailing all animal and human trials—specifically, how the human body responds to the drug and the intimate process of how the drug is manufactured.

Rinaldi eased up a bit at the preliminary good news.

"So what, pray tell, is the remaining hurdle?"

"That's the bad news," replied Marceau. "It seems that the last remaining hurdle is the head of FDA himself. Commissioner John Frederickson is personally holding up the approval."

"What's his objection?" asked Stenson, the heretofore phlegmatic finance man.

"He claims it's the side effects but this is not the true reason. It is nonsense. Data clearly shows, in all countries, that the only side effects most people report are the same ones every drug seems to have . . .

nausea, stomach upset, diarrhea, cramping, headache, dizzy spells. You know the drill."

"What's the incidence rate for these side effects in US trials?" asked Lowenstein.

"The same as in every other country: less than 1 percent."

Rinaldi was well beyond his meeting saturation point. He limped toward the three men, lifted his cane, and pointed it at the CFO.

"Bjorn, remind this illustrious group what the projected sales are for BV3000 in the US."

Stenson sighed. Rinaldi was toying with the CFO; a high-priced bean counter was all he amounted to.

"First year sales in the US market are expected to exceed $8 billion."

"Thank you," Rinaldi said sarcastically. "Eight billion dollars hangs in the balance and you tell me the approval is hung up with one man. This all sounds too peculiar to me. Surely Mr. Frederickson can articulate exactly what his issue is. Don't you think?"

"Well, I didn't want to say anything. I mean, we really don't know for sure but . . ."

"You don't know what?" Rinaldi fired back quickly.

"One of our people working on getting the FDA approval had a conversation last week with the number two man, a Dr. Felipe Pacheco. Pacheco indicated that Frederickson was annoyed by reports of BV3000 having the opposite of its intended effect."

"You mean to say, he believes that our wonder drug will accelerate the aging process?" asked Rinaldi.

"That's right."

"What do we know about that? Is there any credence to the allegation?"

"I doubt it. There was one such claim from a woman in Belgium, another from Brisbane and one in London. Nothing concrete, I assure you. A tiny, infinitesimal fraction of one percent. So little time has passed with the drug on the market, I don't even understand how anyone could make such a claim."

Rinaldi paced in front of the seated executives, back and forth, back and forth. He paced silently with his head down as he contemplated what he had just heard. When he collected his thoughts, he looked up, his good eye twinkled, and a slight grin formed on his thin lips.

"I've listened to everything you've had to say. Now, the three of you listen to me. You have ninety days to get the FDA to approve BV3000. If the approval has not been granted in ninety days, your services will be terminated."

Lowenstein, the boldest of Rinaldi's three pawns, made a feeble attempt to push back.

"Dr. Rinaldi. No one can make the FDA go faster than they want to. We are at their mercy."

The insolence emboldened Rinaldi, whose hot breath enveloped the three men like fire from a mythical, medieval beast.

"Ninety days!" he shouted.

The three men stood up, demoralized with heads down, and left the office in a single file line. Giving these fools ninety days to gain FDA approval was lunacy. Rinaldi realized that they would most likely use the time to seek new employment. That would simply be three months of valuable time and lost profit flushed down the toilet. Resigned to taking matters into his own hands, Rinaldi picked up the phone and set the wheels in motion.

CHAPTER 19

Rachel lost it. The dam that had been holding back the tears suddenly burst, drenching her face. Her nose stuffed up and the ability to speak coherently vanished between the heavy sobs. Through watery eyes, she saw Ari quickly moving toward a locked cabinet. He twirled a black-faced combination lock dial three times, clockwise, counterclockwise, and clockwise again until the device guarding the cabinet's innards sprung open. Rachel sat, numb and sprawled out on the floor next to the lifeless body of the man she loved. Her denim skirt was twisted and uncomfortable. The crying had caused a pounding headache. She moved her hands to puffy, bloodshot eyes and began to rub. The nasal congestion helped conceal the overpowering odor from Ben's earlier regurgitation. Her body and mind were helpless, no better than sugar spilled on a floor.

Rachel watched Ari retrieve a metal box from the cabinet. The box was small, maybe eight by ten inches and, at first blush in her diminished state, struck Rachel as rather ordinary. The only defining feature she saw was a small white button on the right side. The device appeared to be nothing more than common sheet metal and the button resembled someone's front doorbell.

Rachel wanted to understand what Ari was doing but couldn't yet form the words. She gazed in wonder as Ari moved quickly to Ben, hovered the metal box over him and pushed the crude button, holding it in. A glowing series of colored lights emanated from pinholes on the bottom of the box. The light bathed over the dead body of Ben Abraham, back and forth, over and over. Rachel didn't understand. Moreover, she was astounded by Ari's lack of emotion. *Where was his compassion?* His colleague and close friend just dropped dead unexpectedly. *Had this man lost his capacity to feel?* she wondered. Through the fog of despondency, she started to question if she really knew Ari at all. *Had he lost his mind?*

"Wh—what are you doing?" she finally managed to stammer out through the tears and running mascara.

But Ari didn't answer. He just maintained the same laser focus and meticulous pattern of activity. *Pull yourself together,* she commanded herself. Part of her wanted to tackle Ari, tell him to stop, respect the moment. The other part of her knew Ari enough that his actions were always well intentioned. She sat on the cold marble floor, lost in conflicted thought somewhere between hope and despair.

When Ben's head began moving, ever so slightly, left to right and then back again, Rachel considered that she might be hallucinating. Rachel thought she heard Ben softly moan. Then, she saw his eyes open and her hopes rose to a crescendo. A tiny smile began to form in the corner of her mouth and a new tear, one of joy, ran down her cheek. She made eye contact with Ari, whose own crooked smile had surfaced. He had the look of a scientist basking in the glory of an unexpected breakthrough.

While still struggling to comprehend what just happened, Rachel felt everything beginning to slowly return to a state of semi-normalcy. She moved closer to Ben, wanting to provide comfort as he came back from wherever or whatever he had just experienced. Before she could traverse the few feet between them, her stomach rolled over and her heart twisted inside her chest. The unusual events had taken yet another wild turn. Ben's eyes were open, and then spun back violently to his forehead, his hair appeared to spike as a raging seizure overtook the placidity of the past few moments. Rachel looked up at Ari. Her face contorted in terror.

"Rachel, let it pass," Ari guided.

She backed away from the convulsing body of Ben Abraham, reverting back into a full-fledged emotional meltdown. Rachel was transfixed on the body. The spasms reminded her of television shows where a doctor desperately zaps a patient's chest with a defibrillator. Unlike the movies, no one was yelling, "Clear!" and Ben's seizure was "zapping" him repetitively with no end in sight.

"Make it stop!" she blurted out.

Once again, from deep within, she summoned her capacity to breathe deeply and collect herself. Her father was an avid sailor and had taught her that winds can change suddenly. If the sailboat broaches, the captain had to accommodate quickly or face a potentially deadly rollover. She contemplated what she could do to keep Ben from returning to a silent, black abyss. Before she could move, Ben's murderous storm passed and the winds suddenly became calm.

She glanced at Ari who looked as relieved as she felt. They both gathered around Ben to check his vitals. Rachel felt a pulse. She clutched his right hand in both of hers, silently praying that this nightmare had concluded.

As if her prayer had been answered, Ben looked up at them through soupy eyes and asked, "What happened?"

Before she could respond, Ari took over.

"You fainted. I think you got sick, became dehydrated, and just passed out."

Rachel decided to play along with Ari's deception . . . at least for the moment. With Ben out of earshot, she intended to corner Ari and learn what in hell was going on.

CHAPTER 20

John Frederickson was bored. In just ten years, he had experienced a lifetime of Washington bureaucracy. Now he was stuck in Chicago for four days attending an obligatory conference hosted by the Department of Health and Human Services. As the head of the FDA, he was required to attend, be at all functions, and put on his best smile. The trip wasn't all bad. He liked Chicago and its great steak houses and it got him away from the drudgery of his thirty-five years of marriage to a clinging, nagging wife.

Tonight, Frederickson was attending the opening reception for the HHS Conference. The theme of this year's session was something cheesy, like Working for the Betterment of Mankind. He supposed it looked good on marketing collateral but to him, it made little sense. Frederickson was not an introvert but he rarely sought out new people at events like these. He preferred small group interaction with less superficial conversation. After nearly two hours of "networking," as they now called it, he had camped out at a high table with a tablecloth draped to the floor in the corner of the large hotel ballroom, drink in hand, contemplating whether to have one more or call it a night.

At the age of sixty-two, Frederickson had become a creature of habit. If he were home in Bethesda, he would likely be preparing for bed, an old-fashioned newspaper in hand, trying to catch up on the day's events. He elected to forgo the additional cocktail and head up to his room.

"John? John Frederickson?"

Frederickson perked up when he saw a shapely young woman approach in a low-cut black dress leaving little to the imagination. Her long, flowing red hair made for a sharp contrast against the black dress and her alabaster skin. He was captivated by her beauty and thought that perhaps the evening might yet hold a spark of pleasure.

"I'm so sorry. You have me at a disadvantage. Have we met?"

"We just did," she replied. "My name is Portia, you know, like the car."

"Your parents named you after a car?" he inquired.

"It's more like a nickname," she replied. I took the liberty of asking the bartender what you were drinking and brought you another. You don't mind, do you?"

He was mesmerized each time her full, ruby red lips parted. Her eyes were a stunning, vibrant shade of blue and she moved like a cat. Before he could reply, she had set the drink down in front of him, pulled a chair close to his, and gently caressed his leg with hers underneath the table. Frederickson was almost breathless. No woman had paid any attention to him, well, pretty much ever. He knew he had to let his mind overtake the instinctive urge his body was feeling.

"What brings you to the HHS conference? Are you a doctor, a researcher, or . . ."

She placed a long, slender finger with a finely manicured nail over his lips and cocked her head in a seductive manner, looking like she was ready to lean in to kiss him. But she didn't. She just held the position. Their faces were just inches apart. He was intoxicated by the aroma of her perfume. Frederickson felt his body temperature elevating by the second. He looked around the room to see if anyone he knew was witnessing this bizarre occurrence. He hadn't done anything wrong but he felt guilty for just being in the scene. After all, he was the head of the FDA.

As he tried to get a grip on reality, he felt her hand move under the white tablecloth to his groin. She began to caress. Any strength he had to protest was rapidly vanishing.

"John, you haven't touched the drink I brought you. Leave it. We can continue the conversation in your room. That is, if you think you might enjoy some more."

Frederickson was numb. He couldn't speak and frankly, could not find it within himself to apply reason to such a crazy situation. He had been to a million of these monotonous government get togethers but nothing like this had ever happened before. Hell, he was sixty-two years old. This beauty might have been in her early thirties, at most. He was old, with a beer belly, balding and gray and certainly no one's prize. Yet he had heard of women who were turned on by men in powerful positions. Did she want something? Was this some sort of game? He couldn't know for sure but, at this stage of his mundane life, he decided, for once, not to think and just roll with the moment.

He left the drink untouched on the table and told her to meet him in room 1247 in fifteen minutes. Although he was living in the moment, he thought it crazy to be seen leaving the ballroom with this salacious beauty. Frederickson headed to the elevator, took a deep breath, and loosened his tie. He pulled a handkerchief from his left breast pocket and wiped his brow and nose. He didn't even realize how much he had been sweating.

After he was settled in the room, a soft knock fell upon the door. To Frederickson, it sounded more like she somehow stroked the door with just enough impact to make an announcement. He concluded this as being ridiculous. Of course, his mind was still in the numb zone from their earlier encounter. He opened the door and held it as she walked in and, with her mere presence, commanded the room. In just the few seconds it had taken for the door to close, she had slipped off her high heels and black dress. Before he could move, he found himself overtaken by her sexuality, her scent, and her every move. She locked eyes and brought her mouth to his and he felt her tongue penetrate his lips. His mind was completely lost in her allure.

Seconds later, he felt her right hand behind his back form in the shape of a fist. Her finger moved as she depressed a small button in the palm of her hand, activating a stud on her tongue. Before he could make sense of what was happening, Frederickson felt a small pinpoint prick on his tongue. The last he ever heard was the sound of the Bluetooth activated needle receding back into the safety of its origin.

CHAPTER 21

Rachel was on a mission. The prior night had been nothing but a long toss and turn. Knowing that Ari was an early riser and would be in the office by 7:00 a.m., she abandoned the further notion of sleep, readied herself quickly, and, after arriving at the Lab, made a beeline to Ari's office. Rachel entered and closed the door behind her.

"Uh oh," he said. "I know that look. Am I in trouble?"

"Are you seriously asking me that? Don't play innocent with me. You obviously didn't want Ben to know what happened to him and you obviously wanted me to go along with your ploy. So start explaining."

Rachel stood in front of his desk, hands on hips, fuming, while waiting for any plausible scenario to make sense of the unimaginable occurrence of the prior day. Ari stood up and parked himself on the corner of his desk, directly in front of her. He was wearing sneakers with his dress slacks. If she weren't consumed with anxiety, she would have made fun of him.

"As best as I can determine, we witnessed Ben having a brain aneurysm."

"An aneurysm?" she asked incredulously. "What makes you think that?"

"I did some research after you both went home. It's the only thing that makes sense. He exhibited all of the symptoms."

"What are you talking about?" she exclaimed. "An aneurysm? Wouldn't he be dead?"

"Rachel, he was dead. The device I used on him afterward is an experimental prototype of an advanced Liferay that eliminates the need for a preservative, a curing period, and a one year wait."

Unconvinced and out of sorts, Rachel felt like she had left her own body. She was clinging to the last functional part of her consciousness to continue an intelligent query. This still wasn't making sense.

"Are you 100 percent sure it was an aneurysm?"

"If you look up the symptoms and think back to the events of last night, you'll see it for yourself. He threw up, seemed confused, and said he had the worst headache ever. Did you notice his eye drooping? All classic signs of a cerebral aneurysm."

She replayed the horrific scene in her mind and gradually recalled Ben experiencing the symptoms as Ari stated.

"Rachel, the fact of the matter is that if I hadn't acted quickly to use the prototype, Ben Abraham would be gone forever and the world would be worse off."

"I know, I know, you're right." The thought of losing Ben forever gripped her heart like a vise.

Gaining a stronger grasp on reality, she found logic beginning to take hold of the conversation.

"Last night, before all the drama began, you said you weren't anywhere near a solution for an instantaneous awakening. You lied to me."

"Actually, I didn't. You simply asked if we were close. My reply was to ask you if the mess on the board looked like anything meaningful. From there, you drew your own conclusion."

She knew he had her on a technicality but still felt deceived. Why would Ben and Ari hide this from her? If she hadn't walked in on their late night session, they would've kept her in the dark. She decided to contemplate that issue at a later date.

"So if the prototype obviously works, why not just tell Ben what happened, move the device along the production continuum, and reevaluate the commercial center business model? We could offer the service as it's presently being marketed and also another to emergency physicians."

"Whoa! Slow down and take a deep breath. First off, Ben can never know what happened to him. I know him. He would rather be dead than know he was a living guinea pig for an experimental device. On changing the business model . . . maybe one day. We're potentially years from perfecting the prototype."

"What makes you think it will take years? You saw it work just yesterday!"

"You are forgetting the seizure Ben experienced after he came back."

"What about it?"

"It could be blood from the aneurysm's rupture affecting the motor functions of his brain but I am more concerned about it being an effect of the imperfect prototype."

"Oh my God," she said. "If we don't get a CT scan on his brain, we can't know for certain."

"Yeah," he replied wearily. "That's where I'm stuck. I'm not sure how to get Ben a CT without sharing all of this with him and a neurologist."

"What's the worst that could happen if we tell him the truth? He'll get mad, yeah, but he'll have the best chance to live a long and healthy life."

"You don't know Ben as well as I do. If we tell him the truth, he's likely to lose it, disown us both, and retreat to a secluded corner of the world to solve the problem on his own. We can't let that happen."

Rachel tried to make sense of the dilemma in which she found herself fully immersed. If she told Ben the truth, he would be upset and she could lose him forever. If she went along with Ari and Ari couldn't figure out a way out of the box they were painted in, Ben could drop dead from another aneurysm or brain damage he suffered from the first one. The best of the bad options seemed to be the one in which she helped Ari to figure out the path forward. At least that way, she reasoned, she could play a role in determining how to get Ben his CT. But even if the CT was clear, it would place him in a position where the prototype was causing debilitating seizures. They had no idea how to deal with that problem. Could the seizures kill him? She simply didn't know.

She was torn. The situation was fraught with seemingly unsolvable riddles. For a moment she imagined herself in an empty field, the paper with all the answers had been ripped in a million pieces and the wind caused them all to swirl above her head in an unreachable manner.

She hated keeping secrets from anyone, let alone Ben, the man she loved. But at least for the moment, she saw no other choice. Rachel felt the torture of keeping not only the potential pregnancy secret but also one that was even more explosive.

"Rachel, are you with me on this?"

"Yes," she replied with reticence.

CHAPTER 22

Rinaldi was ecstatic. The day began with major news outlets covering the unexpected death of FDA Commissioner John Frederickson. Frederickson's death was determined to be a heart attack. *Not uncommon for an overweight man in his sixties who probably hasn't seen a cardio workout in the last twenty-five years*, Rinaldi thought. How ironic, he considered, that this out-of-shape senior was managing the unit of America's Health and Human Services, which maintained the responsibility for keeping people well. *Pity*, he thought sarcastically.

Rinaldi turned his chair toward the office door to see Marceau in an ear-to-ear smile.

"Henri, I don't think I have ever seen you smile so heartily."

"Our BV3000 roadblock dropped dead yesterday. I mean, I don't care to revel in the misfortune of others but, frankly, we had no clue how we were going to convince Mr. Frederickson to approve the drug within your ninety-day deadline."

"Well," Rinaldi replied snidely, "sometimes prayers do get answered."

Knowing full well what the answer was, Rinaldi queried Marceau as to who would succeed Frederickson.

"The American president has appointed the FDA's chief of staff, Dr. Felipe Pacheco, as the new commissioner. It is expected that Congress will proceed with his confirmation hearing on an expedited basis. For all intents and purposes, as the number two man at the FDA, he is functioning as commissioner already."

Rinaldi feigned surprise. "Splendid. I trust you and the others will be in touch with Dr. Pacheco in short order to gain approval for BV3000."

"Yes, needless to say, they are not taking calls or answering emails today, given the circumstances but we plan on being on a plane to DC next week."

"Excellent. Good work, Henri."

Rinaldi dismissed Marceau and laughed to himself. That very morning, Pacheco was receiving a discreet delivery: a briefcase stuffed with cash—one hundred grand, to be exact. It seems, Rinaldi thought, that Dr. Pacheco's monumental gambling debt would be extinguished before he was sworn in as commissioner. He smiled to himself. Throughout his entire career, doing his homework had always paid off. Learning about the enormous debt Pacheco had developed was a nice tidbit to come about. Rinaldi was patting himself on the back. The DC lobbyist he secretly kept on the payroll was bearing fruit. Eight billion in US sales would soon be rolling in.

CHAPTER 23

Two Tylenol washed down by a Red Bull ought to conquer this headache. Perhaps not the remedy of choice for early evening if he had any notion of sleeping tonight. Ben didn't mind. He had much work to do. It had been two nights since he passed out while working late with Ari. He remembered very little about that night. Maybe he hit his head when he blacked out. That would explain the headaches. Other than that, he felt decent—a little washed out, a little jittery, but decent nonetheless.

Rachel was pushing him to go to a doctor about the headaches. Ben would have none of it. He reasoned that doctors would poke and prod him to no end. With a generic symptom like an intermittent headache, doctors would be looking for a needle in a haystack. He would tough it out.

Before starting in on his self-assigned work for the evening, he sat down in his La-Z-Boy, reclined, and closed his eyes. The conversation with Rachel from earlier in the day was foremost on his mind.

It started out with the push to see a doctor. Then she dropped the bomb. She thought she might have been pregnant. Harrison would have a field day with this, Ben thought. Harrison was the guy who lived carelessly, had fun at every turn, and never got in trouble. Ben, on the other hand, submitted to one night of drunken sex with a colleague—a subordinate, no less—and she thinks she got knocked up. Turned out her monthly guest had just arrived late. *That's a relief,* he thought.

As he waited for the Tylenol and Red Bull to take effect, he started to wonder what would have happened had Rachel been pregnant. Questions flooded his mind. *Would we have to get married? What kind of husband and father would I make? Would we still be able to work together? What about Hiatus Centers? Am I too old to be starting a family?* The business was about to take off. He would have to start traveling extensively across the country. The swirling menagerie of conflicting thoughts was making his head hurt even more. He reached for the TV remote and powered up the flat screen. The guide automatically illuminated the MLB package and Ben scanned for the channel that offered the Dodger broadcast of their game against the Cubs from Wrigley Field. Baseball was a great escape when his mind started the race to nowhere.

His head was beginning to clear from both thought and pain. He became restless and decided to stretch his legs outside. His apartment was nestled in the backwoods of Maplebrook. The day's sun was setting slowly on a clear and rare humidity-free evening. A walking trail began behind his building and ran one and a half miles to a park with a children's playground and several ball fields. Ben liked walking to the park and watching the Little League games. There were no games on this particular evening but it took his mind back to Rachel being pregnant. Ben didn't have to reach deep to discover what he knew but wasn't ready to say out loud; he was in love with Rachel. Why not settle down and start a family? Ben thought of Gramps and how he taught Ben to play catch and then to swing a bat. One day, he could be the dad coaching the tee ball kids. A smile came across his face. He pictured himself with Rachel in an old Victorian style house reminiscent of so many lining the wooded streets of Maplebrook. A millionaire's family would be nice: a boy and a girl.

A middle-aged woman with a Golden Retriever was about to pass him from the other direction on the tree lined path. Ben was snapped back into the present when the dog stopped to sniff him. The dog's owner apologized profusely but Ben didn't mind. He loved dogs and this one looked like a cute old teddy bear. When he married Rachel, they would have a Golden Retriever and he would name it Teddy.

As he turned around to head back, a low hanging tree branch smacked him in the face. *That was my reality check*, he thought. Ben knew he was years away from such a dream come true. Would Rachel wait? He wasn't sure but he did know his first priority, maybe even his first love, was the science. Romance would come somewhere down the road. First, the work. The aroma from the old White Owl cigar box filled his brain. Deep in his soul, he was being pushed by his grandfather's secret. And, he knew, even with the strides associated with Hiatus Centers, he stood completely powerless to act on the secret Gramps entrusted to him. All these years later, it was still his driving force, the reason he had worked so hard. He wanted to ease the pain and suffering associated with the death of a loved one.

He reached the end of the path and stepped onto the cement walkway that led back to his building. As he climbed the steps to his apartment, the world began to tremble.

Maryland doesn't have earthquakes, he knew. Although it felt like the whole planet was shaking, Ben quickly realized that the tremors were occurring only inside his own body. Another seizure was upon him.

CHAPTER 24

Eighteen months later

Molly Kendrick had never gotten over the horror of the way her mother died . . . the second time. Upon Sylvia Bresling's initial death, there was a calming sense of peace that came with Molly's faith in the clinical trial offered by Dr. Abraham and his staff. She recanted the story and her feelings on the matter for her new attorney.

"They all seemed so confident in what they were doing," she said.

With Jeff by her side, Molly walked the attorney through the entire process, every grueling detail, from the time she saw an ad in *The Baltimore Sun* for clinical trial applications right through the hideous final scene when her mother awoke with a neurodegenerative disease. The lawyer peppered her with questions about everything, including the original ad, all of the paperwork they signed, emails they might have exchanged with Dr. Abraham or his staff, conversations that were held, and the actions of the team during the final, fateful night. This included the accident wherein Harrison Bock was struck by the Liferay. Molly recalled how Dr. Abraham and his staff all raced to help their friend while her mother was left unattended.

So far, she had been in his company only for an hour, but Molly was impressed with the lawyer she had hired. Before this, Molly had never hired a lawyer for anything. Heck, she didn't even have a will.

This lawyer had been recommended by Jeff's boss. Jeff was a truck driver and his boss was the terminal manager who once used this attorney to successfully pursue a claim against the manufacturer of a truck he drove with faulty brake lining. Jeff's boss had sustained minor injuries in an incident wherein the truck failed to brake properly and hit a telephone pole at ten miles per hour. The lawyer also sued the employer. The case had never gone to trial but Jeff's boss had received a settlement of $250,000. Not enough to retire on but enough to pay off his mortgage and live more comfortably. Molly was intrigued with the possibilities.

Having no real experience with lawyers or the legal system, Molly thought all lawyers dressed like Lyle Poston. Poston wore light gray slacks with a dark purple dress shirt and a navy blazer with gold buttons on the front and sleeves. The shirt was open at the neck. Poston was a portly fellow with a beer gut and a bad comb-over job. His face was easily recognizable from his ads on the Mass Transit Administration buses and park benches in and around the city. His modest office was in an aging retail district on the western edge of Baltimore.

Molly thought he was cunning, just what they needed to take down Hiatus Centers. She even liked his slogan: *Get ahold of Lyle and there will be no trial.* She didn't really understand what it meant; she just liked the rhyme.

"Mr. and Mrs. Kendrick, I'm not going to lie to you. You signed a battery of waivers and disclaimers absolving Dr. Abraham from liability from any imaginable circumstance, including permanent death. Now, that doesn't mean we can't make something good happen for you. I'm known for getting results."

"But how do we get around the disclaimers and waivers, or whatever you called them? Is there a jury that has to decide? You know, like on television?" she inquired.

"My goodness, no. I haven't seen the inside of a courtroom in more years than I care to remember. These matters get down to the art of negotiation powered by a little old-fashioned know how."

"So, you are saying there's a chance we could collect some money?"

"Definitely. I'm not saying it will be easy but the odds are better than average."

Molly sat back on the lawyer's vinyl sofa and began to feel content. She sat up when Jeff chimed in with a question.

"Mr. Poston, what are you actually going to file suit for?"

"Oh, we'll make some noise about wrongful death, pain and suffering, the usual sort of legal strategy in a case like this."

Molly's sense of curiosity got the best of her.

"In a case like this? Isn't this sort of new ground we're traveling upon?"

Poston smirked. "Of course it is, dear. You are absolutely right," he replied in his most patronizing voice.

Molly was nonplussed but she was also a believer and anxious to get the lawsuit moving.

"When you entered the clinical trial, Hiatus Centers was not yet formed as a corporation. Your contract was with a medical LLC owned by Dr. Abraham. We will sue the LLC, Dr. Abraham personally, and, for good measure, Hiatus Centers."

"How can we sue Hiatus Centers if they didn't exist when Mom was in the clinical trial?"

"Oh, there are many legal precedents. The theory of deep pockets, the doctrine of related party interests and a few more. My law clerk will dig up all the dirt. Don't worry, we'll go after them hard."

Molly smiled. She took Jeff's hand and squeezed. They would get what's coming to them. That bastard Abraham would pay for what he did to her mother.

CHAPTER 25

It had been another insufferable day. The fulfillment of a lifelong dream squarely collided with an ongoing barrage of seemingly endless business barriers. These were challenges for which Ben felt totally unprepared. Solving impossible scientific equations felt easy compared to the rudiments of day-to-day responsibilities as the CEO of a rapidly growing business enterprise. In just under two years, Ben had overseen the opening of new locations in Fort Lauderdale, Orlando, Phoenix, New York, Atlanta, Chicago, Los Angeles, and Dallas. The travel schedule was exhausting. Ari, Rachel, Harrison, and Tomi were all onboard with overseeing the opening of new locations. They had built a template for location selection, interior design, and layout. Opening a new location involved a good amount of oversight, including hiring a manager and training that person while making sure construction and/or remodeling were on schedule and at or under budget. Harrison called him from every new city with a tale of yet another encounter with a member of the opposite sex. *The guy was a magnet*, Ben thought. *Fun just seemed to find him wherever he went.*

Each of them was settling into the routine of it all but inevitably problems arose, like local municipalities throwing permit problems their way. The cost of replicating equipment increased, including the Liferays, which were once developed in the Lab as single location devices but now had to be custom manufactured by a contractor. This presented problems in order fulfillment, logistics, and higher-than-planned transportation costs. In each city, religious zealots would stage protests in front of the new location, causing delays and disruptions. The leader was a reverend named Alonzo Cashman. Cashman was an African-American in his late forties who enjoyed shouting from the rooftops about the indignity of the Hiatus Centers offering. Ben wondered what Cashman's play was. Was he really outraged? Did he see money in this for himself? Was he just a publicity hound who sought the limelight? Any way you cut it, Cashman looked like he was going to be another problem Ben would have to deal with.

As ominous as it had been, Ben had aggressive plans on the drawing board to open a new location bimonthly until every major metropolitan area in the United States was covered. After that, in all likelihood, they would tackle Canada and perhaps the United Kingdom. In his entire life, Ben Abraham had done everything in a big way.

He was glad to be finishing a difficult day in his office on the top floor of a posh office tower on E. Pratt Street in downtown Baltimore. Just five minutes away from Hiatus Centers' location in Baltimore, the corporate world for Ben and his team was taking shape.

Ben's long wall in the corner office contained a window that overlooked the beautiful inner harbor. The sun was beginning to set as Ben relaxed with a bottle of water and his left buttock on the credenza resting below the storied window. He gazed out at the hustle and bustle of the perpendicular shopping pavilions residing on E. Pratt and Light Streets. Although they were a few blocks from Oriole Park at Camden Yards, Ben's office was decorated in the unmistakable tones of Dodger blue with Brooklyn/LA memorabilia on every wall and surface. These symbols paid homage to his favorite team and the memory of his grandfather, a Brooklyn native and die-hard Dodger fan. They were reminders of why he worked so hard to achieve the impossible. The breakneck speed at which he attempted everything was his own choice.

Ben's mind wandered, as it tended to do, as he observed the seagulls diving toward the harbor just alongside Baltimore's vaunted water taxi, which was heading toward the green glass triangular peak of The National Aquarium. Tourists walked along the familiar red brick walkways inlaid in a crisscross pattern. Ben could see musicians entertaining the crowd in the small plaza where the two walkways met. He glanced left and saw the World Trade Center and across the harbor, the age-old factory where Domino Sugar was made. Ben loved the water and admired the many boats lining the marina.

The day's first moments of solitude were disrupted when Traci, his administrative assistant, knocked on the frame of his open door.

"Dr. Abraham, I have a large FedEx envelope for you. Rather heavy for what feels like documents," she said.

Ben thanked her, took the heavy document pack, and stripped it open. As he began to read, he exhaled and let his body fall into his desk chair. The force of his body receding toward the chair caused the unorganized mess of paper on his desk to fly. Ben had never experienced the gripping, physical symptoms of anxiety but he was about to in a big way. His breath became shallow, as if a weight rested upon his chest. There was numbness in his right arm. He began to sweat and his throat became tight and dry. He felt his eyes involuntarily roll up and toward the left. His will to overcome his difficulties had vanished and he succumbed to panic.

The administrative assistant, who had left Ben's office, was able to observe his sudden lapse into despair through the large picture window and became alarmed. She reached for the phone and dialed the cell phone number for Dr. Rachel Larkin.

"I'll be right there," said a frightened Rachel Larkin. "Go check on him and make sure he doesn't need an ambulance."

When Rachel arrived at Ben's door in record time, a recovering Ben Abraham looked up at a scared Rachel Larkin and asked her what was going on. Ben's concern for Rachel immediately diverted his attention from his own problems.

"Ben, Traci thought you were having some kind of attack."

Ben collected himself, straightened up in the chair, and did his best to pretend nothing had happened. He showed her the enormous FedEx envelope.

"The hits just keep on coming, Rachel. Remember Sylvia Bresling?"

"Yes, she was our first attempt at awakening. Why?"

"Well, since Hiatus Centers has expanded nationally and is getting a lot of publicity, I guess her family has decided there is some money out there for them."

"You mean they're suing us?" she asked. "I thought our contracts were ironclad. You know, the waivers and disclaimers they sign. Aren't we protected?"

"Well, theoretically, yeah, but that doesn't stop anyone from the physical act of filing a lawsuit against another party. The strategy is to hope we don't want the bad press and the expense of defending the suit and we will opt for an out-of-court settlement."

"That sucks! So, basically, it's a money grab," Rachel remarked.

"As I understand it, Rachel, most lawsuits are."

○ ○ ○ ○ ○

In Fort Lauderdale, Anna Torres, Marcus Roberts, and Melody Rose all suffered severe effects of neurodegenerative disease upon awakening. Families were outraged. Lawsuits were threatened. In Orlando, the same had happened to Manny Rojas and Stuart Hampton. This news reached Ben Abraham's desk shortly after the Bresling lawsuit had arrived. Ben wanted to say, "Screw it all" and head off to the watering holes in nearby Fells Point. His sense of responsibility won out. He summoned Ari to his office. After filling Ari in on the developments of the day, he said, "Ari, this is baffling. Awakenings at other newer centers have gone off perfectly. We need to figure out Florida in a hurry. The board is pressuring me to begin preparations to go public. We need the money an IPO will raise but I can't do it if we are getting sued at every turn and our clients' contracts keep terminating due to unsuccessful awakenings."

"Ben, when I was in Ft. Lauderdale and Orlando to perform final quality checks on the Liferay devices last year, both seemed fine. When we made the first one in the Lab, it was so much easier to keep our arms around the issues. Now, we have the devices made by a Swiss contractor. The Swiss are known for precision and if they followed our mechanical drawings, everything should be perfect. The machines are designed to self-calibrate before every use so I can't imagine what the problem is. I'll head down to Florida first thing in the morning and report in as soon as I know something."

"Thanks, Ari. In the meantime, I am going to have Rachel put a hold at all locations on any scheduled awakenings for tomorrow. I'd rather not take any more chances."

On his drive home to Maplebrook, Ben chose to ignore the news on the radio. He couldn't wallow away in alcohol so he chose a different outlet: music. Ben liked all kinds of music but when he really needed to unwind, he liked smooth jazz. Satellite radio was the perfect vessel for tonight's dour mood. Thank goodness that modern technology could easily be installed in his old, blue bucket of traveling bolts.

Once back in the comfort of his humble abode, Ben put on a pair of old sweats, grabbed a Corona and some cold pizza from his fridge, tumbled into his favorite blue recliner, and reluctantly switched on the news. He figured he'd better absorb the days' events with a beer in his hand. He watched as the anchor reported on the stories everyone was accustomed to hearing on a daily basis, corruption in Washington, terrorist activity around the world, and controversial stories surrounding political correctness. He tensed up, however, at the next segment.

And now from Baltimore, the corporate offices at Hiatus Centers were abuzz today with all sorts of bad news. Hiatus Centers, as you may know, is the young company headed up by acclaimed scientist Dr. Benjamin Abraham. Abraham's company preserves newly deceased people and "awakens" them once a year for twenty-four hours in a controlled environment. Well, today, the daughter of the first person ever awakened by Dr. Abraham has filed suit in a state court in Maryland seeking unspecified damages for the botched results. It seems that when Dr. Abraham and his staff attempted to awaken Sylvia Bresling, she displayed disturbing symptoms of neurodegenerative disease, such as Parkinson's, rendering her unable to know who she was. Dr. Abraham's staff was forced to place Mrs. Bresling into a state of permanent death. Making matters worse for Dr. Abraham, Hiatus Centers' locations in Florida have experienced similar results with five clients as recently as this week, suggesting that the technology simply is not ready for public use. The families of those Florida clients are also considering lawsuits against Hiatus Centers. One of the failed awakenings in Florida is the daughter of US Senator James Rose. Senator Rose and his family are outraged and have asked the press to observe their need for privacy during this difficult time. Those close to Senator Rose, however, have said he has vowed to launch a congressional investigation on Hiatus Centers' practices and most likely, will introduce legislation to regulate these types of services. For more on this breaking news, let's go to our reporters on the ground in Baltimore and Florida.

He wasn't sure why but he continued to watch as family members of their permanently deceased clients expressed sorrow and outrage. Lawyers were interviewed to give opinions on the merits of the lawsuits and Reverend Cashman expressed concern for the implications of playing God. He referred to those who failed to awaken properly as "victims" of Hiatus Centers. Ben recoiled at this notion. *Victims,* he thought. *These people came to us and voluntarily entered a program full well knowing every risk.* The news onslaught continued with interviews from senators and congressman citing the case of their colleague's daughter and supporting the need to regulate this unprecedented awakening activity. "These people have rights that need to be protected," one said. The sensationalizing of the story went on and on, with interviews from psychiatrists attesting to the potentially long lasting damages inflicted on the families of Hiatus Centers' failed experiments with the extension of human life. Ben was about to switch the channel to anything else when the segment went to Switzerland to interview the CEO of Swiss Pharma Ingenuity, Dr. Anstrov Rinaldi.

"Dr. Rinaldi, you are the CEO of one of the world's largest pharmaceutical companies. Your company is known for tremendously successful product introductions in numerous fields including antiaging. Your BV3000 antiaging drug just became the bestselling pharmaceutical product in history. What do you make of all this?"

"As a scientist and a businessman, I applaud the beauty of the Hiatus Centers' value proposition. Much like SPI, they are entering into uncharted waters. I believe strongly that people in our space must do this. After all, if we don't, the world ceases to move forward. So, the science used by Hiatus Centers, I heartily applaud. The business acumen, on the other hand, leaves much to be desired. There are strong corollaries between business and science. Both require focus, planning, and extensive testing before launch. Sometimes, the zeal for business success leads even the most prudent of people to shortcut these important measures."

After watching Rinaldi, Ben felt the bile rise in his stomach. He wasn't sure if it was the news, the disturbing image of Rinaldi, or the congealed grease from the leftover pizza. He was sure about two things: he was done watching the news for the foreseeable future and he would double down to make everything right.

The next morning, Ben was in the office before the sun rose. The old blue Honda looked sorely out of place in a parking garage shared by the city's most successful lawyers, accountants, and businesspeople. Coffee in hand, he stared at his cell phone as he walked toward the elevator in jeans and a plaid sport shirt.

"Dr. Abraham, it's illegal in Maryland to walk and text," joked Rachel, who had just gotten out of her car.

"As you know, Dr. Larkin, I rarely text. This might be my only opportunity of the day to read the sports headlines."

They chatted on the way up to the office. Ben expressed his frustration with events of the past week, the news headlines, and the ongoing legal issues. Sometimes, he said, he'd like to just go back to working on scientific research in the Lab. Although the Lab was independently owned by an LLC of Ben's, the lawyers had set up a contract between Ben's LLC and Hiatus Centers to perform research and development. Working in the Lab brought him a feeling of success and solitude at the same time. He often thought of returning there.

"Cheer up, Ben. Your attitude will shape your day. Make it a good one."

It was that type of advice that made Ben appreciate Rachel. Not only was she a brilliant scientist, she was evolving into a savvy businesswoman and, to boot, she had a way of keeping him grounded when his ego got out of control.

When the elevator reached the top floor, they went their separate ways. Ben arrived at his office door, observed the unorganized mess, and smiled because he felt right at home.

Just before noon, his office phone rang. It was Ari.

"Ben, I took a red eye to Florida, went right to our center in Ft. Lauderdale, and worked through the night." This didn't surprise Ben.

Ari continued, "I literally took the Swiss made Liferay apart and compared every part and the assembly to our mechanical drawings and what I remembered from our original construction. You won't believe what I found."

"You've got my attention."

"At first glance, everything looks perfect. It was baffling. Then I studied every piece under a magnifying glass. Eventually, I found a Schlemm's rod that was bent almost imperceptibly so the human eye would not be able to detect it. However, when you view it side by side under magnification with one from the Lab, you can see the slight difference."

"Ari, you're such a mechanical tech head. What in hell is a Schlemm's rod?"

"It's a tiny metal pin that holds a mechanical assembly together and enables it to make precise movements in almost unmeasurable amounts. If the Schlemm gets altered, or in this case, slightly bent, the Liferay will deliver its rapid rotational pulses in uneven bursts. As we know, that will cause neurodegenerative alterations in the client."

Ben was deeply troubled by the discovery. On the one hand, he felt a modicum of relief that a solution was potentially within reach. On the other, he didn't quite understand how ominous the path forward might be.

"Are you saying that the Swiss manufacturer used defective parts in making the Liferay?"

"No, the vendor is the best in the world. They wouldn't do that. I am saying the Schlemm's rod was deliberately tampered with."

CHAPTER 26

Rachel slept in till 8:00 a.m. She hadn't set an alarm. The pounding rain against her bedroom window, coupled with the wind with a mind of its own, had something to say on that particular Sunday morning. Rachel clicked her bedroom TV on and was instantly mesmerized. The dreaded infomercial. She always found them so tasteless and now, here on her own TV set, was what she had perceived would be the denigration of her own hard work.

"We thought ahead. Our friends told us we were crazy but we registered our son and daughter as well as ourselves. When our baby girl passed away unexpectedly from a bronchial disorder, we were devastated. She was only eighteen years old! Can you imagine? We were grateful that Hiatus Centers was able to bring her back to us."

"When Aunt Edith was awakened for the first time, I swore it was nothing short of a miracle. I didn't believe it was possible, but there she was, looking spry as ever. I had missed her loving touch. I can tell you this. That first hug made me feel like she had never been gone."

"My sister was one of the first to sign up when Hiatus Centers came to town. My brother-in-law was skeptical but, Jen, she was a headstrong woman. I guess she wanted to come back and tell us all what to do."

One after another, the testimonials continued. Rachel had always disregarded infomercials as nothing more than paid filler to occupy obscure channels' slower viewing periods. But now, much to her chagrin, the public relations firm they engaged had their company front and center, somewhere between the lands of cheesy and tacky. The show progressed with scenes of simulated awakenings—edited, of course, to give prospective clients a sense of "normalcy" around what was deemed ridiculously impossible just a few years ago. Their early results in the marketplace had been disastrous. Rachel had to admit, the PR campaign, including the lame infomercial, was beginning to have a positive impact. Client registrations were booming in locations all over the country.

Rachel had a few hours before she had to make herself presentable. She had lunch and shopping planned with Tomi. For now, she was content to bum around her apartment with a bowl of fruit mixed with strawberry yogurt and granola. Not feeling especially energetic, she was still wearing her flannel PJs, her hair was undone, and her contacts still in the carrying case. She couldn't bring herself to watch any more of the infomercial so she channel flipped until she found a movie much older than she. *Yours, Mine and Ours,* a 1968 classic, starred Henry Fonda and Lucille Ball as two single parents who get married and raise eighteen children together. This epic tale was her mom's favorite. They had watched it together many times. It made her miss her mom but it was still too early to call home in California. She curled her legs behind her, settled in with her breakfast and basked in the glory of a few low-pressure hours to herself.

When the movie ended, Rachel was feeling melancholy. Watching a movie featuring eighteen kids in one family reminded her that her biological clock was ticking. She wanted kids of her own . . . one day. *Would that be with Ben?* she wondered. *Who the hell knows?* Melancholy turned to disdain as she thought, *I guess he is still waiting for the time to be right. Whatever the hell that means.* The line of thinking led her back to depression. So she cheated on her diet with a hot chocolate. For added measure, she filled the space between the beverage and the brim with a splash of mini marshmallows.

The original plan called for a day on the outside shopping avenue in downtown Maplebrook. The weather killed the idea so they met at The Maplebrook Mall, a distant second in terms of experience, dining selection, and shopping choice. Rachel, as a rule, hated indoor shopping malls. For the most part, every suburban shopping mall had the same crap. The avenue stores had personality. She didn't shop often but when she did, she preferred shops with something unique to offer. That experience would wait until another day. This "play date" was about a much needed girls' day out. Two friends who both worked way too hard, enjoying each other's company and having the chance to discuss life and any other topic they cared to trample on. Tomi swung by Rachel's place and picked her up. Rachel had always admired Tomi's fashion sense. It was evident in the way she dressed and accessorized and even in the car she drove. Her new Lexus ES was loaded. It was a bold, metallic, eye-popping red that announced her presence in a way befitting her sense of style. Rachel basked in the soft charcoal interior Tomi had chosen.

"Love this car! Ooh, new car smell! They should put this scent in a spray can," said Rachel.

"That will be the next project at the Lab," replied Tomi.

"It doesn't seem to fit Ben's 'scientific contribution to the world' mantra," remarked Rachel.

"Don't quote me but I doubt he even knows what new car smell is. The jalopy he drives was probably ancient when he bought it a million years ago," answered Tomi.

They made it to the mall in less than fifteen minutes and were both ready to shop. After two hours, Rachel had purchased nothing. Tomi was loaded down with what she deemed the latest hot buys. They wandered into Specifically Salads, one of the few mall restaurants that wasn't part of a chain. A quiet back booth was theirs for the taking.

"So, I was cuddled up in bed early this morning and happened to see the infomercial," said Rachel.

"And?" replied Tomi.

"And, even though I had seen it long before it got distributed to media outlets, this was the first time I had seen it randomly on my TV."

"And?" replied Tomi again.

"I don't know. Even though everything in it is genuine, it comes across as fake."

"I hate to tell you this but I like it. And from what I can tell, it's helping to turn things around in a big way."

In advance of submitting their IPO, a strategic decision had been made to turn around public perception. The infomercial was one piece of a multilayered phased-in strategy. In the coming weeks and months, every success was glamorized and released to the press. "Independent" blogs were popping up across cyberspace espousing the merits of the service. Mini versions of the infomercial invaded every radio station in their target markets. Coupons for free consultations and facility tours appeared in every electronic and snail mailbox. Flashy, digital billboards were impossible to miss along the most congested arteries in every major city. Family members who had good experiences with their loved ones' first awakenings appeared on talk shows, all with close guidance from a member of the PR firm. They had to control the message.

Each new location now featured a "grand opening" blitz strategy involving an elaborate open house and a demo area where the best imaginable awakening experience could be "felt" through simulation. Next up was the fastest written book in modern history. The PR firm actually worked with one family and a hired gun author to tell the story of their loved one. It hit hard on the emotions surrounding death, its impact on each family member, and the jubilation of awakening. The PR firm pulled out all the stops. Ben spared no expense in enlisting their help to turn things around. Rachel knew he was motivated by insinuations that a brilliant scientist could not succeed in business. Ben finally said no when the PR firm wanted to book a "live" awakening session on a national talk show. He wanted to preserve the dignity of their offering.

"I can't deny the results. Business is booming," said Rachel.

"I wish my life was booming," replied Tomi. "I think it's been a year since I've been laid."

Rachel, not usually shy or timid, felt herself blush. Not because of Tomi's frank admission but because she knew what question might soon follow. One she didn't care to answer.

"When I was a girl, we used to spend summers in Italy. Man, those guys were some kind of hot. I miss those days. So, how's your love life? I know where you spend most of your time so I assume your situation isn't any better than mine," said Tomi.

Thank God! thought Rachel. She completely let me off the hook.

"You nailed it. Maplebrook isn't exactly the hot dating scene for single scientists in their thirties. Bars suck, I won't do internet dating, and Mom is three thousand miles away so she can't try to fix me up with anyone," Rachel said.

"When I was younger and living in the Bay area, it seemed like great guys were popping out of the woodwork. I thought living near a city like Baltimore would be like that," remarked Tomi.

"I think it could be. The problem is these two California girls never see much of Baltimore outside of the office."

"I never thought I'd say I'm too tired to go out and play in the city after work but that sizes it up. I think the last time I enjoyed the city was our night in Little Italy with the team. How long ago was that?" Tomi said. "And even then, Harrison, that doofus, made me leave early. I don't know why I rode down to the city with him. I never asked—did you and Ben hang out for long that night?"

Right back into awkward, thought Rachel. Knowing Ben would never tell, she figured she was safe in telling a white lie.

"Oh my God, it was so long ago, I barely remember. We hung out for a while longer and had a drink and then made our way home. No big deal."

Tomi was clearly fishing. Did Tomi suspect that she and Ben had a one nighter or something more? Rachel was relieved when Tomi transitioned the conversation to a review of the days' purchases. Still in inquisitive mode, Tomi ventured onto new ground.

"You said Ben wants to prove himself as a businessman. He's well on the way. He just doesn't look happy."

"It's funny, I see the same thing. He's focused and determined, like with all his scientific breakthroughs but that twinkle in his eye, that's just not there," said Rachel.

"Twinkle in his eye?" asked Tomi.

"You never noticed that? Think about it. Every time we would have an early morning review session in the Dugout, Ben would come in with some overnight epiphany. When he would lay it out for the team, he got a little shit-eating grin on his face and a twinkle in his eye. I can't believe you never noticed that."

"No, I remember. You're right. That's funny. He does seem to be missing the part where he enjoys the success. How long do you think he'll stay in it?"

With that, salads arrived. For Tomi, The Caveman's Delight, a dark leafy mix with raspberry vinaigrette. For Rachel, it was the Green Fruity Nutjob with a light honey-based dressing. They giggled again at the silly names of the salads. Both asked for a second mineral water.

"Who knows? Ben isn't the best at sharing his innermost thoughts," said Rachel.

"What about you?" asked Tomi. "How long do you see yourself doing what you are doing? You're not exactly playing physicist these days. You are more like the chief operating officer."

Rachel stopped to contemplate her response. She had been working so hard at so many different things, she had not taken the time to consider such a question. Recently, work had been more about doing whatever needed doing. She was hiring people, choosing computer systems, playing interior decorator, buying furniture, and solving logistics issues. Anything to take a tactical, daily burden off Ben. As she pondered the question, she realized she missed the Lab but she was enjoying the unending challenges in the business world.

"I like it. Every day is some new adventure. Things move really fast. I suppose one day if it becomes too routine, I'll have to consider the next phase of my career. How about you?"

"Since we've hired more people, I don't have to work on opening new locations all over the country. I'm mostly back at the Lab with Harrison and Ari trying to hone in on breaking the barrier on the twenty-four-hour threshold," said Tomi. "Still having fun, still raking in the big bucks."

Rachel didn't want to go deeper into a conversation on research being done at the Lab. She, of all people, was fully aware of the progress relating to the twenty-four-hour threshold.

They were all paid well. Rachel spent enough to make herself comfortable. For a young single professional, she had managed to build a pretty good investment portfolio. *I guess I have a mind for business*, she thought. The conversation waned for a few minutes while they ate.

"Know anything about how to interpret weird dreams, Tomi?"

"No," she laughed, "but I took a psych class in undergrad."

"Last night, I dreamed I was alone in a serene, wooded area and came upon a babbling brook, you know, like one with clear spring water. Right there, in the water, a turtle was sitting on top of one of the rocks and he was looking up at me and sort of smiling. And, oh, the turtle was much bigger than a normal land turtle. The shell was really pretty, filled with colored blocks of soft pink, yellow, and white. The whole thing went by in a flash. What do you suppose that means?"

"That you've been smoking too many funny cigarettes?" laughed Tomi.

"It made me feel like I had been. I did some research and learned that turtle dreams can have a lot of different meanings depending upon what's going on in your life," explained Rachel.

"What is going on your life that relates to smiling pink and yellow turtles?"

"I can't nail it down but if I had to guess, I'd say it was a message to slow down and be patient. I think it means that good things are in store for me but I can't try to rush them along."

Tomi listened and smiled back at her. There was no deep analysis forthcoming from her friend. Now that it was out, she felt a little silly even bringing it up. Rachel returned the smile and decided to drop the subject. Just then, her cell phone began to vibrate. Rachel looked down at the display. It was a rare text message from Ben. All it said was, "Need to talk."

○ ○ ○ ○ ○

"Ben, are you okay?" asked Rachel.

"Hanging in there. I hope I'm not pulling you away from your Sunday. I am on the road and just need a friendly voice," replied a weary-sounding Ben Abraham.

Rachel, always one to place others' needs before her own, responded, "I just got home from lunch with Tomi. I'm back at my place. What's going on?"

"Are you alone?" he asked.

"Mmm, hmm," she answered.

"I'm just feeling bummed out." This was an unusual admission. "The travel, the problems, the business, sometimes it just gets overwhelming. I'm having trouble sleeping and I feel like I'm always on the edge of losing my cool. And then there's the recurrence of the panic attacks or seizures or whatever they are. I'm putting up my best strongman front but sometimes it's hard to fake it."

"Oh, I'm sorry you are going through all that." She knew he was on the road but couldn't recall his itinerary. "Where are you now?"

"Ottawa. I have a meeting tomorrow morning with the Minister of Health to try and clear regulatory hurdles to begin opening locations in Toronto and Montreal."

"You know you can always unload on me. I mean that. Anytime."

"I appreciate that. I normally dump this kind of stuff on Albert but he's away at a conference in Jakarta and it's the middle of the night there."

"When was the last time you took some time off?" She already knew the answer before she was finished asking it.

"Wow, I've never taken a vacation. Taking time off is foreign to me. Thank goodness my parents still live on the East Coast or I would unwillingly neglect them. My life is my work."

Inwardly, Rachel groaned. Didn't she know it? "I want you to make me three promises," she said somewhat demandingly.

"Okay," he replied.

"Number one, you are going to let me teach you some deep breathing techniques to help you relax." She knew, medically speaking, that wasn't the answer but it couldn't hurt.

"Second, you will put together a plan to slow it down a bit. Even Rome wasn't built in a day." She thought of her turtle dream and knew that slow and steady would be a wiser course for Ben. "Third, when you get back, figure out when the Dodgers are visiting in DC, Philly, Pittsburgh, or New York. I'm treating you to a baseball game."

She could feel his smile coming through the phone line. She knew she had broken through the malaise which had enveloped him.

"Rachel, I don't know what I'd do without you."

She playfully replied, "You don't really want to find out, do you?"

CHAPTER 27

"Frieda, get Bill Smithson from New York on the phone," barked Rinaldi.

He had plucked Frieda from the executive receptionist pool and made her his administrative assistant. She was hard working, loyal, and extremely respectful. He valued these qualities in others despite the fact he chose not to live them. Bill Smithson was an investment banker with whom SPI had a long-term relationship. Predating Rinaldi's involvement, Smithson had played an integral role some years ago in getting SPI listed on the New York Stock Exchange. He had managed their affairs on Wall Street ever since.

Rinaldi informed Smithson he would be arriving in New York in two weeks' time to visit their US headquarters in New Jersey. Smithson mentioned a private party full of Wall Street brethren, investment bankers, venture capitalists, high financiers, powerful lawyers, savvy accountants, and the like.

"Have you considered inviting the fellows from Hiatus Centers to this private party as your guests?" quizzed Rinaldi.

"Why, no. I don't know them. Are they looking to go public anytime soon? Can you make an introduction?" asked Smithson.

"I don't know them per se but I do follow the news and they are expanding rapidly. The technology for such a venture cannot be cheap. They will soon require the capital offered by an IPO," said Rinaldi.

"I understand they are in a world of hurt right now. Lawsuits, regulations, bad press. I'm not sure if I could get a strong result for them even if they hired me," replied Smithson.

Rinaldi, ever the schemer, grinned and said, "That is exactly why you should pounce now. Cultivate the relationship when they realize their vulnerability. Once they bounce back, your competitors will be hovering like a pack of hungry vultures. Nurse the relationship along, coach them on how an IPO works and remain by their side to make it all come together. If their company falls apart, you have lost little. If it succeeds, you make a fortune."

Smithson paused in contemplation. "Anstrov, I guess that's why you are so good at what you do. It's timing, right?"

"Yes, yes, of course my friend, timing is what is," said Rinaldi with a slight air of smugness.

"Do you know who the best contact is at Hiatus Centers?" asked Smithson.

"If it were me, I would reach out to the board chair, Dr. Albert Harmon. He will prove more accessible than the CEO, Dr. Abraham. Abraham is all about science and has less of a head for business. You can find Dr. Harmon in Maplebrook, Maryland. He is the provost of The Harmon School for Gifted Scientific Youth. I suspect that if you get Harmon on board, Abraham will come along."

○ ○ ○ ○ ○

Rinaldi polished off a Porterhouse at the acclaimed Bull and Bear Steakhouse inside the Waldorf Astoria. Thirty ounces of finely aged beef would have proved too much for most men of his size but Rinaldi's appetite knew no bounds. Preceded by an order of Oysters Waldorf and his favorite beer, Kronenbourg, the meal was right up Rinaldi's alley. The dark wood styling of the restaurant was old New York but to Rinaldi, its

Italian leathers and fabrics made it feel European. He asked the waiter for another Kronenbourg and dabbed the linen napkin over the corner of his mouth. Just blocks from Wall Street in Midtown, the grand old hotel was a short walk from Bill Smithson's office. They had agreed to meet for dinner before the private Wall Street party, also at the Waldorf Astoria.

"I took your advice," remarked Smithson. "I reached out to Dr. Harmon, you know, the board chair at Hiatus Centers. He was reluctant at first but after some razzle-dazzle, a little name dropping, and their overwhelming need for a capital infusion, he agreed to come to New York for a visit to our offices and tonight's party."

Rinaldi, of course, through independent private investigators, already knew this. He played along.

"Ah, so this is good, no? I presume you will owe me a sales commission," joked Rinaldi. "You must introduce me to Dr. Harmon."

"I shall and also to Dr. Abraham, the CEO. He also made the trip."

"Splendid," said Rinaldi, although he already knew. "Meeting the world famous Dr. Abraham will make my trip to America complete."

Not wanting to be early, they lingered at the table, enjoying after-dinner coffee and a modicum of pseudo business conversation. Smithson had to engage in some degree of anal banter to justify the meal expense, thought Rinaldi. They boarded the small elevator and ascended to the fourth floor. Smithson walked into the Louis XVI Suite and held the door for his colleague. Rinaldi strolled though and was immediately taken by the noise level in the room. The maximum capacity of the Louis XVI Suite was listed at 241 but to Rinaldi, it seemed like the room held double that amount. The wait staff was challenged serving hors d'oeuvres. Platters were held high enabling the difficult navigation through the throng of Wall Street moguls looking to impress. Rinaldi and Smithson were quickly separated.

Not known for being a social butterfly, Rinaldi retreated to the east side bar adjacent to an eighteenth century replica fireplace framed by Griotte marble and ordered another Kronenbourg. He found a burgundy-colored velvet bench where he sat to rest his bum leg. He wanted to leave but not before he accomplished the evening's purpose. *Discipline*, he thought. *Discipline yields results. Impatience breeds chaos.*

He was determined to get up and make a few rounds through the crowd where he knew no one. His objective was to meet with only two of them. As he was rising, he spotted Ben Abraham, who towered above the crowd. To his left was the much shorter Albert Harmon. To his right was Bill Smithson. Rinaldi was pleased. Now, he could spend some time with Harmon and Abraham and make his way out of the dreadful, earsplitting room full of egomaniacs.

"Anstrov! I've been trying to track you down since we walked in. Meet Drs. Harmon and Abraham from Hiatus Centers," said Smithson. "Dr. Anstrov Rinaldi is the CEO of Swiss Pharma Ingenuity. He is visiting from his headquarters in Basel."

Rinaldi expertly moved his cane to his left hand and extended his right, first to Harmon and then to Abraham.

"Gentlemen, it is my pleasure to make your acquaintance. I have been reading about your progress," said Rinaldi.

"I am afraid progress is not the word I would choose to describe recent events," replied Ben.

"Nonsense," said Albert. "Every business on a rapid growth track experiences start-up issues. I am sure Dr. Rinaldi has had similar experiences."

"Please, call me Anstrov. And yes, I have had many setbacks on the road to success. Our current top seller, BV3000, was almost scrapped several times before we got it right. You must continue to persevere, Dr. Abraham."

"Thanks, and it's Ben. By the way, I saw your interview a few weeks back. Your comments on Hiatus Centers left me curious."

"I hope that I did not offend you in any way. As I tried to state, I have nothing but respect for your sense of exploration. We are similar in this regard. The world needs more of us, don't you think?"

"I suppose. What did you mean when you said, 'The zeal for business success leads even the most prudent of people to shortcut important measures.'? What exactly were you implying?" asked Ben.

Rinaldi chuckled to himself and took note of Albert discovering Ben's temper beginning to flare.

"I am sure Anstrov meant nothing by it," said Albert, trying to quell the mounting tension. "Ben, these TV news interviews all get blown out of proportion to some extent."

"Ben, your colleague is most perceptive. I have been on these news programs many times. While no one would speak this out loud, there is a certain degree of theater involved. This helps their viewership and establishes some nobody like me as a so-called expert," offered Rinaldi.

Rinaldi knew Ben wasn't buying any of it. He exchanged pleasantries with Ben and the noted American scientist retired for the evening. *He seemed more blasé with this event than I,* thought Rinaldi.

Albert hung back and offered to get another drink for Rinaldi. Rinaldi gladly accepted. The encounter was going according to plan. At Rinaldi's suggestion, they took their drinks and walked down the hallway, across the tan and teal floral rug to a quiet lounge where they could hold a civil conversation.

Rinaldi knew that the best way to get people to open up was to ask them about themselves. Harmon was only too glad to oblige. He bored Rinaldi to tears with the story of his life. Inside a far less painful thirty minutes, Rinaldi had read all of the same stories from the commissioned dossier. For over an hour, Harmon regaled Rinaldi with tales of scientific breakthroughs in his early career, the founding of the school, and the untold number of brilliant students he had mentored, with none more special or accomplished than Ben Abraham. Rinaldi listened with a sympathetic air but inside, he wanted to retch. Harmon even went so far as to boast of his ability to subjectively judge talent based on nothing more than a whim. Clearly, after so many years and hundreds—if not thousands—of applicants, Harmon could not recall them all.

When Harmon finally ran out of steam, he appeared to Rinaldi as if he were spent from his narcissistic monologue. For whatever reason, this boob apparently felt comfortable with him. *It is almost as if he were under a spell I cast.*

Emboldened by too much alcohol, Albert blurted out, "Anstrov, do you mind if I ask you a personal question?"

"Albert, we are becoming friends. Friends can ask one another anything."

"I was curious about how you lost sight in your right eye and what happened to your leg."

Although Rinaldi had consumed far more alcohol than Harmon, he was not fazed. *Americans can't hold their liquor.* Inwardly, Rinaldi scoffed at the forward question and the absence of the old man's recall. Outwardly, he smiled warmly.

"My eyesight was lost to a birth defect and the leg was injured in a motorcycle accident in my native Florence when I was a young and foolish teen."

Upon meeting Anstrov Rinaldi for the first time, most people were predisposed to dislike him because of his appearance. Rinaldi was pleased that Albert Harmon held no such notion. He had sold Harmon a bill of goods in his most engaging, charismatic, and intelligent persona. *Of course,* Rinaldi thought, *we are not meeting for the first time.*

CHAPTER 28

No one ever questioned why Ben still drove the old blue Honda. He was too busy to do anything other than work. Besides, those close to him joked that even if he did buy a nicer car, he'd be worried he wouldn't find the exact shade of blue matching the Dodger uniforms. The Honda met this most important criterion. The sedan sputtered to a stop in a visitor's parking space on the grounds of The Harmon School. Over the years, Ben had lectured to students many times. His accomplishments were celebrated on many of the school's walls. In fact, he was a legend, commonly acknowledged as the most acclaimed graduate in the history of the school. The students held him in reverence but even that didn't stop them from making fun of his car.

"Hey, Dr. Abraham! Don't you think you should invent a new car?" asked one youngster.

Ben played along. "Well, in my free time, I'm actually working on the Star Trek thing to defy the laws of physics and beam myself from one place to the next. Until I perfect that, I'm pretending that the Accord is really a time machine, like in *Back to the Future*."

"Back to the Future?"

"Before your time," he replied, smiling.

He loved visiting the school. He adored the students and the innocence of youth. It took him back to an earlier time when life was simple; a time when the science was all he had to take seriously; a time when he was free to be himself, creative, and a little flip. Sometimes he was the class clown, other times he liked to play harmless pranks. Although he knew he had long ago abandoned the immaturity, he wanted badly to reclaim that feeling of being free.

Ben casually meandered through the school's hallways, taking his time and reveling in good memory. His reminiscing came to a halt when he arrived at the provost's office door. Without knocking, he entered and warmly greeted his mentor. The forthcoming conversation would be uncomfortable—awkward, perhaps—but he was determined to press forward. His sanity was at stake.

When the two men were seated and pleasantries had been exchanged, Albert opened the conversation.

"Ben, can you believe we are going public?" he asked excitedly.

"It's been a helluva long road, Albert. Since we discovered the sabotage of the Liferay machines, fixed each of the offending units, found a new Swiss supplier, and embarked on the PR campaign, things have gone relatively smooth."

"Any resolution on the sabotage issue?"

"International investigators were never able to find evidence of wrongdoing. I can tell you this, Ari is adamant that the machines were intentionally altered. Switching vendors was a painful but prudent move we had to make. We've been doing our own quality checks on every machine before opening. I just don't want to lose any more clients unnecessarily."

"So, what other updates do you have for your friendly old board chair?" asked Albert warmly.

"Got a ton of things to go over with you. Let's see. We have had no adverse incidents since the Schlemm's rod debacle. The PR campaign has been amazingly successful. All US locations are performing at a high level. We are opening up six more locations in the upper Midwest. I got clearance from Canada's Ministry of Health to open Toronto and Montreal. And Smithson said he's ready to pull the trigger on the IPO when we are."

"You've been busy, I see. Nice work, Ben. Despite what anyone in the media says, you are one great businessman. You certainly have my respect and admiration. What's happening with the lawsuits and regulatory threats?"

Ben rubbed his head slowly in a circular motion, a nervous habit he found himself engaging in whenever he encountered stress. He exhaled noticeably in an attempt to let the steam escape.

"The lawyer for Sylvia Bresling, a guy named Poston, smells blood. He wants a truckload of cash to make the lawsuit go away."

"Are we going to pay?"

"As much as it sickens me to do so, it's the path of least resistance. Our lawyers are trying to diffuse the situation but Poston is now threatening to get ahold of the other families who have lost someone in our care and turn the whole matter into a class action suit."

"This guy sounds like a real slimeball."

"Our lawyer refers to him as an ambulance chaser. We are discussing settlement amounts for Bresling and the others. We should be able to make most of these issues go away except for one . . ."

"Let me guess. The good senator's daughter?"

"Yeah. That one is going to be an ongoing problem. Senator Rose is pretty fired up and he's got the entire Congress on his side. It sucks to be on our side of the matter but, from a human standpoint, I actually feel for the guy."

"I understand. Your sympathies, however, need to remain completely aligned with what's in the best interests of the company."

Ben nodded to acquiesce.

"No worries. I have done everything to date that I or our board members can think of. We have expensive regulatory lawyers, a lobbyist, and our PR firm working on the matter. I just don't have a resolution in hand yet."

"What are they recommending?"

"The lawyers and the lobbyist think that ultimately it will get down to me sitting with Senator Rose, face to face, and agreeing to submit to some sort of manageable regulation enabling him to feel a little better about his daughter's loss and save face with the public. My objective would be to escape the negotiation without ominous restrictions prohibiting us from operating and growing the business. The PR firm is just focusing on pumping out positive messaging."

"And what about the religious zealot plaguing our every effort?"

"Yes, Reverend Cashman. We still seem to be his primary focus. The PR firm says he will likely continue to dog us until something else arises which he deems more important."

"Is there any way to get a restraining order on the guy? You know, claim interference with a business relationship, libel, anything like that?"

"Been down all those roads. He is apparently within his rights to do what he is doing. Our legal and PR teams are trying to negate the rallies outside our locations by making sure they are the appropriate distance from our property and continuing to project the good in our offering. So far, mixed results, at best."

"Sounds like there is still a lot to do though in the near term."

Ben paused, drew in a deep breath, and collected his courage. "That's what I came here to tell you. What's left on the plate and beyond will be the responsibility of the next CEO."

Albert's expression turned to stone. The blood drained from his face. "You're resigning?" he said in disbelief. "What about the IPO?"

"I know the timing isn't ideal, Albert, but when will it be? I spoke to Smithson in hypothetical terms, of course, and he said we would need to discuss the leadership change in our SEC filing so investors have full disclosure."

"What does that do to the IPO's chances for success?"

"Truthfully, it will have a definitive impact. But the IPO, even with this news in tow, will still raise damn near a billion dollars. That's more than enough to fuel the company's near future, attract a new CEO who will demand a lucrative compensation package, and make each of the founders pretty damn wealthy," replied Ben.

"You're right Ben. Forgive me. I should be placing you first. That's what's most important to me. You deserve to be happy. What do you think you'll do next?" he asked.

"For starters, I need to resolve the issue with the panic attacks or seizures or whatever it is I've been experiencing. I haven't taken any time off in my entire career. I might just veg for a while. I also see myself getting back to the Lab and maybe assuming the role of head of R&D. That's what I really enjoy and if I am working in some official capacity and continue to serve on the board, Wall Street should be assuaged."

"Thought about finding the right 'someone' to settle down with?" asked Albert in his paternal way.

"You mean like you did?" Ben mused.

"You got me," said the lifelong bachelor as he raised his hands in the air in mock surrender.

"Why repeat the mistakes of the prior generation? Being lonely isn't all it's cracked up to be. Ever thought of asking Rachel out?"

Hel felt his skin pull tightly. His forearms responded with an intense, nervous itch. Unable to hold a conversation about his dormant love life and wanting to scratch the skin from his arms, he replied, "Sure, Albert. She's like my best friend. I'm afraid taking it beyond that will screw up the friendship."

"Ben, how long have your parents been married?"

"Coming up on their fortieth wedding anniversary."

"I'll bet if you held individual conversations with both Jon and Marcy, they would each tell you that before the relationship was anything else, there was a special friendship."

Ben mulled the advice but, in the depths of his mind, he could only concentrate on extracting himself from the stress of running the company. "I hear you. I'll give it some thought." He paused and said, almost as an afterthought, "Rachel and I are going to a baseball game together. She even offered to treat."

"Sounds like a great opportunity Ben. I just hope you don't strike out looking."

The two old friends got back down to business. Ben pledged to stay on as CEO until a successor could be found. He also told Albert he believed Rachel would stay on board for the foreseeable future to serve as COO. The same went for the scientific team. They enjoyed their work and were out of the mainstream at the Lab. After two hours, Ben was due downtown for a meeting. He said goodbye to Albert and headed back down the hallowed hallways. He stopped to admire an image of his younger self from senior year. The photograph's frame bore the inscription, Benjamin Abraham, Scientist of the Year.

As he approached the door, he threw his shoulders back, stood upright, and thought, *I'm almost out.*

CHAPTER 29

Ben had declined Bill Smithson's invitation to come to New York on the day of the IPO. Ben wasn't much for fanfare, crowds, and celebration. When his office phone rang, he found Smithson on the other end. Despite the news of Ben Abraham's impending departure, the IPO raised $1.4 billion. Ben was relieved. Smithson was ecstatic. Smithson's commission, at 5 percent of the amount raised, was worth nearly $70 million. *Not a bad day for him*, thought Ben.

Ben still retained a lion's share of the outstanding stock and his portion of the proceeds from the IPO had just made him fabulously wealthy. He almost didn't care. It was great to have the security of knowing he was now financially set for life but money was never his big motivator. He was in it to make a positive difference in the world, fulfill his dream, and maybe one day figure out a path to cryogenic restoration.

In the weeks since he had resigned as CEO, Albert had begun work with an international search firm to find viable candidates to succeed Ben. Internal candidates were considered but no one was deemed strong enough to meet the stringent requirements bridging both science and business. Candidates were now flying into Baltimore from all over the world to interview with the search committee of the board of directors. Ben was participating in all of the interviews.

Albert felt it was important to have Ben sit in. After all, no one else had ever been the CEO of Hiatus Centers. Who knew the job better? Ben reluctantly agreed to participate in the interviews but became quickly frustrated with the tedium and repetition of the process. His disdain for meetings was well known. He opted to spend his remaining days as CEO on more pressing operational matters such as tending to the development of the Canadian market and setting the stage for European expansion. After just three of twelve scheduled first-round interviews, Ben had enough.

"Albert, I trust you. You pick the next CEO."

Over the course of the next three months, Albert and the committee interviewed a wide variety of diverse candidates. Since there was nothing else like Hiatus Centers, it became evident that the search for the successful candidate would prove more difficult than originally imagined. The search firm had sent them current and former CEOs from companies in industries dealing in cemetery management, funeral homes, cybersecurity, retail, and healthcare. The process went on and on. Albert and the committee became disillusioned and fired the search firm.

It seemed that Ben might be serving longer than he had planned. He stayed on top of all his responsibilities, maintaining faith in Albert to resolve the problem.

After another month passed, Ben was still hard at it. He wondered if he had really resigned or whether that had just been a fantasy. The feeling passed when an email from Albert lit up his computer.

Ben,

We've made a hire! The new CEO will start in sixty days. He just signed his employment contract and needs time to wind down current responsibilities and relocate to Maryland. He has experience as the CEO of a prominent multinational company, a background in science, and is

most anxious to begin. Please join us for a celebratory dinner tonight at 7:00 at Fleming's in Harbor East.
Best,
Albert

Funny," thought Ben, *he didn't include a name or a bio. I guess he wants me to be surprised.*

Ben arrived at Fleming's downtown a little early. While it was technically walkable from his E. Pratt Street office, he drove so he would have his car nearby as soon as the dinner concluded. The valet snickered when Ben handed over the keys.

"Take good care of her," he said. He enjoyed the abuse he took over the old car.

The hostess said he was the first to arrive. He was invited to wait in the bar. He grabbed the last remaining barstool and ordered a Corona. He had just squeezed the last bit of juice from the accompanying lime when Albert walked in with his successor.

"Ben, you remember Anstrov Rinaldi?"

PART II

CHAPTER 30

Ben had cleared out his E. Pratt Street office in the city weeks ago, immediately after Rinaldi was hired to take his place as CEO. He would take refuge in his original office, the much more compact and unorganized space at the Lab. He hadn't told a soul but he was looking forward to his planned escape to southern Italy. He had heard Capri, an island in the Bay of Naples, was beautiful and serene. He had always wanted to go but never took time for himself. In his mind, he was already there. In just a few days, he was off to Rome, then a train ride to Naples and a boat across the bay. First things first. He had a transition meeting to tend to with Rinaldi.

It was Friday. Rinaldi officially took the reins of CEO on Monday. When he arrived at his old office, Ben noticed that movers had already loaded dozens of boxes into the office. The most startling change was the lengthy Plexiglas container which already held a ten-foot-long Komodo dragon. Ben was astonished at how the office had transformed so quickly. *Looked better decked out in Dodger blue,* he thought. Rinaldi was hobbling around on his bum leg, trying to get the office in order for his first day on Monday. Ben suspected it would take him most of the weekend to accomplish that feat.

"Good morning," said Ben in an effort to show collegiality he didn't feel.

"Ah, good to see you!" replied Rinaldi who extended his right hand after transferring the cane to his left.

As with most people meeting Rinaldi in his office for the first time, Ben's eyes and attention went directly to the cage on the front wall.

"Meet Drago, my pet Komodo dragon. He accompanies me to every job."

Ben moved closer to examine the Komodo's prehistoric features. Unfazed, he continued staring at Drago while pursuing the conversation.

"He is an interesting choice for a pet. You are keeping him here?"

"Oh yes, he will enjoy the view of employees passing by in the hallway."

"What does he eat?"

"People I don't like."

Ben raised an eyebrow at Rinaldi's illicit sense of humor.

"In the wild, he would prey on birds, deer, and the like. I feed him specially ordered dried meats meant for exotic contained pets of this nature."

"Have you always had a penchant for keeping exotic pets, as you call them?"

"I find comfort and perhaps kinship with Drago. He is not like any other so-called pet. The origin of his species is believed to date back some forty million years. If nothing else, he proves to be a wonderful conversation starter."

"I imagine importing a Komodo dragon into the United States was a challenge."

"Oh, the US Customs regulations are strict, to be sure. I am adept at navigating my way through such difficulties."

Ben let the last comment go. He figured that, on that point, he was best left in the dark.

"So, there are a number of things I need to review with you. We will likely need the better part of the day to go over it all. Rachel Larkin, who functions as my COO, will be here Monday to go over the details of everything and also to take you to our commercial center here in the city and our research facility in Harford County. She will also introduce you to the members of your team. I assume you've already met your admin, Traci?"

"Yes, we became acquainted earlier."

"Great. I'd like to start by just giving you a high-level overview of the company, its genesis, our current state of operations, and our planned expansion for the near term."

"Splendid. Like you, I am a scientist before anything else. I would also like your insight on the R&D and what you think you might accomplish beyond the near term."

Ben knew he had to be forthright with Rinaldi but decided to be somewhat conservative with the truth. Albert had once told him to be 100 percent truthful. Just keep 10 percent for yourself, he said. Ben employed that advice when he met someone he wasn't yet sure of. This was definitely one of those occasions. He certainly wasn't prepared to discuss his evening research sojourns with Ari. He would coach the team to also hold their most advanced research in reserve. *For all we know*, Ben reasoned, *this guy might up and quit in thirty days.*

"Sure thing. For the time being, we are trying to crack what we refer to as the twenty-four-hour threshold enabling an awakened client to remain in that status for a period longer than one day."

"What happens if an awakened client is not put back to rest within twenty-four hours?

"It hasn't yet happened where we've failed to hibernate a client before twenty-four hours have passed. We believe, however, that if hibernation does not occur within twenty-four hours, it will get ugly. The client will collapse, fall into a state of irrecoverable death, and, in all likelihood, begin deteriorating abnormally fast."

"It sounds positively ghastly. Are you making progress with solving the riddle?"

"Not really, we are afraid that it might take years. Based on what we know right now, it might never be solved."

Ben noted that Rinaldi's expression yielded surprise. He wasn't sure if this was because Rinaldi doubted the veracity of his statement or if he thought he just knew better. Ben didn't appreciate what he perceived as a smug response. *Our team broke the barrier. What does this guy know?*

"That is unfortunate," Rinaldi offered. "So I am left to assume that breaking this twenty-four-hour threshold will consume your team for the near and long terms?"

"For the foreseeable future, yes."

To Ben, Rinaldi looked almost annoyed. "Rachel and the team can give you more insight. Ari Weiskopf has been leading the effort since I have been CEO. He is more up to speed on the details at this point than I am."

"I shall look forward to meeting them next week and learning all I can."

"Let's go over the litany of pressing business matters you will need to address. The issues break down into three categories: legal, regulatory, and social."

Ben spent the next several hours briefing Rinaldi on the multitude of legal issues, primary of which was the suit from the family of Sylvia Bresling and the other former clients in Florida, the unfortunate loss of Senator Rose's daughter, Melody, and the legal and regulatory entanglements that ensued as a result. Last, but certainly not least, was the matter of the crusading Reverend Alonzo Cashman, who was starting rallies and dogging them at every turn. Ben reviewed the countermeasures to every problem and then proceeded to address expansion challenges outside North America. When he finished, he wondered if Rinaldi had been paying attention. He almost seemed bored with the business issues.

"Do you think that perhaps you may have gone too fast?" asked Rinaldi.

"You mean with the explanation? I can go back over the detail of any of these topics for you."

"No, I absorbed it all. I meant with the business. Opening so many commercial centers so fast across a vast geography might seem a bit . . . reckless. Wouldn't you say?"

Ben began to do a slow burn. It took a lot to get him angry but this asshole had managed to do it quite easily. *Courage, strength, patience, wisdom.*

Before Ben could respond. Rinaldi kept on throwing barbs.

"I mean no offense. I was merely suggesting that your early business success might have affected you like an addiction. You simply couldn't get enough. It is good that you realized your limitations and stepped down from the top spot before you ruined the company you founded."

Ben was now fuming inside. He hoped it didn't show but he knew he stunk at concealing his emotions. He had encountered "Rinaldi types" before. He understood that Rinaldi, for his own warped sense of purpose, was merely trying to push his buttons. *Courage, strength, patience, wisdom,* he repeated to himself.

"What is too fast and what is too slow?" Ben replied. "Aristotle said it takes courage to be successful. In business, unlike in science, a leader cannot afford to get bogged down in analysis paralysis."

"You speak of business and science as if they are completely different enterprises requiring departing viewpoints. To the contrary, if you approach business as if it were a science, that's where real success occurs."

This guy's crazy. What was Albert thinking?

"I think we've covered all of the ground I wanted to review. You have my mobile number; give me a call with any questions."

"Thank you for your time and knowledge. I shall look forward to having someone of your esteem work for me," replied Rinaldi.

Hearing the words out loud made Ben dizzy. It was the first time it had dawned on him that he would, in fact, be reporting to Rinaldi. The thought made him sick to his stomach. Ben hiked out of his former office vowing to do his job the way he wanted. Nothing would change. After all, he was the founder and remained on the board. The operating hierarchy was just a technicality.

CHAPTER 31

The decision was agonizing. For the life of her, Rachel could not figure out why she tossed and turned half the night. Today was her new boss' first day as CEO. They had yet to meet. Understandably, she was nervous. *What was the big deal?* she thought. She had been beating herself up over what to wear to work. *The green dress or the navy pant suit? Not that it matters. I doubt anyone will really give a shit what I'm wearing.* It had been a mighty long time since she had reported to anyone other than Ben. And reporting to Ben was like not even having a boss. He treated her like an equal.

Rachel knew that Rinaldi was from Europe. She couldn't find colleagues who knew what it was like to work for him. After Googling him and reading everything she could find, there wasn't much to learn save for his infrequent media appearances and addresses to shareholders. It seemed that not a whole lot had been written about the reclusive Dr. Rinaldi.

She chose the navy pant suit and white blouse with black pumps—the ones with low heels. She knew Rinaldi was not very tall. As always, she was conservative with her makeup and fixed her hair in business presentation mode. She thought briefly about perfume but dismissed the idea of even the lightest scent. She had heard that European CEOs were still not used to the idea of women in corporate leadership roles and didn't want to give the new guy the wrong first impression. Taking one final look in the mirror, she was satisfied. She told herself it would be a great day and pledged to keep an open mind about her new boss. No preconceived notions! She checked her watch. She had an hour to get downtown in rush hour. Without traffic, that was easy. This time of day, she expected a hefty backup at the Fort McHenry and Harbor tunnels. The traffic would slow her trek to the city. Rachel supposed it would be worth the extra toll to ride in the express lanes.

When she finally arrived, she ran to her office from the parking garage, threw her purse down on her desk, and made her way to Ben's old office. This is where her 9:00 a.m. meeting would take place.

She arrived at the long glass window looking into the CEO office. The once unobstructed view from the hallway was now blocked. Traci, the administrative assistant, looked queasy. She told Rachel she wanted to vomit. As soon as Rachel looked over Traci's shoulder into the clear Plexiglas of the window obstruction, she understood. Directly behind Traci, along the front window of the CEO's office, was a cage containing a Komodo dragon whose black eyes and forked tongue were quite menacing. Rachel asked another employee to take Traci out for some fresh air. She would discuss the issue with the new boss. Rachel knocked on the closed door and waited for clearance to enter. She poked her head in first, tentatively, and said, "Good morning, Dr. Rinaldi. I'm Rachel Larkin, here for my nine o'clock meeting."

Rinaldi was seated at the desk. He rose to greet her. He was dressed in a simple, signature black outfit. He wore heavily tinted glasses to hide the startling effect his right eye had on new people. Somehow, it made him more presentable. The remainder of his receding black hairline was combed straight back and held in place with gel. He extended his hand and greeted her warmly.

"Ah, Dr. Larkin. I am so pleased to make your acquaintance. I have studied your dossier and feel like I know you already. And may I say, you are as beautiful as your corporate bio photo implies."

Her hand met his and she tried to smile. The touch of his hand gave her a chill.

Boy, his comment was weird, she thought. *I don't know whether to be flattered or offended.*

"Dr. Rinaldi, please call me Rachel. I thought it might be a good idea to spend part of the day touring our commercial location here in the city. It's within walking distance or we can grab a taxi, if you like." She was trying to be mindful of his disability.

"An excellent idea, my dear. But we will not require a taxi; I have a driver assigned to me. He picks me up at my new home in Ellicott City and brings me here. You see, I have never operated a motor vehicle."

She had no idea he didn't drive. *The company was paying for a driver? Wow, Albert caved on the fringes.*

They sat and talked about Hiatus Centers' early days, from scientific theory to their first laboratory success and through to human awakenings. Then she described the details surrounding the opening of the first commercial location in Baltimore. She gave him the ins and outs of that first rocky year or so and then how things came together after they solved the Schlemm's rod defects.

"So, you say these rods in the Liferay were defective?" he asked.

"That's one theory," said Rachel. "Ari . . . that is, Dr. Ari Weiskopf, a colleague of mine and our senior physicist, believes someone at the manufacturer in Switzerland deliberately messed with the parts."

"That strikes me as a bit farfetched, no?" said Rinaldi. "After all, we are hardly living in an industry marked by such covert, dastardly acts."

"I hear you," she said, "but given the nature of our service, there are a lot of people around who feel it's immoral. That might be enough of a motive. Ben certainly thought so."

"Perhaps the good Dr. Abraham is a wee bit paranoid. To build a business, there must be trust," said Rinaldi. "I will summon my driver and meet you in front of the building in fifteen minutes," he said.

Rachel left the office, checked on Traci, who was still visibly shaken, collected her purse, and went down the elevator. She had forgotten to address the Komodo dragon with Rinaldi but made a mental note to do so. She waited on the E. Pratt Street sidewalk for Rinaldi. Five minutes later he walked toward her, unable to hide the obvious limp as he relied on his trusty walnut cane. Not a minute later, a black Lincoln Town Car pulled up to the curb. The chauffer, Baxter, hopped out of the driver's seat to assist Rachel and Rinaldi. The ride took less than five minutes. Baxter would be called when they were ready to go. As they entered the Hiatus Centers' commercial location, the receptionist greeted Rachel warmly. Rachel introduced the new CEO, whose attempt at charming the young lady fell decidedly flat.

There were no awakenings scheduled and no client intakes to witness. Rachel started the tour downstairs in the Containment Area. At a high level, she provided Rinaldi the genesis of containment, beginning with Bock's preservative and the discoveries leading to a normal awakening. As they stood in the sterile environment of the main Containment Area, Rinaldi went into scientist mode.

"I understand the cell curing process you described. This makes good sense to me. But tell me, dear, why does a successful awakening fail to sustain itself beyond twenty-four hours?" he inquired.

Rachel bristled at being called "dear." *This guy isn't that much older than me.* Although it was another minor turnoff, she reminded herself to stay positive and keep the day moving forward.

"It seems that we presently have the exact formula for a successful awakening. The three components are the preservative, time, and the Liferay. When we have experimented with any of the components, the results go south. Breaking the twenty-four-hour threshold is still a long range goal for Ben and our scientific team. Just no luck so far," she replied. She thought better of sharing any of her knowledge of Ari and Ben's evening research and its progress. She had been sworn to secrecy.

"Interesting," is all he said.

As they walked through the large flagship location, Rinaldi peppered her with questions regarding the client experience during intake and awakening. He asked her thoughts on how they might enhance the virtual experience program and whether they ever considered letting awakened clients return to their homes for the day or other places offsite. He wanted to know what she knew about liability policies and legal problems. Then his quest for knowledge moved into her thoughts on advertising and promotional tactics and how current strategy might play out in other areas of the world. Once the conversation got past the superficial, Rachel became more and more impressed with the brilliant mind of Dr. Anstrov Rinaldi. Now, she was beginning to see what Albert saw. The man's mind was almost like a computer, processing multiple complex equations at extraordinary speed.

After standing for quite a while in the Awakening Suite, they moved toward the Virtual Experience Theater where Rachel had planned a demonstration similar to what they had done for Albert. In her preparation for his first day, she had been unable to find out anything of this man's early life. All she knew was that he grew up in Florence. To show Rinaldi the impact of their technology, she walked him through Albert's boyhood years in Kansas and then ran the "Harmon demonstration," allowing Rinaldi to imagine he was Albert. While this was not as effective as she would have liked, she knew it would convey the impact of the technology to their new CEO. When it was done, she watched his unflinching expression. It was a look of indifference. Miffed, she told herself to administer this tour with a steady hand despite his bleak, forced smile.

"I must say, Rachel, I feel most fortunate to have earned the position of CEO for a company with such vision. The work you and your colleagues have done here is profound. It is humbling to have the ability to join this monumental effort."

She felt herself beginning to relax. She told herself that some people take extra time to warm up to. She was guessing Dr. Rinaldi was one of those.

He interrupted her thought process by requesting that they next go see the research facility. Her day was set aside to help him acclimate to his new position so she readily agreed. Rinaldi texted Baxter and, like magic, he seemed to appear in no time to pick them up. They climbed into the back of the black Lincoln and drove out of the city, north on I-95 to Maplebrook.

The ride into the county was pleasant enough. They spoke mostly of Rachel. Rinaldi asked a lot of questions. Where did she grow up? Did she enjoy her childhood? What led her to science? Where did she want to be in five years? Did she prefer research to business? Had she ever been married? Did she have a boyfriend? What hobbies did she have? She tried to answer these questions openly without revealing too much of herself. Normally, Rachel considered herself a "top down" trust person, meaning she gave new acquaintances her trust immediately and didn't withdraw it unless they violated the offering. For whatever reason, call it a sixth sense, she did not immediately extend him her full trust. Rinaldi, she could tell, was a "bottom up" trust person. He trusted no one until they earned it. Rachel sensed this as she tried to reciprocate in learning more about her new boss. He politely answered in short, bland explanations regarding his background and life's tastes.

"We are a few minutes away from the Lab. Just ten minutes from here, along the main road, is The Harmon School. That's where Albert spends most of his time."

Rinaldi barely acknowledged that she had spoken. She found his response, or lack thereof, odd. She wasn't sure but it felt like one of those moments when silence indicated something other than indifference. To her, it appeared that the mention of The Harmon School was a trigger that whisked him away into some sort of daydream. Despite continued pangs on the "weirdness radar," she kept reminding herself to stay the course and not let her mind go where it needn't travel.

The Lincoln rolled into the almost imperceptible driveway of the Lab on the outskirts of Maplebrook. Rachel watched Rinaldi's expression as he gazed out the window and the mechanized fence.

"Ben is adamant about security," she said.

"I see, I see. As I mentioned earlier, perhaps a wee bit paranoid," he replied.

Rachel opened her window and pushed a button registering her fingerprint and the magnificent wrought iron gate came to life. Baxter took them as close as he could to the front door to minimize the walk for Rinaldi.

The inside of the Lab upon entering was fairly ordinary in appearance. To the casual observer, it might have resembled the lobby of a municipal building. With Ben's simple tastes, this was not a surprise. Rachel noted that Rinaldi also avoided excess in his office décor and thought he would appreciate the simplistic functionality of the Lab. They passed a series of offices and visited the various research centers dedicated to emerging technologies and scientific discovery. There were areas dedicated to biology, physics, and chemistry, but the heart of the facility was reserved for programs being undertaken by the scientific team of Dr. Abraham. Rachel found the Lab particularly quiet. She had yet to find Ari, Harrison, or Tomi. That changed when they wandered into the Dugout. Ben's team was having a later than normal daily conference sans Ben and Rachel. Rachel didn't question the timing; she just assumed Harrison overslept. She hugged her three colleagues and then introduced Anstrov Rinaldi.

Rachel watched as, one by one, he greeted the team. He looked into their eyes, held their gaze as a show of respect, gripped their hands firmly, and impressed them with his knowledge of their careers and accomplishments—first Ari, then Harrison, and finally, Tomi. Rachel observed as Tomi gave Rinaldi a big hug and that heartwarming smile she was known for. Knowing Tomi the way she did, Rachel understood she was always a little suspicious of new people, particularly authority figures. *Maybe Tomi was just sucking up to the new boss*, she thought. Rachel made a mental note to rag on her about it next time they were alone.

No one knew where Ben was. Over the past few weeks, he had been showing up sporadically in unpredictable patterns. They had their research assignments. With Rachel functioning as COO on the business side, Ari led the scientific team in Ben's absence. Rachel hadn't spoken to Ben much lately. She worried that perhaps his frequency of seizure had increased and he didn't want to tell anyone. Ben was like that. Always wanting to help others but when he had a problem, he became a recluse.

The tour concluded. Rinaldi again had dumped a thousand questions on her about the research facility. Her brain hurt from processing the interaction with him. It was almost over; time to head back to Baltimore so she could finish out her day, collect her car, and drive right back to her home in Maplebrook. *That could have been planned better*, she thought.

They sat in silence for the twenty minutes it took to emerge from the recesses of Harford County back to I-95 for the journey south to the city. Once on the highway, Rachel remembered that she needed to deal with the Komodo dragon issue.

"Dr. Rinaldi, you may have noticed this morning that your administrative assistant, Traci, was a little freaked out over your Komodo dragon. Is there any way he might be repositioned so she is not seeing him all day? I'm afraid she will quit if we don't accommodate her."

Rinaldi laughed and gently rested his left hand on her right knee. "Drago should not bother the young lady. Don't you think he's rather cute? I thought the people in the office might enjoy the unique display at the CEO office. It helps signify that things will be different from here on in."

You're not kidding, she thought. She tried to hide her extraordinary discomfort with his hand on her knee but knew she failed. Rachel always wore her emotions on her sleeve. She jerked her body to the left to get as far away from him as she could. Rachel quickly composed herself.

"So, you will relocate the Komodo?" she asked.

"I will take it under advisement," he replied. "If she resigns, we shall find a suitable replacement, no?"

Rachel was now completely disgusted. She reminded herself to speak with Albert. Despite her affirmations over the day, she now knew with every fiber of her being that this guy was going to be trouble.

"Oh, by the way, my dear. I wanted to let you know that next week, we shall have a new employee starting with the company. He is relocating from France and will report to me in a yet unnamed capacity, sort of a right-hand man. His name is Maxim Ivanov. You will be reporting to him."

Rachel was appalled. Was it possible to feel betrayed by someone you just met? If so, that's how she felt. *The bastard is bringing in his own guy and giving him my job!* For the first time, Rachel seriously questioned whether she would continue working at Hiatus Centers.

CHAPTER 32

Rinaldi sat back in his office chair and reflected on his first encounter with Dr. Larkin. He was satisfied yet, amazed at the simplicity of her approach to the new boss. He never trusted anyone, at least not fully. Larkin, on the other hand, was proving to be quite the opposite, a gullible pawn, eager to please.

The train of thought was broken when Ivanov entered the room. The two men, who had experienced a topsy-turvy relationship, greeted one another congenially. Ivanov expressed relief that Drago was contained within the Plexiglas. Rinaldi could see that Ivanov looked different somehow—not physically, but there was definitely something different. The choice had been to bring either Marceau or Ivanov to America. Marceau was too old. SPI had really been his last hurrah. Ivanov, on the other hand, was younger and would prove more malleable to his agenda. Rinaldi warmed inside. He had made the correct choice.

"Maxim, you are fully relocated?"

"Yes, Dr. Rinaldi. My things have arrived and I am getting settled in my apartment here in the city. Baltimore is quite different from Colmar. I like it, though. It is comfortable. It is also taxing my English. I haven't spoken this much English since the days of university in Russia. But yes, I think I will do just fine here."

Rinaldi poised his good eye on Ivanov. The man still appeared to be the quintessential sniveling coward he had always been yet somehow he seemed to have gained a measure of self-confidence. Perhaps it was the prestige of such an important position in a growing company. *Could it be that Ivanov has grown a backbone?* Just as quickly as the thought arrived, it was dismissed. He really didn't care. Ivanov was simply a loyalist who could be trusted—within limits, of course—to be his eyes and ears around the company. He knew he could not entrust Rachel Larkin to be his right hand person. *According to my information, she has a thing for Abraham. I will keep her around so long as she serves a purpose*, he reasoned.

"This pretty little Dr. Larkin will report to you, Maxim. So will all of the people at the research facility in the suburbs. You make sure they stay focused on the projects I say. If Abraham shows up and tries to interfere, let me know. If they refuse your orders in any way, let me know."

Rinaldi was as shrewd as ever. Every action had a purpose. For every action, he anticipated the reaction. If he was on top of his game, the reactions of others would be predictable and thus controllable.

They spent the next several hours reviewing the operations of the company. The conversation drifted into research.

"What are they working on now, Dr. Rinaldi?" asked Ivanov.

"Abraham has directed the top scientific team to break the twenty-four-hour threshold. This effort is being led by a Dr. Ari Weiskopf, a physicist from Philadelphia who, like Abraham, is a graduate of the so-called Harmon School for Gifted Scientific Youth."

"Have they progressed in their efforts?" asked Ivanov.

"It would appear not," replied Rinaldi. "When I asked Weiskopf for a report and an estimate for completion, he prattled on about how it was impossible to determine the time it would take and that their methodology has been reduced to what he called 'logical tinkering,'" said Rinaldi.

"Logical tinkering?" stated Ivanov. "What does that even mean?"

"I have no earthly idea," said Rinaldi. "It will be your job to assess what is happening. I want a full report inside of one week, Maxim."

In an instant, the little bit of warmth Rinaldi had offered Ivanov vanished like a sound in the wind.

"Need I remind you, Maxim, I have brought you here for my purpose. The money and power this position affords you no one else would provide. Were it not for me, you would still be in Colmar, overseeing mundane research to help make the next great cough syrup. Do not let me down, Maxim. Do I make myself clear?" he said with an escalating tone and reddening cheeks.

○ ○ ○ ○ ○

One week later, Ivanov returned to headquarters on E. Pratt Street. The two men spoke in the privacy of Rinaldi's office. Rinaldi, in his own paranoia, had the office swept for bugs. Nothing was found. Trusting others was difficult—only on a limited basis and only when absolutely necessary. He wanted to be sure that conversations like the one he was about to have with Ivanov would never be overheard.

"What did you learn, Maxim?"

"I interviewed everyone on Abraham's team. I was not very impressed. It is hard to imagine this group got as far as they did. I have not yet met him but I must presume that Abraham is the genius behind the operation. The group has no discipline, Dr. Rinaldi."

"Are they making progress on the twenty-four-hour threshold?"

"It's hard to say. Bock, the big slovenly one, a chemist, would not last a day in Colmar. Every question I ask of him is met with a wisecrack. He does not appear to take his work very seriously."

"He is the one who discovered the preservative enabling bodies to avoid deterioration during hibernation."

"Perhaps," answered Ivanov, "but he does not seem to have much to offer on the current effort."

"What about the others?" Rinaldi quizzed somewhat impatiently.

"Larkin is busy tending to operations here and at the commercial locations. She is doing a good job but her personality appears listless. She contributes nothing to the current phase of scientific research. Weiskopf, the senior man, is unconventional in his methods. I asked him about his approach and he told me about three components: the preservative, time, and the Liferay. He continues to describe his logical tinkering malarkey. I became disgusted and asked to see his private journals, notes, anything that might make sense. He balked and said he would get back to me when he had something of substance to report."

"And what of Oka, the biologist?" asked Rinaldi.

"She was somewhat helpful. I asked her if she was familiar with Weiskopf's thinking on how to crack the twenty-four-hour threshold and she told me she would see what she could learn. I understand from Oka that the team holds daily research review sessions in the room they call the Dugout. She told me I should drop in on one of these meetings to learn more."

"And did you?"

"Yes, Dr. Rinaldi, three times. Once I arrive, the group either clams up, shifts to innocuous conversation, or disbands the meeting. It was fruitless."

"Stay in touch with Oka. I sense that she will be eager to help. She has a caring nature about her. I see that."

"Yes, I will do that. I must tell you that, one week in, this is a most frustrating group to lead. Americans are so stupid. They lack focus. I question whether they understand the science at all. Perhaps, to get this far, they were simply lucky."

"Do not underestimate them, Maxim. They are very smart. They are playing you. I suspect Abraham is pulling their strings from the background. I don't think he values money at a personal level. This gives him the ability to not care whether we succeed with the company he founded. I would not be surprised if there is a covert attempt to sabotage my leadership. This, as you know, is completely unacceptable."

As his anger began to rise, Rinaldi's good eye started to bulge. His cheeks gradually but noticeably transformed from their natural tone to crimson. The odd voice was clearly agitated. Barely in control, he said, "These people are not fools. Do not take them as such. They must not view you as a spy. They must see you as their leader. You will gain their trust. Become one of them. Demonstrate value to the team. I do not care how you do this. Just do it."

○ ○ ○ ○ ○

As he emerged from the office tower, Rinaldi located Baxter waiting along E. Pratt Street. Baxter had quickly learned that Rinaldi was an independent sort. Despite his handicap, Rinaldi did not wish to have any assistance and took note of how Baxter stood outside the car, in a modest nod of respect, and did not take his seat behind the wheel until he was comfortably seated in the large rear compartment.

"Ready to head home, sir?" asked the driver.

"Not quite yet, Baxter. We must make a stop not far off our normal route."

About twenty minutes outside the city, the Lincoln turned into an old, decrepit strip shopping center off Route 100, not far from BWI Airport. Clearly, this was an economically depressed area, as evidenced by the number of boarded-up storefronts. After pulling into the parking lot, Baxter was forced to maneuver the large sedan away from a pothole measuring at least a yard in diameter. Rinaldi instructed Baxter to stop in front of one of the few ongoing businesses, a retail outlet for one of the large courier companies.

While Baxter waited in the car, Rinaldi stepped toward the retail establishment, pulled open the glass door, and went left toward a wall of small, golden-colored steel vaults. These storage units for rent were similar to the wall of lockboxes one might see in any US post office. Rinaldi reached into his right pocket and removed a small, dull, gold-colored key and looked for the engraved box number 142. He inserted the key, opened the small door, and extracted a tiny insulated shipping envelope. It was sealed per the instructions he had provided. He tucked the envelope inside his jacket, closed and locked the little door, and returned to the car.

Back in the Lincoln, Rinaldi switched on the overhead light and removed the insulated envelope from his breast pocket. He gently tore open the top and peered inside. It was as he had ordered. A small flash drive was nestled in bubble wrap, waiting to reveal its secrets.

○ ○ ○ ○ ○

Two weeks later, Rinaldi was exasperated. He felt as if he and Ivanov were having some sort of broken record conversation. He was not known for patience with others.

"I don't think you understand me, Maxim. I am tired of the bullshit. I want you to tell me exactly what these characters know about how to crack the twenty-four-hour threshold."

Ivanov continued to report little of substance and Rinaldi was questioning whether he made the right decision bringing him to the company. *Maybe his brain just cannot get beyond cough syrups and pills,* thought Rinaldi.

From the flash drive he had acquired, Rinaldi had been surprised to learn his suspicion that Weiskopf had not gotten very far with the mandate to crack the twenty-four-hour threshold was wrong. Rinaldi had in his possession the contents of Weiskopf's private scientific records detailing the team's research methods and progress. More importantly, he held in his possession a digital copy of Weiskopf's personal journal.

This journal told the real story of their research and its progress. The clandestine data exchange was an inconvenient but necessary evil to avoid any arousal of impropriety.

"Maxim," Rinaldi said calmly but deliberately, "I want you to tell Weiskopf that by early next year, Hiatus Centers will begin offering an awakening service that lasts indefinitely. Instruct Larkin to begin working on the client-facing details, including allowing the awakened to leave the grounds and return home if they wish."

Rinaldi knew the look on Ivanov's face and he was intimately familiar with the tone. He assumed Ivanov was suppressing his fear and would muster the courage to respond in a voice indicative of his newfound sense of self-worth.

"But Dr. Rinaldi, we both know that an indefinite awakening is not scientifically feasible at the present time. It may be years until we are ready. Dr. Larkin will tell me she is too busy to plan for something that is unimaginably impossible."

Rinaldi appeared calm. Before responding, he sighed and clasped his hands together in a steepled fashion.

"Maxim, small minds focus on barriers. Great minds dream of what is possible and discover how to make it so. The latter is what I expect."

Ivanov, emboldened by Rinaldi's dearth of anger, plowed forward. "This is mere fantasy. You expect the team to create science out of the dust on the floor? There is a huge gap between imagination and reality and rarely can it be filled because someone orders it so."

Rinaldi's left eyebrow went up. "While what you say has merit, I refuse to accept the specter of doubt as an excuse before anyone has lifted a finger to genuinely try."

"Dr. Rinaldi, they have been trying, long before you and I arrived on the scene. The world's most powerful computers have been unable to solve a puzzle where error rates are measured in mere femtoseconds. I urge you to be reasonable in your requests."

"The plan is firm. It is April. I expect results by the end of the year; sooner is preferable."

Ivanov felt the need to keep pushing back. This was not like Colmar. Rinaldi needed him as his man on the inside. He grasped the perceived latitude by the reins and kept going.

"And if the scientific team decides this is madness and walks out the door?"

"It is of no concern to me, Maxim. As you said a few weeks ago, these American scientists are not so disciplined. Perhaps that would be a benefit. I shall consider this. Now, go. Make something happen!" he snapped.

CHAPTER 33

Rachel was glad Ben had agreed to go for an early morning hike. While they had been talking by phone here and there, they had been on different schedules and hadn't found the time to get together. They were to meet at Rocks State Park, at their usual auxiliary parking lot along Route 24. Ben, of course, was late.

She wanted to see Ben. She missed him. Since their night in Baltimore, things had been different. In some ways better, in some ways, more distant. On the positive side, she could sense that when they were both together, they shared the desire to rush to each other's arms. On the other hand, fear kept them from doing so and had created a wedge. She just wanted everything to be perfect. But that was never easy. The conflict regarding their relationship status was wearing on her. Not as much as working for Rinaldi but it was an ever present contributing factor. Her nerves were frayed, partly due to her current life situation and partly because Ben was late. He was always late. Why should she be surprised? While she waited, she closed her eyes and tried to get herself to a better place.

The words flowed effortlessly through Rachel's mind. It never ceased to amaze her that poems filled her brain when she experienced extreme states of emotion. Had she tried to sit and write a poem for fun, she most likely would draw a blank. On this day, words came easily.

The stress of working at Hiatus Centers under Rinaldi's leadership was too much to bear; definitely not what she signed up for. She took a deep breath, opened her eyes as wide as she could and drank in the beauty of her surroundings. Ever since she came east to work at the Lab, Rocks State Park had been a place of solitude, somewhere she could gather herself and rediscover the energy and focus she required to plow through difficult situations.

It was early Saturday morning and the ground was damp from the prior evening's rain shower. The air had the crisp, clean feel of an early spring day, deep in the woods. Rocks State Park was known for its densely wooded acreage, the beauty of Deer Creek, and natural rock formations, including the iconic King and Queen Seat, the biggest formation in the park at 190 feet, which offered climbers breathtaking views of rolling Harford County. It was difficult for Rachel to imagine that these hard beaten foot trails were once home to the Susquehannock Indians and the Baltimore and Pennsylvania Railroads that steamed through with carloads of grain from local farms. What was once a bastion of activity was now a secluded and peaceful sojourn for a woman with a weary mind.

Her back was to the parking lot so she could face the park and the majestic beauty it had to offer. She was lost in her thoughts when Ben finally arrived.

"I like that outfit. Much better than a white lab coat."

She turned around and smiled. She quickly thought of how she was wearing nothing but a white lab coat during their night in Baltimore. He couldn't have meant that night. Just her day-to-day attire. She vanquished the errant thought from her mind and gave him a tighter hug than normal.

She was wearing a light red windbreaker and jeans. Her hair was pulled back into a short ponytail which she let hang freely through the rear opening of the white ball cap atop her head. While they weren't a couple, she needed him this morning and took the liberty of winding her arm through his and staying close. Ben didn't seem to mind. In fact, she hadn't seen him this relaxed in years. Unselfish as always, Rachel listened while Ben told her about his couple of weeks on a beach in Capri. The color in his face was indicative of the newfound energy and enthusiasm. He had told her on the phone why no one had seen him recently at the Lab. She understood his need to simply disappear for a while. To Rachel, Ben looked refreshed. Somehow, it made him even more attractive than she already found him.

"Man, listen to me. I've been going on and on about myself. Is work getting any better for you?" he asked.

Rachel felt her stomach gurgle. A tear filled her eye and her voice was a bit shaken. Ben saw the change and they stopped walking. He took her in his arms. For a few minutes, they stood in a comforting embrace, taking in each other's warmth, enveloped by the early morning mist of the forest. They agreed to go sit on one of the large rock formations and just talk. Ben was about to park his rear end on the rocks when, suddenly, Rachel instructed him to halt. Her caring nature didn't want his jeans to be soaked from the wet rock. She pulled a rolled up plastic rain poncho from her small backpack and laid it out over the rocks for them to sit.

"You know, it would be embarrassing for me to be seen walking through the park with a man who has a wet butt mark," she quipped. Rachel frequently fell into humor when she was stressed. Where Ben was concerned, it was less a release than something that naturally came to her in the course of verbal interplay.

Ben tried once more to get her to open up. Although she knew she was likely to begin blubbering again, she started in.

"Oh Ben," she tried to smile as she said this. "It truly sucks." She pulled a giant wet leaf from the bottom of her shoe and looked into his eyes. His warm glow and ability to listen empathically were already beginning to break down the protective wall she built around herself.

"I tried, you know, I really honestly tried to understand and appreciate what Rinaldi would bring to the company. I got so many weird vibes on the first day. He's condescending, arrogant, and a chauvinist. Oh, and you can also throw in a penchant for sexual harassment. He keeps that Komodo dragon in his office scaring the shit out of everyone and he has major trust issues. I think that's why he brought in that lackey, Ivanov, from France. It's someone he can control. I barely get to speak with him. I report to Ivanov who is basically a courier. Rinaldi tells Ivanov what he wants and Ivanov carries out the demands."

"The guy's a major dick. Maybe you need to get away from it. Just go do something else. The stress of working for that ass isn't worth your health. You've put in way too much hard work to feel unappreciated. You don't need the money and you don't need the aggravation."

"Trust me, I'm thinking about warming up my résumé. It's just been so long since I've had to do that . . . and I think about all we've built. I was hoping I could see it through."

"To what end? We developed the science. We did something miraculous. We brought a miracle to the world and it's making people happy."

"Yeah, I hear you, Ben. I feel like . . . if I leave . . . the whole thing will fall apart."

"If it does, Rachel, you don't want it falling apart on your watch. Get out before the shit hits the fan. Maintain your scientific and business credibility. You can always tell a prospective employer you left because you disagreed with the philosophy of the new CEO. They'll respect that. Is anything else going on?"

"You haven't heard the half of it."

"What do you mean?"

"Ivanov came to me yesterday and told me that Rinaldi wants the company to prepare for a new service offering for awakenings of indefinite duration . . . and off the grounds."

"But Rinaldi doesn't have the science in hand to make that happen. I've been speaking with Ari. I know he has no clue how to do that."

The knot in Rachel's stomach tightened. Once again, concealing the truth from Ben was crushing her. The guilt she felt was overwhelming. She knew that, for the time being, and for Ben's sake, she had to keep the secret.

"That's what I'm talking about, Ben. The guy is deranged. What happens when he tries what he thinks will work in an effort to build more profit and stay ahead of would-be competitors? What happens when you start letting awakened clients go off the grounds? How on earth will we control the awakening process? There are so many issues I can't even comprehend them right now. And worst of all, I can't express any of these reservations to Rinaldi. I told Ivanov and he told me that Rinaldi doesn't care for excuses, just results. He told me if I went to Rinaldi, he was likely to blow a gasket. Apparently, in addition to his many other charming qualities, he has a bad temper, too."

"And Albert is aware of all of this?"

"Ivanov has me running around with so much crazy shit. I haven't had time to find out what Albert knows."

"I'll speak to him. He needs to know. In the meantime, get your résumé warmed up. I can't stand what this is doing to you. In fact, just quit. Say 'fuck 'em' and take a year off. We can spend some time together."

With that suggestion, her eyes lit up and she felt her heart begin to sing. Maybe this was the silver lining on the darkest cloud she had ever experienced. Her troubled mind seemed to clear like the sun breaking into a congested sky. Rachel reached over and took his hand. She gave it a little squeeze, leaned in, and pecked him on the cheek. It made her feel even better when Ben blushed like a schoolboy.

With more life than she had felt in months, she smiled enthusiastically.

"I was hoping for dinner and a movie and maybe the chance to work closely together again," she mused. "But I may be able to be talked into something more."

With Rachel in higher spirits, they got up and made their way further down the old dirt path. They held hands and enjoyed the gathering warmth of the morning's glow. For Rachel, a morning full of stress had turned completely around.

Suddenly, she felt the grip of his hand tighten around hers. It didn't feel normal. In the second it took for her to turn her head to ask if he was okay, she understood what was happening. She saw his eyes roll upward as he lost consciousness. She tried to help him as he collapsed but she was too small and slight to gently ease him to the ground. As he went down, his head snapped sharply against a small rock protruding from the dirt path. Rachel reached into her backpack, grabbed her cell phone, and dialed 911.

The paramedics arrived quickly and skillfully pounded the path with a stretcher that would enable them to transport the long, unconscious body of Ben Abraham. Before lifting him, they had determined that his pulse was weak. Because they were fairly deep in the woods, the two paramedics were taxed to move Ben to the closest spot the ambulance could be parked. Rachel climbed in behind Ben. She would take the fifteen minute ride to Upper Chesapeake Medical Center in Bel Air. Although he was unconscious, she held his hand and silently said her prayers.

Ben was still out cold when the ambulance rolled into the driveway at the hospital earmarked for emergency vehicles. Rachel was quizzed about Ben's medical history by the paramedics, the triage nurse, and the attending physician. She felt helpless but told them all the same thing. She and Ben were friends and colleagues. They hadn't seen each other for a while and decided to spend the morning together at Rocks State Park. She had no knowledge of his detailed medical history. She relayed that she saw his head twist and hit a rock as he crumbled to the ground. *That alone*, she thought, *would force the ER docs to order a CT.*

Ben's parents were retired and traveling in Australia. She didn't have their contact information but made a mental note to scout through Ben's cell phone when things settled down at the ER. In a way, she was relieved that Mr. and Mrs. Abraham were traveling. They would be freaked out. She called Albert. She knew he would understand. He arrived at the hospital in record time.

"What in the world happened?" asked a disheveled and worried Albert Harmon.

Rachel told him the story. She said she was holding up and that Ben's vitals had returned to normal. He had not yet come to. The doctor suspected a possible concussion or maybe even a slight brain contusion. They were still running tests.

"So it was like the seizure he had in the office before he stepped down as CEO?" he asked.

"I came in after that one occurred. This one, I saw from the start. When he had the episode in the office, he never lost consciousness. This time, he was out before he fell and hit his head on that rock. The doctor mentioned the possibility of a coma."

Rachel hoped Albert wouldn't blurt out anything regarding the office seizure to the ER doctors. She didn't want to go there. The CT would be telling. In the meantime, she would need to keep Albert from speaking with the ER staff.

Rachel's stomach began to knot again. Her eyes became moist. The morning had felt like a rollercoaster of emotion. She knew she needed to be strong and keep it together for Ben. With nothing more to do but wait, Rachel left her cell phone number with the nurse and walked off with Albert to the cafeteria where they could sit with a cup of coffee or tea. In the cafeteria, Rachel left a voicemail for both Jon and Marcy. She had located their cell phone numbers from Ben's phone. Australia was fourteen hours ahead so they were likely asleep. Ben had no siblings and no other relatives she knew of. She didn't see the sense of disturbing

Ari, Harrison, or Tomi on a Saturday. She would wait with Albert at the hospital for as long as it took.

Seven hours later, Ben regained consciousness. Through the fog, he saw the worried faces of Rachel and Albert. He knew instantly what had happened and where he was. Ben's right hand instinctively went to the back of his head.

"Worst headache I ever had," he said.

Rachel had heard him say those exact words the night he died in the Lab. Hearing them again sent a chill down her spine.

"Ben, we've been so worried. Let me get the nurse and tell her you are awake."

After the nurse and attending physician examined, poked, and prodded Ben, Rachel and Albert were allowed back in. The original diagnosis had been the correct one; concussion with a slight contusion. Ben was to be kept at the hospital overnight for observation and fluids but would be fine. The doctors had listed the cause of the incident as "fainting, probably due to dehydration."

After learning he was okay, Albert left and promised to check in with Ben the next day. Once they were alone, Rachel began to probe.

"Okay, it's just the two of us here now," she said. "Is there something more going on?"

He grinned and playfully replied, "Well, if you're asking if I've been experimenting with hallucinogens, the answer is no."

"Ben, I'm worried. How many of these seizures have you had?"

"I lost count. They seem to be coming with a greater frequency and each one is a little more severe. This was the first time I lost consciousness. Usually, I feel it coming on and can sit, close my eyes, and let it pass. Most of the time, it's done in fifteen minutes or so."

"Are you going to tell the doctors here what's going on?"

"Hmmm, let me think about that one," he said. Then, just as quickly, added "No."

"Are you insane? The blackout changes everything! Think about this, Ben. Suppose you are driving a car and an attack occurs? Or some other activity requiring motor skills that all of the sudden disappear?"

"Rachel, you are right. Trust me—I won't do anything to place myself or others in danger. I'm working on a solution."

She recoiled at the mere suggestion he could somehow heal himself from an unknown condition. Not even the great Ben Abraham could pull that one off.

"What exactly does that mean, Ben?"

"Let's just say that I am doing my research."

"Ben, this is your life on the line. I need to understand what the hell you are talking about."

"Okay, okay. Stay calm," he said. "Today, I had a CT scan. Since these seizures began, I've had one other. Every time I have sought or unexpectedly receive medical attention, I get a complete set of medical records so I can track the data. I have been studying pharmacology and considering it with everything else we have learned while developing the Liferay and the entire Hiatus Centers experience. The combination of the knowledge and my medical data is fed through a computer program I wrote that is associated with the world's most extensive databases on known medical conditions and their treatments. The program identifies a precise diagnosis and recommended treatment regimen based on differing types of medicine practiced by every known culture, current and ancient, throughout the world. No single doctor could know more and no single doctor could possibly do the amount of research my program does. So, at best, going to a doctor for what's happening to me will boil down to the experience of the individual doctor and his or her ability and willingness to research endless possibilities. I like my chances with the program better."

Rachel listened in amazement. In dealing with the events of the day, she had foolishly deluded herself into rationalizing treatment options the way anyone would. She understood Ben Abraham all too well. Of course he would want to find a way out of his own mess.

"I guess I shouldn't be surprised," she said.

"I love the beach but I love science more. There was no way I could just goof off indefinitely. In a strange way, this condition has given my work a new sense of purpose I haven't felt in a long time."

Upon hearing all this, Rachel felt relief and sorrow all at once. On the one hand, she understood that no one on the planet was better suited than Ben to find his own medical solution. For this, she was grateful. On the other hand, if he was enveloped in work, the "plan" they hatched at the park to take a year off and spend some time together had just become far less likely. She immediately chastised herself. *You can't be selfish here! Be there for Ben. Help him get well.*

On a good note, he had now had two CT scans since his death. Neither one indicated any negative resultant effect from the aneurysm that had killed him. That was a huge relief. Ari needed to know. At a minimum, they now knew that Ben was not a walking time bomb awaiting another lethal aneurysm. But who knew if the seizure-driven condition from the experimental Liferay would prove fatal? The pressure of not knowing was likely to destroy her. She would call Ari when she got home.

"I want to help," she exclaimed. "I can quit my job and work on this full time. Ben, you are all that matters to me."

Ben's tanned expression bestowed the reciprocity of her feelings.

"I may very well take you up on that. For now, my next step is to create a ruse of sorts for Albert's current crop of scientific prodigies at the school. I will ask them to crunch some data for me as part of a project to create a new antiseizure medication. They just won't know it's for me."

"Brilliant," she replied. "Based on what you just described, you also have the makings of the world's most powerful tool for medical treatment. You could start a company that dwarfs the revenue of Hiatus Centers."

"You know I'm not in it for the money. I can't spend what I've got now.

I like being able to support some favorite charities, though. I'm far more excited about the help the program will provide the medical community. You know, by taking the guesswork out of diagnosis and treatment. Once I get past the seizure issue, I can focus on that."

What'll you do in the meantime?" she asked somberly.

"Not following you," he said.

"How do you know that the next seizure won't kill you before you figure out the solution?"

"I don't."

CHAPTER 34

Rachel had been to Ari's house only once before. Shortly after she began work at the Lab, he made a lame attempt at a costume party on Halloween. She remembered wanting to make a good impression on her new colleagues and had purchased a Pocahontas costume from a local shop in nearby Abingdon. With the long, black wig and the faux animal skin dress, she felt ridiculous. Her memory confirmed the feeling when she remembered the photo from the party that was still tacked to a corkboard in Ari's office. She gained an immediate sense of belonging after the good-natured razzing they gave her. Harrison told her that pale girls don't make good Indian goddesses.

Rachel gave it right back to him.

"How, exactly, do you know what Pocahontas looked like?"

Harrison sheepishly looked at her with a dopey grin on his face and replied, "What? I saw the Disney movie. She was a babe."

Ari, as he was prone to do, rang in to assail Harrison with a corrective remark. "That's a cartoon, dumbass."

Rachel parked her car and walked along a stone path inside the townhome community. Like so many Maplebrook developments, Ari's house was nestled gently into the beginning of a densely wooded area. As she walked up to his front door with a purpose in her step, she noticed that the body of his ten-year-old Jeep Cherokee looked a little more decrepit each time she saw it. She thought that the forest green color might have been really nice when the car was brand new. Now, the faded paint job, road dents, and blotches of rust made it look worse for the wear.

Ari lived in one of those communities with a homeowner's association that insisted all of the units be displayed in earth colors. This, she knew, meant that only acceptable shades of brown, green, and yellow would dominate the exterior paint, siding, and roof.

It's pleasant enough for a wooded community, she thought. *It makes for a peaceful, perhaps even sleepy, neighborhood.* Rachel approached the front door, lifted the brass door knocker from its base, and brought it back to the flat plate three times.

It was early Sunday morning. Clearly, Ari had not been expecting a visitor. He opened the door and greeted her barefoot, in his jeans and an old untucked T-shirt with the Liberty Bell depicting his Philadelphia roots. Before Ari could open his mouth, Rachel said simply, "We need to talk."

He opened the door and invited her in. She immediately took note of the mess. Ari apparently had no regard for cleaning. His home resembled the cluttered chaos she frequently saw in his office. Clothes were strewn everywhere, as were books, magazines, computer equipment, and trash. It looked like something from a post-tornado scene. She could tell that he was embarrassed, most assuredly, from the look on his face.

"Why don't we go sit on the deck?" he asked. "It's a pretty morning and it's very quiet."

Ari brought a bottle of water for each of them and they sat on his aluminum furniture, the kind you would get on sale at a discount retailer.

Rachel quickly filled Ari in on the prior day's events.

"Ben has had not one but two CTs," she exclaimed. "He made no mention of any doctor telling him about the aftermath caused by an aneurysm. You do realize what this means?"

Ari nodded. "Yes, it means that although I saved his life, I am the cause of his seizures."

Rachel understood why Ari would feel guilty. She felt for him but her clear priority was helping Ben. She needed to get Ari to focus on the solution.

"This is where you said you were stuck. A CT would help clear the path forward. He's had the CT. We know the results. Now what?"

She was despondent when he dropped his head and his posture in the aluminum chair noticeably degraded.

"I've been thinking of little else. I wish I knew what to tell you."

Rachel thought that telling Ari about Ben's own idea to cure himself might aid the progress of the conversation. She relayed what Ben had told her and was interested in Ari's reaction. Ari sat upright and his mood brightened.

"Wow, Ben's a fuckin' genius. Who else would think of an idea like that?"

"Yes, it's fascinating but wouldn't his effort be easier if he knew everything?"

"We've been through this. Ben would seriously kiss us both goodbye if he knew what we did."

Rachel contemplated the comment before replying. *You mean, if he knew what you did.* She had been a witness to a macabre scene in which she was now being held hostage. Before she could say anything, Ari chimed in with, "Maybe it's best to continue letting him figure it out on his own."

Rachel considered the possibilities. If she continued to acquiesce to Ari's suggestion, given what they now knew, she would be banking on the fact that Ben would somehow heal himself, a process that could likely take years. And he could drop dead in the process. She simply couldn't get comfortable with either of the two options: keeping a secret with Ari or telling Ben what had happened. Then another idea materialized.

"Maybe we can tell Albert. He might have a good idea or have a contact somewhere around the world who might be able to help," she said.

"I can't fathom what Albert would be able to do to help. All he will likely do is worry and ultimately tell Ben, taking the decision out of our hands."

Rachel decided Ari was probably right about telling Albert. His loyalty to Ben would dominate his ability to help them on the other side of the equation. She wasn't willing to end the conversation with Ari until she found an acceptable answer. The back and forth was maddening.

Rachel got up from the uncomfortable chair and walked over to the deck railing. She looked out over the woods for a minute and tried to clear her head. A squirrel darted up a maple tree and hit a crossroad of branches. He stopped. He apparently couldn't decide which way to proceed. Rachel understood.

The crossroad of tree branches she was experiencing fell between a measure of culpability and preserving her integrity. Rachel grappled with the strain of it all. The muscles in her face tightened. She took a deep breath to relieve some of the tension.

"I heard what you said. We have to tell Ben. There's really no other choice."

"You are willing to risk your job and the love/friendship thing you two have going on?"

"At the end of the day, it means more to me to help Ben save his own life . . . even if I won't be a part of it going forward."

"It's a huge decision, Rachel."

"What if Ben were here with us right now and he began having a seizure. Would we just stand by and watch, all the while knowing we might hold the key to resolving the cause?"

Ari winced. She wasn't sure if she struck a nerve or if he just disagreed. She decided the latter. Ari merely lacked the courage to do the right thing. Regardless of what happened to Ben, Rachel knew she needed to do what she thought was right or she would never be able to live with herself. Letting another person's lack of courage ground her morals to a halt simply wasn't a choice she was willing to make. If Ari doesn't agree, then to help Ben's cause, she might need to throw him under the bus. She silently wondered if throwing Ari under the bus truly helped Ben or just vindicated her in Ben's eyes. The conflict rattled around in her head like a steel marble in a pinball machine.

Ultimately, she decided, Ben's health was her priority. Being truthful with herself, if there was a way to help Ben and preserve her future by his side, Ari was a sacrifice she would grudgingly make.

She picked up her purse from one of the deck chairs and turned toward the sliding glass door.

"I need to go. There's a lot to think about."

CHAPTER 35

"I understand you have been vacationing in my native Italy," remarked Rinaldi. "You look well rested. Ready to rock the scientific world, I trust?"

Rinaldi prided himself on being a student of human behavior. Like a predator in the wild, he could sense what people were really thinking and feeling. He considered the body language and tone of Ben Abraham, who merely replied, "I'm here."

Rinaldi decided to let it slide. He held a certain dominance over Abraham by virtue of the fact that he occupied his former office, the seat of power built by the man who stood before him. *The fool probably wonders how he got into this position.* Rinaldi enjoyed the game. The prey was within his sights and now it was time to move in for the kill.

"I grew up in Florence but spent many a summer's day on Capri. Did you enjoy our island gem, Ben?"

"Yes, it was nice," he replied stoically.

Rinaldi pressed on just to drag out the torture he was inflicting. He enjoyed forcing people to endure discomfort. He didn't know why. It was part of the game, he supposed.

"You know, the island's name has been 'Americanized' here. In Italy, we say CA-pri, with the accent on the first syllable. Americans pronounce it as if it were a pair of ladies' pants."

Rinaldi enjoyed the bored expression on Abraham's face. He knew he was pushing the right buttons.

"I hope you were able to frequent the Blue Grotto," said Rinaldi. "Or perhaps you are too tall to fit in the rowboat that offers the only admission to the small cave opening on the face of the island. Even short people are required to lie flat in the rowboat to gain access."

"Perhaps we could get down to the reason you asked me here."

As Abraham looked even more uncomfortable, Rinaldi decided to press on.

"The grotto offers a spectacular illusion of blue cave walls caused by the sunlight's reflection off the azure water. Quite remarkable."

"I didn't get to see it."

"Oh, truly a shame. You must partake if you go back. Of course, ask for an extended boat; a man of your height would have his legs hanging over the normal-size tenders."

Rinaldi kept on jabbing. He wanted Abraham uncomfortable and off balance for his intended purpose.

"I understand you enjoy the outdoors. I hope you didn't miss the opportunity to climb Vesuvius. The view from the top is magnificent. It's only a short climb from the bus platform."

"Nope."

"Tell me you saw Pompeii. The aftermath of Vesuvius' eruptions has certainly made its mark. Such a fascinating part of the world."

"Please," exclaimed Ben, "can we get down to the reason you asked me here?"

Rinaldi was satisfied. Abraham was agitated. That was right where he wanted him.

"Of course, of course. There are several matters for us to discuss. Let's begin with the lawsuits."

"What about them?"

"I am working on settlement offers for the affected families. The lawyers would like your input on the legal documents. They were looking to wrap this up last week. I held them at bay until your return."

"Tell them to email the documents. I'll review them this week. Is Senator Rose among the settlements?"

"Unfortunately, no. He is seemingly the lone holdout. Settling would derail his regulatory train. I believe this to be his higher purpose." Rinaldi watched as Abraham appeared to squirm. The expression on his face told the whole story. He decided to twist the knife a bit more. "In fact, Senator Rose has scheduled hearings on the matter. I have tried to clean up your mess but they still want you to appear."

"When do the hearings start?"

"Oh, you will have plenty of time to prepare," Rinaldi said sarcastically. "The hearings begin in two weeks."

Ben's tanned and relaxed manner had turned south. In just a few short minutes, stress had overtaken him. *That didn't take much effort at all.* Rinaldi considered the lack of challenge somewhat disappointing.

"There is also the matter of this crazy preacher who has made it his business to embarrass us at every new center we open. I have arranged a face-to-face meeting with this individual."

"What are you hoping to achieve by such a meeting?"

"Learning what it will take to silence him."

"What makes you think he can be bought?"

"Everyone has a price."

"Not this guy. Before you got here, I had our lawyers reach out to him for the same reason. He's not going away for any amount of money."

"Perhaps, perhaps not. Money is only one recourse."

Rinaldi rolled out the last comment for effect. He noticed the surprise come across Ben's face and decided to continue.

"You see, Ben, in America, people always worry about what is politically correct. This holds true in business dealings. In Europe, when you are head of a multinational billion-dollar pharmaceutical behemoth, the CEO cannot afford to bear such burdens."

He noted Ben's expression transform from surprise to concern, maybe even panic. He applauded his own judgment in opening the meeting with these "cleanup" items from Abraham's inept leadership period. Once the goody two-shoes before him was sufficiently outraged, he would reveal his true purpose.

"What exactly are you implying?"

"I imply nothing!" he remarked with a slightly raised voice, done so for added emphasis. "I only mean to communicate that I, as CEO, will do whatever it takes to resolve the problem."

Abraham was now in a place where comfort with the conversation was no longer possible. Rinaldi pressed for further advantage as he watched Drago, across the room, observing Ben with a suspicious eye. "Let us continue on to more important matters. You may have heard that I plan to expand our service offering to something far more magnanimous."

"If you are referring to some harebrained scheme to offer a permanent regeneration service where awakened clients leave the premises, I think the idea is insane."

Rinaldi smiled back at him. The conversation was moving along according to plan. He stood up and walked around the desk to get closer to Ben. He wanted his adversary to see every pore in his face for the crescendo of the conversation.

"Yes, this is the same type of feedback I received at SPI when I began discussing the idea for BV3000. All of the experts said it couldn't be done. Everyone had their reasons why the idea would not work, why the market wouldn't support it, how the FDA would never approve it. Let me tell you this: a CEO must be a bold visionary and reach beyond the limits of what 'is' to the world of 'what could be.' You, of all people, I thought would understand this."

"What I understand is that stretching the limits of what is possible is great but it takes time. We do not have the scientific data that gets us anywhere close to making your plan a reality. As the head of R&D, I am telling you that this 'vision' of yours will take years and years to explore."

It was time to drop the bomb. Rinaldi looked down on Ben and delivered the blow.

"Are you not living proof to the contrary?"

He could see he had Abraham on the ropes. Ben's expression turned to anger.

"What in hell are you talking about?" he almost shouted.

"You seem surprised!" Were you not aware that Dr. Weiskopf and Dr. Larkin used an experimental Liferay to bring you back from the dead after you perished from an aneurysm?"

Ben was blown away. Rinaldi knew he had played his hand to perfection.

"I don't know what you are talking about."

"Oh, but I think you do. You and Dr. Weiskopf were working late in the Lab in pursuit of the very same experimental Liferay that saved your life that evening. Apparently, you were under the false impression that you had just blacked out."

"Wait, how could you possibly know that?" Ben looked confused but continued. "Experimental Liferay? Yes, it is true that we were discussing such a thing as a concept but there was no prototype. There still isn't."

"I believe your so-called friends are withholding the truth from you. The reality is that you died nearly two years ago, that very same night in the Lab, and you were brought back by an advanced prototype. The technology exists to now offer this commercially. I am looking at the proof."

"This is unbelievable. How did you come by this information?"

Rinaldi was in the zone, thanking himself for the foresight to procure the omniscient flash drive with the contents of Weiskopf's private journal. He was ready for the coup de grâce—the move that would set up his plan for revenge on Abraham and his blowhard mentor, Albert Harmon.

"How I came by this information is of little importance. The fact is that I am telling you the truth and I have no problem telling the world that Dr. Benjamin Abraham is a living, breathing abnormality, a one-of-a-kind, how would you say it? Ah yes—freak of nature."

Rinaldi could see that he had stunned his opponent. Like a boxer, he had punched Abraham into submission. The dazed look upon Ben's face told the whole story.

"You wouldn't dare. What do you gain by such an action?"

Rinaldi felt the inner glow from the warmth of success. He delivered his best attempt at a smile and simply said, "Because, my good man, it is what I do."

Abraham had no reply. He was defeated.

"And so, here is what I expect. From this day forward, you will not oppose any action I take in this company. You will provide your faithful and undying support for everything I say and do. If you fail to comply, I shall be forced to expose you, ruining your scientific credibility and placing you in a position of controversy in the media and with people such as your friend, the good Reverend Cashman. He, I am sure, would feast on you like a buzzard on fresh roadkill."

"That's why you are meeting with Cashman?"

"We will discuss anything that works to my advantage . . . even the downfall of the mighty Ben Abraham."

"You are out of your mind. I will take this up with the board."

Rinaldi anticipated this. He lifted his cane in the air and waved it around for effect.

"As you wish. The board will not take kindly to the deception from your inner circle colleagues. Nor will they appreciate your withholding knowledge of the secretive, advanced research by you and Weiskopf that will support my permanent regeneration idea. Just how do you think each board member will feel when they have to waste time testifying, under subpoena, in front of Senator Rose and his committee of bulldogs? You forget, we are a publicly traded company. Everything must be driven by the pursuit of the almighty dollar. Your withholding of key research will convince the board that you, Dr. Larkin, and Dr. Weiskopf should all be fired, to leave in disgrace from the company you founded."

"You might think you can control me, but you can't," Ben yelled as he stood up to leave.

Rinaldi had won.

"Control you? Oh no, Dr. Abraham, I don't seek to control you. I intend to own you."

CHAPTER 36

Ben couldn't recall ever feeling this angry in his life. He had been betrayed by two members of his team, one of whom he had mistakenly thought he was in love with. He would deal with them one at a time. Outside Rinaldi's office, he pulled out his phone and sent Rachel a text, all in caps, to announce his anger: *WHERE ARE YOU?*

He stared at the phone until he saw the blinking ellipsis indicating a reply was on its way.

In my office catching up on email. Is everything okay?

Ben didn't reply. Like a tornado, he barreled through the hallway, ignoring all in his path. He didn't lose his cool often but when he did, he returned to the familiar words from his grandfather: *Courage, strength, patience, wisdom. One of these four concepts will get you through any situation*, the old man had told the young boy.

Intellectually, Ben knew he should retreat and let a cooler head prevail. Maybe he should go for a drive, head to Maplebrook, and talk to Albert. No, the unprecedented anger had trumped the age old advice from his grandfather and his sense of what was right.

He entered Rachel's office and loudly slammed the door behind him. He had her attention and that's exactly what he wanted. He was pissed and he was hurt. In Ben's blinding rage, his only objective was to give Rachel some of the same in return.

As he looked down at Rachel, sitting behind her desk, her inquisitive look made him question what he was about to do. For just the briefest of moments, his anger receded when he took in the look of concern in those beautiful emerald eyes.

With an empathic tone, she asked, "I've never seen you like this. What's wrong?"

The calm before the storm had passed. The fury once again consumed him and unleashed itself with the force of a thunderbolt attacking an innocent tree along a country road.

"What's wrong? What's wrong? Are you seriously asking me what's wrong?" he screamed hysterically.

"Ben, you need to calm down and tell me what is upsetting you."

"How could you?" was all he could intelligently spout.

"How could I what?"

"Don't play innocent with me. You and Ari have been living a lie for nearly two years. Late night research with Ari has been a fraud. All that time working to develop a prototype that he already had . . . and then to use it on me! And not tell me about it?"

Ben took note of the shocked look on her face. It confirmed what he already knew. That bastard, Rinaldi, had been telling the truth.

"Try to understand," she said, with tears beginning to run. "If Ari hadn't acted when he did, you would be dead."

His eyes grew wide and he leaned down to get closer. When his face was close enough for her to feel his breath, he said, "Maybe I would prefer to be dead. Maybe," he continued, "it would have been helpful to know the truth from day one, especially as I have been trying to resolve the ongoing seizure problem. Now I know why I am having them!"

"I wanted to tell you from day one."

"So why didn't you? I thought we had something, something really special. Do you have any idea how much it hurts to discover that the woman I thought I loved and one of my closest friends have betrayed me?

To make matters worse, I have to hear all about it two years after the fact from my pal Anstrov Rinaldi."

"Rinaldi? How does he know any of this? Only Ari and I know."

"Apparently not," quipped Ben sarcastically, "and to top off all this great news, Rinaldi is trying to blackmail me with undying support for his crazy-ass schemes. If I don't cooperate, he claims he will ruin my scientific credibility."

"Can't Albert stop him? He is the board chair."

Without elaborating, he replied. "Rinaldi has that covered."

"Ben, I love you. I would give up my own life for yours if it would take the pain away. Ari wanted me to keep this from you and I reluctantly agreed."

"What on earth was the point of hiding it from me?"

"He said you would blow up and disown both of us forever. He said you would want to solve the seizure problem on your own. I begged and pleaded with him."

Ben looked back at her with a cold stare and for the first time in the turbulent conversation, he replied calmly, "Well, maybe Ari knows me better than *you* do."

"What are you going to do next?" she asked through running mascara.

"I'm done," he yelled.

"Done? Done with what?"

"With Hiatus Centers, with Anstrov Rinaldi, with Ari, and with you!"

He stormed out, slamming the door as he thundered back down the hallway.

CHAPTER 37

Rinaldi adjusted his dark glasses and placed the phone back on its base. The chief of staff for Senator Rose had not yet heard from Ben. The senator's office had expected Ben to confirm his appearance at the upcoming hearings. Rose was growing uncomfortable with what he believed were stall tactics from Hiatus Centers. Rinaldi had assured the senator's office that Ben would appear as scheduled and that there really were no problems. He jotted a note to himself to remind Ben of their new "arrangement" and how he did not like to be let down.

When he looked up from his desk, he found his next appointment before him.

"Good morning," he said with a genuine smile and a gesture of warmth. Although this was rare for him, he admitted to himself he had always found a certain allure in Asian women. Tomi Oka's Japanese heritage made her burst with sex appeal. He refocused his mind to the work at hand. Why waste thoughts on the improbable? He knew she would never have him. What woman would? Like other people, Tomi Oka was simply there to be used.

"Good morning, Dr. Rinaldi," she replied. He recognized that Oka's voice belied her confidence.

Despite his attempt at self-discipline, he took note of her appearance. He was captivated by her dark eyes. Her hair was down and free and swept gently across her forehead, making her look even sexier than normal. She wore a black-and-white dress, somewhat conservative but cut low enough to reveal just a hint of cleavage. The rich red lipstick she wore accentuated her full lips.

Focus! He commanded of himself.

"I trust you are enjoying the Lexus?" he asked.

"Yes, it is the nicest car I have ever had."

"Well, I am glad that I could help procure something that makes you happy."

Despite his real purpose, he genuinely did want to give her everything. The truth, he knew, was that this was merely business to be transacted.

"The pressure of being debt free must be liberating," he offered.

She looked blatantly uncomfortable now as she replied, "I appreciate your help."

Rinaldi came from around the desk. He motioned for Tomi to join him on the leather couch perpendicular to the wall nearest Drago's cage.

"Perhaps we will be more comfortable over here."

She appeared uneasy at the suggestion but moved anyway. He had planned this scene hours earlier. They sat at opposite ends of the couch. Rinaldi angled his body toward her by shifting his left leg across the middle cushion. The combination of sitting on a couch with him and the close proximity to Drago would be enough to eviscerate any sense of strength she might choose to muster. For further effect, he stretched his left arm across the top of the couch. His hand was only a few inches shy of her right shoulder.

"I must tell you, your assistance to date has been extraordinarily helpful to me," he said.

"I take it you received the flash drive I placed in the mailbox by the airport?"

"Most certainly, my dear. The contents were filled with informational riches. Dr. Weiskopf's journal and its immense detail was indeed a treasure to behold."

"I'm glad it was helpful. I did want to tell you, Dr. Rinaldi, that I have been doing a lot of thinking. I appreciate all you have done for me but I would like to discontinue the arrangement we have had. It just doesn't feel right. I feel like I am spying on my friends."

Rinaldi expected this. Sooner or later, they all start to have doubts.

"You have nothing to feel guilty about. At corporations much larger than Hiatus Centers, this is how business gets done. You are helping the CEO achieve his business objectives, nothing more, nothing less."

"That's all well and good," she replied "but why not just go to my colleagues at the Lab and simply ask for the information you want?"

Rinaldi paused to consider his reply. He had trusted that idiot Ivanov to do just that. They shut him out. Then he asked Ivanov to get the information covertly but he was too stupid to pull that off. Like always, Rinaldi needed to take matters into his own hands.

"I wish it were that easy. Senior people often shun the new CEO. Overcoming their reticence and building trust can take months or years. We are a publicly traded corporation looking for rapid growth. You are helping me to accelerate the timetable."

"I understand but if it's all the same to you, I'd like to beg off and just concentrate on my own research."

Rinaldi bristled. He had expected her to cave easily. Besides, he wanted to keep the arrangement going just so he had an excuse to be close to her.

"Your feelings are understandable. I will have another little "job" soon. There may be a six-figure payout for you."

He watched as her eyebrows arched in contemplation. She inhaled deeply and replied, "Thank you but no. I just want out."

Rinaldi was losing the battle. He would need to switch tactics. Charm had failed. He always got his way with intimidation.

"Perhaps you would prefer to be arrested on charges of embezzlement?"

"Embezzlement? I haven't stolen anything," she proclaimed. "It's absurd."

"Absurd? I hardly think $150,000 missing from the company's account is a matter to be taken lightly."

"I don't follow."

"Let me see if I can help you. The money wired to your account for the "bonus" extinguishing your mounting credit card debt was never processed through payroll, yet it came from Hiatus Centers' operating account. Officially, we have no idea where this money went or why. No corporate officer officially signed off on the transfer. If you cooperate, I can make sure this accounting anomaly is cleared right up."

When every feature on her face sank like a stone, he silently reveled in another victory.

CHAPTER 38

"Oh my God, Ari. Ben knows. He knows and I think he's headed to see you."

Rachel was relieved that she had been able to reach Ari as soon as Ben stormed out of her office. As was her trademark, she held up well in times of crisis. While she had the presence of mind to call Ari immediately, she was completely freaked out at Ben's behavior. She tried but could not recall a time where he had been so angry...and at her! Ari was right. Rachel now feared that Ben would disown them both forever and retreat to a remote corner of the world to work on resolving his seizures.

"Slow down; get a grip. Tell me what happened," replied Ari.

Rachel took a deep breath and stood up. She paced around her office with the cell phone pressed to her ear. Somehow, the telling of the tale was easier to relay while she was moving around. When she finished, Ari failed to answer.

"Hello? Ari? Are you still there?"

"Yeah, I heard you. I'm just blown away by the whole damn thing. You think he's on his way over here?"

"He didn't say that but that's what I would do if I were him. You have about forty minutes to brace yourself, or get lost, whichever you prefer."

"I frankly don't know what I will do if Ben storms in here. I don't care much for angry confrontations, especially with close friends. I may just opt for contrition."

"It may be too late for contrition."

"Maybe, but my instinct tells me to throw myself at the mercy of the court. I will offer to help him in any way I can, his acceptance of which is a major long shot."

"Getting back in Ben's good graces feels like a long shot for both of us right now."

She plopped into her desk chair with a thud. The thought of losing Ben forever caused her muscles to collapse into jelly. She began contemplating what, if anything, she could do to regain Ben's trust. How could she possibly repair the damage she had helped cause? Rachel had no idea but she surmised she would think of little else until the solution arrived.

Rachel felt like Ari had dragged her into a web of deceit and lies in which she remained caught. She reverted to an idea from their previous conversation and relayed it to Ari.

"I'm going to call Albert. There's no reason not to at this point. If Rinaldi is blackmailing Ben, then Albert has to get involved. He's got to have Ben's back."

"Want me to join the call?"

She considered his offer but decided it best to speak with Albert alone. With worry beginning to consume her, she didn't want Ari's logical mind interfering with her need to express emotion in front of Albert. Plus, she wanted to be able to speak frankly with Albert about her relationship with Ben. These were details she was ill prepared to share with Ari.

CHAPTER 39

As he navigated the winding roads leading up to The Harmon School, Ben wondered if his efforts to exorcise the lifelong guilt over his grandfather's illness had gotten out of control. Had he properly processed these feelings as a boy, there wouldn't be a Liferay or a Hiatus Centers—or, for that matter, an Anstrov Rinaldi. He was kicking himself for screwing up his own life and the lives of so many he held dear.

Albert would understand. He was Ben's rock; the one person to whom he could spout anything. Albert had always helped him return to reason. Today, he needed that rock more than any other time he could recall.

When Ben arrived at Albert's office, he found his mentor behind the desk. Ben noticed immediately that Albert didn't look right. His eyes were glassy and his remaining hair askew. It was the end of the school day. The administrative end of the building was quiet. Ben chalked it off as the old man just being tired and well, old. He plowed forward with the purpose of his unexpected visit.

"You won't believe what Rinaldi is up to," Ben proclaimed.

Albert looked up but didn't reply. Ben decided to keep going. He paced back and forth in front of Albert's desk until he had relayed the entire sordid tale.

"You were right, Albert, about the Law of Unintended Consequences. So much has happened that I never could have anticipated. And now this . . ."

Ben was still supercharged from the meeting with Rinaldi. With no real response forthcoming from his friend and mentor, he assumed Albert was being the good listener. So he continued.

"I want to perfect the advanced Liferay and when it's ready, to deploy it for its intended purpose. Rinaldi doesn't seem interested in the technology. He has something else up his sleeve; I just don't know what that is."

Albert remained still, almost catatonic. He said nothing.

"I just can't believe this guy left the prominent CEO position with SPI to come here. That's one of the reasons I wanted to speak with you. When you ran the interviews with him, did he say anything that you would consider odd? You know, some offhand comment that might have seemed out of place at the time but you couldn't quite figure out why?"

Albert didn't flinch. He just stared straight ahead, looking right through Ben.

"Albert, what's wrong with you? Answer me! I need your help here." Ben was exasperated.

Ben saw him there but the old man did not emerge from the distant land to which his mind had traveled.

"Goddammit, Albert, snap out of it! This bastard is trying to get me for some reason and I don't know why."

Without a response, Ben leaned over the old man and smelled the alcohol on his breath. Then he saw the small, metal flask in the partially open desk drawer. *Was Albert drunk?* Ben had never seen him take a sip in all the years he had known him. *What the hell was going on?*

Ben gently shook Albert by the shoulders and placed an open hand firmly against his cheek, trying to gain his attention without hurting him. Finally, Albert looked at him with a small measure of response. A tear was beginning to form in one eye. Ben had never seen Albert cry. Ben had never seen Albert as anything but a man with the strongest of resolve. Albert lifted a set of documents from the surface of his desk and shoveled them toward Ben. Ben picked up the paper and began to read.

The documents were from a lawyer in Virginia. The lawyer was representing someone named Jeffery Borland. Borland was claiming that while he was a student at The Harmon School twenty years earlier, he had been sexually abused by the school's founder and provost, Albert Harmon. The letter threatened a suit seeking unspecified damages. When Ben finished reading and looked up, Albert began to speak with a shaken voice gripped with fear and grief.

"You have to believe me. I would never do anything like this."

Ben felt horrible for Albert but also because the guilt he entered with was now compounded. How could he not see his friend in such obvious pain? How could he blather on and on about his own misfortune when the man he considered his second father was dying inside? *What kind of person am I?*

"Don't," he told Albert. "You don't need to provide me with any sort of affirmation. I know this isn't you. The real question is why come forth with this type of allegation now?"

"Until thirty minutes ago, I couldn't answer that. The papers arrived today via courier. I didn't open them until an hour ago. Almost as soon as I finished reading, my phone rang. It was Rinaldi."

"Did he have something to do with this?"

"It's all him. He told me you were likely on your way to see me to help displace him as CEO of Hiatus Centers. He told me that more students like Jeffrey Borland would be coming out of the woodwork if I helped you or in any way disrupted his plans. He told me if I 'behaved,' the Borland claim would quietly disappear."

"This guy is sick. We need to figure out what his motivation is."

Ben could tell that Albert had stopped listening. He was receding back into the malaise.

"If a story like this gets out, even though it's not true, it would ruin this school forever."

Ben's heart was aching for the malady facing Albert. He couldn't help but assume the guilt for this. He didn't understand Rinaldi's motivation for any of his actions but he couldn't shake the feeling that somehow this was all his fault.

"Stay with me. I need to ask you a few questions so we can understand what's happening here. Okay?"

Albert nodded slowly in the affirmative.

"Do you remember this Borland guy?"

"I've been wracking my brain. I have a distant recollection of him as a quiet kid, average student, nothing spectacular in terms of scientific accomplishment during his time here. After he finished college, I heard he went to work for the Centers for Disease Control in Atlanta but then I lost track of him."

Ben had the picture. Rinaldi was a snake. He found a former student with questionable character and offered him a truckload of cash to go along with the scheme.

"Albert, you are in no condition to drive. I'm going to take you home. Promise me you will stop worrying. With your help, I'll figure all this out and get both of us free from Rinaldi's grasp."

"You don't understand. This school is all I have. I've poured my heart and soul into this place." He paused for a moment and looked up at Ben in his first moment of clarity and said firmly, "I can't help you this time."

Ben was stunned. He never envisioned those words emanating from Albert's mouth. Just then, his cell phone began to vibrate. It was Ari. *Rachel must have called him.*

He would deal with Ari later. His first priority was getting that sonofabitch Rinaldi out of his company and out of his life.

CHAPTER 40

With the sword of Damocles wavering perilously above his aching head, Ben prayed it was just the aftermath of tension and not the onset of another seizure. He had no time for that. Four hours had passed since his macabre meeting with Albert. He had to keep moving forward. Recalling Gramps' four tenets for conflict resolution, he knew he would need to call upon them all to get through the biggest challenge of his life.

Courage to defeat a formidable foe, strength to lead the effort, wisdom to know what to do, and patience to see it all through. He summoned a deep breath and, using the disposable prepaid TracPhone he purchased that afternoon from the local Walmart, dialed Ari's cell phone number.

"Ben, thank goodness you called me back. Before you start, let me get a few things out."

"There will be time for all that later. We have bigger problems right now."

Ben knew how to compartmentalize emotion. He had been doing it all his life, not always to his advantage. He quickly recalled how this ability haunted him when Gramps got sick, during the Bresling debacle, and even in the aftermath of his one great night with Rachel in Baltimore. He hoped that the ability to suppress emotion would serve him well, given the present set of difficulties. Ari obviously felt guilty for what he did. *Good,* thought Ben. *Let that guilt work in my favor right now.* Ben needed the brilliance of Ari's mind to help take down Rinaldi. Although Rachel wasn't his favorite person at the moment, she, too, would have a role to play.

First things first. Ben had to learn why Rinaldi was doing what he was doing and also how much he knew about their work and their lives. *Not that it really matters*, he thought. Just like he did with Albert, Rinaldi simply "manufactured" skeletons and attributed them to his prey. It was frightening how someone could ruin another person. Apparently all you needed was a lot of money and a mind geared toward evil. Wary of Ari's phone being bugged, Ben instructed Ari to meet him in thirty minutes on a park bench along the Ma and Pa Trail that wound through the wooded areas of Maplebrook and Bel Air.

When Ari arrived, Ben was already waiting impatiently, pacing nervously back and forth. To passersby, he probably stood out. This was exactly the opposite of what he wanted. Pacing, however, was the only outlet he had for the cache of frenetic energy. Joggers and dog walkers might call him out if he didn't get his nerves under control. Then he spotted Ari. Without so much as a friendly greeting, he blurted out, "Tell me how Rinaldi knew about my death and the experimental Liferay."

"I wish I could tell you. This is tearing me apart. The only people that knew were me and Rachel. I persuaded her to keep the secret. I was worried how you would react. If you have to hate someone, hate me, not Rachel. It was all my fault."

"We can deal with all that later. Rinaldi has launched some sort of blackmail scheme against Albert and me. I need your help in figuring out his motive."

"Sure, anything. Just name it."

"For now, I want you to get ahold of the team and move the morning meeting tomorrow to the large gazebo by the pond at Friends Park. Remember, your phone might be compromised so I need you to swing by Rachel's and Tomi's homes and speak to them personally but not in their apartments. Do it outside. I will go see Harrison."

"Okay, but do you mind me asking why?"

"I can't be sure but I wouldn't put it past Rinaldi to have also bugged the Lab. I still don't know how he knows what he knows. Until then, I am taking extra precautions." Ben handed him a prepaid TracPhone. "I also have prepaid TracPhones for Rachel, Tomi, and Harrison."

"Good point. I will tell everyone to disable the location service on their company-issued cell phone. That way, he can't track our movements."

"Smart thinking. Given that we all have company cell phones, Rinaldi could easily issue orders to have our phones and email accounts monitored. Let's advise the team to stick to face-to-face communication in secure locations for the time being. If that isn't feasible, everyone can use the TracPhones. As a precaution, I will have a security firm I know sweep our homes, vehicles, and the Lab."

"Best to keep that expense off the books and have the security firm come when Ivanov isn't there."

"I'll have them send the bill to me personally and we can schedule the Lab sweep for after hours. Oh, by the way, don't tell Tomi or Rachel anything. Just let them know the location has changed for the morning meeting and if they ask why, say I have something delicate to discuss with them."

"Got it."

Ben bid Ari adieu and began to relax. He hated the paranoid precautions but viewed them as a necessary evil. Until the sweeps were performed, meeting outdoors or in public places seemed prudent. Nearby Friends Park was fifteen minutes from Maplebrook. Once the team was assembled, he would lay out the details of what he knew. He needed their help. He didn't have enough hardcore evidence to involve the authorities. If he called the police, they would probably file a report and that would be the end of it. Maybe they would interview Rinaldi. The bastard would charm his way out of trouble. Ben never resented anyone the way he did Anstrov Rinaldi. Together, his team would figure out Rinaldi's motive and what they could do about it.

He walked back to the Honda. Time to pay a quick visit to Harrison, who would press him for the meeting's true purpose and the strange venue, but Ben would hold steady. He knew it would piss off his longtime friend but, for now, it was more important to lay the whole mess out to the group all at once.

CHAPTER 41

When Ari had mysteriously appeared at her front door and said that the morning meeting had been moved from the Lab to Friends Park, Rachel didn't know what to think. Ari wouldn't provide a reason for the strange move and it made Rachel curious. If things were normal with Ben, she could just call him and ask why. That wasn't an option. Rachel hated it when stuff like this happened. It was like when someone called and said they needed to speak to you about something really important but they couldn't do it till later. She correctly predicted a night's sleep lost. Worry and wonder consumed her mind for the better part of the evening hours.

Rachel entered Friends Park and passed the reticent pond and accompanying gazebo where they would be meeting. A flock of Canadian geese surrounded the pond and entrance to the boarded walkway that led to their meeting spot. The parking lot was on the road just beyond the path situated near the ball fields where kids regularly played baseball, softball, field hockey, soccer, and lacrosse. This early in the morning, with school in session, there was only one other car in the parking lot, a spit-shined red Lexus. Maybe Tomi knew something about today's bizarre shift in venue.

Rachel parked her car and walked down the old path, which consisted of dirt, pebbles, protruding tree roots, and disgorged feathers from the geese and Mallard ducks that frequented the pond. As she approached the gazebo, she saw Tomi sitting alone on the built-in wooden bench that faced the water. Tomi saw her and stood up for a welcoming embrace. It felt mechanical. Rachel stepped back and noticed that Tomi had barely put on makeup, her hair was in weekend mode and her face bore stress. *She knows*, thought Rachel. The problems with Ben aside, if Ari, her co-conspirator knew, and Tomi knew, why wasn't she told the subject of this meeting? It couldn't be good. *Tomi looks like someone just shot her dog.*

"So what's up with the sudden change in venue? Is the Dugout being painted or something?"

Rachel figured she would make light of it. Maybe that would get Tomi to relax and tell her what was going on.

"No clue. Ari just said we were meeting here instead of the Lab and that Ben had something to tell us."

Damn. Same innocuous crap Ari had given her. Maybe Tomi didn't know. But something was up with her. She looked too uptight. Rachel decided not to press. Being friends with Tomi, Rachel knew she couldn't hold the problem in for long. Rachel was sure the issue would spill itself before they left the park. She would simply let it play out naturally.

They sat in the quiet of the morning and, for a few minutes, just watched the pond in its abundant beauty. Small sunfish and guppies danced about the surface while the morning sun glistened across the water. The ducks were enjoying an early swim and geese milled about the pond's edges, looking for the remains of the ripped bread commonly offered by neighboring kids and their parents. In the distance, the serenity of the morning was disturbed by a screech. When she first arrived in Maryland, Rachel had heard the unmistakable sound of the Eastern Barn Owl and learned that they never hoot, just shriek. It was eerie until you knew what it was.

Her mind came back to reality when Ari's beat up old Jeep rolled in and right behind him, Harrison's black Range Rover. Harrison was in his usual morning fog and had to slam on his brakes to avoid running over an errant duck. *At least he's on time*, thought Rachel.

Once they were situated on the wooden benches affixed to the inside walls of the large gazebo, Rachel chuckled at how Ari started right in on Harrison.

"Jeeezus, Bock, it's not duck hunting season, you know."

Harrison just smiled and calmly replied, "That was a duck? Aw, man, I thought that little critter was you! I was kind of sorry I missed."

Rachel intervened. She was hoping to quiz the group before Ben arrived. Her inquisitive mind had gotten the best of her. Before she could get the first words out, she heard a car backfiring and she knew Ben was on his way into the park. She would just have to be patient for a few more minutes.

She watched Ben make his way down from the parking lot. He wore faded jeans and an untucked, unbuttoned sport shirt with a gray T-shirt bearing the logo of the Los Angeles Dodgers. His jumbo Wawa coffee was ever present. What really struck Rachel, however, was that Ben had a good week's beard growth. She knew that was a sign he was deep inside a problem—in the zone, as he liked to say. If she had to bet, she was willing to wager that today's meeting had something to do with his seizures. Maybe he was going to ask the team for help. But if that were true, why move the meeting offsite?

Ben stepped into the gazebo and thanked everyone for acquiescing to the unusual venue on short notice.

"This team has been together a long time. We've accomplished more than I could have ever imagined. To me, you guys are more family than colleagues . . ."

Oh shit, thought Rachel. *It sounds like he's checking out. Ari was right. He's going to disappear and try to resolve his medical problem on his own.* Rachel had been holding onto the hope that this meeting would somehow be the catalyst to help restore Ben's trust in her.

"But now I need you like I never have before. Anstrov Rinaldi has targeted both me and Albert, for reasons still unknown, and is trying to ruin both of us."

Rachel hung on every word. Despite all she and Ben had been through recently, how could he not tell her this sooner? Rachel was still wrestling with the fact that, where Ben's personal life was concerned, she was squarely on the outside looking in. She listened as Ben recalled the underpinnings of the problem. In a most gracious manner, he explained how he had died and that she and Ari had brought him back to life with the experimental Liferay and how, for his benefit, they had kept the secret from him. At first, she was mortified when he dove into that night but once she heard of Rinaldi's blackmail attempt, she understood that he needed to disclose the heart of the issue.

As she was listening, she conducted a visual poll of the team to gauge their reactions. Ari seemed pleased that Ben had chosen to diplomatically frame his actions. She concluded that Ben could have addressed this any way he wanted and Ari would have been okay. He was so afraid of Ben exiling him from the team. Knowing Ari, just being asked by Ben to help with the problem had to be a huge relief. She wished Ben had asked her for help. Harrison, on the other hand, looked a little peeved. Rachel theorized that Harrison, as the one who was closest to Ben, was understandably upset he was hearing in a group setting how his longtime friend had died and maybe even that the experimental Liferay did not require his scientific contribution. Rachel's eyes shifted to Tomi. She still appeared stressed, perhaps even more than when the meeting began.

Ben finished up by recapping Rinaldi's blackmail of Albert with a false molestation claim and his suspicion that the Lab, their homes, phones, and email accounts may all be at risk insofar as privacy is concerned.

After hearing the whole of what Ben had to say, Rachel was blown away. She knew Rinaldi was a dick but she never saw this coming. Ben wanted to start working on the motive and figuring out how Rinaldi knew what he knew. Only then, he had said, can they figure out what to do about any of this.

In developing the immediate first steps, Ben informed the team that he had engaged a security firm to address the leaking of information. Ari and Harrison pledged to keep their eyes and ears open at the Lab. Now that they were aware of the situation, maybe some action or words from Ivanov could be viewed in a different prism. Tomi remained silent.

"You and Ari have known Albert a whole lot longer than any of us, and I hate to ask this, but is there any possible chance these allegations could be true?" asked Harrison.

Rachel watched as Ben's defensive mechanisms immediately kicked in like thrusters on a rocket.

"Not a chance," he replied sternly. "It's an easy thing to suggest because Albert is old and has been single his entire life. Therefore, one could argue, something must be wrong with him. It would be improbable for society to view him for what he is, a man who has simply dedicated his life to science and education. Rinaldi sees this and will exploit it to his advantage."

Rachel believed in Ben. Just as much, she believed in Albert. The story of Albert molesting a student was not comprehendible. Albert Harmon was so honest and honorable, he would probably feel guilty about jaywalking.

Ben told the team he wanted them to think about everything and that they would reconvene in the next day or so to assess where they were. He handed everyone other than Ari a TracPhone and gave instructions for contacting one another. After he adjourned the meeting, Rachel saw Tomi approach Ben.

"Can I speak to you privately before you go?" she asked him.

Rachel said her goodbyes and left the gazebo. She intentionally trailed behind Ari and Harrison. She wanted them to leave before her. She was determined to learn what was eating at Tomi. While spying was not in her nature, she wanted to know everything she could in her efforts to aid Ben. Once Ari and Harrison had driven away, she positioned herself behind a massive, aged oak tree just beyond the gazebo. Ben and

Tomi were seated with their backs to her. They were facing the water. She couldn't see their expressions but she could hear every word of their conversation.

Tomi was crying and struggling to get the words out. Ben put his arm around her in a gesture of comfort and tried to help her catch her breath. She was sobbing. Rachel could see her shoulders bouncing up and down as the emotional storm enveloped her slight frame.

"I've done something terrible," she told him.

"It's okay. Whatever it is, I'll help you. It can't be that bad," he replied.

Rachel wished she could get closer. She could still hear the conversation but it was challenging through Tomi's tears along with the nearby traffic from the main road and the sounds of a day coming to life. She hugged the old oak and continued to listen.

"I'm not sure you will want to once you hear."

"It doesn't matter. Just tell me and let me see how I can help."

Rachel wasn't sure the conversation was still audible. She was dying to know what Tomi had done. But for a moment or two, she heard nothing. She concluded that, in her emotional state, Tomi was just collecting strength to release the demons that now possessed her.

"I'm the leak," was all she said.

Rachel was flabbergasted. She could only imagine what Ben was feeling.

"You're the leak? How could you be the leak? I don't understand."

Ben's voice took on a troubled tone. Rachel sensed he was moving from sympathetic friend to one who just learned he had been royally screwed by a member of his inner circle. Heck, she was pissed on his behalf and they hadn't yet heard the details.

"I . . . I needed money," was all Tomi managed to stammer.

"Money? Money for what?"

"Debt. At least that's the way it started and then, the car and the promise of more money."

"Back up. You're not making any sense. Why were you in debt and who gave you the money?

"The money came from Rinaldi. I don't know how he knew but I had run up six figures of retail debt. I can't stop spending. Clothes, shoes, spa treatments, electronics. Things I don't really need but I am compelled to buy. It's some kind of sick obsession." Tomi paused. "He gave me the money to get me out of debt and then bought me the Lexus."

Rachel felt for Ben. This was unbelievable. The poor guy never seemed to be able to get out of the shit storm.

"Okay," he said. "Tell me exactly what it is you gave to Rinaldi."

"It all began before he even worked for the company. He had someone approach me with the knowledge of my debt and an offer to pay it off if only I would provide the name of the Swiss contractor we hired to make the Liferay. I didn't know at the time that it was Rinaldi. He told me that later. I wasn't thinking. At the time, it didn't seem like a big deal."

"And that's how the Schlemm's rods were being altered. Ari was right. Someone was doing it deliberately. Rinaldi was plotting against us even before he came here. But why?"

"I don't know. Before he got here, he contacted me, told me that he was my benefactor and he bought me the Lexus. I didn't worry much about it once I learned he was our incoming CEO."

"What did he want in exchange for the cash and the car?"

Rachel couldn't believe what she was hearing. She knew Tomi had a penchant for spending money but she never imagined she was capable of anything like this.

"I was required to copy Ari's private journal from his laptop to a flash drive and leave it in a retail post office box off Route 100."

"And that's how Rinaldi knew about the experimental Liferay and my death. But it doesn't explain why he is taking on such elaborate measures to get at me and Albert."

"Ben, I don't know anything else. I feel like a piece of crap. I know you will never forgive me. I went to Rinaldi and told him I wanted to end the arrangement. He told me if I did, he would have me arrested for embezzling money from the company."

"But you didn't steal money."

"I know but he had the transactions recorded in such a way that I could be framed. He won't let me stop."

Rachel wasn't sure what Ben would do next. If it had been left to her, a right cross on Tomi's jaw might be in order. Then perhaps shoving her unconscious body into the pond.

"Tomi, to say I am disappointed doesn't describe how I feel. This is unbelievable. Part of me wants to hold you here while I call the police and have you arrested for corporate espionage."

"You should. I deserve it. Call them now. Going to jail would be preferable to doing any more of Rinaldi's bidding and hurting the people I care most about."

Tomi was one of her closest friends but Rachel valued her integrity above all else. She stood behind the tree disgusted, silently rooting for Ben to call the cops.

"No. I won't do that. You are going to continue playing the part. See what he asks of you next and report directly to me. We will feed him information. Just not the information he is looking for."

Rachel had heard enough. She didn't want to be seen. Her spying mission was causing her to call her own integrity into question. Now her dilemma was, *Do I keep my knowledge of this from Ben, another secret that would harm their damaged relationship or do I let him know I know and offer to help?* Rachel wasn't sure how she could resolve that paradox. What she did know is that she would need to potentially figure out how to deal with Rinaldi on her own. It may be the only way for her win back Ben's love and trust.

CHAPTER 42

It was 3:00 a.m. The task at hand was important and so, despite the odd hour, Rinaldi would not risk being seen by late night scientists with no life. It's one thing to show dedication and get results; it's quite another to stay late because you wanted to avoid something or someone on the outside.

His driver, Baxter, had proven adept at complying with whatever he wished without asking questions. Rinaldi admired this. When the black Lincoln Town Car approached the final stretch of driveway nearest to the Lab's main door, Maxim Ivanov was waiting. Walnut cane in hand, Rinaldi got out of the car unattended and, with the gait of a man much older than he, hobbled toward the front lobby.

"Good evening, Dr. Rinaldi. Or should I say 'Good morning?'"

Rinaldi scoffed at Ivanov's banal attempt at humor. Although there was work to do, he was tired. "It is late, Maxim. You are sure the facility is empty?"

"Yes, quite sure. The security system verifies that no one is in the building at the present time. If someone were to enter while we are inside, an audible tone will sound throughout the building. This is the normal protocol for late night security. I have taken the liberty of temporarily disabling the nighttime security cameras."

"Abraham made getting into this place difficult, even for the staff.

Given the backwoods location and the lack of signage, I am sure the general public has no idea this facility even exists. And even if they did, they would not know what went on here."

The two men walked through the lobby and made their way toward the main theater used only by Ben's team. Ivanov placed his right eye to the retina scanner, enabling the two men to enter. Rinaldi had seen this space only once before. It was when he first joined the company. Rachel Larkin had taken him on a guided tour. It wasn't Colmar, which was a world class research facility, but they had invented the Liferay here and that was something. He held himself back from admiring the work of his enemy. That was a compliment he was unwilling to pay. Rather, he thought, it was better to hold onto the hatred that had built up for all these years. The "what could have beens" had driven him to near madness. His intellect, coupled with psychosis and subdued anger, had fueled his actions since that fateful day at The Harmon School, just a few minutes from where they now stood. How far he had come in his master plan to exact revenge on the men he held responsible for his physical disabilities. How much more could he have accomplished in this life were it not for Abraham and Harmon? Never mind—the truth would soon be known. The day of reckoning was just around the corner.

"Show me the Liferay that is currently employed in all HC locations," he ordered in an impassive manner.

Ivanov had learned nearly everything about this place. He wasn't the brightest bulb in the pack but at least he was loyal. Rinaldi always favored those who proved loyal.

"This way, Doctor."

The main theater, at ten thousand square feet, was cordoned off by portable walls to separate projects. The largest of these spaces was adorned with a sign, obviously made in a moment of restlessness, which read: LIFE JUICE . . . FRESHLY SQUEEZED. Rinaldi thought this a childish and unprofessional gesture. *Americans don't take anything seriously*, he thought.

When they passed under the crude, hand drawn sign, Rinaldi, again, was unimpressed. The Liferay itself was mounted on a metal platform atop an ordinary lab table. The platform stood only six inches high. That was enough to distinguish it from the plethora of parts, tools, and trash that surrounded the device on the countertop. Rinaldi looked on in disgust and wondered what kind of slobs could abuse a magnificent scientific environment like this.

"You have not yet told me why we are here at this late hour," said Ivanov.

This brought Rinaldi back into the moment. Even at 3:00 a.m., he had retained his innate ability for laser-focused precision. It was the secret to his success. Rinaldi knew how to remain disciplined in the face of a task, no matter how daunting it may be. Tonight would be no different.

"Dr. Abraham is about to deploy new technology enabling all awakened clients to remain so for three days. They will also be permitted to leave the grounds while they are awakened. He just doesn't know it yet."

Rinaldi watched for Ivanov's reaction. He had no mind for deviousness. His expression was almost devoid of comprehension. His assessment was validated when Ivanov stated, "But Dr. Rinaldi, I do not understand."

"You see, Maxim, it is my intention to bring this company to its knees by having the awakened across the country drop dead in the streets. With altered Liferay settings, bodies will decay and rot instantaneously. HC staff and client families will just 'think' their loved ones will be alive for more than twenty-four hours. Disease will spread throughout the United States. Lawsuits and regulatory hammers will come thundering down. There will be public outrage. It will ruin Abraham."

The shock on Ivanov's face was evident. Rinaldi began to worry that perhaps he had erred in taking Ivanov into his confidence.

"Buh . . . buh . . . but your plan . . . you will be killing all these people."

Rinaldi delivered a poetic laugh and said, "No, no, no, my friend. You forget, these people are already dead. Now show me the Liferay device settings. I need to completely understand how they are set and how they might be altered."

They began to work. Rinaldi asked many questions and took notes. The information Oka had supplied via Weiskopf's journal had made the comprehension a lot easier. Hours of advanced study had provided an in-depth understanding of femtosecond lasers, the related physics and associated chemistry, and biology of the complex equation making the Liferay a success. Tonight was about nothing more than comparing his book knowledge to the physical device. No detail would be left to chance.

After nearly ninety minutes of study, he was satisfied. He knew that the first scientists often arrived at 5:00 a.m. The building's security system had not alerted them to another entrant. He did not wish to push his luck by staying much longer. It would be difficult to explain to an arriving scientist why the CEO was in the company's main research facility in the middle of the night. He theorized that if someone had shown up, he would have had to kill them and worry with the details later. That didn't fit his M.O. He had loosely formatted a plan where if he had been forced to kill an employee, he could blame it on Ivanov somehow. Loyalty is valued. It enabled someone like Ivanov to make sacrifices he had no idea he was prepared to make.

As they were navigating their way down the long main corridor, Ivanov reverted back to the sniveling cowardice he had regularly displayed in their Colmar days.

"What is it, Maxim?"

"I am not sure of your plan. I don't understand why you would go to such lengths to destroy Dr. Abraham. Are you not worried about what happens if you get caught?"

Rinaldi breathed a deep sigh. "Let's just say that I am settling an old score. Once the plan goes into effect, I shall resign as the CEO, stating

I can no longer be associated with Abraham's incompetence. The board will pay me millions in a mutually agreed upon severance agreement and you and I shall depart Maryland with reputations intact. I will make sure you are handsomely rewarded for your faithful service to my cause. You will never have to work again. Can you not imagine yourself lounging in a quiet beach villa in a remote part of the world?"

Ivanov still seemed distraught. Hopefully, he would come around. As Rinaldi settled into the back of the Lincoln and Baxter was closing the door, he thought that he might need to dispose of Ivanov sooner versus later.

CHAPTER 43

The security firm he had hired found no evidence of electronic surveillance. Ben was flabbergasted. After hearing Tomi's confession, he was sure they would discover something. One of their homes, cars, phones or offices ... something. Even the Lab checked out. He wasn't sure how to process it. It was now clear that Rinaldi had some sort of vendetta against him and Albert. It was also obvious that he knew things beyond the information he duped Tomi for. So if there were no bugs ... was Rinaldi having him followed? He hadn't noticed anything suspicious but then again, he hadn't been looking.

Ben wondered whether he was coming apart. His world was crashing. At one point, life came so easy. Now, he felt like he was under constant siege. Each time he was certain he had his arms around a problem, another would bubble up and then one he thought was solved would blow up again. In the center of everything was Anstrov Rinaldi. Ben hadn't yet determined why or how but he knew now that Rinaldi was behind almost every one of his current problems. If he wasn't the cause, he was exacerbating the issue.

Front and center was Senator Rose and the upcoming hearings on Capitol Hill. The hearings were next week. Ben had been forced to spend considerable time with the company's lawyers to prepare. Rinaldi caused that issue by orchestrating the defects in the Swiss made Liferays and since then, he had stoked the fire. The fact that the altered Schlemm's rods had victimized a senator's daughter had just been a bonus for Rinaldi. Ben had assumed that after he stepped down as CEO, Rinaldi, as his successor, would take on the burden of the Senate hearings. *Now it made sense why he essentially stuck me squarely back in the center of the mess.* The lawyers had sent him reams of documents to read in preparation but he was too preoccupied with Rinaldi. He hadn't yet picked up any of it.

Rinaldi told him he was meeting with Rev. Cashman. He even admitted that he would do whatever it took to get him to quiet down. *He pretended to be on my side.* What did he really say to Cashman? Odds were, Ben surmised, the Cashman problem was going to rear its ugly head and be worse than it was before Rinaldi became involved. He was sure of that now.

The train of thought led him to wonder what had happened to the lawsuits. Rinaldi had said he was settling them. Ben hadn't seen any correspondence between Rinaldi and the lawyers. If settlements were progressing, surely the lawyers would have mentioned it during all the Senate hearing prep. He picked up his cell phone and dialed George Diamond, the lead attorney for Hiatus Centers. Ben still had the TracPhone but since his mobile was cleared, he preferred to use it.

"Hiya George, its Ben Abraham. Hey, I was just wondering what was happening with the settlements on the lawsuits."

"Settlements? There are no settlement discussions. Rinaldi told us a few weeks ago that Hiatus Centers would never settle. In fact, he said you were adamant and to tell the plaintiffs we would see them in court."

"What? George, *that's total bullshit!* I never said anything of the kind. Rinaldi told me he was settling the cases and I needn't worry about the details."

"You guys better have another conversation. It doesn't sound like you are on the same page."

"Well, that may be the understatement of the century," Ben exclaimed. "What would it take to settle these cases?"

"A whole lot more than before Rinaldi issued his tough guy stance. We've already sent communications to the plaintiffs that would constitute 'fighting words.'"

"Thanks, George. I'll get back to you."

The conversation with George Diamond confirmed his suspicion that Rinaldi was trying to screw him every way imaginable. It felt like he was being placed in a room and the walls were closing in. Just for a moment, his chest constricted. It became challenging to take a deep breath. Ben urged himself to relax. *Courage, strength, patience, wisdom* . . . the familiar words rang true in his head.

Back on track, the thought occurred to Ben that it was Rinaldi who broke the news about his own death and the experimental Liferay. This had led to the downturn in his relationship with Rachel. While he and Ari had mended fences to some extent, Ben was still on the outs with Rachel. *I loved her, dammit. Or at least I thought I did.* He knew he could never truly love someone he didn't fully trust. Yet, undeniably, despite the fact he was deeply hurt, he still had feelings for her.

All this shit with Rinaldi and then the seizures. He had practically no time to work on his plan to resolve the seizures. Fortunately, of late they had been few and far between, with diminished intensity. With all the stress he had been enduring, the seizure issue in a mild state of remission was one of the few blessings he was grateful for at the moment.

He returned his attention to the task at hand. His kitchen table was full of notes scribbled on printouts of research he was assembling on Rinaldi. Trouble was, there wasn't much of substance available. He had scoured the internet for anything and everything and come up with almost nothing. He recalled Rachel telling him something similar from her less intense effort just after Rinaldi was hired. He was crashing into the same brick walls.

Ben found high-level bios from SPI, media interviews, and business magazine articles covering his career but literally nothing on his personal life and nothing about his early days. Ben threw his head back, raised his arms toward the ceiling and stretched his upper torso. He had been at it for hours and was getting nowhere. He needed a fresh idea. Then it came to him. One of his best friends from college, Jess Miller, might be able to help. Ben recalled how he had met Miller at MIT. While he and Miller did play a lot of basketball together through their college years, they had actually met across an old ping-pong table in the hallway of the auxiliary gym. Miller was a fierce competitor and hated losing. Ben couldn't remember who challenged who to that first game but he did recall beating Miller, 21–19. Miller was so pissed off after losing, he cursed and broke the wooden paddle on the edge of the beat-up table. Ben had laughed his ass off. From that first game, a lifelong friendship and competitive sports relationship had emerged.

These days, Miller worked counterintelligence for the CIA in Langley. More specifically, he was a threat analyst. Knowing Jess the way he did, he would take it upon himself, as a personal mission, to find out everything he could about Anstrov Rinaldi.

He went back to his mobile phone and dialed Miller. Miller picked up on the second ring.

"Hey, are you calling for a basketball lesson?"

The banter with Miller always made him smile. They had that kind of relationship.

"That'll have to wait," he replied. "I need your help."

It took Ben nearly thirty minutes to brief his college friend on the details of recent events. When he was done, Ben didn't need to ask. Miller said with confidence, "I'm on it. Give me a few days. I'll give you a dossier so detailed, you will know every public can the guy ever took a shit in."

Ben thanked Miller and clicked off. He felt relieved. He wished he had thought of Jess earlier. He supposed it was his nature not to intrude on friends' goodwill. Times had changed. Desperate measures were called for.

If Miller could fill in the blanks about Rinaldi's life before SPI, maybe there would be a clue regarding his hatred for him and Albert. He thought of the obvious. Maybe Rinaldi had been a student at The Harmon School but he quickly dismissed it when a check with the school's registrar eliminated the possibility. No one named Anstrov Rinaldi had ever attended The Harmon School. He mentally tracked back over his entire life, searching for some potential overlap between himself, Albert, and Rinaldi. Some scientific conference, maybe? Even if Albert and Ben had met Rinaldi at some scientific conference, what could have happened to have made him so angry as to take on his current elaborate plot? He made a list of every supplier they had used in developing the Liferay. Maybe there was some tie to Rinaldi. Could some other adversary have hired Rinaldi? Was he just a front for someone else? Ben was beginning to think that Rinaldi was merely insane and that there was no further explanation. Nothing clicked.

He turned his attention to Tomi. How best to use her current situation against his foe? What information could he have her feed Rinaldi to throw him off the trail? He pondered this awhile and decided it was too early to play that card. Tomi could be invaluable to him in this battle; if for nothing else, to help buy time in the war in which he now found himself fully embroiled.

Ben had always been a fierce competitor. He hated to lose. Through his entire life, his mischievous side had been both a blessing and a curse. At times, it was the impetus to plow forward when odds were long and the pursuit appeared elusive. At other times, it made him reckless and prone to error. The conflict with Rinaldi was like nothing else he had ever taken on. As a scientist, Ben knew that patience and data collection were of paramount importance in the genesis of discovery. He felt like he had undertaken every reasonable avenue to get his arms around the issues. He just didn't have enough data with which to draw a logical conclusion.

His brain felt like it was filling with mud. It was time to get out of the apartment. He would hit the drive-through for a large coffee. Patience, he reminded himself, will be his savior. Gather more data, allow some time for things to work and reassess the situation. After he grabbed some coffee and got some fresh air, he knew he would have to dive head first into the massive quantity of legal documents. The Senate hearings were next week. Senator Rose was one angry man. Ben didn't know what it was like to lose a child but he understood the angst it caused a parent. Senator Rose lost his daughter not once, but twice, and was pissed beyond belief.

CHAPTER 44

A California girl never quite gets used to colder weather, Rachel thought. Fall was arriving once again and she felt a sudden chill go right through to her bones. A cold front had moved in and transformed the pleasant temperatures of summer's end into a chilly burst of autumn. The shiver it sent up through her spine reinforced what she already knew; it was a workday but she wouldn't be driving to Baltimore. It was time to have a one-to-one conversation with Ben. Rachel walked outside and pressed a button on her key fob to start her car remotely. In addition to warming the car's interior, her steering wheel and driver's seat would also be nice and toasty in a matter of minutes. She stepped back into the apartment, buttoned up her black and white wool jacket, checked her makeup one last time and, in a final, departing instinct, applied a touch of Obsession, the Calvin Klein fragrance she had been wearing the night she and Ben made love in Baltimore. She knew what it did to him and figured, with the current state of their relationship, she needed every bit of help she could get.

The short drive through the winding back roads of Maplebrook was pretty. Leaves were changing color and had begun to drop. While she remained focused, the serenity of the drive offered a modicum of peace. As with many a Maryland fall morning, the air was dewy. It wasn't raining but her windshield wipers, with a mind of their own, came on automatically until the force of the fan's warm air against the glass convinced them to stop.

Even though her primary location was in Baltimore, she still maintained an assigned parking spot at the Lab. It was next to Ben's. She was relieved to see the blue jalopy in its customary spot. Had it not been there, Rachel would have turned her car around and headed south to the city. But he was there! She gathered her determination, along with her purse and a shopping bag, and made her way through the main corridor to Ben's office.

It was still early, 7:17 by her watch, but the Lab was already abuzz. She greeted colleagues with her disarming smile and hoped that her persuasive abilities would be firing on all cylinders when she approached Ben. She didn't tell him she was coming by. Ben didn't like surprises but, all in all, she concluded it was wise to just show up. A call ahead might have resulted in an excuse of some sort as to why he couldn't see her. She was taking a chance that he wouldn't be tied up in a meeting but it was early. This was a conversation she did not want to have on the phone. Rachel was confident that she could win him back. It would have to be in person. Her weapons against Ben's stubborn resentment were her powers of persuasion, their history as friends, colleagues, lovers and of course, the Obsession. She knew how to move him. While the conversation would not be easy by any stretch, Rachel knew that Ben was attracted to her. A well-placed smile with an arched, singular eyebrow, was a look he always fell for. She could do this, she told herself. *He needs you. You just have to make him see it.*

When she arrived at his door, she took a deep breath and instinctively brushed her left hand across her forehead, sweeping her falling hair back into place. She knocked on the doorframe and delivered the warm smile she relied upon when she needed Ben to acquiesce. He looked up from his desk, failing to return the smile and appearing aggravated at the intrusion. But for a second, she mentally recoiled.

His expression announced that he was repulsed by the mere sight of her. She anticipated this as a possible reaction and decided to keep plowing forward.

"Good morning, Sunshine," she said in a sing-song voice.

Ben didn't crack a smile. She ignored the customary arm chairs designated for office guests and saddled up behind his desk. She parked her rear end on the glass-topped workspace. They were inches apart. Her sitting position versus his gave her the ability to neutralize his height and look down into his eyes. They looked haggard. Crow's feet were evident in the corners and with that beard getting heavier by the minute, he looked ten years older than he was.

"What can I do for you?" he asked monotonically.

"I'm worried about you and I want to help."

"I appreciate it but I'm good."

"You look terrible and, from what I can see, you are immersed in paperwork, which I know you hate."

She wondered if she had just made a critical misstep. She promised herself she would not lead with anything other than supportive comments. Telling him how bad he looked might not have fit that bill. She decided to quickly reverse course.

"Ivanov has been preoccupied with something else and has left me alone. I have a quiet few days ahead. Maybe I can take some of that paper off your desk?"

"It's all prep for the upcoming Senate investigation hearing. Unless you want to read all this crap, go to Washington, and pretend you are me for the day, I think I'm stuck with it," he replied dourly.

"Are you almost done? Can I come back later and take you to lunch, or better yet, dinner tonight?"

The shoulder he gave her was colder than an ice cave stalagmite piercing her veil of confidence.

"No, I'm nowhere near done. Just beginning, in fact. Until this Senate hearing is done, I won't have time to do much else except take an occasional piss."

The conversation was on the fast track to nowhere. She wasn't reaching him. *How do I get through?*

"Let me help you prepare. We can work out of my apartment to avoid distraction. I can read the documents and create briefs for you so you are up on all the pertinent details. I'll tell Ivanov I'm taking some time off. I'll make sure you are ready and you'll get a meal or two along the way."

"Rachel, you don't need to mother me. I need to do this myself. Is there anything else?"

She was crashing. Her confidence was waning and desperation was beginning to take hold.

"Ben, at some point, you need to talk to me. I'm your friend. I know you can't see it right now but I've always placed you above everything else ... even with that night. Some choices I made backfired and believe me, I would do some things differently but you were the center of my reasoning, the center of my universe."

"I can't do this right now. If you have any real feelings for me, leave me the hell alone for a while and let me work through this mountain of shit and the eighty million other problems I have to solve."

Rachel was crushed. He had never spoken to her that way. He was full on resentment and anger. She fought the swell of emotion building inside her breaking heart and urged herself to go back in. *Place his feelings above your own,* she told herself. She retreated from her position on his desk and inched slowly toward the door. Moving away from their relationship, she opted to take a different tack.

"Okay, okay . . ." her voice was shakier than what she would have liked. "But I do want to ask one question before I go."

"Shoot," he said coldly.

"The other day at Friends Park, after the meeting, what did Tomi want to speak to you about?"

This got to him. She could tell. It was a flicker of light beyond a brick wall but she held onto the hope that she had ignited a spark of real conversation.

"She wanted my advice on how to resolve a personal issue."

"Does it have anything to do with Rinaldi?" she asked as innocently as she could.

"Why do you ask that?" he said with suspicion.

"No reason. It just seemed odd that Tomi wanted to speak with you right after the revelation about Rinaldi."

"Why is that unusual?" he asked.

"I don't know," she replied, "things just feel weird. I mean, has Tomi ever sought advice from you before, about anything? I'm her closest friend and, for some reason, she chose not to confide in me. That got me wondering if it was about work. That's all."

"Maybe Tomi doesn't trust you, either."

Ouch! She guessed she deserved that shot but Ben was being noncommittal. He was playing it cool all the way down the line.

She was now caught up in the dilemma she had hoped to avoid. The agonizing choice between revealing what she knew and further ruining his trust in her, as if it could be ruined any more than it was. *He would freak if he knew I had been hiding behind a tree and listening to their conversation.* She decided to hold onto the information. Since she had made a tiny bit of headway in the conversation, she thought she would take one more stab at rekindling the personal relationship. She knew it would be like hurling a silver dollar across the wide expanse of the Potomac River but if George Washington could do it, why couldn't she?

"The Dodgers will be in DC in a few weeks to wrap up the regular season. Still up for a game?" she asked.

"Doubtful, what with the Senate hearings and everything else going on."

"I was hoping this might change your mind. I bought it with the game in mind."

She reached into the plastic shopping bag and held up a Dodger home jersey in Ben's size, complete with the number 32 and the name "Koufax" on the back.

"I remembered how you told me Koufax was Gramps' favorite Dodger. He would be thrilled to see you in this."

A smile. A small victory!

Ben thanked her, stood up and held the jersey against his chest, as if trying it on for size. He seemed pleased at the gesture. He laid the jersey over a chair and gave her a hug that, in her opinion, was just slightly better than what she would have gotten from a long lost third cousin. But she didn't mind. The conversation, although painful, had her further down the road than before it had taken place.

Rachel collected her purse from the same chair upon which Ben had laid the jersey. It may be too soon to invest the goodwill the jersey had earned but she was in a gambling frame of mind.

"My office in Baltimore is right near Rinaldi's. Maybe we could bug his office. He keeps it locked all the time but maybe I could slip in there without him noticing."

"We are better off, for the time being, to let Rinaldi think he has the upper hand."

Rachel concluded she overstayed her welcome, not that she felt welcome in the first place. She once again reiterated her offer to help in any way she could. She said goodbye and turned to leave.

"Rachel, hang on a minute," he called.

Her spirits began to brighten. She did it! She broke through. She knew she had it in her. Things between them were going to be all right, after all.

"I wanted to ask about the research you did on Rinaldi when he was first hired. What exactly did you find?"

Her enthusiasm plunged but not to the depths. At least, she told herself, he was asking for her help. It was a start. She knew getting back in Ben's good graces would be a journey and not a single leap.

"Not much. I can share the research I have. It's all fluff, routine PR. You know what struck me at the time? It's like the guy didn't exist before SPI. It made me suspicious at the time but I dismissed the thought because I immediately got immersed in work."

She understood his temperament. He was preoccupied with Rinaldi's plot but was also a reluctant participant in a Senate hearing heavily weighted against him.

"I have an old college buddy who works counterintelligence for the CIA. He is looking into Rinaldi's background for me. On the QT, of course. Like you, I found no trace of Anstrov Rinaldi before he went to work in Colmar for SPI."

That's a good friend to have in your hip pocket, she thought.

"Has he come up with anything?"

"Not yet. We just spoke yesterday."

"Hey, before I go, how are the seizures? Are you okay?"

He told her that he was in remission and some of Albert's prodigies were working on the computer program without knowing its true purpose.

The conversation had taken on an odd ebb and flow effect, business and personal, business and personal. "I know you don't trust me and I understand why but just know that I still love you and it was never my intent to violate your trust or betray you."

Ben smiled weakly but said nothing reassuring. All she got was a benign "thank you."

"Ben, I still believe we have a future."

"Rache, we all have a future."

"No, I mean, 'us.'"

"There is no 'us.'"

She left feeling shitty, her head down. It was not what she had hoped for but at least she got her feelings out in the open. She said what she needed to say. The conversation reaffirmed in her own mind that she would need to take matters into her own hands if she was to fully regain his trust. The problem was, she didn't quite know what that really meant.

CHAPTER 45

It only made sense for Ben to have spent the prior night in DC. The Senate hearing was scheduled for 9:00 a.m. Living forty-five minutes north of Baltimore would have meant navigating both Baltimore and DC rush hours. Instead, he had driven down the prior afternoon, checked in at The Willard and met George Diamond for dinner at Old Ebbitt Grill. He figured any restaurant with a name reminiscent of the Dodgers' history in Brooklyn couldn't be bad. He had not been disappointed. Old Ebbitt's history dated back to 1856. The saloon had served presidents, senators, congressman, and a host of other impresarios. Ben and George both enjoyed a smorgasbord of oyster preparations featuring shellfish from New York to Maine. Ben proceeded to have a grilled filet mignon while Diamond partook of shrimp cappellini. Ben would have preferred a Corona but in deference to his attorney, they split a bottle of Pinot Grigio.

Over dinner, the two men discussed the next day's scheduled hearing. Ben was hopeful it would be his only one before the powerful Senate Subcommittee on Consumer Protection. This subcommittee and its chair, Senator James Rose, a Florida Republican, had earned a reputation for crusading. Ironically, the subcommittee's most famous crusade also involved Senator Rose's daughter, Melody. Only thirty-two years of age, the brakes had failed on Melody's car, causing her to lose control of her vehicle and plunge into a lake. As Ben recalled from the national news frenzy, the incident was witnessed by a teenage boy who happened to be fishing nearby. The boy tried to save Melody but was too late. She had drowned. The boy called for help and the state police arrived in minutes, identified the body, and notified the senator that his only daughter had died. Senator Rose called Ben within an hour of the incident. Ben could not recall having encountered a man so distraught over the loss of a loved one. The Senator asked whether Ben could bring his baby girl back to life. Ben had told him it was theoretically possible but without one of his people examining her remains, he could not make any promises. Within ninety minutes, Harrison was on a chartered plane taking off from the tiny Maplebrook airstrip. He would meet Senator Rose and his daughter's remains at Hiatus Centers' Ft. Lauderdale location. Time was of the essence. Human cells had only eight hours to be properly preserved.

Six and a half hours after the accident that took the life of Melody Rose, Harrison applied his intravenous preservative and the local team assisted in getting Melody's body into a specialty casket for her year-long hibernation. Harrison expressed doubt as to whether the process would work. They had never before attempted it on a drowning victim. Harrison feared that the ingestion of too much water would dilute the preservative and promote a slow decay. That did not happen.

What did happen was Senator Rose's most famous crusade against the automaker and the brake manufacturer. Both companies denied liability and a prolonged and heated battle took place on a worldwide stage. The automaker, in particular, took a beating in the public's eye. After numerous subpoenas and threats of criminal prosecution, as well as new legislation to "protect innocent consumahs," as Rose, originally from Alabama, put in his protracted, southern drawl, The Melody Rose Automobile Safety Act had been passed by Congress. The automaker and brake manufacturer had survived years of ugly public rhetoric, plummeting sales, and millions in legal fees. Ben saw what Senator Rose and his deputies could do when vengeance was the goal. Now, it was he and Hiatus Centers squarely in the crosshairs of this angry and volatile predator.

Ben remembered how grateful Senator Rose had been. "You saved what little of my daw-tah that you could. I don't know how I will evah repay you." The two men never met. All of their communications had been by phone. Ben was now hopeful that, upon meeting face-to-face for the first time, Senator Rose would look at things more logically than emotionally. Ben acknowledged the farfetched notion.

The letter from the subcommittee arrived shortly after Melody Rose's terminated Hiatus Centers contract, in effect, resigning her to a state of permanent death. After conferring with George Diamond, they decided to fully cooperate. The bad press from being subpoenaed was an invitation for more disaster. Ben had had his fill. Cooperating fully meant turning over the digital equivalent of a truckload of documentation and the CEO's appearance at a hearing in Washington. Fortunately, the requested documents did not include his private journals or those of his team members. This meant that Ari's theory on sabotage, which he now believed to be true, was safe . . . *at least for the time being.*

Ben invested dozens of hours in preparation for the hearing. When he resigned as CEO, he wrongly assumed that this was one of the burdensome issues his successor would take over. Little did he know his successor was doing just the opposite.

Ben retired to his room to cram. It felt like old times in college. George had counseled him on being careful with his testimony. It was important to be honest, he said, without jeopardizing the end game. For Ben, that was a three-headed monster; not having his testimony used against him in the civil suits, avoiding the threat of criminal prosecution, and mitigating the need for legislation. He felt as prepared as he could be.

George advised that the chairman of the subcommittee sets the tone for the hearing. This subcommittee was chaired by James Rose—trouble for Ben.

The morning of the hearing was met by the brilliant autumn sunshine beckoning outside the lobby of the historic Washington hotel. Diamond had a private limo to carry them the 1.5 miles to the Senate building. Armed security guards were hired to escort them in and out of the building. Diamond expected a media circus and they were not disappointed. Outside the Senate building was Ben's nemesis, Rev. Alonzo Cashman, with a throng of one thousand or more protesters. Ben was sickened by the sampling of homemade signs he saw sprinkled throughout the angry mob:

HIATUS CENTERS KILL
YOU ONLY DIE TWICE
REST IN PEACE? WHAT A JOKE!
NO MORE PLAYING GOD!

Cashman was on top of a makeshift lectern with a microphone, firing up the raucous crowd. The reverend was screaming into the mic: "We need this Congress to get off its duff and pass legislation making this immoral practice a thing of the past."

Diamond had apparently suggested to Rinaldi that a new PR firm be brought in—one that specializes in diffusing the negative PR. He had recommended a DC-based firm called Zentarsky and Blumenthal. They charged top dollar but specialized in Congressional investigations and got results. Of course, Rinaldi dismissed the suggestion without discussing it with Ben; just one more way to nail him inside the coffin.

Ben wore his "special occasion" suit, which was usually reserved for weddings and funerals. It was dressy but not too flashy. Diamond cautioned him to look professional but not in a braggadocio manner. The suit was a charcoal gray with a subtle pinstripe. He wore his white, long-sleeve oxford button down with a conservative, wide stripe tie alternating bold red and pure navy. His black Bostonians were spit shined, courtesy of a stand inside The Willard. He wore the gold Seiko watch his parents had given him as a gift upon receiving his doctorate. While not superstitious, somehow, the watch had always served as a good luck charm. On this day, he would need all the luck he could get.

Ben observed the Russell Senate Office Building as the limo slowly came to a stop along Constitution Avenue. The building was an American classic hailing back to the early twentieth century. The hearing was scheduled for the historic Kennedy Caucus Room. Originally called the Russell Caucus Room, it was renamed in 2009 for John, Robert, and Ted Kennedy. The iconic space had been used for other hearings of note, including the sinking of the *Titanic*, Watergate, and the Melody Rose Automobile Safety Hearing. Today's session was standing room only. All of the national media was there and the hearing was being telecast live by C-SPAN. *What a circus,* thought Ben.

When they entered the building, they were taken through security. Pockets were emptied, jackets removed, bodies scanned, and briefcases x-rayed. Ben, with his attorney by his side, entered the grand elegance of one of Washington's most famous spaces. The room held three hundred people. There were at least that many jammed into the rectangular configuration. Ben was taken with the marble floors, the Greek motif gracing the ceiling, and original wooden furnishings from the turn of the last century. Hand carved eagles adorned the mahogany benches that were, to Ben's untrained eye, a true work of art. The walls were at least thirty feet high and featured three grand windows offering the benefit of natural daylight to help illuminate the majesty of the room.

Ben was shown to one of two opposing rostrums. His contained seating only for himself and George Diamond. Nameplates were placed on the surface reading "Dr. Abraham" and "Mr. Diamond." Longneck microphones stretched before each man's spot. A pitcher of ice water sat between the mics. Fifteen feet across the floor sat a much more elaborate wooden dais that would hold the members of the subcommittee, none of whom had yet entered the room. Ben could read the nameplates facing their table, from left to right; Mr. Breck, Mr. Strong, Mr. Rose, Mr. Oliver, and Ms. Prentiss.

Three Republicans and two Democrats. All five would get their turn to ask both reasonable and unreasonable questions. Apart from Rose, his handpicked Republican colleagues for the hearing were Hollis T. Strong of Louisiana and Bronson Oliver from Missouri. The two Democrats were chosen at the behest of the senior party member on the committee, likely with little or no input from Senator Rose. The Democrats were represented by Arnold Breck from Colorado and Maya Prentiss of Maryland. Ben was up to speed on all of them. Strong was an ordained minister and was known as a conservative bible thumper, while Oliver had led the charge in an earlier Congress to defund Planned Parenthood and their "heinous waste of taxpayer dollars." His effort failed even with the Republicans in control of both houses of Congress. Breck was likely to get behind Hiatus Centers. Colorado was the first state to legalize marijuana. Ben silently hoped that progressive thinking like that would come to his aid. Prentiss was from Abraham's state, Maryland, which Ben knew was bluer than blue. She supported Hiatus Centers and did not want to risk the loss of jobs in her state. In a recent interview, she was wavering just a bit at the bad publicity the nature of the services had brought. In the shadows of Washington, however, a Prentiss aide had been covertly feeding George Diamond enough of the behind-the-scenes chatter to get the extent of the subcommittee's venom. This proved invaluable in the prep.

Ben was seated next to Diamond. He poured himself a glass of ice water and took a look around. It was standing room only. Every major media outlet was there. The C-SPAN cameras were poised and ready. The room was getting noisy. Diamond cupped his hand around Ben's ear and pointed out a gentleman in the audience wearing an olive suit. Ben took note of Elijah Horsman, the Deputy Attorney General for the United States. The only reason Horsman would be in attendance is at the urgings of Senator Rose. George had thought that a US attorney might be asked to attend. Horsman's presence, as the number two man at Justice, said that DOJ was serious and wanted to learn a lot more in consideration of potential criminal charges at the federal level. Ben wished George hadn't pointed out Horsman. He preferred not to know.

Courage, strength, patience, wisdom

Like an opus heard in a symphony hall, the familiar words played effortlessly in Ben's brain.

The boisterous assembly in the Caucus Room began to settle as the five members of the subcommittee entered the room from the west side and, in order, mounted the time-worn rostrum and took their seats. Senate aides were already seated in a row of chairs behind the subcommittee rostrum. They would feed the subcommittee members information throughout the hearing. Ben was seated across from the middle of the opposing rostrum. This meant he was looking directly at Senator Rose. While he had seen this man numerous times on television and in pictures, he had never realized what a striking resemblance he bore to Paul Newman. His short, silver locks were perfectly styled with a part on the right. Rose's eyes were a piercing shade of blue. His cold stare drilled a hole right through Ben. He had to admit, Rose was an intimidating figure with a flair for theater. This reputation was clearly upheld when Rose brought the hearing to order and began his opening monologue.

Rose, with tortoise-shell reading glasses perched along the tip of his nose, read his opening statement while barely looking up. He cited the name of his subcommittee, introduced the members of his panel, and stated that today, on the first day of the hearings, only one witness would be appearing. Then he introduced Ben and George and thanked them for cooperating fully, abating the need for time consuming subpoenas. Ben knew pretty much what Rose would say but hearing the words spoken out loud set off alarms in his brain. In addition to citing the charge of the subcommittee to protect the health and welfare of the American consumer, Rose made a point to say, "if criminal activity is found during this hearing, the Department of Justice could elect to pursue prosecution." The presence of Elijah Horsman loomed large. Ben listened as Rose went on dragging out syllables in his slow southern dialect.

"Now, many in the media, and quite frankly, some of mah colleagues in the Senate, have suggested that Ah step ah-side in this mattuh as Ah have a cleah conflict of interest. This investigation, in paht, emanated from the death of my only daw-tah, Melody. Let it be known that Ah have volun-teeahed to do just that."

For a moment, Ben thought his luck was about to change. Getting Rose to recuse himself from the subcommittee would be a blessing.

"How-evah, the great mah-jaw-rity of mah colleagues have uhrged me to plow fohr-wahd and Ah intend to do just that."

So much for the turning of the tide. Ben took notes on the opening monologues of Rose and the other four members of the subcommittee. There were no time limits placed on any of them. He found most of their opening remarks to be benign but he knew the party was just getting started. Finally, Rose called on Ben to make his opening remarks. He reached into the breast pocket of his suitcoat and removed a wad of paper, neatly folded in thirds. Ben began to read, trying to sound conversational and humble, anything but monotonic.

"To the honorable Senator Rose and the other esteemed members of this subcommittee, I wish to offer my thanks for allowing me the privilege of presenting to the American people our view of Hiatus Centers' mission and values, as well as the unfortunate events leading to the loss of a limited number of clients."

His comments spoke at a high level. George had instructed him to avoid unnecessary details. He spoke for ten minutes. The crux of his remarks centered on why he embarked on the journey to create the Liferay and bring his dream to life. He cited the loss of his grandfather and the calling he had felt to help others escape the pain of losing a loved one. He teetered on thin ice for a bit when he dove into clients' and their families' understanding the risks with an emerging technology. Ben was worried that he might inflame Rose with these words. After much debate, he and George decided it best to leave the comments in but to keep them extremely brief. Upon advice from counsel, his opening remarks were only to set the tone. There would be ample opportunity to set the record straight while answering questions from the subcommittee and also to add anything else in a closing statement. The opening statements had killed the first two hours. Rose began the questioning.

"Son, what gives you the right to play Gawd?"

Ben had anticipated this question, just not as the leadoff inquiry. His answer had been well thought out.

"Senator, with all due respect, we would never presume to play God. We believe that the choice to enter our program is a personal decision. Personal to the client, his or her family, and most importantly, personal between those people and God. We are simply providing a means."

Senator Strong, the religious zealot from Louisiana and also with a southern drawl, albeit less pronounced, chimed in. "Dr. Abraham, if it's personal between God and the intended client and his or her family, what gives you the right to provide the means?" Strong looked anything but what his last name implied. He was a throwback to the late 1800s. His thinning hair was slicked back with too much styling gel and his gaunt face and thin lips made him look more like a mortician than a politician. The polka dot bow tie he wore did not help his cause.

"I'm not sure I follow your question, Senator."

"I'll rephrase it for you. Did God speak to you in some manner telling you to provide 'the means,' as you call it?"

"No, sir. The means are a matter of scientific discovery. My earlier response was meant only to convey that the decision to enter our program is a personal choice between a person, his or her family, and God."

The first half-hour of questioning centered on religion and potential violations of religious rights. Ben knew to expect these questions but didn't understand how this directly affected the rights of consumers to make a free choice. Freedom, he thought, was still a tenet of American life.

Next, it was Senator Oliver's turn. Ben's inner child made him want to smirk when Oliver turned his head. At profile, Oliver's long nose resembled a child's sliding board. His beady eyes, far recessed into his head and too close to one another, made him look like a messed up cartoon character. The Coke bottle glasses magnified his eyes but instead of making them look more natural in appearance, it gave him the look of an insect on steroids.

"Dr. Abraham, I would like to better understand what type of licensing you hold to operate these 'centers,' as you call them."

"In most states and provinces in Canada, we are licensed as a mortuary."

"A motch-U-ARY," bellowed Rose. He had a definitive penchant for bluster, Ben thought.

"Yes, Senator. After conferring with state bureaus of licensing and health departments, it seemed the most prudent and closely related license we could procure."

Senator Rose frowned. "I hahdly think it's the same thing," he exclaimed to no one in particular.

Senator Prentiss, the junior senator from Maryland, was formerly the governor of The Old Line State. She held the distinction of being the state's first African-American governor and its first female governor. Along with Mayor Goldstein, she had been instrumental in helping Hiatus Centers establish its corporate office and first location in Maryland. She was nearing sixty but her penchant for exercise, and perhaps some plastic surgery, made her appear no older than forty-five.

"Dr. Abraham, can you tell us how many people you employ in the state of Maryland and overall?"

"Yes, ma'am. In our Baltimore headquarters, we employ 250 people, 60 in our Baltimore and Rockville centers and another 150 or so at our research facility in Maplebrook. An additional 2,540 employees work in our North American locations outside Maryland."

"So, if my math is correct, you employ 460 in Maryland and 3,000 overall?"

"That's correct."

"And how many locations do you have across North America holding dead people, Dr. Abraham?"

"We refer to our clients as being in a state of hibernation. Currently, we have 115 centers operating in the 48 contiguous states and five Canadian provinces."

Prentiss continued. "How many people are hibernating, as you call it, in your North American facilities?"

"Approximately 130,000, at the present time."

"And how many people have failed to awaken properly since you opened your doors?"

"In Fort Lauderdale, during the period in question, Anna Torres, Marcus Roberts, and Melody Rose all suffered severe effects of neurodegenerative disease upon awakening. In Orlando, the same had happened to Manny Rojas and Stuart Hampton."

"So a total of five? All at the same time?"

"Yes, a total of five and all in the same week, shortly after each location had passed its one year anniversary."

"Does this concern you?' she asked.

"Of course. To the men and women of Hiatus Centers, the loss of any client is the worst of all tragedies. We strive for perfection. At the same time, we are proud that our success rate is 99.9 percent."

The senators on the subcommittee effortlessly picked up where the last one left off. They were like synchronized swimmers in some sort of bizarre relay. Senator Breck began where Prentiss had finished.

"Is losing only less than one-tenth of 1 percent acceptable to you, Doctor?"

"No sir, it is not."

"Losing a single life is unacceptable to me," offered Strong.

Before Ben could address Senator Strong's statement, Rose jumped back onto center stage.

"When these five inno-cent lives wehre ex-tinguished un-necessarily in your care, what, pray tell, went amok?"

Ben paused for a moment to consider his reply. His hesitance lasted perhaps a bit too long and he finally said, "I don't know, Senator."

"Well, Ah know fohr a fact that yohr current CEO has a theory."

Holy shit! Ben quaked in his chair. The thought that Rinaldi would launch an offensive with the subcommittee had not occurred to him. He looked over at Diamond. Nothing reassuring came back. He was kicking himself for not having considered the possibility. He began to sweat. He was sure it was noticeable to everyone in the Caucus Room, as well as the TV audience. Hell, at that moment, Ben was betting people listening on the radio could *hear* him sweat.

Ben had to consider his next move carefully. To accuse Rinaldi in this forum could easily backfire and might inhibit their chances in the civil cases and promulgate a criminal investigation. He decided to play possum.

"Senator, I am not sure what you are referring to."

"Ah think you dooo," replied Rose. Ben was sure he dragged out the *ooo* for effect.

The session had been going on all day. It was 3:45 p.m. Almost to the finish line. Ben was out of ideas. The tank was empty. He felt cornered. All of a sudden, with every ear hanging on Ben's reply, George Diamond took control.

"My client would like to request an immediate 'in-camera' session with the subcommittee."

Diamond's action was tantamount to turning the relief valve. The steam poured out of the room. Ben had learned the prior evening that "in-camera" was a legal term for a private, in-chambers conversation. When Ben had laid out the details of Rinaldi's vendetta over dinner at Old Ebbitt Grill, Diamond had suggested the procedure as a safety net, if they needed it. His timing was perfect. They would proceed to a private room inside the Russell Senate Office Building after a forty-five-minute recess.

Ben waited for the room to clear. Then he and Diamond walked out a back door to avoid the reporters. Diamond's hired bodyguards kept everyone at bay. Ben inhaled and took in a big helping of the crisp, late afternoon fall air. He couldn't wait to lose the necktie and shed the dress shoes. George wanted him back in the private office they were assigned for the day. There was much to discuss before the in-camera session began. Ben followed George back into the building when suddenly, he felt the vibration of his cell phone. The caller ID read simply: The Harmon School. Probably Albert wanting to know how the hearing went.

He looked over at George and said, "It's Albert. Let me tell him I'll call him on my ride home."

"Albert, I can't talk just yet," he chirped into the phone.

"Ben, it's Elsie." Elsie Simmons was Albert's longtime secretary. She had been with Albert at the school almost since the beginning.

"You sound upset. Is something wrong?"

"Well, I hope not. Is Albert with you? He didn't come to work today and he doesn't answer his cell phone or landline."

Ben's heart sank. Albert never missed a day at work during the school year.

CHAPTER 46

Not wanting to risk being caught with evidence indicative of his plan, Rinaldi worked out the details during off hours in the peaceful confines of his home office. It was early Saturday morning. Although he lived alone and never had visitors, he kept the dark wood and glass double doors to his office locked at all times. A domestic employee, Trixi, who cleaned, did laundry, and sometimes prepared light meals, was not allowed in the office unless he was there to supervise. Trixi had her own code to the alarm system so he could always tell when she entered and left. Little did she know that he had cameras hidden everywhere. About the only place she couldn't be tracked was the bathroom. He actually had considered that but thought it too unchivalrous.

Rinaldi ambled across the office, over the woven area rug that replicated the Grand Canal in Old Venice. The expansive floor covering, coupled with the morning sun, which shone brightly into the room each day, illuminated the space.

An oil painting of a black stallion on its heels hung behind the desk, occupying one half of the twelve foot wall. A long, rectangular gold plate light mounted above the painting produced a complimentary sheen on the horse's dark coat. While he shunned objects of irrelevant opulence, Rinaldi enjoyed art and its history. While still a youngster in Italy, he remembered studying da Vinci's Gran Cavallo. A project commissioned by the Duke of Milan in 1482, it intended to create the world's largest equestrian statue. While da Vinci had been unable to complete his grand sculpture due to an unplanned interruption from the French, Rinaldi would not be deterred from his own plan. The painting was symbolic—a reminder of why he was in America.

Spread across the Italian writing desk were census data on hibernating populations at each Hiatus Centers location across North America. These papers were ordinarily kept in the hidden safe on the opposite wall behind the gold foil, double hemisphere map highlighting famous Italian explorers, including Marco Polo. Polo, of course, influenced early efforts to create detailed cartography. It was an elaborate piece with exquisite detail, for which Rinaldi had paid an art dealer $75,000. When he became taken with an object reminiscent of his native Italy, money was no object.

Rinaldi leaned back in the overstuffed antique chair. The leather, extremely soft and dyed a dark emerald, was reinforced with classic brass rivets. In this chair, he fancied himself a king. The desk was something Rinaldi found by chance when he had first relocated to America. A day's exploration through Annapolis had landed him in a European-owned antique store. The desk had immediately caught his eye. The dark mahogany was burnished with a rich, genuine leather top restored to its original luster but with an appropriate hint of distress remaining. Carvings on the corners celebrated the age of Roman prosperity in the days of Marcus Aurelius.

When he had purchased this stately manor in Ellicott City, the room layouts fit his needs perfectly. The interior decorating, however, needed a European touch. For this task, he needed no outside help. Rinaldi had always possessed an innate ability to shape a room and make it his own. While he was proud of his efforts with the Ellicott City home, he knew it would never match the elegance of what he once had in Alsace.

He placed his reading glasses on his nose in order to help his good eye see the fine print on the Hiatus Centers documents. As he began to absorb the data, Rinaldi's mind wandered. He, some might say, was no better than an embedded terrorist, lying in wait for the best moment to strike. He preferred to think of it as simply playing one of life's many required roles enabling him to reach his chosen objective. The terrorists were known for assuming an identity and working for months or years in an environment marked for destruction. *Wasn't that what he had been doing? Did it really matter?* No, he concluded. He banished such thoughts from his mind. His course was clear. It was just a matter of making the timing and numbers work.

With 130,000 souls resting in the confines of 115 North American facilities, there was a lot of potential to wreak havoc. How to inflict maximum damage and not have it impugn his reputation was the key. He couldn't risk the possibility of spoiling his escape route; the golden parachute from the board of directors promising a secure financial future and a clean break from the trouble Abraham would find himself in the thick of.

Rinaldi thought about the time he had already invested. It had been significant. He chuckled at the irony. He had worked so hard as the CEO of Hiatus Centers, building the corporation he would ultimately destroy. While he admired the technology and the ingenuity, Rinaldi ultimately regarded the entire value proposition as unsustainable, at least in its current form. Theoretically, Hiatus Centers could awaken someone once per year forever. At some point, the person being awakened wouldn't have any reason to be brought back. They would have survived, in a matter of speaking, all of their known descendants. Given Abraham's secret, the one-year waiting period was not really needed any longer. But even then, Rinaldi thought, we would just be hastening a population explosion in a world of ever-diminishing resources. The newer technology could best be exploited in a number of ways, he thought. Perhaps after all this was over, he would pick back up on that notion.

When he had first arrived as CEO of Hiatus Centers, he doubled down on prior efforts to open locations across the continent as quickly as he could. An efficient template was created and teams of the world's best were trained. They went at it with a blistering pace. Rinaldi had simplified the entire process. Abraham's team was tending to every last detail before opening a new location. Rinaldi accurately assessed that a center could open and begin taking applications immediately. Bringing in bodies as registered clients who had died was not a problem. The gift of time came in the year before they would have to awaken the first client. In this timeframe, they had ample opportunity to install the Liferay and the Virtual Reality Theater systems. These, Rinaldi knew, were the most complex and time consuming aspects of opening a new location. He had mastered the art of expanding the company's footprint in record time. It would take far less time to bring it to its knees.

His plan was to be implemented on a specific day in the near future. He hadn't yet decided on the date. He was still struggling to solve the problem of critical mass. Ultimately, Rinaldi wanted the maximum number of people possible to drop, rot, and decay, preferably in the heart of the continent's most dense populations. He wanted an infallible plan that would cause an irreversible tailspin for Abraham and the company. He was willing to be patient but felt the beginning angst of the long awaited climax.

As Rinaldi returned his attention to the data covering his desk, he contemplated the numbers. Large metropolitan centers held fifteen hundred hibernating clients at any one time and the smaller locations in less populous areas about five hundred. The large centers averaged seven awakenings per day and the smaller ones two. This did not constitute the critical mass he desired but it might just be enough.

On any given day, he anticipated that approximately six hundred awakenings would occur. He wanted ten times that number but without building dozens of additional locations and waiting for them to reach capacity and one-year anniversaries, he knew he would work with the materials he had in hand. The good news was this: once his plan launched, on that long anticipated day, every major city in North America would have awakened people off the grounds, inexplicably dropping dead, rotting in the streets, and spreading airborne disease before authorities in the United States and Canada would know what to do about it. He snickered out loud, "Abraham will be ruined. If I play my cards right, he will wind up in custody the day everything breaks, powerless to save the day."

CHAPTER 47

Ben was exhausted. A long day of DC hearings in uncomfortable dress clothes and tight shoes was a calcification of everything he hated. He was finally back in the Honda, motoring north on the Baltimore-Washington Parkway. He activated his hands-free and instructed his smartphone to call Albert's home. There was no answer. The machine did not pick up. That was unusual but not necessarily alarming. He tried Albert's cell phone; again no answer. Ben decided to call Elsie, Albert's secretary, to see if there had been any further developments. It was after hours so he dialed her home number. Elsie answered on the third ring. She told Ben she was hoping that he was calling with some good news. He told her he was just leaving DC and was anticipating that she was going to give *him* some good news. Ben assured Elsie that he would drive directly to Albert's house and make sure he was okay. Albert had long ago entrusted him with a spare key. Ben was always regarded like a son. As he drove, his mind flooded with worry. Gramps used to tell him: Life will present you with enough problems; you don't need to create any on your own. The sentiment helped shake him back into reality. Maybe Albert just took a day trip somewhere. Perhaps the recent stress and the extortion attempt by Rinaldi had taken its toll and he just needed to get away. *But without telling anyone?* As much as he tried to reassure himself, his skin tingled, a physiological reaction to his innate sense that something was wrong. It would take him another hour and fifteen to get back to Maplebrook. *Stay cool until you know there's a problem*, he urged himself.

Upon leaving the Russell Building and firing his phone back up, Ben had noted several missed calls. One had been from Elsie, another from Harrison, and two from what the phone's caller ID listed as Private Caller. He wondered who that could have been. As he was getting ready to return Harrison's call, the phone, tucked securely into the drink cup holder, lit up and began to ring. The caller ID read Private Caller. *Well, here we go*, thought Ben, *no further need to speculate*. He answered and awaited a reply.

"Ben, it's Jess Miller. I've been trying to reach you all day."

Ben smiled to himself. He should have thought that Jess's CIA office would not offer a traditional caller ID. He gave Jess a high level overview of his day, explaining his lack of availability.

"Forgot about that. I don't watch C-SPAN," he replied. "Too boring."

"Not today. Lots of intrigue, even for those who are easily bored."

"Hey, the reason I was trying to reach you is that I have some news on your buddy, Anstrov Rinaldi."

"Great. I can use a break. Give me the lowdown."

"You may not like it. In fact, there isn't much to tell."

"Whaddoyoumean?" Ben replied in one long, lazy retort.

"I can tell you everything you would ever want to know from today back to when Rinaldi began working as a chemist for SPI in Colmar and even back to graduation from the university in Munich. Before that, the guy simply didn't exist."

Too tired to process the revelation, Ben asked, "What does it mean?"

"That Anstrov Rinaldi is an alias. For some reason, he saw fit to change his name."

"Man, that's wild. I never would have imagined. Is there anything else we can do?"

"Not unless you can get me a DNA sample, no."

Ben paused a moment for contemplation. Then, lightning struck! He had the answer . . . Tomi. In her confession to him at Friends Park, she told Ben that Rinaldi gave her a creepy feeling, like he was attracted to her; just a sense she got. If that were true, Tomi was about to regain her stripes. A plan was forming.

"Jess, I know this sounds crazy but I might just have a way to get the DNA. I'll be back to you. Thanks for all your help."

Ben clicked off and instructed the phone to dial Harrison's mobile number.

"Yo, buddy. You looked like you were having a blast on C-SPAN today."

"Yeah, it was slightly more fun than having a hot poker jammed into my eyeball."

"So, I didn't see all of it but I did watch the last hour or so with Tomi and Ari at the Lab. Why did your lawyer end things so abruptly? The talking heads didn't seem to be able to offer anything logical."

"My attorney asked for an in-camera session. Basically, it was a legal maneuver to bring the session to an end and have a private conversation with the committee behind a closed door without the world watching."

Ben went on to explain to Harrison that the hearing took an unexpected turn south when Senator Rose dropped the "Rinaldi bomb." That had been a curveball for which they had been unprepared. Ben figured that Rinaldi was content with just throwing him back into the fire of the Senate hearing. He had not imagined that his foe's quest was that he did not emerge from the flames. With this realization in hand, it became clear that Rinaldi would say or do anything to anyone to claim victory, inclusive of lying to a powerful Senate subcommittee. George Diamond had no choice but to try to throw Rinaldi under the bus. Diamond had told the subcommittee they had a witness who would testify that Rinaldi had bribed an engineer at the Swiss contractor Hiatus Centers hired to build The Liferay. The engineer altered a key component of the device, the Schlemm's rod, which produced the ill-fated demise of Senator Rose's daughter and four others. Senator Rose was flabbergasted at the revelation and reluctantly suspended the hearing pending further investigation into the allegation. Ben explained, in confidence, Tomi's confession and the ongoing role she would need to play to help them defeat Rinaldi.

"Man, every time I think life has thrown you all you can handle and then some, another meteor comes hurtling in your direction."

"Just good luck, I guess," he replied in the sarcastic tone Harrison would expect from him. "Harrison, I can't get into it now, but I'm going to need your help in a big way."

"Anything, you know that. Is there something I can prepare for?"

"Not quite yet. I'll be back to you in the next few days. Right now, I gotta check on Albert. Elsie called and said he didn't show up for work today and he isn't answering his home phone or cell phone."

"You want me to go check on him? You have to be at least an hour away."

"I appreciate it but you don't have a key. I'll check it out and call you if there's a problem."

Ben took solace in talking to Harrison. They had been friends for so long and had leaned on each other throughout the years. Ben had felt like shit when he saw Harrison's face upon learning the news of his death and "rebirth." He had never intended to keep it from Harrison, it had merely worked out that way in the throes of everything going on. He knew he could implicitly trust Harrison.

Ben shoveled his left hand through his unkept hair and drove with his right. He had a dull headache. Not the kind of pain that usually precedes a seizure but he was always mindful that something could erupt at any moment, especially when he was driving a car. No dizziness, so he kept on going. Ben switched on the smooth jazz and tried some of the deep breathing exercises Rachel had recommended. *Damn if it didn't really work.* He started to unwind. His inhibitions flew out the window reeling backward into the cool night air. He felt his luck change when he arrived at the mouth of the Fort McHenry Tunnel and there was absolutely no traffic. He breezed through the tube which lay below the surface of Baltimore's harbor. It was 6:30 p.m. If there were no traffic delays, he could reach Albert's house by 7:15, make sure everything was all right, and grab some food by 8:00. He was famished.

The Honda emerged from Bore 4 of the tunnel and through the E-Z Pass lane. Ben's phone began to chirp. It was Rachel. While she hadn't been his favorite person of late, he warmed just a bit at the sight of her name on the phone display. They had been close and until she had violated his trust, Ben felt like "she got him."

"Hey Rache, what's up?"

"Just wanted to check on you. It looks like you had a rough ending to your day."

Ben appreciated the call but didn't feel like retracing the day one more time.

"Doing okay," he said. "In fact, those breathing exercises you taught me that I didn't take seriously at the time—I just did them and they actually helped."

Her voice brightened. "Well, that makes me feel good. Dr. Larkin knows what's best."

Ben did tell her about Albert. He didn't mean to worry her unnecessarily but if something were wrong, Rachel was good under pressure. He hated asking her for anything but it seemed, lately, he was calling in chips from all over the place.

"Let me meet you at Albert's. After we check on him, we can grab a sandwich somewhere."

Too tired to deflect the overture, he reluctantly agreed.

"I'll see you there in thirty minutes."

When he arrived in front of Albert's home, Rachel stood on the sidewalk. She was wearing jeans and the red windbreaker with a white shirt. He liked that look. *Don't abandon your defenses*, he reminded himself. *You're tired. Keep your guard up!*

They embraced loosely, as friends. The sun had set. Albert's front porch light was dark. His car was still in the driveway. That was disturbing. Ben rang the doorbell several times. No answer. He knocked loudly and peered through the narrow, vertical glass pane adjacent to the door. Nothing. Rachel shone her phone's flashlight on Ben's hands as he fumbled for Albert's key on a jam-packed ring. He finally found the crimson colored key with the University of Kansas logo Albert had cut at The Home Depot in Bel Air. He placed the key in the door, first in the deadbolt and then the handle. The door opened. The house was quiet, no sign of activity.

Ben flicked on the hall light.

"Albert," he called. "Albert."

There was no answer. Everything was in place. They made their way through the living room, looked into the kitchen and dining area, still nothing. The house had a small finished basement but they decided to investigate the main hallway of the compact rancher toward the three bedrooms, one of which served as Albert's home office. When they entered Albert's bedroom, the room was dark. Rachel flipped on the light and they saw that the bed was undisturbed. The master bath was just ahead. Rachel moved forward, hit the light switch, and let out a blood-curdling scream, the likes of which Ben had never before heard.

CHAPTER 48

Rachel knelt down beside the body of Albert Harmon. By the look of him and the feel of his skin, he had been dead for quite some time. She guessed that it had been at least twenty-four hours because his color had faded and rigor mortis had set in. On the white ceramic tile floor, next to Albert's body, was a bottle of sleeping pills, most of which had spilled across the cold surface. For good measure, Albert had washed the pills down with a bottle of Crown Royal. Clearly, he had wanted to take his own life. In her state of emotional trauma, she couldn't comprehend it.

She felt for Ben. She had never seen him cry but he edged toward the precipice of tears when they discovered Albert's body. Ben had been through so much. Was there no end to the pain for him? Rachel worked hard to overtake her emotion and gain control of the situation. She dialed 911 and did her best to comfort Ben while they waited for the coroner. They sat on the foot of Albert's bed.

"I'm so sorry, Ben. I know how close you two were."

Ben didn't reply. He sat next to her, shoulders slumped, his head dangling down near his knees. She placed an arm around him and tried to offer a small measure of comfort. Across from the foot of the bed sat Albert's dresser. Atop the old wooden piece was a rounded mirror. Against the mirror's base was an envelope. The number ten enclosure sat at attention, seeking an audience of only one. It appeared to be sealed and it stated, for anyone who cared to see, one simple word: Ben.

Rachel stood up and retrieved the envelope clearly intended for the man she was now trying to console. For a moment, she had contemplated stuffing it in her purse and presenting it later, when his emotions were calm. Then, in a moment of clarity, she realized that such a maneuver is exactly what got her into trouble with Ben in the past. Envelope in hand, she returned to her position next to him on the bed.

"I found this. Albert left it for you."

Ben looked up slowly. In the short time since they had discovered Albert's body, he had taken on a haggard look. The color had drained from his face and, in the dim light of Albert's bedroom, he again looked ten years older. Her heart ached for him. She wished she could take it all away.

Ben took the envelope from her. He didn't open it right away. He just stared at the front. It was as if the mere writing of his name in Albert's familiar hand had transfixed him. Rachel wanted to take the envelope and rip it open to reveal its contents but she knew she had to be patient.

He turned the envelope over, stuck his pinky under the tiny opening where a letter opener would ordinarily go, ripped the top of the flap and removed the folded letter. It was handwritten. Rachel surmised that Albert had written this before he had begun drinking. The cursive was too neat.

She watched as Ben began to read. She moved closer so she could read along with him.

Dear Ben,
All my life, I have placed my personal feelings and desires aside in the pursuit of scientific discovery and education. This time, I regret I was unable to adhere to this lifelong creed by which I have lived my life. While completely untrue, the stress of defending the baseless claims orchestrated by

Anstrov Rinaldi has taken too great a toll on my resolve and my psyche. I have succumbed to a state of selfishness, electing to wither and not to fight. I know you will feel I have let you down. I believe it to be true. I have also let down the students and the board of directors, not to mention our shareholders, to whom I feel a great sense of responsibility. I hope that you and the others will find it in your hearts to forgive an old man who elected to simply take the easy way out.
Albert

Rachel felt her resolve beginning to crack. Ben finished reading Albert's note and simply let the paper drift to the floor. Rachel picked up the paper, snapped a photo of it with her smartphone, and placed it atop the dresser.

"Hello, anyone here? Harford County Sheriff's Department."

In their haste to begin looking for Albert, they had left the front door open. The Sheriff's Department would have to file a report as a matter of routine. There was no doubt that Albert's death would be ruled a suicide. She had snapped the photo in hopes that somehow, maybe, the authorities would be able to file some sort of charge against Rinaldi for promulgating an innocent man's suicide.

Rachel went out to the front of the house and greeted the officer. After they both gave the police a statement and the coroner had come to remove the body, Rachel ferried Ben out of the house. He was numb.

"Leave your car here."

She drove him to his place and walked him inside. While Ben went to change, she inspected the fridge with the intent of making him something to eat. Other than some eggs and individually wrapped slices of American cheese, the cupboard was bare. *An omelet it is.* When he came back out, he sat down at his kitchen table and looked up at her.

"I'm not too hungry," he said. "I have to call Harrison, Ari, and Elsie. My parents will want to know too. I think Albert has some nieces and nephews in Kansas somewhere. I'm not sure what their names are or even how to find out. And then there are funeral arrangements."

"Shhh . . . all that can wait. Eat your omelet. I made you some tea. Let's get your body and mind in a better place and then I will help you with everything."

Ben offered a reserved acknowledgement of gratitude. She knew he needed her tonight regardless of their recent difficulties. Watching the man she loved in pain was heart-wrenching. It reinforced her resolve to do whatever it took to get at the source of all his troubles: Anstrov Rinaldi. Clarity befell her in a way she had never before experienced.

CHAPTER 49

Rinaldi waited. It was 6:30 a.m. The fall sun had not yet risen. He sat alone in a booth by the front window and watched the burly, flannel-clad men enter and leave the busy diner along the hectic truck stop corridor in Gorman's Creek, fifty miles north of the city. Tomi Oka was late.

Their last meeting had left his confidence in her discretion waning. He needed to test her allegiance. Although he was battling a head cold and had no desire to get up in the middle of the night and travel ninety minutes from his home, it was worth the inconvenience to not risk being seen in public with Oka. The truck stop was perfect. Of course, he didn't mind that Oka was aggravated with the time and location. Having her off balance at the start of their session worked to his advantage.

His cane began to slip from where it leaned against the booth's bench. He caught it just in time. He sat back up, sipped his black coffee, and spotted the red Lexus pulling into the trash-laden parking lot. As she got out of her car, Rinaldi thought she looked a bit nervous, and she should. A beautiful woman getting out of a red sports car would attract the wrong kind of attention in these parts. All by design, he thought as he smiled to himself. He had dressed down for the meeting but he afforded her no such protection from what she would perceive as hostile environs.

When she entered the diner, he waved to indicate his location although he did not rise to greet her. Maybe he would have, if she had shown the mildest spark of interest in him. *Fuck her*, he decided. He was navigating a war and she was but a pawn—a piece to be maneuvered at his will. He would not waste one ounce of charm on this bitch. He removed his dark glasses to expose his prosthetic eye. He knew he was more intimidating that way.

"You are late," he commanded sternly. The effects of the cold mixed with the odd pitch of his regular speaking voice made him sound eerily terrifying.

She looked put off. He had flustered her right out of the gate and this pleased him.

"I incorrectly loaded the name of this place in my GPS. I apologize."

"I am not interested in your apologies. I am interested in your cooperation and your loyalty—nothing more, nothing less." He paused to sneeze. A serial sneezer, he reeled off four in a row. Looking for a handkerchief and coming up empty, he reached for the napkin dispenser. He wiped and blew and placed the wadded up tissue on the table beside his coffee.

"When the waitress comes over, order something. We are trying to be inconspicuous."

She ordered a bowl of fresh fruit and an English muffin, lightly toasted with jelly on the side. He ordered two eggs over easy, a side of bacon, and toast. While they waited for the food to arrive, Rinaldi decided to probe.

"What did you tell Abraham about our little arrangement?"

"Nothing," she replied, "I swear. I haven't told anyone."

"You are lying. I can see it in your eyes."

"No, no . . . please believe me."

"Why should I?"

"Because I don't want to be arrested for embezzlement."

Rinaldi was enjoying the repartee. She had no way of knowing, but he was merely playing with her, killing time until the food arrived.

He gave her an intentional look of suspicion. His left eyebrow arched, his facial muscles tightened and his bad eye bulged, just a little. She looked like she was going to hurl. *Now*, he thought, *this was getting fun*. He decided to throw her a curve ball.

"Tell me, what do you do for fun?"

"Fun?" she asked incredulously. "What do you mean?"

"I mean, when you are home alone and there's nothing to do and no one around. What do you do for fun?"

Rinaldi was in high gear. Oka looked positively mortified at his implication. Everything was done with a purpose. He wanted to make her as uncomfortable as he possibly could.

She appeared shaken and stammered out, "I like to read. Sometimes I watch a movie."

"Are your books and movies about fantasies that most single women your age must have?"

Now she looked like she wanted to cry or run or both. He grabbed another handful of napkins from the spotty metal dispenser and blew his nose, placing the soiled remains on the table with the others. He reached into his jacket pocket and removed a foil-backed package with two green cold lozenges. He popped them out and swallowed both simultaneously. *I hate colds*, he thought.

"I must use the men's room. Do not even think of leaving. We still have important things to discuss."

With that, Rinaldi put his dark glasses back on, grabbed his cane, slid out of the booth, and worked his way to the back of the greasy diner.

As soon as he was back at the table, a thirty-something waitress in a mustard yellow uniform delivered their food. She smiled as she told them to enjoy their breakfast. Rinaldi took note of the pronounced gap between her two front teeth. He was starved. He liked to eat breakfast as soon as he rose each morning. Today, for reasons of importance, he was several hours off schedule. He tore into his meal while Oka poked nervously about her plate. When he finished, he wiped his mouth and sneezed three more times. She looked so disgusted. It was time for the test.

"The last time we met, I told you I would have a task of significance for you."

He sniffed, plunging the running mucus northbound through his left nostril. She did not reply so he kept going.

"You will need this." He reached into his inside jacket pocket, removed a small padded envelope, and gently slid it across the table's surface.

"Don't open it now," he commanded.

"What's inside?"

"Inside the envelope is a micro drive. It contains preloaded software that will automatically upload once inserted into a USB slot."

"Software to do what?"

"Just some routine improvements to our awakening protocol for all commercial locations."

"You're the CEO. Why do you need me to upload software clandestinely if these are just 'routine improvements?'"

He smiled the dastardly smile that only he could. He paused, sneezed again, and elected not to answer. She already knew.

"I will contact you with a specific day and time. It will be off-hours, most likely the middle of the night. You will report to HQ and insert the micro drive into the main server. You will wait two minutes for the program to upload as indicated by a green light on the tip of the drive. Then you will remove the micro drive, place it in the envelope, and mail it to this address."

The address on the envelope was for Box 142 at the rundown parcel center off Route 100 where he had secured her first drop . . . the flash drive with Weiskopf's journal.

"I don't have authorization to the main data center at HQ."

"You will. This I can easily arrange."

"If I agree to do this, I will forgo payment in exchange for a release from further tasks. I don't want to be involved."

Rinaldi breathed in, the cold causing a hissing sound, like a wheeze, and replied, "Execute this task without error and we shall see."

He remained in the booth as she stood to leave. He watched her walk out the diner, admiring her legs. She definitely stirred something in him. By the looks of things, she also aroused the multitude of locals watching her exit. Rinaldi enjoyed the angst he had put her through, directly and indirectly via the location. He knew the locals were likely harmless but to Oka, they would appear menacing. He sat back for a few minutes, reveling in the wolf whistles she endured on her way out. *Dumb bitch!*

All he had given her on the micro drive was a program with a benign worm. While she would see a program upload, all it would do is send a meaningless executable crashing into a firewall. The meeting accomplished two things: (1) he needed to test her loyalty to do as he commanded, and (2) he would have her on the company security cameras uploading malware into the main server from an unauthorized drive. Another opportunity for blackmail.

How naïve this woman was to think he would trust her with his real plan.

CHAPTER 50

The death of Albert Harmon hit Ben hard. Unlike many of his friends and colleagues who had lost relatives, he had been fortunate. Despite the proposition of the company he founded, Ben had not dealt with death on a personal level as an adult . . . until Andrew. And now this! His emotions and grief were cycling through classic phases including denial, anger, and even depression. While Gramps' loss had hit hard, he didn't know at the time how to properly grieve. Heck, he wasn't sure he knew now. He just knew he felt defeated. Feeling like he had been sucker-punched in the gut, he forced himself to keep moving forward.

It had been two weeks since the Senate hearings. It was Ben's first time in DC since that stressful day at the Russell Building, a day that had ended with the grisly discovery of Albert's body and a suicide note. So much of what Ben Abraham knew and loved was coming apart at the seams. The root cause of it all was Anstrov Rinaldi. Maybe it was part of the grieving process but he had never felt so much anger toward another human being. Ben was determined to use every resource at his disposal to unravel the mystery behind his adversary. If he failed, Rinaldi was going to ruin him.

He had agreed to meet Jess Miller at a Georgetown bar on M Street. Following suit with the entertaining names of local drinking establishments, this place bore the moniker Billy Goat's Beard. If you spoke to the founders of bars like these, they invariably had entertaining stories to tell about how they selected names for their saloons. Ben didn't really care how the place got its name; his quest was information and an hour or two of reminiscing with an old friend. He was halfway through the first brew when his mobile lit up. A text from Jess: "Running late, there in fifteen."

Running late? No shit, thought Ben.

A half hour later, Miller strode through the door. The bar had an entry level, a basement, and an upstairs. The hostess said the upstairs bar was usually the quietest at this time on a weeknight.

Ben followed his friend up the narrow flight of stairs. Miller took two at a time. He always did like to show off. He wore black boots, jeans, and a dark jacket with a black T-shirt that read, *"I'm in construction, call me Stud."* His long sandy blond hair bounced as he attacked the staircase.

When they each had a beer and the lite fare menu, Miller dove right in. "Your friend did a good job getting DNA from Rinaldi."

Ben was no germophobe but he had to admit that the thought of Tomi scarfing Rinaldi's used table napkin while he was in the restroom was gross. "Yeah, she owed me a favor."

Miller liked to boast. He grinned and said, "Most people know that DNA testing evolved in the 80s. A geneticist in the UK was the father of modern day DNA testing. But what most people don't know is that long before that time, European hospitals, in the interests of furthering medical science, took blood samples of newborns and preserved them in a manner where, years later, they could be typed for DNA with the results stored in a global database for not only science but criminal investigations. We're talking samples collected in the tens of millions. All very controversial. All without consent or knowledge of the parents."

With all of his training and study as a scientist, what Ben was hearing was beyond comprehension. "What you are talking about sounds like something from a futuristic sci-fi movie."

Miller shrugged his shoulders bidding acquiescence to Ben's remark. "Does the name Niccolo Abandonato mean anything to you?"

Ben paused in a moment of contemplation. He rubbed his head, a nervous habit.

"No, should it?"

"Maybe, maybe not. That is Rinaldi's real name. He apparently left it behind after high school when his father, a finance minister from Milan, was taken down in a national embezzlement scandal."

Ben was still puzzled. "What else were you able to find out?"

"Apparently, the good doctor grew up in Italy and left Europe only one time prior to high school. This is where it gets interesting."

"Interesting? How so?"

"His one trip outside the continent was to the United States. Maryland, specifically."

"Maryland?" Ben replied in a surprised manner.

"Yes, through medical records, we were able to discover that, thirty-plus years ago, he was treated at Upper Chesapeake Medical Center in Bel Air for injuries to his eye and right leg, among other bumps and bruises, all sustained during a horseback riding accident."

"Upper Chesapeake is the hospital nearest Maplebrook." Ben still couldn't make the connection. "Do hospitals keep records back that far?"

"Not officially." Miller smiled. "But in my line of work, we have access to databases that don't officially exist."

Ben chugged the remaining quarter of his beer and set the glass on the hardwood tabletop.

"Take a look at these." Miller slid an 8½ x 11 envelope across the table. Inside were several photographs of a young boy bearing a mild resemblance to the man he knew as Anstrov Rinaldi.

Ben stared at the photos. His brain was attempting to cut across the fog formed by the passage of an eternity. There was something there, he could sense it. In the recesses of his mind, he recalled bits and pieces of a vague recollection. *Yes,* there was a horseback riding accident during his days at The Harmon School. It was an unusual accident and Maplebrook was a small town. An occurrence like that spreads through the community like wildfire. *Damn. If Albert were alive, he could perhaps remember. Maybe Mom or Dad might recall something.*

Miller interrupted his brief departure from their conscious level conversation. "Does any of this information help you?"

Ben hesitated and then replied, "I think it does." He pointed to the photos spread across the table and asked, "Can I take these with me?"

Miller gave his consent. Ben picked up the tab, thanked his old friend, and began the walk back down M Street to the garage where he had left the old blue Honda. The next order of business was a visit to Elsie at The Harmon School. He had a nagging feeling that Niccolo Abandonato had once been a student at the vaunted institution. His only hope was that the school had access to decades-old files.

CHAPTER 51

Ben asked Rachel to meet him at The Harmon School. They went to the administration office and found Elsie Simmons in her familiar spot outside the now vacant office once occupied by the school's founder. To Ben, Elsie looked like he felt. She was moving around but she appeared to be going through the motions, like she had been shot. The thought crossed his mind that, in a literal sense, Albert's death had blown a hole in all of their lives.

Knowing it was the longest of long shots, Ben inquired about the records from three decades earlier.

Elsie Simmons, always wanting to be of assistance, allowed a faint smile to purse her lips. "You know Albert," she said. "He never threw anything away. All the old records are stored in the shed on the back end of the property. No one ever goes back there. I have a key and can show you where it is."

Ben felt a slight sense of relief. Going through all the old files would take forever but at least it was a place to start. "I know where it is," he replied. "When I was a student here, we used to pretend the old shed was a fort and we would hide behind it and sometimes climb on the roof."

He took the key from Elsie and he and Rachel went back to his car to drive the short distance. It was an easy walk but Ben wanted the car nearby in case they needed to remove file boxes for viewing at his place. The drive took less than five minutes. Red and gold maple leaves lined the narrow access road leading to the small, gray-sided structure. Ben parked and they walked up to the front door, which Albert had painted bright red. The shingles on the triangular roof were a classic gray/black pattern. Ben inserted the key and opened the door. The diminutive structure had both lights and HVAC and was meticulously organized. Ben was relieved. Perhaps the task would be easier than he thought.

Rachel went directly to the steel shelves with hang tags for the decade they were most likely to need. The long white file boxes were tied down with black string secured by loops encumbering plastic discs on both ends. They each took a box and began working through files of applications processed on paper that had turned yellow with age. Thankfully, each box was alphabetical and the name they were seeking, Abandonato, began with A.

After only fifteen minutes of searching, Rachel hit the jackpot. They removed the file and took it to a small wooden table, gray in color and faded with years, at the front of the shed. They both leaned over the file and watched as Ben matched the photo in the application to the ones given him by Jess Miller. There was no doubt it was the same face. Ben began reading the application.

Niccolo Abandonato was an accomplished student from Italy. The file was laden with accolades and certifications from grade-level schools in Florence. Grade transcripts, in Italian, accompanied the application. Albert was not able to speak Italian and had made handwritten notes in the margin translating key points to English. Knowing Albert, he had probably gone to the local library or bookstore for an Italian-English dictionary and done the translation on his own. Other notes probably came from conversations with the boy and his parents. Ben kept going and found the Italian birth certificate and underneath it, at the bottom of the thin manila folder, two other pieces of paper. The first was a processing form describing the details of the applicant's visit from Italy and Albert's handwritten notes from his interview with the boy. Above that, it listed the name of Abandonato's assigned student liaison, Ben Abraham.

Ben read Albert's notes indicating that the Abandonato boy was being rejected. Albert's commentary indicated that the boy was brash and recounted his belief in shortcuts and taking chances. He felt that being first to scientific discovery was more valuable than exercising patience to get it right. Albert's notes revealed disdain for this approach.

Underneath the processing form, a yellowed newspaper clipping from *The Maplebrook Community Press* described a horseback riding accident involving a young, Italian boy who had been visiting the area as a candidate at The Harmon School for Gifted Scientific Youth. The article described the boy's injuries as severe, inclusive of a crushed knee and the loss of an eye.

Ben felt sick. The gates of his memory opened and flooded his brain like a tsunami. He remembered. All those years ago, he, the practical joker, pulling a fast one on this naïve kid from Italy. Ben recalled, as a sometimes rambunctious twelve-year-old, that the Abandonato boy struck him and his friends as being weird, funny looking, and someone who probably would not fit in. Everything was starting to crystallize.

Was it possible that these events from so long ago had fueled Rinaldi's need for vengeance over so many years? Ben thought it unlikely but what other explanation was there?

Ben was visibly shaken but had not yet spoken.

"Ben, what does all of this mean?"

"It means that it's all my fault. I'm to blame."

"What's your fault?"

"Rinaldi, or Abandonato—I intentionally gave him bad advice for his interview with Albert."

"So? How does that make any of this your fault?"

"Piece it together. As a kid, I was very competitive and judgmental. The group I hung with didn't like Abandonato. So I told him to say the opposite of what Albert liked, knowing full well it would get him rejected."

"Okay, so he got rejected. I still don't see how you can blame yourself."

"According to this clipping, his parents took him to a local farm to ride the horse that caused his disabilities. His mother is quoted as saying that the horseback riding session was an attempt to ease the boy's troubled mind after he had been rejected as a candidate from The Harmon School. What this means is that Rinaldi blames me for his disabilities and for who knows what else."

A look of realization dawned on Rachel. "Ho . . . ly shit," she said in a slow, drawn-out manner.

"This guy has made it his life's work to get even with me. It explains why he is so motivated to ruin me and everything I've built and those I love."

"And to think Albert hired this shithead as CEO of the company you founded."

"I can't fault him for that. There's no way that Albert would have recognized Rinaldi as Niccolo Abandonato from so many years ago. Even without the disabilities, he would have looked remarkably different. Besides, Albert interviewed hundreds if not thousands of kids over the years. He couldn't be expected to remember them all, especially the ones who were never actually students here."

"I'm sure that's what Rinaldi was banking on."

Ben replaced all the papers back in the manila folder and closed it. He put all of the file boxes back where they were, shut off the light, and locked the door on their way out. With the Abandonato file tucked under his arm, he settled into the driver's seat of the Honda and drove Rachel back to the main parking lot to retrieve her car.

"So, what comes next?"

Ben sighed and thought of all the crap he had endured at Rinaldi's hands: sabotaging the Liferay and the resultant deaths; the lawsuits; the Senate investigation; the blackmail of Tomi, Albert, and himself; the breakdown of his relationship with Rachel; and now, Albert's death. He was sure of one thing: Rinaldi had no plans to stop there. He would keep going until Ben had been eviscerated.

In response, he said with explicit lucidity, "Now I have what I need to defeat the sonofabitch."

PART III

CHAPTER 52

Baxter navigated the black Town Car alongside the curb on E. Pratt St. Rinaldi opened the door to exit the vehicle, his walnut cane leading the way. With his weight firmly staged on the cane, he stepped out of the car and onto the sidewalk. At that very moment, Harrison, walking briskly down the pavement, barreled into Rinaldi like a defensive end upending an unsuspecting quarterback. The cane shot skyward and came to rest thirty feet away. Rinaldi lay on the ground, motionless, trying to regain his wits. Bock, not even fazed by the collision, turned back and kneeled beside the fallen CEO.

"Dr. Rinaldi. I am so sorry. Are you okay? Should I call an ambulance?"

Rinaldi looked up. He felt dizzy and somewhat disoriented. The metallic taste of blood was forming in his mouth. Something had cut his lip. He touched his finger to his mouth and saw the tip turn crimson. Baxter was at his side with a box of Kleenex.

"No, no. I think I am okay. You should watch where you're going," he replied with a distinctive tone of disdain.

He sat up and looked around. The world was spinning. He saw the normal morning hustle, people in a hurry to get to work, coffee in hand. Cars and buses were racing down E. Pratt St. *Was that a street cleaner picking up trash?* No, he must be hallucinating. He never saw street cleaners in Baltimore. Perhaps just a homeless person seeking a newfound gem. Normally proud with an indomitable will, he allowed Baxter to help him to his feet. Bock handed him his cane and stood by while he dusted himself off. When he was satisfied with his balance and appearance, he bid Baxter adieu and proceeded into the office building.

The collision with that oaf, Bock, had placed him in a foul mood. He blew by his administrative assistant, ignored Drago, and sat down behind his desk. The incident with Bock aside, he reminded himself to stay in the moment and concentrate on the exciting day ahead.

In his inbox was an email from the head of IT security. Oka had placed the micro drive into the Hiatus Centers' server. He had her on film. The harmless worm bounced against the firewall and was immediately quarantined. He had her in his hip pocket. Rinaldi replied with instructions to keep the tape indefinitely and that he would personally handle the security breach with Dr. Oka. He really didn't need to think too much more about her. Soon he would be gone. It was time.

After a lifetime of plotting, waiting, and flawless execution, Rinaldi's moment was finally at hand. This was the day he would set the wheels in motion—the ticking bomb, as he like to think of it. He was already planning his getaway. Between SPI and Hiatus Centers, he made millions and invested wisely. He laughed out loud. Before it was all over, Hiatus Centers would be compensating him with severance of $10 million. He had already secured his destination.

Although Rinaldi thought about returning to Alsace or even his native Italy, those places did not permit him complete anonymity or a safe escape from the aftermath of his final plan. His new home would. He had purchased a nine-thousand-square-foot complex in Villa La Angostura along the Patagonian Lakes Route in Argentina. Through a proxy and a newly created identity, he had completed the purchase of a luxury estate and its accompanying landscape spanning 875 acres. In addition to a winery, the property held separate servants' quarters. Rinaldi liked this. Service close at hand but not in his living space. He closed his eyes and let his mind drift off to the image of his soon-to-be new home. The front of the multicolored stone wall estate was stunning. To the left of three large bay windows was a lighthouse-shaped structure enabling a remarkable view of the surrounding crystal lake, which was suitable for boating, fishing, and even swimming. The Great Room sat behind the bay windows and held an endless water view. Drago would enjoy that. He imagined lounging on the ridiculously long waterside deck with a Kronenbourg and pictured the sun swept sky and its late afternoon rays dancing across the lake. A sense of calm began to wash over him.

Rinaldi's thoughts wandered to an image of the equally serene back porch that faced the mountains and its foothills full of Lenga trees and accompanying fields. The thought of the serenity and seclusion the location offered was a magnificent exit from the completion of what he considered his greatest feat: the total destruction of Dr. Benjamin Abraham.

Rinaldi sat back in his chair and reviewed the draft one final time. It was the text of an email he had been formulating in his mind for months. The email was about to be sent to all Hiatus Centers managers. Only he would not be the sender. The email would be seen by its recipients as originating from the mailbox of Ben Abraham, the head of R&D.

To: All HC managers
From: Abraham, Benjamin
Subject: URGENT – Immediate Changes are Required for Your Liferay Settings

HC is ready to unveil its latest technological advancement: a seventy-two-hour awakening. HQ has already notified the families of those scheduled to be awakened in the next thirty days. To make this new service as successful as possible, we are, for the first time, encouraging the awakened to leave the grounds and spend time in public and in the homes of their families.

299

Vouchers to local restaurants and other venues in each market have been emailed to family members.

Families have been reminded that they need to have the awakened back to the HC location approximately twelve hours before the expiration of the seventy-two-hour period in order to prepare for a proper hibernation.

To ensure the new seventy-two-hour awakening protocol, you will need to make immediate changes to the setting of the Liferay(s) in your center. Instructions for making these precise changes are shown below. The new settings must be implemented immediately but no later than Saturday morning prior to noon local time.

If you have any questions or need assistance with this procedure, please speak directly with our COO, Maxim Ivanov.

Thanks for your assistance in making this exciting new change a reality.
Ben

In Rinaldi's estimation, the email was good to go. By Monday, what was left of Abraham's world would come crashing to pieces. The revised Liferay setting would cause those awakened to drop, rot, and decay in less than six hours after hitting the street. Even better than that would be the instantaneous creation of a plague spreading through the developed world like wildfire. It was the ultimate payback for a life's potential squashed by an impetuous fool.

Rinaldi envisioned state and provincial health departments and the CDC getting involved, the FBI launching an investigation, and Senator Rose becoming incensed. Cashman would lead the public to anarchy. Lawsuits would fly. The press would sensationalize the story to no end and the US president and Canadian prime minister would begin calling for heads to roll in the name of public safety. He couldn't help but admire the brilliance of his own scheme. And it will all be blamed on Abraham! The email he was about to launch would be the smoking gun. *By the time they figured out what happened,* he thought, *I will be long gone.* His escape plan was flawless.

Rinaldi planned to leave his position in a most unconventional manner. He would email his resignation letter to the acting board chair, feigning indignation at what Abraham had done behind his back. He would explain that he was leaving immediately. In the letter, he would state that, in accordance with the terms of his employment contract, he had authorized the transfer of the required $10 million in severance. While this was a somewhat unusual tactic, Rinaldi did not want to chance that the board might investigate his involvement and place the severance on hold. Instead, the money would land safely in a numbered account at The National Bank of Greenland. From there, he would move the money in a series of transfers, routing it through different world banks under various numbered accounts, making it virtually untraceable.

Yes, he thought, *Abraham will be blamed for everything and I will escape . . . scot-free.*

In his meticulous planning, Rinaldi had told a mid-level IT manager that he had concerns about Dr. Abraham leaving to go to a start-up competitor. Therefore, effective immediately, Abraham's email permissions were to be diverted and restricted to only Rinaldi. This way, he would be able to monitor any email coming back to Abraham on this issue and respond as if he were Abraham . . . all without Abraham's knowledge. By the time Abraham learned his email privileges had been diverted, it would be too late.

Ivanov had already been briefed and understood his marching orders. Content with the progress of his plans, Rinaldi lit a rare cigar, leaned forward in his chair, poked his right index finger onto the left section of the mouse, and clicked SEND.

CHAPTER 53

Never in her wildest dreams did Rachel Larkin imagine the solution to all her problems would be a bottle of deer urine. The research was conclusive. She had been experimenting in her kitchen for days. Deer urine, a common attractant used by hunters, mixed with an appropriate amount of household vinegar, would be nearly odor free. All that would remain would be a hint of ammonia. Her plan was simple. The solution would be placed in a spray bottle akin to those normally containing blue window cleaner. A few drops of blue food coloring converted the odd mixture into the perfect shade of skylight.

Rachel had lost countless hours of sleep. *What to do? What to do?* Her life had turned into a constant state of worry. It was agonizing. She lay awake most nights, tossing and turning, every sound in her apartment was magnified by a thousand. Her mind flooded with "What if" analyses. When she looked in the mirror, Rachel had begun to doubt she knew the person staring back. Ben was so overwhelmed—even lost, by her estimate. With all of his Rinaldi problems and medical issues, she couldn't fathom how his actions might meet the expectations of the determined words that sprang from his mouth as they were leaving the storage shed at The Harmon School. She believed the death of his mentor would add an even greater burden to his alleged resolve to defeat Rinaldi. Ben was an idea guy but it had always been her who implemented the plans, the one who got things moving. Ben often got lost between the idea and the execution. This time, there really would be an execution and she would provide both the method and the means.

She never fancied herself a killer. She had never hurt any living thing. This was different. Her one true love and all that was dear to him had been threatened . . . *with no end in sight*. Like a lioness, Rachel felt the calling to protect her cubs and swore to herself she would do whatever was necessary. Rinaldi was clearly planning to cause trouble and escape, leaving others to take the blame and clean up the mess. The authorities were useless. They would disregard any accusations as being meritless. Rinaldi needed to go and it had to look like an accident. Any protest from her conscience was defeated in the latest round of consternation. She had a plan and, if all went well, the good doctor would be gone by Monday.

Using a small funnel, she transferred the solution into the cleaning spray bottle and placed it inside a plastic bag. She grabbed her coat off a hook by the front door and headed out to the agreed-upon meeting place on Eastern Ave.

Rachel had debated performing the deed herself but wisely concluded that her presence in the scene was a nonstarter. She had a bit of money socked away. She would bestow some of it on a cleaning person. The unsuspecting office cleaner would pretty much do their normal thing. The only difference was the brand of cleaner they would use during the routine weekend office cleaning. As the former COO, she still had access to all of the personnel files, including those of the contracted cleaning service. Because of the sensitive nature of their services, Hiatus Centers required these detailed profiles for all contractors performing any type of work on the premises. It was a security measure, pure and simple. Once the plan had formed in her mind, she began researching the cleaning crew. With their Social Security numbers in hand, she was able to run background and credit checks on all of them. Rachel had chosen Damon Bell.

Bell was forty-seven and had worked for the cleaning contractor for just over a year. He possessed a ton of debt, had been evicted from his last two apartments for non-payment of rent, and owned a long record of arrests for petty crimes. Rachel concluded he could use the money and he likely had no problem bending a few rules. She had left Bell a note on his locker, typed on a plain white sheet of paper, with nothing identifying herself. It essentially told him that if he wanted to make $5,000 in cash, then meet her at a designated time and place in Patterson Park, come alone, and tell no one. The note assured him that he would not be breaking the law to earn the money.

She sat and waited. It was a windy Saturday morning. The temperature felt ten degrees colder than it actually was. She was getting anxious, wondering whether Bell would show. *Maybe the whole idea is stupid. Maybe I should try something else.* She was about to bail on the plan when she saw the thin, gaunt figure of Damon Bell approaching. He wore a wool cap on his head bearing the logo of the Baltimore Ravens. He walked like a man with a bum knee, not really a limp but a hitch in his step. A little grizzled gray beard was visible on his chin. The jeans he wore were faded and torn. A tattered gray sweatshirt hung on Bell's skeletal frame. His shoes were full of holes. To Rachel, he looked like a homeless man and for all she knew, he may well have been.

"Mr. Bell?"

"Yeah, that's right. You the one who left me that note?"

"Yes, I need your help."

"I ain't doin' nuthin' illegal. I'm keepin' my nose clean, you hear?"

She smiled to reassure him he had nothing to fear. She hated lying but, she concluded, in any war there were always casualties. "Nothing illegal involved. You work for the cleaning contractor that takes care of the Hiatus Centers corporate office on E. Pratt Street. You are cleaning the offices later today. Right?"

"Yeah, so?"

"Mr. Bell, I have here a bottle of window cleaner. All I want is when you go to clean the CEO's office, you use this bottle to clean the windows, the office chair, and spray a little on the carpet."

"Why you want to use that stuff?" he asked.

"Let's just say the CEO prefers this brand. He's very eccentric and likes things a certain way. If you agree, I have a paper bag with $5,000 cash. It's yours. You can take it with you right now."

She worried that he would take the cash and walk out on the job but she was banking on the fact that, with his history and the need to stay employed, he would accept and honor the terms of the agreement. Five thousand dollars was more than Damon Bell would make in three months. It was enough to serve as an enticement but not so much that he would just take it and run.

"Lady, I dunno know what kinda shit you tryin' to pull but if that's all you want me to do, use a different cleaner and spray it around the carpet some, man, you got yourself a deal."

"Good. I appreciate your help. Just in the CEO's office. Nowhere else. When you are done, empty the rest of the solution in the men's room toilet, flush it, and dispose of the bottle outside the building."

"I understand," was all he said.

"One more thing, on the way out, when you are completely done and don't need to reenter the office, pretend to dust the cage with the Komodo dragon. Conceal the lock and your hand with a feather duster or a rag and turn it counterclockwise. Then leave the office and lock the door. Got it?"

"Got it." He took the two bags, one with the money and one with the cleaner, and turned to walk down Eastern Ave.

"Oh, and Mr. Bell," Rachel called to him, "never speak of this to anyone, understand?"

He placed two fingers to his forehead in a mock salute to acknowledge his agreement.

For a few minutes, Rachel sat there on the Patterson Park bench on the east side of the city. She had forgotten how cold she was. Somewhere during the exchange with Damon Bell, she found her resolve. What she was doing felt right. She knew it in her bones. Disposing of Rinaldi was the path to make everything she held dear right once again.

Rachel was satisfied. She would never be caught. Investigators would not be able to determine any difference in the smell of her solution and that of any common window cleaner. By the time forensics hit the scene, the solution and its remnants would have completely evaporated. The dragon's cage, it would be assumed, was simply left unlocked after a feeding, an innocent error on the part of the owner.

Rinaldi's reign of terror would soon be over. She would free Ben, indirectly help Tomi, and forge a path for her and Ben to be together again. She envisioned the scene. Rinaldi walks into his office; the dragon, sensing the odor of his natural prey, attacks Rinaldi's ankles, pulls him to the ground and uses his powerful claws and serrated teeth to tear into Rinaldi's flesh. Her research indicated that dragons could ingest large hunks of flesh in a single feeding. It would not take long for the dragon to reduce Rinaldi to a bloody pulp. The macabre image made her queasy but in an odd way also offered a strange sense of ill-gotten victory, one in which she would get what she wanted but would then have to live with. Rachel prayed she could do just that.

CHAPTER 54

In a torrent of angst, Ben Abraham was denied sleep. Ordinarily, when sleep would not befall him, he would succumb, dress, and head to the Lab. On this night, Ben had uncharacteristically resorted to tossing and turning. His mind aloft, his conscience raging, and his heart aflutter, Ben simply could not reconcile the need to do what must be done and the morals with which he had lived his entire life. He would ultimately push himself, he knew, to the edge and over. Here he stood on the precipice of using his God-given talent for destructive purposes. *What would Gramps have thought? And his parents? Or Albert?* To date, he had dedicated his time and talents to the betterment of mankind. Now, the moment at hand, he was about to complete the plan to vanquish his staunchest foe.

Harrison's E. Pratt Street "tackle" was executed to perfection. Ari, always the inventor and never one to shy from an immense challenge, created the replica cane, using one of his newest toys, a high-end 3-D printer. Inside the uppermost section, Ari had inserted the tiniest amount of C-4 explosive and in the lower section, a remote GPS transmitter. The plan was to track Rinaldi's movements and, at the appropriate time, when he was most likely to be alone in his Ellicott City home, transmit an activation code to the cane. The activation code would trigger a fibrous heating element. Along with the simple force of Rinaldi's own body weight, the necessary combination of heat and pressure would cause an effective explosion.

Ben was proud of his team for their ingenuity and discretion. Tomi, dressed as a city street cleaner, had done a great job of retrieving the real cane and handing Harrison the replica before Rinaldi had gathered his senses. Sitting across the street, Ben had watched the whole scene unfold through a pair of high-powered binoculars at an outdoor cafe on the second level of Harborplace's E. Pratt Street shopping pavilion. If all went as expected, Rinaldi would soon be dead and the cause would be ruled a gas explosion. The intense heat of the fire would destroy any opportunity to detect the minute amount of C-4. It should work like a charm. Still, Ben wrestled with the morality of it all. He once again contemplated notifying the authorities. For the thousandth time, he dismissed the notion. Rinaldi had built an airtight bubble around himself. He'd been planning all of this shit for years. With no discernable evidence in hand, Ben was doing the right thing. For all he knew, even if the authorities wanted to investigate, it would take months. Time was a luxury he did not currently enjoy.

He thought about Rachel. He knew she would do anything to help. Something prevented him from asking. At some level, he just didn't want Rachel to think less of him. Harrison and Ari would run through brick walls for him. In a sense, they were loyal soldiers. Tomi owed him. Rachel, even after all their troubles, was still piercing his veil of indifference. Maybe after it was all over, he would tell her what he had done.

It was 8:00 a.m. when Ben rolled up to the Lab. As soon as he broached the main lobby, his cell phone began to vibrate. It was Tony Pulaski, the center manager in Chicago. Ben had hired Tony to manage their first Chicago location in those early whirlwind days of expanding the company. Pulaski, Harrison, and Ben had gotten wasted more than once after long days getting the huge Chicago center ready for business. Tony was a fun guy. Ben always enjoyed hearing from him.

"Good morning," Ben said. "How's kicks in The Windy City?"

"Going good, brother. I wanted to apologize. I was away for the weekend and just saw your email. I know it said to call Ivanov with questions but hey, I just don't like the little weasel."

"Email? What are you talking about?" With the words barely out of his mouth, Ben got a sick feeling in the pit of his stomach.

"The one you sent Friday afternoon about changing all the Liferay settings to prepare for the new seventy-two-hour awakening protocol starting today. It'll only take a few minutes and our first awakenings aren't scheduled for another hour or so."

Immediately suspicious of another Rinaldi scheme, Ben said, "Tony, don't make any changes. I didn't send any email out on Friday and there is no new seventy-two-hour protocol. I am going to need you to do me a favor."

Ben instructed Pulaski to forward the email in question to a private account. He turned around, got back into his car, and drove home. Ben would need to access his personal email away from the prying eyes of Hiatus Centers' servers.

The short drive home took forever. School buses, farmers on heavy equipment, and every slow driving asshole imaginable was in his way. When he finally arrived, he shifted the Honda into park and bolted up the stairs, two at a time. Ben logged onto his personal laptop and hit the envelope icon to retrieve his email. A flood of incoming email arrived. He looked at this stuff so infrequently. His parents occasionally sent email. The rest were retailers from which he made sporadic purchases. Dozens of emails to delete. Another time. For now, only one email was important. The one forwarded by Tony Pulaski. And there it was, second from the top. He clicked on the entry and began to read.

Oh my God, Ben thought. Looking at the specifications for the revised Liferay settings, the plan immediately became clear. He actually wants Hiatus Centers' awakened clients to drop dead in public. Ben instantly comprehended the enormous ramifications of the plot. The problems he now faced at Rinaldi's hand would look like child's play compared to the aftermath of this scheme.

Too many lives hung in the balance. It was no longer about Rinaldi going after him and his inner circle. To completely ruin him, Rinaldi was now going after Ben and anyone or anything who stood in the way. Hundreds of hibernating clients and their families were now squarely in Rinaldi's crosshairs, not to mention the potential public health problem that would ensue across North America and potentially the rest of the developed world. No, Ben had to place his personal code of ethics aside. Rinaldi's plan was in play right now. He knew that if he stood by and watched, hundreds of thousands, maybe more, might die from the rapid spread of airborne disease.

The revised Liferay settings indicated the core of Rinaldi's plan; to use the awakened clients as "hosts" for his true goal, the creation of an epidemic. The sick and twisted mind of Anstrov Rinaldi had envisioned the spread of a deadly disease across the continent and beyond. Ben would not allow that to happen. He still prayed he could save them all.

Ben reached into his pocket for his cell phone to call Jess Miller.

"Jess, I'm short on time. If I sent you an email, can you track the sender's IP address for me?"

"Sure can. If you forward it to me now, I might be able to get you an answer while we are on the phone."

"Coming your way."

"What did you wind up doing with the information I shared in Georgetown?"

"I used it to go back to old records at The Harmon School. I found the original application file for Abandonato. He's apparently blaming me for the disabilities he incurred after his rejection from the school. I gave him bum info for his interview with the headmaster."

"Well, he certainly has gone to great lengths to get even, wouldn't you say?"

"I would. In fact, I think you are going to tell me that it's Rinaldi's IP address that sent the email this past Friday."

Miller hesitated. "Wait a minute, hmm, oh man! I got a definitive IP at Hiatus Centers HQ in Baltimore. Here is the originator's IP address. You'll need to find someone at the company to identify whose computer is associated with this IP address."

Ben was an advanced computer user and programmer. He knew that a computer's internet protocol, or IP address, was like a person's DNA. The IP address uniquely identified a single computer with a specific numeric sequence. Ben took down the IP address and thanked Miller. Now, how to determine who this specific IP address belonged to? Maybe Rachel could help. *Or maybe she can find Ivanov and we can get him to see that he doesn't want to spend the rest of his life in jail for being Rinaldi's lackey.* Ben had no choice. He needed help and Rachel was uniquely qualified to assist.

Ben dialed Rachel, who answered on the second ring.

"Rache, I need your help. If I give you an IP address from within HQ, can you discreetly nail down who the owner is . . . and fast?"

"Sure, I have security privileges to figure it out in about two minutes. What's going on?"

Ben explained the offending email and his suspicion that Rinaldi was trying to terminate awakened clients to create a deadly plague.

"Are you sure? I mean, of course you are sure. Oh my God. Hang on with me. Let me see what I can find out."

He held on while she researched the IP address. Through the phone, he could hear the furious banging of keys on Rachel's keyboard.

"I did a search of the number to see which employee is matched to the specific IP address. It was yours."

"I keep a second laptop in my Baltimore office. He must have used a master key to just walk into my office. I gotta go. I need to get Ari to help reverse the damage Rinaldi is trying to inflict. I think we can reverse every location's Liferay settings from Maplebrook."

As he was about to hang up, another thought occurred to him.

"Hey, one more thing. I need to speak with Ivanov but he doesn't answer his phone. I want to try to get him to turn. He can likely corroborate Rinaldi's plan and give us valuable information. Can you track him down and get him to return my call ASAP?"

Rachel agreed.

Before Pulaski had called, Ben thought he was in control. The simple push of a button on a remote control would end it all. The Pulaski call had changed everything. If he pushed that button too soon, they might not learn all they needed to know about Rinaldi's intended plague. Was there more he hadn't yet contemplated? *I might need the bastard alive for a while longer.*

Ben dialed Ari to begin dialog on how to overturn the pending apocalypse. After he got Ari started on reversing the Liferay settings, he made one more call. This one was to Senator James Rose.

CHAPTER 55

When Rachel hung up with Ben, her head was spinning. A plague? No one saw that coming. They knew that cell mutations occur rapidly without reapplying Bock's preservative a few hours prior to the expiration of a twenty-four-hour awakening. Heck, she and Tomi proved that out before the first commercial center had opened. If awakened clients were left to mutate, their cells would decay so rapidly that they would not only enter a state of permanent death but their bodies would take less than ten minutes to look as if they had been dead for months. But decaying bodies would not spread disease just by dropping and rotting, at least not on a mass scale. Was there really a reason to worry about a plague? As soon as she found Ivanov and got him to call Ben, she would get to a computer and begin researching. As long as they could get the awakened back to each location within a few hours, all of the trouble should be avoided.

Rachel walked down to Ivanov's office. She was so preoccupied by the conversation with Ben, she momentarily forgot about her anxiety regarding Rinaldi. He might even be dead by now. Her brain felt as if it were swelling. She was great under pressure, carrying a heavy burden. When Rachel arrived at Ivanov's office, her mind was in a distant place. She failed to realize she hadn't placed her hand on the knob to open the door. Rachel's forehead hit the glass pane hard and she was knocked backward. She stayed on her feet but was dazed. Feeling a bruise rapidly developing on her forehead, Rachel approached the door once again but this time, entered in the conventional manner.

"You okay there, Dr. Larkin?" inquired Maddie, Ivanov's assistant.

Feeling foolish, she replied reticently, "Yup, just wasn't paying attention. I'm okay. Hey, is Dr. Ivanov in his office?"

"No. Last I saw him, he was heading over to Dr. Rinaldi's office to pick up a FedEx envelope. You might find him over there."

The pain in her head from the encounter with the door felt like a picnic compared to the storm that now ensued. *How stupid.* The thought of someone else entering the office had never really occurred to her. She had surmised that, outside the cleaning crew, Rinaldi had the only key. The guy was obsessive about his privacy. When Ben moved out of the office, Rinaldi had immediately changed the lock. Would he have given Ivanov a key to his private office? Maybe the FedEx envelope was sitting in the reception area with Traci. But suppose the FedEx envelope was *in* the office? *Oh shit!* What would she find? Was Ivanov dead or did he discover Rinaldi's remains?

She slowed her walk to a crawl. Sweat was forming on her brow. *Act naturally! Don't give anyone a reason to be suspicious of you*, she reminded herself. Her cell phone began to vibrate. She looked down at the display. It was Ben. She would have to call him back. If she answered now, her voice might reveal her anxiety. She ducked into a restroom, splashed cold water on her face, and collected her resolve to keep moving forward. *You've come this far*, she told herself. *See it through.*

Rachel's senses heightened before she got to Rinaldi's office. From around the corner, she could hear the commotion. A crowd had formed outside the office. Yellow crime tape cordoned off the entrance to the reception area and Rinaldi's private office. Rachel looked through the picture window normally offering a clean view of Drago in all his splendor. It was empty. Had her plan worked or did it backfire in the worst imaginable way? *Stay cool*, she thought.

She spotted Traci, Rinaldi's assistant, amongst the crowd. Traci had a handkerchief to her face. The tip of her nose was red, as were her eyes, from the hysterics following the discovery. A policewoman was leading her to a hallway bench and offering a cold bottle of water. Rachel made her way over and motioned to the officer.

"I'm a friend. I can sit with her, if you like."

Rachel sat down beside Traci and placed an arm around her shoulders. While she knew what had probably happened, she needed to play her part. Despite her own feelings of guilt over what she caused, her nurturing manner genuinely felt for what Traci was going through. She wanted to offer comfort while continuing to precipitate the ruse.

"Did something happen to Dr. Rinaldi?' she asked gently, already believing she knew the answer.

Traci lifted her head and, through her sobs, managed to utter the words that crushed Rachel Larkin. "No, Dr. Rinaldi didn't come in today. He left me a message saying he was working from home. The Komodo dragon got loose somehow and attacked Dr. Ivanov."

Her plan had failed. Rinaldi was alive. She killed the wrong man. How could she tell Ben? He was looking for help from Ivanov. Just like with the experimental Liferay, her well-intentioned extraordinary measures to help Ben had once again crashed and burned. She started to cry. It was okay. No one would suspect anything. She was empathizing with Traci over the horrid loss of a colleague.

When they both collected themselves, Traci recounted seeing the empty cage when she arrived that morning. She immediately became alarmed and notified Dr. Rinaldi, who told her that he had instructed Dr. Ivanov to go into his office and retrieve a FedEx package. Ivanov had the only other key. It had to be him, Traci had said.

"Didn't they find Dr. Ivanov's body in there?" Rachel asked.

Traci began to sob uncontrollably. "Not exactly," she stammered. "They brought out pieces of a body. It was impossible to tell who it was.

But it had to be Dr. Ivanov. No one else had a key except the cleaning people and they found Dr. Ivanov's ID badge on the floor."

"And Ivanov is currently unaccounted for."

Traci was still borderline hysterical. Rachel needed to get back to Ben. She wasn't sure what she would tell him. But she couldn't abandon Traci. She decided to keep her talking.

"Where's the Komodo?

Traci looked up. Some men came with a net. I think they were from Animal Control. They may have said something about taking it to The Maryland Zoo."

Rachel didn't know what else to say. She stayed close and then, mercifully, saw Traci's husband coming down the corridor. He was her escape route. She handed off the comforting duties to Traci's spouse and left to contemplate her next move.

Her mind was flooding with conflicting thoughts. Did Rinaldi often work from home? She had no idea. Did Rinaldi somehow know to stay away this morning? Even Damon Bell couldn't have told Rinaldi anything meaningful. But wasn't his story, on its own, enough to raise suspicion in Rinaldi's mind? Yes, she concluded, most definitely. Still, she wasn't convinced. Bell wouldn't even know how to reach Rinaldi. Did he have a guilty conscience after he did what she asked? But what exactly would he have told Rinaldi, anyway? A lady whose name I don't know paid me to use a different brand of cleaning fluid in your office? All she really knew was that Ivanov was dead and she was responsible. The good news was that no one would ever rule this a homicide. That was her intent all along. She could just keep her mouth shut. She didn't need to tell Ben, the police, or anyone else.

She needed to return Ben's call. Rinaldi's plan was in motion. Rachel told herself to try and focus on helping Ben stop Rinaldi. Everything else could come later. She had never felt so confused. Inherently, Rachel knew she had to tell Ben the truth. There could be no more secrets. She owed him that much. They were finally starting to get back a little bit of what they once shared but now she foresaw any chance of a future with Ben vanishing before her very eyes.

In an instant, Rachel's cognitive ability to form a rational thought completely dissipated. She would call Ben and perhaps, after that, she would walk back down the hallway and turn herself in to the investigating officer.

CHAPTER 56

It was the beginning of the end. Rinaldi sat back in his leather recliner and watched as CNN reported that Hiatus Centers' awakened patients had been passing out all over the eastern United States and Canada. Rinaldi clasped his fingertips together, creating a steeple, and marveled at the news of a middle-aged woman named Linda Martin who had been awakened for just over four hours before she keeled over in downtown Philadelphia. The CNN reporter paused and reminded the audience that what they were about to see contained graphic images not suitable for young viewers or those with a weak constitution. A crude video showed Martin and her daughter and grandchildren at a restaurant having lunch. At first glance, it would have appeared to the average person that Martin had suffered some sort of heart attack. After becoming unconscious, her body slid from the chair and crumpled to the floor. A waiter delivering food to an adjacent table had poor reaction time and tripped over the corpse. Food went everywhere. Linda Martin's face appeared to be covered in some sort of greenish-gray sauce from the spilled meal. Rinaldi took heart at what was really occurring. The rapid decomposition process had begun. Restaurant patrons were aghast. Many were seen holding table linen to their noses to guard against the sudden noxious odor emanating from the remains. The video cut away when the victim's grandchildren, aged ten and eight, began to scream in horror.

In Atlanta, a report ensued about a young awakened client named Jen Summers who was blonde and beautiful and just twenty-eight at the age of death. She asked for and received permission from her husband, Jed, to drive his car back to the home they once shared in the suburbs. Ignoring that the awakened no longer had driving privileges, Jed Summers reasoned that the existence of a license was inconsequential. The field reporter described how the awakened Hiatus Centers' client expired behind the wheel, causing a twelve-car pileup on a major highway. The weeping husband was being interviewed, haunted by the sight of his once-beautiful bride decomposing before his eyes and the accompanying overpowering odor. Rinaldi cracked a smile when other stalled drivers in the snarled traffic provided accounts of the rotting corpse. One man even exclaimed, "Her body began melting away, like a special effect in a horror movie."

In Florida, the media was in a frenzy as the Cane family took their awakened ten-year-old, Trevor, to Disney World for the day. *That is perfect*, thought Rinaldi. *An amusement park!* He couldn't have scripted it any better. Cane's decomposition would instantly spread the plague to thousands of carriers.

Scenes like these were unfolding across eastern and central time zones. Shortly, the same episodes would be manifested on the West Coast. Like a restaurant chain with a contaminated food supply, Hiatus Centers' reputation was being systematically and irrevocably destroyed.

Rinaldi didn't have much time. Watching the news was a small luxury he had allowed himself. After all, years of plotting were coming to a head. Who wouldn't want to witness the events as they unfolded? He flipped channels. Fox News, MSNBC, they were all on top of stories similar to the scenes in Philadelphia, Atlanta, and Orlando. He watched as Fox reported on an elderly awakened man who began decomposing in a crowded coffee venue in Harrisburg. MSNBC had a similar story about three cases unfolding simultaneously in New York City, one along

Fifth Avenue, another in Times Square, and a third in Brooklyn. While all the networks were covering the pungent effects of the decompositions, no one had begun to report on the possible spread of disease. That suited Rinaldi just fine. The longer it took to figure out the real problem, the greater the damage that would be inflicted.

Ultimately, he knew that someone would identify the destructive agent his plot depended upon: Cadaverine. The putrid-smelling toxic compound containing two different amino groups was common in the decomposition of animal carcasses, not so much in humans. Rinaldi reflected on the marvel of his own brilliance. For the man who had cracked the fountain of youth and commercialized the results in the form of BV3000, altering the Liferay settings to cause the opposite effect, rapid decomposition, was a walk in the park. He loved that his human Cadaverine formula would confound the most astute of world scientists. The majority of the scientific community would dismiss the notion of Cadaverine for the simple reason that it was not common to human beings. No one would outsmart Anstrov Rinaldi. Yes, his own Cadaverine formula was the coup de grâce. Now that it had begun to spread, there was no known, effective way to neutralize the impact.

Rinaldi's lone bag was packed. The early afternoon was already upon him. He would soon depart for the chartered plane that would whisk him away to a life of luxurious oblivion. It was time to anonymously send the "Abraham" email to the media. Using a fake identity and a credit card by the same name, Rinaldi logged onto the website of a pay-by-the transaction press release service. He uploaded only the text of the Abraham email and paid the premium price for an immediate, national release to all major media outlets. Within the hour, every station in the country would have a copy and a manhunt for Ben Abraham would begin.

CHAPTER 57

Ben couldn't deny it. His remission had ended. The intense headaches, insomnia, and dizzy spells were all telltale signs. While he hadn't had a full blown seizure in nearly six months, he knew a storm was in the offing. All of his troubles were reaching a crescendo. Basic human physiology told him that extreme stress would exacerbate his condition. Even though he fully understood the consequences, he willed himself to press forward. If things worked out the way he planned, there would be time in the near future to get back to the intricate work of solving his medical issue. Assuming, of course, the aftermath of the experimental Liferay didn't kill him first.

Ben stretched and yawned. He was bone tired. *Courage, strength, patience, wisdom.* Gramps' familiar tome permeated the malaise. Right now, it was the strength part he needed most. After hanging up with Senator Rose, Ben made sure Ari began looking into the altered Liferay settings and then made his way back to the Lab. He could use the facilities as his base of operation and make his greatest impact there. Having his trusted team members and closest friends nearby in a time of crisis didn't hurt, either.

Ari worked well under pressure. He was able to quickly revert all Liferay settings remotely from Maplebrook. All Liferays were equipped with wireless connectivity enabling an encrypted call from an authorized user anywhere in the world. Until now, this had never been attempted. Ben had always preferred to have Liferay settings changed locally by the center manager. Using the internet, even with the best encryption technology, left open the possibility of Liferays being hacked. Although the risk was slight, Ben had never wanted to take the chance.

Today, of course, was different. The company was under attack. Center managers would all be in damage control mode. Even if they wanted the Liferay changes to be made locally, there was no guarantee that each center manager could be reached to make an immediate change. No, it had to be done this way. The download process had begun. Ben watched Ari's computer screen as it indicated the status of each location's download. The larger cities with robust connection speeds were completed faster. The smaller locations would take a little more time. Ari assured him the process would be complete across the continent within the hour.

Ben retreated to his office. He decided it best to construct an email to the center managers describing what measures were being taken regarding the attack on the company. Ben needed to convey that the Friday afternoon email sent under his name had been a security breach instigated by the perpetrator of the attack. Even though he knew Rinaldi was behind everything, it was not yet time to publicly place blame. The center managers would learn the truth soon enough. Ben also wanted to reaffirm the directive to suspend all scheduled awakenings and to have all clients awakened that morning be taken to a quarantine location. After logging his credentials, an error message flashed on his screen. It read, "Insufficient security privileges. Please see the system administrator."

Damn! Rinaldi had his access pulled. *Probably at the same time he sent the bogus email under my name.* Ben went into a word processing program, typed out the email, he wanted to send and printed a copy. He took the sheet of paper to Tomi and had her send the email on his behalf. As he walked out of his office to find her, he was intercepted by an animated Harrison Bock.

"We need to talk. Your theory about Rinaldi making the awakened clients into carriers for disease was spot on."

Ben remained stoic. "Were you able to isolate the reaction? We need to know exactly what we are dealing with here."

"Oh yeah. And you're not going to like it."

"Come on, Harrison." Ben was tired and agitated. "I have no time for theatrics. Just spit it out."

"Are you familiar with Cadaverine?"

Ben had heard of it. He recalled some distant level of minute detail involving the putrefaction process in animals and a foul smell from the compound.

"Isn't it inherent only in animal carcasses?" he asked.

"It is, generally speaking. And in those instances, it can initiate the spread of airborne disease. Your friend, Rinaldi, figured out how to have the Liferay create a human form."

"Are you shitting me? How bad is it?"

"No, I'm quite serious. Cadaverine from an animal carcass would be nonlethal if it were less than .25 parts per million. Rinaldi created a supercharged version of Cadaverine. It fires on all cylinders at 3 parts per million. Way beyond a reasonable short-term exposure rate for humans."

Ben was beside himself. This was unfathomable. "Do you know how to reverse the effects?"

"That's the rub. This is uncharted territory. It will take months, if not more, to figure it out."

"So, everyone exposed to the lethal amount of Cadaverine is going to fall prey to rapid decomposition and become a carrier themselves?"

"That sounds like the plan."

"Harrison, this could wipe out the human race!" They stood there in silence, soaking in the crushing reality of what they were discussing. "I know the odds are long but you've got to find a way to turn this around."

Ben pulled his cell phone out of his pocket. He needed to ask Rachel about getting the awakened back into the fold and into quarantined areas. Rachel picked up on a single ring.

"No time for talk. Harrison determined that Rinaldi's altered Liferay settings will create a lethal spread of a compound called Cadaverine. We believe it will cause everyone in contact with an awakened client to be infected. Separate quarantine facilities need to be established for the awakened and those that may have come in contact with the awakened. Tell the local authorities to make use of schools, churches, synagogues, and community halls. Corral any large facility available and for God's sake, keep the two groups separated. No one should be near the quarantined groups without full gas mask and oxygen apparatus."

His next call would be to Dr. Ellington Lawson, the Director of The Centers for Disease Control. Dr. Lawson could mobilize resources that his team could not. In addition, CDC would tap the knowledge banks of the World Health Organization and their own teams to hopefully find a solution to this nightmare. Before he could dial, a hallway speaker came to life.

"Dr. Abraham, please call the front desk. Dr. Abraham, call the front desk, please."

Now what? He picked up a courtesy phone on a wall mount and dialed the front desk.

"Amy, it's Dr. Abraham. What's up?"

"Dr. Abraham, the FBI is in the lobby. They want to see you," she spoke in a hushed tone.

"Did they say what they wanted?"

"I might suggest you turn on a television news channel before you walk down here."

Ben walked back over to Ari's lab section. He had a TV in his area. He found Ari and they clicked on Fox News. Ben saw his own face all over the screen. The reporter was droning on about the email that had been sent Friday afternoon. Ben was being placed in the center of the controversy. Rinaldi had sucker punched him once more. His head began to pound and his chest tightened.

"I have to go the lobby to be arrested. Call Lawson at CDC, alert FEMA, and call George Diamond."

Then, in a moment of absolute clarity, Ben Abraham reached into the left pocket of his trousers and retrieved the small remote control Ari had created to accompany the replica walnut cane. He checked the locator app on his smartphone. Satisfied, he closed the app, unlocked the keypad on the tiny remote, pushed the red button, and handed the device to Ari.

"Destroy this."

CHAPTER 58

When his assistant called to let him know about Ivanov's unfortunate demise, Rinaldi could not help but wonder if there was a deeper meaning beyond the face of the morning's events. *Was Ivanov's death a botched assassination on his own life?* Drago had never attacked anyone in the years he had been with Rinaldi. *What would have caused this? And why was the cage unlocked?* He was the only one who fed Drago. He never left the cage unlocked. No, all of his senses were screaming. This was deliberate! But who? Abraham? He had the motive but in Rinaldi's estimation, Abraham was too much of a coward to take such action. Could Abraham have hired someone to take him out? He was perplexed, for sure. He decided that, with his imminent departure at hand, he didn't need to tax his brain on the matter.

Truth be told, Ivanov had always been expendable, an insignificant token who merely played a supporting role in his grand master plan. He concluded that he would actually miss Drago more. In a strange way, the Komodo dragon had been the best friend he ever had.

Anstrov Rinaldi was ready to depart. Everything would be left behind. His one bag was a small leather duffel. All he would carry was a single change of clothing and some basic toiletries. And, of course, a fake passport, along with $100,000 in cash. Rinaldi chose Argentinian and Chilean currencies. These would be of use once he reached his final destination.

Rinaldi was confident that his conscientious engineering would reward the effort. In little more than an hour, he would be on the first of three private jets, winging his way to Argentina via the carefully chosen, circuitous route to his new South American home. He had multiple stops with a leased jet in each of three locations. None of the pilots know of the prior pilot's existence. All of the jets were secured from different charter companies. With each, Rinaldi used a different false identity. All of the charters were paid for with drafts originating from a numbered account in the Cayman Islands. As soon as the last draft was initiated, he would terminate the Cayman account.

First, it was on to Mexico City where he had a two-hour layover and then another flight to the tiny island of Aruba. From Oranjestad, the third leg would carry him to Ministro Pistarini International Airport in Buenos Aires. The plan made for a long and arduous journey but he wanted to avoid the possibility of being traced.

In Buenos Aires, a private 4WD luxury vehicle would be waiting to take him to his new home. He could have taken one last flight but he thought it better to be cautious. The driver would be paid handsomely, in cash, for his discretion and for making the 1,100 km ride across the rough Argentinian terrain, some of which was unpaved. It would be unpleasant after so much air travel but he didn't care. There would be plenty of time to rest once he arrived in the serene splendor of his faraway retreat.

Baxter was waiting outside. The first jet from BWI left in ninety minutes. Rinaldi sighed and stood up to take a last look around. He would miss this place—not as much as Alsace, but he would miss it nonetheless. Rinaldi's thoughts turned to his new palatial home in Patagonia. This made him smile. He picked up his cane and noticed an odd notch where the handle met the base. Maybe the damage occurred when Bock knocked him over. He studied it carefully. *Was that damage or had someone substituted a lookalike? To what end?* He had a bum leg and was blind in one eye, but his sense of hearing was acute. He placed the lower part of the cane to his ear and heard a distinct buzzing sound. It was faint, almost undiscernible. *Someone had bugged the cane!* He didn't have time to dismantle it. He did not want to be late for his getaway charter.

It was time to go. While he treasured the old cane, a gift from a mentor, he would have to abandon it. Perhaps, he thought, Baxter could dump the cane in the nearby Patapsco River on the way to the airport. No, that was an unnecessary precaution. He would just leave it in the house. With no time left to think, he set the cane to the floor one final time, allowing it to support his body weight, and moved toward the front door.

CHAPTER 59

Ivanov's grizzly death had cast a grim pallor on the staff of Hiatus Centers' headquarters in Baltimore. Rinaldi had not yet communicated on the matter and Ben couldn't be reached. If it were up to Rachel, she would have closed the office for the day. Except for essential staff working to reverse Rinaldi's evil doings, there was really no need for anyone else to be there.

Rachel was stationed in her office, working at a feverish pace to reach the center managers and establish quarantine facilities across the large North American continent. It was no small feat and progress was painfully slow. The first thing she did was to call Tomi in Maplebrook and enlist her help. Rachel had already emailed and texted instructions to each center manager to begin the urgent process of locating facilities in their area. She would contact FEMA, who in turn, would alert each state's equivalent agency. The federal and state governments would be able to mobilize private resources much faster than she.

Her cell phone rang. It was Ari. Should she pick up? She had so much to do. They were in an emergency state and time was of the essence. Yeah, he might have a new development that needed to be communicated to the center managers. She'd better answer.

"Ari, what's up?"

"The FBI just left here. They arrested Ben. Apparently, Rinaldi leaked the bogus email from Friday afternoon to the media."

Her voice was panicked and now distressed. A lump formed in her throat as she replied. "What can I do?"

"I am contacting Ben's lawyer, the CDC, and WHO. Can you get on the phone with FEMA and the state emergency management associations?"

"Already on it. Did the revised Liferay settings get deployed?"

"Yes, all downloads are nearly complete. We saved a lot of people. If the Pacific time zone awakenings had occurred today, the magnitude of the current crisis would be much worse."

Before she could reply, Rachel heard a woman shriek from around the corner. With her cell phone to her ear, she walked out to the hallway to see what was happening.

"What the hell was that?" Ari asked.

Rachel walked toward the ruckus. "I don't know. There are some people around a TV set and a lot of noise. Let me try to get in closer."

As she made her way to the lounge where the TV was, she got a closer look at the flat screen. CNN was reporting a gas leak caused an explosion at the home of Anstrov Rinaldi in Ellicott City, Maryland. The Hiatus Centers' CEO was believed to have been in the house at the time.

"Oh my God. You are not going to believe this!"

"Rachel, what's happening?"

"Turn on your TV. Rinaldi's house just blew up from a gas leak. It's destroyed and he was believed to be inside."

No reply came from the other end of the line.

"Did you hear what I just said?"

All she heard were crickets. "Ari, are you still there?"

The reply came slowly. "Yes, I heard you. That's incredible. A gas leak, you say?"

Rachel Larkin had an uncanny ability to sense when people were lying to her. Her skin was tingling. This was one of those times.

"What are you trying *not* to say?" she quizzed.

"Nothing. I gotta go. I need to get on the horn with CDC and WHO." And he clicked off.

Rachel's sense of wonder was on high alert. Ari was clearly fibbing. But why? Could he have had something to do with the explosion? Like her, Ari had fallen into disfavor with Ben over the incident with the experimental Liferay. Could Ari have had the same idea as her? Getting rid of Rinaldi to get back in good graces with Ben? Rachel couldn't dismiss the notion but admittedly, it surprised her to think Ari had it in him. She supposed he would think the same of her. How ironic! With so much to do, she would have to ponder it all later.

FEMA had emergency reporting numbers. But all she got were auto-attendants—press 1 for this, 2 for that. What a waste. Here was a full-blown, five-star, federal emergency and she couldn't reach a live person. Never having to call FEMA before, she had wrongly assumed it would be like calling 911. It was futile. She couldn't waste any more time. Apparently, FEMA had to be called into action by the president of the United States. He wasn't about to take her call so she reverted to the obvious. She called 911.

"9-1-1, what's your emergency?"

"This is Dr. Rachel Larkin. I am an executive with Hiatus Centers in Baltimore. Our awakening processes across North America have been compromised and there is currently a very real health threat that could kill thousands of people across the continent and maybe beyond if we can't contain it."

The 911 operator appeared miffed. She had not received training for this type of call.

"How can we help?" was all she said.

Rachel wanted to explode. "I need the president to call FEMA. A state of emergency must be declared. The same applies for Canada."

Again the operator responded slowly. "Our emergency response system does not provide for those actions, ma'am. I suggest you reach out to the federal authorities." And the operator hung up. Rachel was frustrated that the operator took the call as a prank. *I guess she hasn't turned on a TV today or looked at her phone for a news alert.*

Precious minutes were ticking away. What to do next? She needed a lifeline at the federal level. Then a revelation occurred. Senator Rose! He would know how to move this forward with expediency. She quickly Googled the Washington, DC, phone number for the senator's office and clicked on the link to dial.

"Senator Rose's office," the sterile voice replied.

Rachel repeated the same routine she had for the 911 operator. Only this time, given the adversarial relationship Hiatus Centers had with Senator Rose, his staffer knew exactly who she was and understood why she was calling. The staffer took Rachel's cell phone number and promised that the Senator would call her personally within minutes.

Five minutes passed. It felt like five hours. Her cell phone rang.

"Doctah Lahkin, this is Senatah James Rose. What exactly is happening?"

Rachel held nothing back. Short of her botched attempt on Rinaldi's life, she told him everything she knew, including Rinaldi's sabotage of the Liferay settings and Ben's apprehension by the FBI.

"Senator, I know we've been on opposite ends of the issue but right now, if you don't help me to get the president and Canadian prime minister to declare states of emergency, the entire human race could be affected."

"Ah undahstand. I will call the president pehsonally. Ah presume Ah can reach you at this numbah?"

"Yes and thank you."

Satisfied that she had done all she could for the moment, she called George Diamond. She wanted to know where they were holding Ben. That was where she was heading next.

CHAPTER 60

Ben had never been inside a federal holding facility. He guessed this one was three or four steps up from the stereotypical jail scene he knew from the movies. The FBI building in the Baltimore suburb of Woodlawn was a few miles outside the city line, near the Social Security Administration campus. While it wasn't really a holding facility, a small portion of the building was reserved for detaining people of interest. It was a four-story structure containing mostly office and conference space. Ben was being held in an upper-level detention room by Special Agent Ronald Franklin. The room was fairly empty except for a five-foot wood-top folding table and four aluminum folding chairs. Ben was grateful that he could at least see outside from the fourth floor windows.

Franklin was a man of average height, 5 feet 9 inches or so, by Ben's estimate. He was lean and wore a black formfitting light wool suit to reveal his penchant for weightlifting. Ben wasn't sure if the FBI agent was vain or just wanted to intimidate. Probably both, he reasoned. Special Agent Franklin was loaded for bear. Ben was the target and in his mind, the premise of "innocent until proven guilty" did not apply on this particular day. There would be no benefit of the doubt bestowed on him. Franklin was the senior agent. His partner was Special Agent Tess Ziglar. To Ben, she looked young, fresh out of training. Franklin would do all the talking.

"Tell us, Dr. Abraham, how did you see yourself escaping from the aftermath of this devious plot to end the world?"

Ben paused, sat straight up in his chair, and took in a deep breath. The question was accusatory and dripping with sarcasm. He wisely determined that his best course of action was not to say anything that may incriminate him.

"My attorney is on the way. I think I'll wait for him to answer any of your questions. All I can say is that I was framed and have done nothing except work as hard as I can to stop the madman behind today's events."

Franklin looked back in disgust. "Framed, eh? Yeah, Doc, they all say that at this stage of the game. Don't you worry now, the truth will come out and it won't take long, either."

Ben was pinning his hopes on exactly that. The world was falling apart. Ari was working feverishly with Harrison, Tomi, and Rachel to make things right again. He badly wanted to be in the mix, doing whatever he could. Time was being pissed away. With each passing moment, his anger rose with the ferocity of a wave crashing to shore. Ben's train of thought was interrupted by a buzzer. A small wall panel by the door became illuminated by an amber light. Special Agent Ziglar responded by picking up a handset on the panel.

"Okay, I'll be right down to get her."

She looked at Ben and said, "You have a visitor. I'll go run her through security, badge her, and bring her up."

Ben was so pissed off, he wasn't thinking straight. *Her? Where was George? Didn't he understand the magnitude of the problem? He sent a junior associate?* Franklin muttered something about checking his messages and walked out behind Ziglar. Every passing moment on the old-fashioned analog wall clock reminded Ben that people were dying while he was being detained. Sure, the team was doing all they could. Yes, he trusted them implicitly. But dammit, he could be helping! Ben supposed this was exactly what Rinaldi wanted. *At least that asshole won't be causing any more trouble,* Ben thought reassuringly.

His mind wandered precipitously to how it must have happened. Did Rinaldi figure out who or what was behind his demise or did it just happen? Ben hoped that Rinaldi somehow figured it out in his final moments but then again, it didn't really matter. Rinaldi was gone and the world was a better place without him.

Ben had been detained for about ninety minutes. Add to that the forty-minute ride from Maplebrook to Baltimore. Ben hadn't seen or heard a lick of news since his arrest. He was hoping his plan to rid the world of Anstrov Rinaldi had succeeded, but he still didn't know for sure.

His chain of thought was derailed when a buzzer once again sounded, then a loud door clicked as the mechanical bolts slid horizontally and Special Agent Ziglar returned with Rachel in tow.

"I'll leave you two to speak until your attorney arrives," Ziglar said. Rachel sat down at the only table in the room, in a seat opposite Ben.

"What are you doing here?" he almost bellowed, "You should be helping the team." His words betrayed his undeniable feeling of relief at seeing Rachel's face. In his deepest troubles of late, it was always thoughts of Rachel that brought him back around. Even when he tried not to love her, that smile disarmed him.

"Relax," she said. "I think things are as under control as they can be. I didn't have anything else substantive to do. Someone needed to be here with you." On cue, she delivered that warming smile and his inhibitions melted away.

"I'm glad you are here." He replied and returned her smile. He took her hand in his. "I haven't seen any news since I got picked up. What's happening?"

"To start, Ivanov is dead and Rinaldi's house blew up—they believe, with him in it. The media is saying it was a gas explosion. I don't know for sure, but I think, as crazy as it sounds, Ari might have something to do with it." She whispered the last part for fear of being overheard by the FBI's monitoring system.

Ben was relieved. Calm poured over him. Killing a man was not something he ever envisioned himself doing but he was glad his plan apparently worked. Anstrov Rinaldi was a conniving and evil force, the likes of which he could compare to Hitler. Ben imagined, just for a second, a courageous Jew during the Second World War having an opportunity to take out Hitler . . . and accomplishing the deed. The world would have been far better off. Who could blame him for what he had done to Rinaldi? No, he was at peace with it. He knew he had done the right thing.

Ivanov's death surprised him but he knew he would need to ask her about it later. Franklin would be returning in a few minutes.

For Rachel's benefit, Ben tried to remain unmoved. He wasn't ready to admit his role in Rinaldi's death nor implicate Ari as an accomplice. Rachel would be upset she hadn't been asked to help, especially in light of the fact that Tomi and Harrison had participated. No, he felt an innate sense—a need, even—to insulate Rachel from the negative ramifications. Hopefully, she would understand this when the moment came to explain it all.

For the time being, he decided to simply get more information out of her. "That's incredible," he said. "Tell me about the recall of the awakened and the quarantines—what's happening?"

Ben listened as Rachel quickly explained the day's events. When she completed her hurried and emotional collection of varied thoughts, she looked troubled.

"There's something else, isn't there?"

"Yes. To get the feds moving, I had to make a call you may not be happy about."

"Okay," he said. *How bad could it be?*

"Have you ever tried to call the federal government or 911 with a national emergency? It's not so easy to get a person on the other end of phone and, even if you do, getting them to believe you is a whole other matter."

Being a bottom line guy all his life, Ben replied, "Rachel, just tell me. Who did you call?"

"Senator Rose." To Ben, Rachel looked like a little girl who just admitted to her father she broke a window in the house. He sympathized with how hard it must have been for Rachel to make that call . . . and admit it to him.

He squeezed her hand gently, reassuringly. "It's okay," he said. "I called him myself after Jess Miller was able to use a CIA software tool proving Rinaldi was behind the poison pen email that went out under my name. It seems that he had access to some sort of IP masking program fooling the system to thinking the sender of the email was someone else."

"That's like robbing a bank and leaving someone else's fingerprints at the scene."

"Something like that," Ben lamented. "Senator Rose still isn't thrilled with us but at least he now knows that it was Rinaldi who killed his daughter. At a minimum, we've redirected his vitriol."

"That explains why he agreed to help so quickly when I called. I had assumed that it was just because of all the lives that were at stake, and I'm sure it was, but he was already on the job by the time he returned my call."

The buzzer sounded once more. A loud click from the door and then Special Agents Ziglar and Franklin appeared with George Diamond.

"Your attorney is here. We'll give you a few minutes and then we'll be back to begin questioning. Your company's CEO was coincidentally confirmed dead a short while ago from a house explosion. Better start thinking about how you will talk your way out of that one. Just a hunch but I think you may have something to do with that." Franklin's sneer demonstrated his contempt for Ben.

So this is how justice works, Ben thought. Diamond took over and shuffled the FBI agents out of their own holding room. Prior to their exit, Diamond requested that the room's listening and viewing devices be deactivated to maintain the integrity of attorney-client privilege. The agents complied and left the room. With Ben's permission, Rachel remained. She sat next to Ben and George Diamond assumed her former seat across the table.

"Ben, I need to know everything. Don't leave out a single detail."

With precision and total recall, Ben laid out events and facts as he knew them as quickly as he could. He wanted to get this over with. He was needed back at the Lab. After relaying the part about the plan to kill Rinaldi, he glanced to his right to look at Rachel. The blood had drained from her face. She looked visibly shaken. He looked at her, paused from his oratory to Diamond, and softly said, "Don't hate me. When this is done, we'll talk."

A tear in her eye, she gave him a modicum of a smile and once again squeezed his hand reassuringly. Slowly, her green eyes flickered as if they could speak on their own. A lock of soft brown hair fell across her forehead. "It's okay," was all she said.

George Diamond had now heard it all. Even with the knowledge of proof exonerating Ben and implicating Rinaldi, he looked deeply troubled.

"Despite everything you've told me, we can clear your name on the spread of the plague. That's the good news but you could still be charged with murdering Rinaldi and getting you out of here anytime soon won't be so easy. It could be days before you'd get a bail hearing. To make matters worse, if the feds figure out your team was involved, they will get picked up, too. Your involvement with trying to stop Rinaldi's plague will come to an abrupt halt."

"But George," Ben protested, "they have no proof that I was involved with the house explosion. Nor will they obtain any. It's foolproof."

"I hear you. Did you listen to what that agent said before he left the room? He already accused you! You are right about the evidence. But until they determine they don't have enough to prosecute, they can and will hold you in a federal detention facility. That means 'jail' and we're not talking about anything remotely like the room we currently occupy."

"George, you have got to do something," Ben said pleadingly. "Every minute I waste in here translates to the spread of disease and more people dying."

"You need to stay calm. You just told me that the CDC and WHO are involved. You have the best minds in the world working on the problem."

With that, Rachel broke in and yelled, "The best mind in the world is sitting right here, incarcerated!"

The tension was high. Nerves were frayed. They all heard the door buzzer, then the click. Franklin and Ziglar had returned. Ben's muscles tightened. Here it comes, he thought. The accusation of murder and whatever other shit they wanted to throw against the wall. He braced himself for the worst.

The agents sat down. Franklin stared at Ben. It was a long, hard, cold stare. Ben did not intimidate easily. Part of him wanted to get up and punch Franklin.

"Well, it appears that you have friends in high places," Franklin said icily.

To Ben, it was if the FBI man was disappointed his chase might be coming to an abrupt end. Franklin was the type who thrived on high-profile cases. He enjoyed the limelight. Ben was the opposite. His successes were never intended to be about him.

"We just received a call from Senator James Rose's office. The good senator is on his way to Baltimore and will be here within the hour to speak with you. In the meantime, we were told by the FBI Director himself to stand down . . . for the moment, that is."

Ben didn't appreciate the last part. Franklin was the kind of guy who had probably been the schoolyard bully as a kid. The good news was that Senator Rose would soon arrive. Hopefully this meant Ben would be released shortly. He badly wanted to get back to Maplebrook.

For the next hour, Ben, Rachel, and George Diamond paced around the room, reviewing facts and discussing possible outcomes and strategies, all while going a little stir crazy. Ben walked over to a window. The sky had been painted in shades of gray and rain was beginning to fall. He started to hope for a downpour—anything that would keep the awakened and those they had infected off the streets. There was a better chance of containing the spread of Cadaverine with fewer people exposed. Shit, anyway you cut it, the situation appeared dire. And here he was, stuck, time just ticking away.

Finally, Rose arrived with an entourage of aides. The senator and his staff barged in and took over the room. He immediately dismissed the FBI agents and instructed one of his minions to close the door. When they were all seated, he got right down to business.

"Now, Ah know everything there is to know at this point. Ah know who the good guys are and who the bad guys are. What Ah don't know is whether you had anything to do with today's explosion in Ellicott City. But here's what Ah'm willing to do . . . and Ah nevah said this, for the record."

Ben held Rose's stare and listened intently. He suspected some sort of deal was coming but he had no idea what that might entail.

"Assuming you had something to do with the explosion, Ah'm willing to look the other way. Mah friend at Justice, Dustin Horsman, can make any muhdah charges disahpeah, just like that." Rose snapped his fingers loudly for effect.

He really is quite the showman, Ben thought.

"Ah do this because Ah now know that Rinaldi was the one who extinguished the life from my poor Melody. Howevah, colleagues of mine in the Senate don't care for the nature of your company's service, Dr. Abraham."

Here it comes. Ben braced himself. What would he have to agree to if he wanted a 'get out of jail free card'?

"They don't just want to regulate your service; they want the company completely shut down and made illegal. Now you listen and you listen good. Ah can have you outta here lickety-split. You just gotta agree to two conditions."

Ben leaned forward. "Go ahead, Senator. I'm listening."

"Here's the deal. All accusations of Rinaldi's muhdah will go away. You will get full immunity from all legal liability for existing and fu-cha lawsuits from Hiatus Centahs' clients and their families. In exchange, you have to agree to help the federal government do all it can to contain the damage Rinaldi caused and . . ."

He paused. The first condition was something Ben would gladly do voluntarily but he instinctively knew the final condition was going to be staggering. The room was quiet enough to hear a pin drop.

"You gotta agree to shut down Hiatus Centahs and bring the business to an orderly close."

The room remained silent. Everyone turned to Ben, awaiting his reply. Knowing he had no choice and putting the fate of mankind ahead of his personal interests, he looked dead on at the Senator from Florida and said, "Done."

CHAPTER 61

Rachel was in her car, following Ben from Baltimore back to Maplebrook. They would likely work through the night, in concert with CDC and WHO officials around the world to contain the damage. She was exhausted but she knew adrenaline would carry her through. Her cell phone lit up. It was Harrison and uncharacteristically, he sounded fatigued.

"I can't reach Ben. Do you know where he is?"

"I'm behind him on I-95. The FBI gave him his phone back but he must have forgotten to power it back on. What's happening?"

"Rinaldi screwed up."

"What are you talking about?"

"The Liferay settings he thought would produce Cadaverine at 3 parts per million will only produce the compound at .3 parts per million. Just slightly above the recommended tolerance level for human intake."

"That's great news! So, all of those who came into contact with awakened clients today won't become ill and become carriers?"

"They might get a little nauseated and fight a bout of diarrhea but that's the extent of it. How did things go with the FBI?"

"Well, he's free, obviously. He had to cut a deal with the government. I'll let him tell you but let's just say we'll all be unemployed in the near term."

"Oh wow! But Ben, he's doing okay?"

"You know Ben. He's obsessed with reversing Rinaldi's plot. That's all he can focus on at the moment. Get Ari and Tomi together. We can meet in the Dugout in forty-five minutes to get everyone up to speed on where things are and what we each need to do from here."

Rachel gazed ahead at Ben's blue Honda. She could only imagine what Ben thought of the day's events. Heading north on I-95 at seventy miles per hour, the city skyline quickly melted into the early evening sky. This had been a day the world would never forget. One madman tried to bring a perceived enemy to his knees and, in the process, almost caused a global epidemic. She wondered what type of mental illness lurked in someone's mind to get them to where Anstrov Rinaldi finally went.

With thirty minutes of drive time remaining, Rachel's mind harkened back to her initial encounter with Rinaldi. It was his first day as CEO. They had taken a ride together, first to the commercial center in the city and then to the Lab. She'd been trusting initially but when she thought back, all the signs had been there. Rinaldi had a definite weirdness factor to him that was evident from the moment they met. Alarms went off but she suppressed them, hoping to make a good impression on the new boss. She was kicking herself now. The day's events and all the crap Ben endured might have been avoided if she had trusted her gut. Could everything have been prevented if she had been courageous enough to act when all this started? She told herself there was no use in dwelling upon what couldn't be changed.

What would happen now? Did she still have a chance to build a life with Ben? With the company soon to be closed, could she regain his trust and make him fall in love all over again? She wasn't sure but she knew she wanted to try. That old image of a classic Victorian with a white picket fence and a tire swing came to mind. Not in Maplebrook, though—definitely not in Maryland. Rachel had come to love the Old Line State but knew that it held too many memories. No, she was thinking

Southern California. Not Lobo, but perhaps San Diego or a little north, somewhere in Orange County. That was closer to Mom and Dad. Ben could sell the Lab and open research facilities in California. Maybe he could align with one of the universities. Being closer to Dodger Stadium would be a selling point. She snapped back to reality as she approached the Route 24 exit toward Maplebrook. First things first: she needed to do all she could to help clean up Rinaldi's mess. Then, she thought, she would take some much needed time off to help Ben figure out the answer to the aftermath of the experimental Liferay. Yes, first things first.

The team was waiting in the Dugout when Ben and Rachel walked in. Ari had a map of North America projected on the wall. Green-shaded states and provinces depicted areas wherein no awakenings had taken place. By and large, these locations were all in the Pacific time zone. Rachel was aghast to see the mass of red-shaded terrain: essentially every location east of the Mississippi and the provinces of Quebec and Ontario. By Ari's calculations, 612 had been scheduled for awakening that day. Based on their actions, only 345 were victimized by Rinaldi's scheme.

Rachel knew that Ari wasn't cold or unfeeling but she was uneasy with the statement, "only 345." Ari was a scientist; they all were. Ari, she knew, was a pure and simple numbers guy. He was one for whom everything was generally black and white. Intellectually, Rachel understood and even respected colleagues with this ability. She, however, felt her heart cry out to the families of the 345 clients. These were people who trusted their loved ones to Hiatus Centers. *They trusted us to take care of their mothers, fathers, sisters, brothers, and children. All with the hope of spending just one glorious day a year with an awakened family member. Thanks to Anstrov Rinaldi, no one would ever experience that magic again.*

Thousands of Hiatus Centers' clients would soon be notified to claim the remains of their loved ones for cremation or a traditional burial. The thought of the company's demise and its impact on so many people made her sick. She leaned against a wall to steady herself and tried to focus her attention on Ari's assessment.

"So as far as we know, Rinaldi, in his haste to alter the Liferay settings, miscalculated on the creation of human Cadaverine. Because he couldn't test the settings, he had to rely on his own manual efforts to prove out his theory. Fortunately, his results were off by a factor of ten. Rinaldi's Cadaverine was intended to produce a lethal fume of 3 parts per million. Instead, it was only .3 parts per million. Safe, more or less, for the human population."

Tomi stepped up to the presentation wall and continued with the recitation of their current state.

"We are still waiting to hear from seven locations but, so far as we now know, we lost all of those awakened today. Nearly 80 percent of them died in public. Approximately 10 percent expired in one of the many makeshift quarantine centers set up around the continent. The remainder expired in local hospitals and emergency walk-in medical clinics."

Rachel had no questions and she had nothing to add. Her mind was numb. She could see from Ben's facial expressions that his mind was still very much focused on what needed to be done.

"Have we notified the authorities about Rinaldi's miscalculation?"

Tomi was the first to respond. "I have notified CDC and WHO. CDC said they would contact law enforcement as well as state, provincial, and local governments. All quarantine centers are closing tonight. I also contacted our PR firm and have them issuing an immediate press release stating that no one exposed to an awakened Hiatus Centers' client today is in danger. I've included the minor side effects that may be experienced and advised those affected to visit their regular physician or an urgent care center."

Rachel was relieved. She should have known that, from years of working with this team, they would have things in hand by the time she and Ben arrived. Effectively, the crisis was over.

Ben stepped up to the front of the room. Rachel admired his strength. What other person had she ever known who could be so strong in the face of such adversity? No one came to mind. He had to be physically spent, his mind a bowl of Jell-O. That's how *she* felt. For Rachel Larkin, known for being great under pressure, once the curtain fell on the calamity of the day, she let the tough guy exterior fall away. Not Ben. He was redirecting the team's energy for what still remained to be done.

"You guys all did one helluva job containing the damage today. The best and brightest minds in the world were called in to solve the problem but it was you, this team, who came up with the answers. I can't tell you all how incredibly proud I am. Unfortunately, another chapter of unpleasantness remains to be written."

Rachel understood Ben's need to press on. If they broke now, one of them would see or hear the news. Ben didn't want his inner circle finding out about the deal he had cut with Senator Rose from anyone but him. She sat quietly as Ben articulated the details of the deal, the ultimate closure of the company in concert with the promised destruction of every known Liferay.

Ari now showed some emotion. Ben had invented the Liferay but it was Ari's ingenuity that had created many incarnations of the device. He had just been told his crowning achievement would be locked in a box, thrown into the sea, and made illegal. Normally full of energy and resolve to keep innovating, Rachel had never seem him appear so defeated. To her, the great Ari Weiskopf suddenly looked like a wounded lion amid the African plains, gaunt and hurt.

Tomi took the news as expected. She was sullen. Rachel assumed, because of Tomi's prior involvement with Rinaldi, she felt guilty and would do whatever was necessary to help get things in order. Knowing Tomi, when this was all over, she would run far, far away and escape to a different life.

Rachel gazed over at Harrison. His future seemed the most uncertain. Yes, she thought, he was a brilliant chemist. There were any number of untold opportunities he might pursue. Right now, she guessed, he didn't really care about any of that. Rachel watched the face of Harrison Bock as it expressed only concern for the health and welfare of his best friend, a man he considered a brother—Ben Abraham.

Rachel again was lost in thought. Her mind had leaped to another galaxy. She had no idea that Ben was addressing her.

"So Rachel, are you willing to accept the position?"

Taken aback, not having heard a single word that proceeded his question, she replied simply, "I'm sorry, what position?"

"Weren't you listening? Hiatus Centers is currently without a CEO. I want to recommend that you take the job to oversee the orderly shutdown of the company."

Stunned at the suggestion, she replied, "What about you? Won't the board of directors expect you to do that?"

"Probably. But you are far more capable than I am at seeing to the immense amount of logistical details the job will entail. If you are willing, I would like to recommend you for the job. It will last only six to twelve months."

She was surprised and didn't immediately know how to answer. The job, at this point, was inconsequential. She wanted to be close to Ben. Nothing else really mattered.

"What will you do? Where will you go?"

"My home and the Lab are still here in Maplebrook. I need to resolve my seizure problem before it resolves me. I expect that'll take a while. So . . ." He flashed her a little smile and said, "I'll be around."

Her spirit warmed at the suggestion. A modicum of trust had been restored. He would not have offered the job otherwise. A hint of a future together was dangled before her. That was all she had hoped for.

CHAPTER 62

The Honorable Senator James S. Rose
The Russell Senate Office Building
Washington, DC 20510

Dear Senator Rose:

I am writing to inform you that all conditions of our agreement have now been fulfilled. Dr. Larkin has led Hiatus Centers through the mandated orderly shutdown. All Liferays previously in use at commercial locations have been destroyed. In addition, comparable Liferay equivalents housed within our research facility in Maplebrook, Maryland, have been destroyed. Our Swiss contractor provided the requested certification (copy attached) indicating the same measures have been taken with Liferay devices in its possession.

All of the families of affected Hiatus Centers' remaining clients have been sent certified letters from the Law Offices of George Diamond stating that, under an agreement with the federal governments of The United States of America and Canada, Hiatus Centers, its' officers, directors, shareholders, and employees are fully and completely released from all liability and may not be sued for reasons related to the company's shutdown.

Finally, I would like to make you aware that Dr. Larkin and her team completed the required shutdown of the company two months in advance of the federally mandated deadline. Thank you for your support during this difficult time.

Once again, please accept my deepest sympathies to you and your family on the loss of your daughter, Melody.

Yours truly,
Dr. Benjamin Abraham

Ben stood outside the FedEx Office location in downtown Maplebrook. He read the letter one last time. Then, without folding it, he placed the letter inside the cardboard mailing envelope. He yanked the protective strip, revealing the underlying adhesive that would seal the deal. The letter was the final step. It had not been required of him but he felt it was the right thing to do. He dropped the envelope on the counter, smiled at the young girl who worked there, and headed on to the next phase of his life.

A lot had happened in the ten months since that fateful day when the world was threatened by Anstrov Rinaldi. Ari had agreed to take over The Harmon School. As a former student, he had an emotional attachment. Ben was glad. It kept Ari close. That had been an important consideration because Ben needed Ari's help in his quest for a cure to his own condition. Ari was also working on a book telling the world about femtosecond laser technology. He planned no mention of the Liferay, just the other, feasible applications of the technology.

Tomi, as Rachel predicted, had escaped all the way back to northern California. She was the new biology chair at Berkeley. And then there was Harrison. He hauled his black Range Rover to his hometown of Cleveland where he opened a nightclub down the street from the Rock and Roll Hall of Fame. Harrison had pressed him to come for the grand opening but Ben never fancied himself as a nightclub kind of guy.

As for the beautiful and seductive Rachel Larkin, they were now roommates, on a trial basis. Ever the risk taker, Ben wanted to go slowly on this front.

Ben climbed into his beloved clunker of a car and drove ten minutes to visit Ari at The Harmon School. That iconic campus, really where his life began, was where he would go to start the next phase. The old storage shed, the one at the back of the campus where no one ever went, had been expanded. It was there that he and Ari concealed the experimental Liferay, the device that caused his seizure problem. It would be the key to discovering a remedy. It was his hope that there, in a makeshift lab on the desolate far end of The Harmon School, he would perfect the technology for his own sake and that of mankind . . . and, maybe, just maybe, discover the key unlocking the secret his grandfather had bestowed upon him so many years ago.

EPILOGUE

Free . . . at last, he was totally free! Free from unimagined problems emanating from his most grand plans, free from the pressure of hoping others would act as he might have hoped, free from unreasonable expectations placed upon him, and most certainly, free from the stress of ever having to worry again about money. He had left all of these troubles behind. In the end, he wondered if he had really experienced success. Sure, he had brought the world a discovery that no one else imagined possible. Yes, it was truly effective and would have a lasting impact on mankind. Yet, there remained an emptiness. Was it the absence of female companionship? No, he admitted, that had never been a central part of his life. What then?

He had always been driven by the science. The thrill of discovering a key unlocking the secrets past generations had only dreamed of. That was his adrenaline . . . originally. Later, it had taken on another dimension. His foes had caused him to become someone or something else. It was their fault. How could he be held responsible? He would have been content to make the world a better place through scientific research. By his reasoning, he had been thrust into a predicament calling for retribution in a way only he could administer.

Now, he sat alone. In the cushioned chaise lounge, he reached both arms skyward to stretch the muscles in his back. His body ached. His back screamed for a massage. Supposing it was all worth it, he sighed and took in the surrounding beauty of his final destination. In this peaceful haven, he would have all the time he needed to reflect on what had happened.

Suddenly a commotion erupted from below—splashing and an odd whistling noise. One duck in a small flock was having some sort of disagreement with its brethren. The other ducks were ostracizing him. Memories of his own childhood came flooding back. The lone duck, elevated from the water, rising like a Phoenix, while showing off its thirty-two-inch wing span. His head was a shiny blue-green color with a bill of dark blackish gray. The remainder of the flock had bills of sky blue. The neck and wings were striped like a zebra against a light brown underbelly. As he rose majestically, a long green blade from a water plant dangled in his mouth, both sides hanging symmetrically. The duck was an outcast. Oddly, he seemed to understand this about himself.

A loner most of his own life, at different points he had found kinship with kindred spirits. Those spirits came in different forms, none of which were human. Perhaps a new bond would be formed with this Patagonian outcast. He let his body relax and looked up at the cloud-laden blue sky for some sign of the truth regarding his life and where he would go from here.

If he was being totally honest with himself, he knew, deep down, he had failed. While he sat alone, in his remote paradise, Kronenbourg in hand, a leaf from a nearby Lenga tree drifted onto his lap; another landed softly on the crystal lake and floated slowly with a gentle ripple. Somehow, Abraham was free, vindicated from the jowls of defeat. Instead of retiring contently to his Patagonian paradise and all of its splendor, Rinaldi remained troubled to the core. How close he had come to death. How naïve of Abraham to think that he wouldn't notice that his cane was somehow different.

He reclined on his deck lounger and recalled how he and Baxter watched the house explode from the safety of the escaping Lincoln Town Car. When he contemplated how close he had come to being blown up in his own home, he felt vulnerable, mortal, and, yes, frightened. But he had survived. The beauty of his current situation was that Abraham— and the rest of the world, for that matter—believed him to be dead. Had Abraham been incarcerated in federal prison, he would be far more content. Part of him wanted to let it go, live out his days in luxury, and tell himself he got even. The other part still yearned for what might be.

ACKNOWLEDGEMENTS

My wife, Denise and our son and daughter, Ryan and Leah, who served as my earliest sounding boards and first readers. Their love and support helped me to believe in myself and gave me the strength to plow forward in uncharted waters. Denise encouraged me at every turn while enduring my many hours in isolation spent researching, writing, and editing. Ryan's love of science fiction and the hours of conversation about this book as well as his input on the final cover design were invaluable. I continuously tapped Leah's knowledge of writing, editing, and publishing. Her talents are on display as the author of Rachel's poem entitled "Unbreakable" which appears in Chapter 16. The three of you helped me to achieve a lifelong dream and for your love and support, I am eternally grateful.

Wayne Caskey, my executive coach and mentor. When we began our work together in 2013, Wayne asked me for a personal goal I wanted to achieve. I mumbled something about wanting to write a novel. He then manufactured his trademark eye twinkle and proceeded to challenge me to begin writing this book. Thank you for the push.

Diane O'Connell who helped me see that writing a novel is not like building a house by going off to the woods with a saw, dragging trees back to a clearing and asking, "What's next?" Diane gave me tools and structure and taught me how to write a novel. Her content edits and our many conversations about the right plot twists helped make Hiatus the story it is.

Dr. Ben Shanabrook and Dr. Virginia Shanabrook - my "scientific advisory team" who refreshed my memory on basic science, fed me terminology and concepts to explore and enabled me to make the unimaginably impossible events in this book sound semi-plausible.

Dr. John Mioduski for his help authenticating scenes in Basel and for providing the idea that became BV3000,

Father Sylvan Capitani and Pastor Tom Moen for offering religious perspectives.

Ron Cobert, for helping with legal issues which might surround the application process for a Hiatus Center client as well as the Senate investigation and hearing processes.

Troy Michaels for help with understanding the basics of munitions.

Early readers and proofreaders who provided valuable feedback include my wife, Denise, my son, Ryan, my daughter, Leah, my mother, Sheila Weinstock, Ron Cobert, Ben and Ginny Shanabrook, Bruce Savadkin, Greg Harmis, Chuck Ferraro, and Bill Rowe.

My father, Jay Polakoff, who never failed to ask about this book and my progress.

I would also like to gratefully acknowledge the talents of Gwyn Snider of GKS Creative who did a masterful job capturing the essence of this book in her cover design.

Kim Bookless, my copy editor, who whipped the final manuscript into shape and taught me that what I knew about punctuation could be placed in a thimble.

Finally, I would like to thank all of my friends and family, not listed due to space limitations, for their interest and support in this project. I hope you enjoyed reading this book as much as I enjoyed writing it.

Love to all –
Sam

LOOK FOR THE NEXT NOVEL BY SAM POLAKOFF

Shaman

Dan Alston questioned his sanity. A successful businessman and US senator, his entire life had been plagued by strange visions; brief, flickering snapshots that placed him below the Earth's surface, in remote mountain caves and even in the heavens. The episodes were almost undiscernible and easily ignored. But on his 50th birthday, during a climb in the Peruvian mountains, Dan Alston is involuntarily transported on a spiritual journey and shown something horrifying; an environmental apocalypse.

With guidance from an anthropologist, Dan learns he is exhibiting signs of shamanic powers common to ancient tribes and cultures across the world. His chief of staff, Talia Clayton, tries to help him understand the meaning of his experience and to fight his demons, both real and imagined.

While he learns to harness this power and determine reality from fantasy, Dan and Talia cross paths with Jade, an ancient and evil force unleashed to hasten the Earth's destruction. In a race against time, Dan Alston must overcome trepidation while embracing his innate powers to defeat Jade and save the planet from an apocalyptic end.

Shaman is the story of a man who thought he knew what serving his country meant until he discovered his true purpose and the power required to fulfill it.

www.sampolakoff.com

74028864R00203

Made in the USA
Middletown, DE
19 May 2018